Joss Lynn

R.P. Wollbaum

Copyright R.P. Wollbaum ©2023
ISBN: 978-1-989210-14-7 Book
ISBN: 978-1-989210-13-0 Ebook

Table of Contents

Chapter One

Joss had begun her career like many, singing in a local high school band for the schools around Brownsville Texas. One of the guys in the band had an old beat up stock car he raced, more for fun than anything else. Joss would come along and watch and help out a bit in the pits. At one practice session, the driver had asked Joss if she would like to try driving. Always up for something new, Joss had agreed. Her times were faster than the regular drivers times were.

The next weekend, they entered Joss as the driver. She placed in the top ten! The weekend after, the top five. Using her personality, Joss negotiated with the track owner for more practice time during the week. The catch was, the band had to play for the after race party each race. They jumped on it. The stands were always packed and it was great exposure for them.

The band, and especially Joss, were a big hit. She always made time for the fans, even though most times she was exhausted from not only singing, but from racing. Her mother and sisters were becoming concerned. Joss was always tired. She just shrugged it off. Part of paying your dues, is what she told them.

One of the local bigger bands had caught her act after a race. They did the state fair tours and local dance hall gigs all across Texas. They asked Joss to join as a backup singer. With a somewhat heavy heart, but with the urging of her own bands mates, Joss had agreed. Soon the band had a good following of fans. Of course, this had led to more gigs and finally as the opening act for an up and coming star. Charley Bikum.

That acts female vocalist had become sick and this young local singer from their opening act had been pressed into emergency service for a one time deal. The gig was at a large venue in Austin, one of the biggest music markets in America. Over ten thousand people were in attendance. Joss had done good enough, and Charley had asked Joss to be one of his backup singers, full time. The pay was better, so she agreed.

Then had come the recording session for Charley's new album. One of the tracks on the album, had Joss singing solo back ground that required her to record it alone, so it could be mixed into the song later. The song was about the highs and the lows of being on the road. The only people in the studio that day were, Joss, John, the record producer and Hal, the mixer artist.

How it worked was, over her head phones, Joss would hear the instruments and Charley and she would sing her bit at the right moments. It was nothing fancy, she thought she would be out of there in an hour, two at the most. The producer finally let her loose around ten that night. A full ten hour day. She could not understand why, but heck, he was the producer, she was just a back up singer. What did she know? She had to show up three more times, this time with the other members of the group for back ground voice on other tracks. These were fast and she was quickly out of the studio.

They had two weeks off after the recording session was finished, before they would once again set off for a 200 day tour around the country doing live shows. She was booking out of her hotel, intending on spending some time with her family in Brownsville. She hadn't seen them in over a year. Hal, the mixing artist from the studio, was at the front desk waiting for her. She was to report to the studio. John, the record producer, wanted to talk with her.

Once there, she was handed a sheet of lyrics. It was a whole song. It was an upbeat song from one of the latest Bond movies. She was allowed to hear the musical part of it twice, then told to enter the recording booth and sing. They made her do ten takes, then, gave her a break. When she returned from the bathroom, Hal handed her a soda and patted her on the shoulder. He pointed over to the corner office. John was on the phone and excitedly talking to someone on it. He hung up and approached them.

"You got a manager kid?" He asked.

"Not really," Joss had answered. "I have a standard union contract."

"Perfect," John said. "Wait here."

Joss was wondering why she would need a manager. She was a nineteen year old back up singer who had no experience really. Well, not enough experience to warrant an agent anyway.

John went back into his office and made another shorter call. Then returned to them. He handed her a card. It was a lawyers card from one of the top agencies in the music business. The lawyer was one of their top agents. Scott Akelman and he generally worked out of New York.

"You have an appointment with this man. My car is waiting to take you to him, then back here." John said.

She was driven to a big high rise office building in the producers Mercedes S class car. The car was a large luxury vehicle, with plush leather seats and individual climate control for each passenger. Joss was more used to driving around in ten year old beaters that had seen better days. The building itself was in the higher end of the office towers in the downtown core. A personal assistant dressed in high end designer clothing, had been waiting and escorted her up to the 29th floor and a large reception area right off the elevator lobby. The walls were covered in gold record albums from many of the worlds top musical acts. The waiting chairs were plush leather. The assistant asked Joss if she wanted a coffee and how she liked it, returning shortly with a hot cup that she placed on the marble topped coffee table in front of Joss. Joss was definitely feeling out of place. She had only seen this type of furnishings on TV and movies and she was definitely under dressed, wearing blue jeans and a light blouse she had picked up from Walmart. Even the receptionist was wearing the latest designer business attire.

Joss had not even taken more than one sip of her coffee and the personal assistant was back. She escorted Joss to a corner office. A man in his late forties, dressed in an expensive suit, stood from his desk and offered her a chair. The office was large, so was the solid and well burnished oak desk. All along the walls and in display cases, were not only music memorabilia, but acting and sporting ones.

"Ms. Litzenberger," the lawyer said. " I'm Scott. John has told me wonderful things about you. If you agree, John has asked me to represent you for your up coming negotiations."

"Negotiations?" Joss had asked. She was now very confused. What the heck was going on?

"I am sure the union can handle all that for me. No offence, but I am positive I cannot afford your services sir." Joss said.

"You let me and John worry about that hey," Scott said. He slid one sheet of paper over to her.

All it said, was that she agreed to hire him to provide legal services and advice, for 5% of her earnings.

"Are you kidding me?" Joss asked. "I only make three grand a month."

Scott had just smiled at her and handed her a pen. Once she had signed two copies and handed them back to him. He hit speed dial on his phone. It was on speaker.

"Hey John," the lawyer said. "MS. Litzenberger has just hired me to represent her."

"What's her first name?" Brent asked.

"Joslyn," the lawyer said.

"Ok, for now," John said. "Joss, come on back here, the car is waiting for you."

And so, Joss Lynn was born.

Her first job was to sing the opening credits for a soon to be released movie. It was a cover of Laura Branigan's version of Gloria. She received $500,000 for that. It had only taken two days to record it. Next, she was whisked off to the Cann Music Festival, where she had to perform the song live. She received $100,000 for that and all expenses paid. Joss had never been out of the States before, let alone to France.

Cann is the biggest and most famous music venues in the world. Her wardrobe had been especially designed for her, even her casual wear. Never in her life had she worn this quality of clothing. The jewels and dress she had worn for her performance were by famous designers. Of course they were only on loan, but still. How many people from the wrong side of the tracks in Brownsville Texas ever even had the chance to wear the like?

Joss was flabbergasted when, some of the leading recording artists came and started conversations with her. Beyonce and Drake were very understanding and made her feel comfortable, even making jokes about themselves when they were new and dumb like she was.

The song became popular and she had to make personal appearances on television to sing it. She was on the Late Show, Regis and Kelly, just to name a few. Asked by Kelly how she was handling all the fame, Joss just shrugged her shoulders.

"I have been so busy since Cann, I have not had time to actually sit down and think about it," Joss said. "Maybe I can take a day off soon and relax and let it all sink in."

All in all, she made a million dollars. Then the royalties began to roll in. By the end of the year, she had made five million dollars. All for less than a week of recording studio work. She never had to work again, ever.

Joss bought her mother and her siblings the houses of their dreams in the upper end suburbs of Brownsville. The houses were not big mansion style homes, but much bigger and nicer than the double wide trailers they had been living in. Joss was also looking for a place of her own. Something out in the country, away from prying eyes, where, she could maybe have a couple of horses to ride like she used to before her mom's divorce from her dad.

Then the producer called her again. This time she went to his offices in Downtown Burbank California. Joss had been to California before, just for one night concerts and the recoding session, never to Burbank with its trendy shops, wide boulevards and fancy expensive cars.

Scott, her lawyer, was also waiting for her there.

"Ok MS. Lynn," her lawyer began. "You have just been offered the chance to sing the latest opening song for the latest Bond thriller. John here will be producing it. I advise you to take it. They are offering you five mill up front and 10% royalties on any sales. Plus, of course, a minimum of one hundred thousand dollars for any performances you are required to do on their behalf."

Joss looked back and forth between Scott and John.

"Are you kidding me?" She asked. To make a song for that movie franchise was like having a gold mine for a singer.

"Oh, that ain't all kiddo," Brent said. "Tell her Scotty."

"They also want you to be *The Girl*," Scotty said.

"What??? I don't know how to act!" Joss exclaimed.

The only acting she had ever done was in the typical grade school Christmas and Thanksgiving pageants.

"Neither do most of the new hotshot actors," Scotty said. "I should know, I represent most of them. You have the voice and the look, they are looking for. Plus, another 1 million and two percent of the movie gross. The up front money is not all that good I admit, but the two percent of gross could add up to some substantial numbers. What have you got to loose? It's your part, they aren't looking for anyone else. Yet."

That quickly, her nice simple life had, over night, turned her into a world wide fenom. Her every move was followed and chronicled. Who she dated, where she shopped, what she wore, where she went. She was in every tabloid, movie magazine, influencer Vlogs and entertainment show.

It was fun for the first few years. Then it became tiring. She had a team of personal assistants and publicists, drivers and body guards. Gone were the days of going to the mall for a cheese burger and fries, or to just hang out with her friends. She even had to add appointments in her schedule to meet her mother and siblings.

Most of her so called friends, were hangers on, not real friends. Some, wanted investments in unsound concepts. Others would try and use her willingly, or usually, with out her permission, to enhance their reputations or products, just by being in her presence.

Her long absent father even got in the act. Trying to get her to invest or loan him money on some scheme or other. In reality, just thinly disguised excuses for more booze or gambling.

She had experienced some flings over the years. These generally ended in disaster, hurting her badly. Many were like her father, or the other hangers on. Just wanting to use her, her money or contacts for personal gain. Others tried to control her every moment of the day. A small majority of men, just didn't want to put up with all the craziness of show business. The constant pressure from media and the general public.

Finally Joss came to the conclusion that it was just easier to be without a guy and stopped trying.

She was always invited to the latest trend setting event. Openings of hot new night spots, fashion galas and the like. Generally she didn't have to pay, or was indeed paid an appearance fee to show up. Most of them were attended by more media than regular people, or self important artists or wealthy people. While she went through the motions expected of her, it was tedious and pretentious.

One of the ones she enjoyed, were the Formula One car races. The atmosphere was always vibrant and exciting and because many of the jet set were always in attendance, she was not bothered as much as she normally was at events. The places these races were held in generally had many exciting sights and attractions. For her, the European races were special. All the history, castles, walled towns and cathedrals. Some a thousand or more years old.

The different countries and their varying cultures, music, cultural clothing and dance. How each country and even region within the country, had different customs and parades. Growing up in Texas, she spoke what they called Texican. A derivative of Mexican Spanish. The Spanish broadcasters of the events soon picked up on it and Joss had many interviews in Spanish, which, in turn, led to Spanish speaking fans approaching her.

Joss had to make the rounds of the VIP functions each night. Mostly, more of the same old same old. Some of the drivers, especially the younger ones were funny, acting like most young people she ran into. Wanting selfies and autographs. Unlike the general public, these guys, used to the limelight, actually loved to ham it up. One went so far as to tell her to lighten up. Life is short, enjoy it.

She was generally at the track early every day. She had unlimited access to pit row and enjoyed walking among the drivers, mechanics and engineers. Especially for the lower class support race teams. The sight of these young and usually under funded teams reminded her of her stock car racing days. Everyone on the teams, from mechanics, top drivers and even owners, busy making adjustments or repairs on the cars. The smell of oil, high octane gasoline, burnt rubber, all held memories for her.

When a team was not busy, Joss would ask a mechanic or driver, questions about the car, or why they were doing this or that. The questions she was asking were pertinent, not the expected *bobble head* American movie star type questions, such as why the colour on the car was the way it was. She asked how the suspensions were tuned, or the down force required for that track.

Her first race in Montreal, she had arrived a day early. She had heard about the vibrant night life and the mix of old Europe and modern North America. The old original part of the city still had the narrow cobble stoned streets common in Europe. Expecting only French to be spoken, she was surprised that English was very prevalent in Montreal itself. Also surprising was the ethnic diversity she saw. Dark skinned and light skinned people walking and socializing together. Something she rarely saw at home.

At the race itself, something odd had occurred. In the VIP suite at the race was someone who didn't fit. He wasn't odd. He just didn't fit. He was just over six feet tall, with what looked like not an ounce of fat on him. He sat by himself in a private box for four and kept to himself. Unlike the others in the suite, dressed in their designer clothing, he had sneakers on his feet, blue jeans and a pull over shirt. One of the racing teams jackets was placed on the back of an empty chair and the matching ball cap on the table. Also, unlike the others, he drank beer, not the fancy cocktails or champagne the others drank, but a local beer called Blue. And while a fancy beer glass had been provided, he drank it right out of the bottle.

Again, unlike the others, he was actually interested the race. The others were more interested in socializing. The race was uneventful and never in doubt. No crashes or catastrophic failures happened. The leading team in the championship, finishing one two handily. Once the race was over, he was gone.

She saw him again the next day at the private area of Mirabel Airport where the private plane owners and their guests or passengers went, instead of the airport terminal. Joss and her entourage were there waiting to board their private charter flight to the next race. He was quickly gone though, a back pack across one shoulder.

Joss had been contracted to do some appearances at the United States Grand Prix at Austin Texas that year. Being a Texan, she was in big demand and it was a hectic week, but fun for the most part. She only had to work at night and because she actually liked car racing, she was at the track early each day. And so was he. Once again sitting in a private box, by himself.

She did notice that he had noticed her. It was kind of hard not to. With her gaggle of people around her and in these early practice days and support races, the beautiful people were not in attendance. So she had a lot of attention from the media present and some ardent fans. Not from him though. It was almost like she was invisible to him. This was not normal for her. Men always noticed her. Yet, other than when she had first walked in, he ignored her, seemingly content to sip his beer, this time a Coors and watch the goings on on the track. He began to intrigue her.

After one of the preliminary races had concluded, Joss had to make an appearance with the British broadcasting company that had the broadcast rights for the Formula One Series. She knew it was just for filler material for them and they clearly thought she knew nothing about racing, from the types of questions they asked her. Things like which racing teams colour scheme she liked or a drivers hair style. Joss played along, being the typical Hollywood *bobble head*. Then she saw him out of the corner of her eye. He walked down pit lane to where one of the minor support race cars was parked and was warmly greeted by everyone there.

Her interview completed, she was quickly forgotten about by the media and she moved toward where this man was talking with the young female driver and the crew of the car. Her gaggle of *protectors*, scurrying after her. Once again he noticed her, it was actually very hard to miss her this time as the whole crew recognized who she was.

The car was part of the Porsche GT series and was always in the hunt for wins. The team was well funded and had ten people working as mechanics doing various tasks on the car. She was soon busy taking selfies and signing autographs. Looking around, she saw him walking away.

Joss didn't see him in his box for the next days practice session. He was briefly with the cars crew like the day before, just before the race. Then he disappeared.

He was back in his box for qualifying day. But she was to busy to talk with him. All the beautiful people had arrived as well. The same thing for race day.

She spotted him again at the Austin Airport and the Mexico City Airport after the Mexican Grand Prix.

She didn't see him again at any of the remaining races that year.

Chapter Two

B etween races, Joss led a fairly quiet life. She had been signed for her own action spy thriller movie franchise. It was a spin off of her Bond character. She didn't need much coaching on firearms use. She had gone hunting as a young teen with her father and was familiar with fire arms and firearms safety. She did all but the most dangerous driving stunts herself. The studio absolutely refusing her to take part in the hazardous ones.

The movie had gone on location in Morocco for three weeks to film some action things. Expecting nothing but desert sand, Joss was amazed at the scenery of the location and the flora and fauna of that area of Morroco. It was actually cold. The area they were in even had a ski resort, which is why it had been picked. Joss had learned that for her, she had to actually experience the actions the scenes had. For this one, it was skiing. It was arranged for her to have two days of private ski lessons. There was not much snow in Texas and she had never been on skis before.

While she was far from being a competent skier, not like one threesome that had one of the skiers actually skiing backwards on the slope, Joss could at least stand still on the skis without falling over for those scenes. She also did not look out of place walking in the ski boots, an acquired skill, with the skis on her shoulder and actually wore the clothing in the correct manor.

The four observers were over looking a small clearing in the tall cedar treed mountainous landscape of the Atlas Mountains. Not far away was Michlifen Ski Resort. To the four observers, it was not much of a ski resort. Still, one did not expect such things in a supposed dry and arid country.

Two of the observers had issues breathing the first few days. They were more used to lower elevations than the other two were. Only one was complaining of the cold. The other three laughed at him. Unlike he, they had their jackets open, while his was done up all the way. That individual, was also a city dweller and complained about how quiet it was. Other than the wind rustling the trees and the odd noise from the native macaques in the area, the area was silent.

A credible intelligence report had been received that an Iranian backed insurgent group from Libya was going to do something here this week, or the next. The Moroccan government had been informed. They had asked for help, discreet help, to resolve the issue. As a moderate middle power with ties to the west, the east and the other African nations, they could ill afford the negative publicity that such an attack would attract. They also could not afford to have the west publicly involved.

The decision had been made to contract a well respected and non aligned specialist firm. The firm had accepted the contract. After reviewing official government reports from a number of governments and their own contacts, the decision had been made to dispatch a team.

The team that had been selected, many said, were the best the firm had. The four person team comprised two women and two men. Two were North American, two European. The team had been together for over five years and were very experienced, having served in their perspective governments clandestine special forces groups prior to joining the firm.

The Moroccan government had been informed that a team had been dispatched and that a report would be following the operation. The team had flown in on a Pilatis PC 24 executive jet, every inch the typical upper middle class tourists that came this time of year. With their skis and large baggage. Curiously, a senior Moroccan official performed the customs inspection, which was quick, even for African standards, just quickly looking at passports and stamping them.

Four sets of skis in hard cases were attached to the rented Mercedes SUV's ski racks, the large luggage cases stacked in the rear. At that point, the four entered the overloaded vehicle and headed to the Moroccan interior.

They had taken the first two days to acclimatize to the high elevation, even going so far as to actually go skiing, strangely, on rented skis. The two couples were having a ball, one of the men actually skiing backward in front of one of the clearly far from competent female skiers.

After the first two days, the two couples simply vanished one night. No one thought much about it. Tourists always did weird things. The vehicle was still in the parking lot and all the clothing was still in the rooms.

As far as operations went, this one was like ninety percent of the ones they deployed on. Boring. Two of the team were always watching the film location, the other two resting, or cooking whatever goo was handy from the Meals Ready to Eat packets they had. These were boiled in a small pot over a hikers one burner alcohol stove, using melted snow for the water. For them, it was cold, but all of them had served in much colder situations than this one.

After a week, the days were all becoming familiar. Just past day break, the film crew would arrive, starting generators and testing equipment. At ten, the cast, directors, producers, make up artists and clothing people would arrive. The cast would disappear into now warm camping trailers for makeup and dressing. After that, shot after shot was filmed. Sometimes two or three times from different angles. By four, the day was done. Today had seen a few extras arrive on chartered busses. These were, for the most part, locals hired for the day for back ground. After that, things were shut down. Busses reloaded, and cast and crew would disappear once again to the ski resort for the night.

The film was Academy and Grammy award winning Joss Lyn's latest Jorden Fields spy adventure film. These were a female version of the James Bond franchise and were always well received and anticipated, like the Bond films were. The team had the shooting schedule, tomorrow would just be the main cast. Another boring day.

Almost. Just before dark, six heavily burdened figures arrived. Like the observing team, these set up just behind the tree line. Unlike the observers, the first thing these did was start a fire to keep warm.

"Two RPG's, Two machine guns, six AK's," the European man said.

"Radio it in," the other man said. "Watch and ready tonight."

The European grabbed a back pack and pulled a Satellite phone from it, dialled and reported in German to the person on the other end. Four hard covered ski containers were opened. Four long guns and four HK 416 assault rifles with 20inch barrels.were removed from it. All had two power scopes mounted, three had grenade launches mounted under the main barrel, one had a large capacity fifty round magazine, the other three the standard 30 round magazines. All four long rifles were Barret MOD rifles chambered in Norma 338 caliber. All these weapons had sound suppressors installed and scopes.

The weapons were assembled, examined and cleaned. Weapons harnesses were removed from packs and donned. Each had a Sig P320 chambered in .45, also with sound suppressors. These were mounted high on the outside of the chest side of the weapons harnesses. Four clips for the assault rifles, two for the pistols and four grenades for the three with the launchers were also mounted on the harnesses, ammunition loaded. One clip of the long rifle ammunition was also in a pouch on the harness. Other clips were pulled from the back packs and inserted into the weapons.

The attackers were up well before daybreak, cooking breakfast and readying weapons. They were positioned four hundred meters from the film location and six from the observers. As the first of the film crews vehicles arrived, the attackers moved to the tree line and began observing.

Once the rest of the crew and the cast arrived, the attackers returned to their camp, gathered weapons and went to firing positions. Two men for each machine gun and RPG readied the weapons. The other two, binoculars to foreheads observing.

Then bodies were flying in red tinged mists as high speed high caliber rounds hit them. First the four with the machine guns and the RPGs. Followed by the two with the binoculars. The ones with the binoculars just beginning to react when the rounds hit them. It was all over in less than six seconds.

Two figures clad in white and light grey camouflage from head to toe cautiously approached the fallen from the sides. Each with an assault rifle at their shoulder ready to fire. There was no doubt the attackers were dead. A hit any where on the torso meant catastrophic damage and death. None of the attackers was wearing body armour, the damage was severe.

All were rolled over, pictures taken, weapons unloaded and rendered unusable. Then the two disappeared back into the trees.

Having heard or seen nothing, the film crew carried on as it did each day. The vultures and other scavengers made short work of the bodies. Nothing was ever reported to the media and the Libyans were wondering what happened to their team.

Chapter Three

The movie shooting was arranged so Joss could attend the Formula One races. In fact, the movie people actually wanted her to go. As her character, like Bond, was always at fashionable events like Formula One races, it fit her on screen image.

It had been a year since she had first seen the quiet man in Montreal. It was this years race in Montreal. There he was, in his same box at the very first practice session of the very first day. Like Mexico, Joss was a big hit in Canada and had little opportunity to confront this quiet man. She was unused to being ignored by men, the least she ever received was a nod or a smile in her direction. This man actually shunned her. He was never rude about it, just made it clear he had no interest at all. He was an enigma to her, a mystery that she just had to solve. Joss had her people looking into who he was, but could find nothing out about him. The box was rented out by the Porsche Series racing team with the female driver he had talked to at Austin. They, in turn, were the start up team for one of the mid pack F2 Teams, who were also a part of the Hubba Bubba Formula One team.

Once again, he showed up at the private airport lounge with his back pack. Once again he was gone.

Every second year, the German Grand Prix was held. This year in Hockenhiem. It was two weeks after the Montreal race and one week before the next race to be held in Austria. She liked these two races. While the races themselves were well attended, the practice days and the preliminary races were not. She could actually spend some time watching the races for once.

Joss walked in the first day and after the fast round of autographs and pictures from the catering staff, made her way to her seat. There were about twenty spectators scattered about the large room, most of them sponsors of the race teams or managers of drivers. She was just about to sit down when she saw him. She wouldn't have noticed him, but he had stood and was making his way to the door to leave.

"Hey!" Joss yelled at him. "Where are you going? The lower class racing not good enough for you?"

He had put his sun glasses on. It was a bright day that day. He turned around and looked at her from over top the glasses.

"Nope," he said. "To crowded and noisy in here." Even though the room was far from being full of people.

His English was clear and concise and had a western American Accent. He walked out the door.

She didn't see him again, until race day. Once again sitting alone in his box, once again quickly leaving after. One of her recent co-stars, Nat Carson, had decided he had a crush on her. He was European and wouldn't leave her be. It had started in Morroco, at first Joss thought it was cute. They were, after all, co workers and it was not unknown in the industry for actors to get a little to involved in their characters and to let it run into their personal lives. With not much else to do on the location shooting in Morroco, Joss had gone out for diner a couple of times with him. He really was not her type, the typical publicity hound actor. The studio actually encouraged him and let her know it was good publicity for her to play along.

So, all the next week in Austria, Joss and Carson were seen together at the clubs or having diner or whatever. Carson was becoming a pest, she would have to do something about this soon. Joss had a respite from his affections during the practice sessions and preliminary races the first two days of the race weekend. To early and boring for him he had said. In actuality, he was not the slightest bit interested in car racing, just the publicity he would garner rubbing elbows with the rich and famous at the main race.

Once again, the quiet man was in his box. Once again, when he spotted her, he rose to leave. This time she was having nothing of it. She walked right up to his table and sat down before he had risen. She stuck out her hand.

"Joss Lynn," she said.

He just nodded at her and stood, making to leave.

"What?" she said. "Do I stink or what? My shit not good enough for you?"

"Nope," he said again, putting his sunglasses on. "Have a great day."

He left. Joss was left sitting alone. That had never ever happened to her, somebody just out and out snubbing her like that. That got her Texas dander up. She was not going down without a fight.

Race day came. She was there early. This time when he sat down, he had a cold beer bottle plunked down in front of him. Then another and she sat down across from him. Today, she was dressed somewhat like he was. Of course her blue jeans and shoes etc were all designer, but still, she was slumming it for her. Like him, she was wearing a team ball cap and had sunglasses on.

"Joslyn," she said, clinking her beer bottle of Otakringer against his then taking a swig. "Good beer they have here. You should try it."

He had a grumpy look on his face.

"Oh can the cowboy act," she said. "I'm a Texas girl. You ain't shitting me."

She had let her Texas drawl come out.

"Look Bubba," she continued. "I really like these races and all those yahoos don't let me watch. My latest co star has decided he is infatuated with me and the studio is encouraging him. I told all my *protectors* to take off and leave me alone today. Watch, without them around and me dressed like this today, nobody will even notice us."

"Ya right," he said. "The fabulous and famous Joss Lynn not being noticed. They call me Richard."

She reached into her jeans pocket and brought out some crumpled bills.

"A hundred Euros on it Richard?" She said.

Like she had done, he dug into his right pants pocket and plunked some crumpled bills on top of hers.

"Done," he said.

"Oh ya," she continued. "You get to buy me diner after the race too."

He put his hand back in his pocket and came out with some more crumpled bills, quickly flipping through them.

"Not one of your fancy joints though," he said. "I ain't got enough cash for that."

"Well something better than Rotten Ronnies I hope," she said.

He actually grinned then. She felt her heart skip.

"Ya, Pizza Hut is more my style anyway." He said.

She laughed and placed her right hand on his left forearm. She quickly withdrew it and looked away.

"So who do you like in the GT race," she said. "I kind of like car 38."

Like she had predicted, nobody bothered the two lower-class people sitting by them selves. The two of them had a good time watching the race. He was actually funny, when he wanted to be. His blue almost grey eyes, threatened to suck her into them when she looked to long. The more he loosened up, the more talkative he became.

"Your Canadian aren't you?" She asked at one point.

"Ah crap," he said.

"Your accent is almost American, but you do tend to say eh a little to often at times," she said. "No aboots though."

"Well that's good then," he said. "Wouldn't want to be mistook for an easterner. Well Ya'all, your Texican slips in once in a while too eh?"

She said some choice Spanish to him. He laughed.

"Careful girly," he said in the same language. "You never know who can understand you. You're definitely not Mexican. Texican is close, but..."

"Oh shut up," she said. Then a twinkle came in her eye. "Eh."

"Touché," he said, clinking his beer bottle against hers.

"Whats say we blow this joint," he said. "We know who's gonna win, this way we get out of Dodge before the crowds hit."

They stood and quickly left. Exiting the VIP area and taking the first cab in the line waiting in front of it.

He said something in German to the driver and they were soon on their way out of town.

"Hey," Joss said. "You said you would buy me diner."

"I did so," he said. And laughed.

Soon they were at the airport, the private part. He paid the cab driver and they walked into the private lounge.

"I have to get my gear. Grab a beer," he said. "I'll be right back."

Joss ordered a coffee and looked around her. The lounge was mostly empty and she had a view of an office type area that had many people in white shirts, or uniforms with bars on the epilates gathered around. Richard was at the counter with them. A few minutes later, he returned, with his back pack across his shoulder.

"Come on then," he said. "Diner awaits."

He walked out onto the tarmac and headed down the long line of private jets and expensive private planes. Joss began to think that perhaps Richard had more than a few bucks, or a position that allowed him access to a corporate aircraft. Then they stopped beside a small single engine low wing aircraft. Joss was, well, not shocked, but....she didn't actually know how she felt about it. While it was not a big fancy corporate aircraft, it had a shinny dark blue paint job.

Walking around to the right side of the plane, he unlocked, then opened the door, letting his back pack stay on the ground.

"Just a sec," he said. "Only one door on this thing."

He jumped in, went to the passenger side and flipped some switches on.

"I have to check the old girl over," Richard said.

He made his way to the wing and inspected it, then the rear tail, the other wing and the propeller. He checked around the nose, then grabbed his back pack, took it to the pilots side of the plane, opened a small baggage door there and placed the back pack inside. He removed the ropes holding the plane down and the chocks holding the wheels from moving, also placing them in the baggage compartment.

While all this had been going on, Joss looked the airplane over. There was not a dent or scratch anywhere on it. Other than a few bugs on the wings and the front edges of the landing gear, it was spotless. All three wheels and tires had tear drop shaped devices around them, just leaving the bottom half of the tires visible. The way they were designed and positioned, Joss's racing knowledge told her they were aerodynamic enhancements.

He quickly checked the oil in the engine and motioned her to follow him showing her where to step on the wing, then levered himself into the pilots seat. She clumsily followed him in.

He was flipping more switches while she was doing that and the instrument panel came alive. Once she had gotten herself comfortable, he started to brief her on what to expect. It was much more in-depth than the briefings she received on her private charters. What to do with her feet and hands, when to talk to him, what he was going to do, what to expect if something went wrong, how to close and latch the door.

Then he showed her how to put on the headset he gave her and she heard him speaking to her on it.

"We can talk to each other through these," he said. "Except when the radio kicks in that is. You'll get used to it."

Then he was back to work, this time going over a check list he had on his iPad clipped to his control wheel.

While he was doing that, Joss looked around the airplane. The two seats were covered in a supple leather, as were the two rear seats. The front dash was covered in instruments. Two large glass panels dominated the centre of it. The one in front of Richard had some kind of terrain looking display on it in the centre. There were some lines across it. Around the edges were what appeared to be gauges of some sort. The other display had a map of the airport runways on it. A bank of what looked like four radios were toward the centre. The only spot not covered by switches was directly in front of Joss and it had what looked like a small glove box in it.

She saw him depress a button on his controls and he spoke in German. Then looking around and behind the airplane, he started it. Even with the noise cancelling headphones she had on, she could clearly hear the engine and the propeller and she felt the airplane rocking from the propeller blast.

Soon, he was once again going through the check list, looking at gauges and moving his controls. He spoke again in German and wrote something down when he heard the response and repeated it back. The engine revved up and they began to taxi to the runway. He had her make sure the door was shut and latched and that her seat belt was on, then turned onto the runway, and gave it full throttle.

The engine went to full power, the propeller noise rose. She could clearly feel the rumbling of the tires on the runway. The scenery quickly began to pass beside her faster and faster. The nose rose a little, the tire noise went away and with a little sideways movement, the airplane straightened out. There were a few bumps, much like hitting a pot hole while driving a car, other wise, the ride was smooth. As they went higher, the farms and villages became visible. The highway and rail systems laid out under them. The patterns made by the farms became visible. Things she never usually saw in the bigger faster jet aircraft she was used to. They flew higher.

Ten minutes later, he once again said something in German and the plane levelled off and the engine noise went down.

"Ok," he said. "We have about half an hour until we land again. Ever been in a small plane?"

"No," Joss said. "I saw them from time to time back home, but no, never flown in one. It's kind of noisy and bumpy."

He laughed.

"Ya, we're a little low right now and it's a hot day," he said.

"If you don't mind," Joss said. "Ah, where are we going?"

"Just a nice little pizza joint I know," he said. He patted her knee with his right hand. "Don't worry Joss, I won't ply you with booze and sell you off to the Arabs."

He laughed again.

"Oh them I could handle," Joss said. "The Russians though?"

He laughed again. Then once again, the check list came out and he was back on the radio and soon they had landed and the plane was shut down. This airport was smaller, it had about a dozen hangers and many small single engined airplanes parked in an area out side of the hanger area. The runway was also grass, not paved. Richard went around the plane once again, attached tow straps to hooks under the wings and attached them to rings in the ground. Finally, he put the chocks under the wheels. He beckoned for her to follow and off he went.

He walked up to an Audi parked in the lot, withdrew a key from his pocket and unlocked the door. He even held her door open for her. The car was new and had everything a person would expect from a high end German sports sedan.

Twenty minutes later, driving down country roads, they came to a very German town. He quickly drove through the narrow streets, with their long narrow cream coloured houses with red roof tiles. He came to a stop in the parking lot beside a gymnasium of some sort. He opened her door for her and then walked, not to the gymnasium, but what turned out to be a restaurant next to it.

It was between the lunch crowd and the evening crowd. The place was empty. It was a large restaurant. While not the fancy upper end eateries Joss was used to, it wasn't a small town dive like in Texas either. Rather a mixture of both. Unlike American style small restaurants, there were no booths, a few rows of tables were pushed together making long benches. Others were single. Only four chairs were at the bar. The woman behind the bar clearly knew Richard, she rushed around it and gave him a big hug.

She called him Rikhart and spoke to him in German. Then looked at Joss.

"This is Joss," he said in English. "She's American."

The woman looked at Joss and frowned.

"Oh come on Elka," he said. "She's with me. She's ok."

"If you say so Rikhart," Elka said. "Regular for you?"

"Ya," he said. "Same for Joss, she's from Texas, she can handle it."

"Ja, Ja," Elka said. "We see."

Elka was soon back with two beer with the typical thick foam on top.

"Snitzel like normal?" She asked.

"But of course," he said. "You think I came all this way just to ogle you? Beautiful though you are?"

"Ja, Ja," Elka said and slapped him gently on his right cheek. "Always the charmer this one. You better keep a close watch on him Texas."

A few minutes later, others arrived and joined their table. Two older men, two men about her age and two a bit younger. All of them knew Richard and they were soon laughing and joking. While accented, their English was understandable, only occasionally lapsing into German. The meals arrived. The food was outstanding and obviously prepared on site, not like the chain restaurants she was used to. The potatoes were fresh creamy mashed, the vegetables fresh, the meat tender and cooked just right.

Joss saw how easily Richard switched seamlessly from speaking English, to German. He made sure she was included in the conversations. She was asked what it was like in Texas, how she liked Germany and Europe. No one asked her about what she did for work. For once, she was allowed to be a normal person, not a celebrity and she loved it.

After diner, the beer was flowing and soon the shot glasses of hard liquor, Schnapps and Cognac for the most part, arrived. Rikhart played along for a bit, but after the second shot he stopped them.

"You know this get the Canuck drunk game doesn't work guys," he said. "I drink you guys under the table every time."

"Well maybe one day we get lucky hey," Heiner one of the older men said. Every one laughed.

"How about you Texas?" He said.

"Sure, why not?" Joss said, grabbed the shot glass that had been poured for Rikhart and shot it back.

"Woa, good shit," she said.

Several hours later they poured her into bed.

When she woke up in the morning, she found she was in a large soft bed covered with a down filled comforter. Her shirt was still on, but her pants and shoes were off. And her head was pounding. The bed was large and comfortable. Light came in the window filtered by slates partially open in the outside mounted window wide shutters. The window itself was open, slanted inward at the top, not to the side or upward like she was used to.

She found her shoes underneath a chair by the bed and her jeans folded nicely on top of it. Pulling them on, she saw a control beside the window and hit the top button. With an electric whine, the shutters began to rattle upwards and open. Looking outside, she saw she was on an upper floor. The street below was clear of vehicles. The houses across the street were two stories high and unlike in North America, there was no front green space. The houses coming almost to the front of the street. The street was quiet and very clean. Finding the bathroom, she saw it was neat and tidy. The bathroom included a shower and a bidet, along with a large sink and lighted large mirror over a large counter. Joss washed her face and digging through her small purse, applied some light make up and deodorant. She smelled breakfast being cooked and female voices. Following her nose and ears, Joss made her way down a set of stairs with a wrap around thick oak banister and oak clad walls and found the kitchen. A fourtyish aged woman was sitting sipping coffee, while Rikhart was cooking breakfast. The kitchen was small, but well appointed.

"Well Texas," the woman said, her English accented but very understandable. "We thought we would not see you until tomorrow at the earliest."

"Now now Rosy," Rikhart said. "Be nice. She woke up before your old man."

"Ja, Ja," Rosy said. "It will be noon before Heiner gets down here. Coffee Joss?"

"Oh God yes!" Joss said.

Joss found an open spot at the kitchen table and sat. She took a big gulp of the cup of coffee and looked uncertainly at the plate of eggs, sausages and a very large Pretzel Richard plunked down in front of her. Seeing Rosy begin to eat and Richard tying into his like he had not eaten for a week, Joss took a tentative small bite of the pretzel. It was not at all like the ones she was used to. This one was fresh and soft. She also realized how hungry she was.

She saw that Rosy had cut her pretzel in half lengthwise and had put butter and jam on it and did the same. It was delicious.

"The three of you came home last night arm and arm," Rosy said between mouthfuls. "Walking down the centre of the street, or rather staggering, singing at the top of your lungs as you staggered in. Even as drunk as you were, you've got a good voice, for an American."

Rosy laughed then.

"I haven't seen those two bring a woman back home like you since that time with Matti right?" Rosy said.

Richard's demeanour changed. His face and eyes went blank and while he was staring at his plate, he wasn't seeing it.

Then she was quickly beside Rikhart, putting her arm around his shoulders and whispering to him in German. He nodded his head, stood, then quietly walked out the back door.

"Who is Matti?" Joss asked.

"His wife," Rosy said. "And my niece."

Joss didn't know what to do. Here she was going out with a married man in her relatives house.

"Rosy!" Heiner said walking in the kitchen door and interrupting them. "What have you said now? You like him Texas? Go talk to him. He will be by the back fence like always. He can use a friend right about now."

That's where she found him. A grain field was beyond the fence and he had one foot on a lower fence board and both elbows on the top one. He was looking out across the field.

"You ok?" Joss asked. "Something I did last night?"

"Nah," he said. "Rosy is just pissed. She was at some church deal last night and missed the party. She's a good person Joss, they all are. Matti is ancient history. They are good with it Joss."

She had been rubbing his back while he spoke. He looked back at her, her knees went weak. She took a deep breath, stood back from him and held out her hand.

"Joslyn," she said. "Joslyn Litzenburger."

An internal switch somewhere had gone off and he was back to the Richard of before.

"Ah," he said. "Your folks always from Brownsville?"

"No, further west," she said.

"Thought so," he said. "Richard, Richard Rosenbaum."

He took her hand and shook it, then kissed her knuckles.

"Come on then," he said "I'm hungry."

They walked back to the house along a small path in the large rear yard. A girl and two men from last nights festivities had arrived.

"Oh my God!" A blond girl, about twenty exclaimed. "Joss Lynn! In our house!"

Joss didn't know what to do.

"Who her?" Richard said. "Hell no. She's from Texas not Hollywood and she's one of us. She's a Litzenburger."

"Really?" Rosy said. "Litzenburgers lived just down the road from me where I grew up."

"Like I said, she's one of us. Well, not me obviously. My ancestors made the better choice and went to Canada."

"Says who?" Joss said. "Texas is a hell of a lot warmer in the winter."

"And a hell of a lot hotter in the summer," Richard said.

Then the war was on. America or Canada, or Germany. Germany with it's history and culture, America with it's innovation or Canada with it's wide open spaces. All the while, the blond girl, Anna, Elka's daughter, kept gawking at Joss.

Richard seemed to notice this. "Hey, Anna. Come help me get some beer from the shed hey?"

Richard left with her, and he began speaking to her in German. Anna kept her head down and was nodding. Joss wondered if he were chastising the girl for her benefit.

The two men turned out to be Stephan, Anna's father and Joken, her uncle. Both were the sons of Rosy and Heiner. All of them made her feel comfortable and part of the family. They all had a great sense of humour. Especially Heiner who liked to play practice jokes they told her.

Heiner had been a Master Plasterer and had started his own company. Rosy had worked at a large fabric making shop. Jokin had worked alongside his father at the company, while Stephan had leveraged his university education and former position as an officer in the German army to obtain a position with a large German company that produced, installed and maintained complex medical machinery. He was often on the road and away from home. Heiner had sold his company two years earlier and now he and Rosy were retired. When asked if he still worked at the company, Joken said he did not. he didn't elaborate further.

"Hey," Richard said. "Joss, if you don't have anything going on for the next week, why don't you stay and hang around with us eh?"

"Yes, yes," Rosy said. "You must."

There was a two week hiatus from the Formula one season for the teams to go on holidays. The shooting for the movie had wrapped up and she had no commitments until the next race.

"Well," Joss said. "I'd like to, if it's not a burden. Butt..."

Joss looked down at her clothing.

"Ja, ja," Rosy said. "It's settled then, you stay. Come, get your purse, we go shopping. Anna, you come too."

Parked along side the house was a three year old Mercedes S class car. Rosy got behind the wheel and motioned Joss to the passenger side, Anna went in the back seat.

"Kronau is just a small town," Rosy said. "We must to Hokenhiem go for shopping."

"Hokenhiem," Joss said. "I was there last year for a Formula One race."

"Ja, ja," Rosy said. "As crow flying, not far. Driving, more so is."

"We can hear the race cars when they are racing," Anna said.

After driving for fifteen minutes, they arrived at a large store called Globus. Like Walmart, it sold almost everything. Unlike Walmart, the goods were good quality, the store much bigger and better laid out.

Anna and Rosy shepherded Joss threw the store. Soon the shopping cart they had picked up was full of everything Joss and they, thought she would need for the week. Joss used her own personal credit card to pay for it all. Not the one that Joss Lynn used. Loading all the clothing and a few other items Rosy had picked up in the trunk, they were off once again.

Once back in Kronau, Rosy parked beside a small shop, where they each chose an ice cream cone. Rosy insisted on buying. They sat outside in the sunshine on a bench and chatted while they ate. Anna explained that Joss would rarely see her father and mother in the same place. The breakup had been nasty and both of them avoided each other as much as possible.

Jokin had also been divorced and had a daughter that lived in a town about half an hour to the east with her mother. This one was more amicable, both parents realizing they had been to young when they had married and were not compatible with each other. Both had remarried, Joken lived in Mingleshiem, just over one kilometre to the east of Kroanau.

That evening, Joken had brought his wife Sophi along for diner. Sophi spoke excellent English and she and Joss were soon laughing and joking together. A motorcycle arrived in the back yard. Taking their helmets off, Joss saw the driver was Anna and a girl, about thirteen, the passenger. The girl was Talia, Joken's daughter. She was shorter than Anna and a strawberry blond, compared to the blond Anna. She was warmly greeted by her grand parents and Richard. then introduced to Joss. Anna had obviously briefed Talia. While she had the wide eyed look Joss often received by star stuck teenagers, Talia was polite. Her English not as good as the others.

The rest of the week flew by. Early each morning, after breakfast, Richard took her to see something new.

The first day to Worms, where in the famous castle a copy of the first printed bible was. It was also the home of a centre that rescued injured endangered birds and they watched the birds perform in flying demonstrations. The next day they went to the chateau at Bruksaul. It had been restored to it's previous grander after being almost completely being destroyed in WW2. It was patterned after the great French Chateaus.

Then to Heidelberg and it's great castle. The former seat of the Holy Roman Empire. This was more like the large American cities Joss was used to. It had many American chain stores and fast food restaurants, like McDonald's and Pizza Hut.

Almost at the crack of dawn the next day, Richard had them rocketing down the autobahn at high speed in his Audi headed south east. Two hours later, they arrived at the famous NeuShwanstine Castle that the Disneyland castle was copied from. This was located just to the west of Munich. The original castle was rose in colour and lower down on the mountain. Higher up was the large and imposing new castle. It had been built by the *Mad King* Ludwig when he inherited the Bavarian crown. Even though built in the nineteenth century, it had been built with many, at the time, innovations, like running water, in door plumbing, electricity and central heating.

Joss was amazed at the grandeur of the place. While on the verge of being too opulent, it was just shy of it. She was also not quite able to go un noticed this time. There were many American and British tourists touring the sight. But Richard always seemed to be able to spirit her away before she was even spoken to by them. Joss fell asleep on the ride back. It had been a long day and she was unused to the altitude.

"He likes you, you know," Anna said that night. The two had grown close during the week. "You play your cards right, you'll have him wrapped around your little finger."

"As if." Joss said. She didn't know it, but the tips of her ears turned red.

"And you like him too, don't you?" Anna said. "You could do worse."

"But he is already married," Joss said. "To your cousin."

"No," Anna said. "She died in a tragic circumstance seven years ago. He has two sons my age. They don't talk to him anymore. Oppa's half sister Ilene, was Matti's mother. She and her other two daughters blamed Richard for it. Richard kind of self destructed for a while after that. He was slowly drinking himself to death. Ilene and the two sisters petitioned the courts and gained custody of the boys. I think the in laws hostility to Richard rubbed off on the boys."

Rosy walked up at that point.

"This a private conversation, or?" Rosy said.

Anna told her grandmother what they had been talking about.

"Yes," Rosy said. "It was all very tragic. Unlike what my sister in law and her brats think, it was not Richard's fault. In his heart he knows this as well, but he still blames himself."

The three of them were silent for a moment. Joss was not sure how she felt about all this. She was developing feelings, strong one's, about Richard. Now she was unsure about how she should proceed.

"You are the first woman he has shown any interest in," Rosy continued. "Even Anna's mother Elka had a go at him. You must be something special missy Texas."

Rosy thrust a glamour newsprint at Joss. She was front page news. Missing, it said.

"He know about this?" Rosy asked. "Who you really are?"

"Yes grand ma, he knows," Anna said. "So do I. And I am going to tell you what he told me. Leave her be! Not only that, but she is my friend! So, leave her be!"

"Ja, ja, don't get your panties in a knot Anna," Rosy said. "I like him Texas. Don't you be hurting him now!"

"Ummm...." Joss said. She didn't know what she do next. Apologize, or try to explain. but how to explain?

"I'm sure her parents would say the same thing to me Rosy," Richard said, walking up on them. Joss wondered how long he had been standing there. "Time to get you back I think, Joss. They have Interpol looking for you."

The next day, Richard flew her back to the airport in Austria. They were both quiet on the trip. Richard leaving Joss to her thoughts. Joss trying to figure out what she should do next. To take a chance and tell him how she felt about him. how would he react to that. Then they were stopped outside the small private terminal. Joss had not even noticed they had landed. She took a deep breath and decided to face the inevitable.

"You better not come in with me," Joss said. "I can handle all the BS. Thank you for the wonderful week Richard. I have not had such an experience in, well, never actually. You and your family treated me like a normal person. I think I am going to miss you."

"Ya," he said. "Me too."

Then he pulled her to him and kissed her. Things began to heat up, and he stopped and gently pushed her from him.

"Not here, not now," he said. "Go, before somebody comes over here and spots you."

"Will I see you again?" She whispered.

"Well," he said. "Ya never know eh Texas. Shit happens." He had that twinkle in his eyes when he said it.

Reluctantly, she let him go and exited the plane. She was barely in the lounge door when he was taxiing away. Her life became a living hell for the next month.

Chapter Four

Unfortunately for her, the next race was in the UK. The Jorden Fields movie franchise she stared in was British produced and she not only had many personal appearance commitments on behalf of the production company, but the tabloid media and paperatze were on her all the time. No matter if it were a network talk show appearance or even a simple night out for diner, where she went or what she did, she was barraged by reporters yelling questions at her and flashes from cameras blinding her. She was always surrounded by her and the production companies, security teams.

She had't expected to see Richard. From what Joss could determine, Richard normally never attended any of the races outside of North America, except for the German and Austrian races. He hadn't forgotten her however. After one particularly brutal day, which had seen her co star Carson being overly attentive and even snatching a kiss in front of the media, Joss had arrived back at her hotel suite and found a large bouquet of colourful flowers in her room and a case of 12 German Mankiker beer in bottles.

"How odd," Delta, her personal assistant said, handing her a card. "This was delivered for you in a plain card board box from DHL."

The only thing written on the card was a hand drawn map of Texas, with a donkey below and a cowboy boot kicking the donkeys rear.

Joss laughed and instead of tearing up the card and tossing it in the nearest trash bin like she did with most of those kinds of things she received from an admirer, she put it in her breast pocket. Even more amazing, she grabbed two bottles of beer and headed for her bath.

"Put the rest of them on ice Delta," she said.

Once in her bath alone, she looked at the card and dreamed of what might be.

The next race was in Belgium and the heat from the press was off her somewhat. The host broadcasting network did follow her around a little more than they normally did and she had to give two interviews this time.

Once again, the flowers and the case of beer awaited her after the race and the card this time with a thumbs up drawn on it along with the map of Texas. Joss had seen that Delta had figured out that these were coming from someone special to her, but chose to say nothing about it. While she did think things between her and Richard were heading in the right direction, it was still early in the relationship, if it was a relationship, for Delta to know anything about it.

There was another week off between races and as the next two races were still in Europe, her schedule had her doing personal appearances on behalf of her just released Jan Fields movie. The second in the franchise. She had little time off and answering the same repeated questions on all the talk shows and interviews was becoming tiring. So was Carson her co-star. He really began pushing his luck with her. Putting his arm around her in public and trying to hold her hand, even going so far as to hint to one interviewer that things between he and Joss were much more than they appeared. Joss just smiled. The second they were out of sight and hearing of anyone, she gave him a look with daggers coming out of her eyes and stalked away muttering to herself.

One night instead of the flowers and beer, was a large box of German chocolate bars and a bottle of schnapps. Once again the map of Texas on the card, this time with a six gun drawn firing at a character of her co-star. She laughed at that. Underneath, written in a female hand: *Go for it Texas, he's kinda cute.*

"Ok Joss, what's going on?" Delta asked. "Something I need to worry about? And what's with this Texas stuff?"

The only people who knew who she really was, were her family, Scott her lawyer, Delta and John the record producer.

"Just some friends I made in Germany," Joss said. "They think everybody in the States is from Texas or California."

"Ah hu," Delta said. "I've been with you for ten years Joss. Don't try shitting me. Who's the guy? We need to check him out."

This wouldn't be the first time Joss had fallen for some cute hunk that was after her money and or fame and glory. Joss remembered one time she had fallen for the wrong guy, who was only after her to further his own career. Delta had tried to tell her, but Joss had ignored her. Delta contacted Scotty, who *leaked* to the press how this guy was acting. That's when Joss had realized how bad this guy was for her. It took her several months to get over it. It was right after that, she had sworn off men of any type. Until Richard came along.

"No really," Joss said. "I met some really nice people in a little town in Germany that actually like me as a person. And yes, they really know who I am. If you will notice, everyone is still trying to figure out where I was for that week. So they haven't spilt the beans."

"Yet," Delta said. "Who are they, I need them to sign a non disclosure contract."

"Leave them be," Joss said. "All that would do is piss them off."

Joss really liked the family and didn't want Delta upsetting them. Even though Delta was only doing her job and trying to protect Joss.

The next race was at Monaco. Because of all her recent press exposure, the celebrities that normally chummed with her at the races, like Brad Pitt and Serna Williams, stayed well clear of her. They didn't want the press badgering them to try and gain information from them about her. No flowers, chocolate or booze was waiting for her this time. Delta could see Joss was a little down hearted at not having received anything. But she hid it well.

Next was the Spanish Grand Prix. Joss was always in big demand in Spain. They didn't mind that she spoke Texican flavoured Spanish. This time the British broadcasting network actually had a crew following her around for a day. Joss even got them laughing and joking around some. Even the bobble head fake blond female commentator who liked to ask Joss inconsequential questions all the time. Joss had her doing things the normally stuffed up woman would never dream of doing. Like going for donkey rides and Joss pretending to be a bandit chasing her on donkey back. Or in front of a castle, tossing the woman a broom stick and one for her self and having a sword fight with them. Joss had the woman laughing about it, enjoying every minute of it.

Joss took her aside at the end of the day.

"Look, Candice" Joss said. "In five or ten years, you and I are going to be tossed aside and replaced with the latest cute bobbleheads. Get out and enjoy it once in a while. You get to go to all kinds of wonderful and exotic places, all around the world. Take advantage of that while you can."

As she made to leave, Johnny the other commentator, an ex Formula One driver, took her to one side.

"I've been trying to tell her that," he said. "She really is a pretty nice person."

"Well," Joss said. "We can lead a horse to water, but you can't make it drink."

Then in a flourish, surrounded by Delta and her security people, Joss was gone.

Two days after the race, she was in Scotty's office. They had a week before the race in Austin.

"How hard would it be to break the contract for the rest of these races?" Joss asked.

"Not hard," Scotty replied. "They are race by race. You sure you want to do that? They are netting you a million a race. Some two million."

"Ya, I'm sure." Joss said. "I'm tired. I need a break from all this crap. Especially the talk show dog and pony shows."

"I'll call the studio and let you know," Scotty said. "You ok kid?"

"Just need some time off Scotty," she replied. "Living in hotels is getting old."

Later that afternoon, back in her hotel room, Joss had a bite of the meal that had been sent up and made a face. After a while, all the food, no matter where from, all began to taste the same. Just like the hotel rooms. Many times the only differences were just the city they were in.

"Are you getting tired of all this nonsense like I am?" Joss asked Delta. "The food all tastes the same. the hotel rooms are all alike."

Delta shrugged her shoulders. The phone rang at that point. Delta walked toward it and shrugged her shoulders.

"Where you go I follow Joss," Delta said. "But ya, I could use some time off."

Delta picked up the phone and spoke into it, then handed it to Joss, it was Scotty.

"The promoters asked if it would be possible for you to do the Mexican and Russian races Joss," Scotty said. "Two mil for the Mexican race, four for the Russian. I guess the Russian president kind of insisted you go."

"Ya, ok I guess," Joss said. "More money for the pension fund is always welcome Delta keeps telling me. But then I'm out, got it?"

"Ya ya," Scotty said. "What about the next movie? They are just getting the story line together. They upped your contract to ten mill and ten percent of gross."

"As long as the personal appearance dog and pony show is kept to a minimum this time Scotty," she replied. "Let them know I am reevaluating my commitment to the franchise."

"And next years race schedule?" Scotty asked.

"I'll cross that bridge when I come to it," Joss answered.

"Call up the house," Joss said to Delta after hanging up. "Take the wraps off the house. I need some me time after the Russian race. And I am sure you need some me time as well Delta."

Joss was upbeat for the whole pre race week in Austin. Delta even told her she seemed to be having a good time for once. Until the first practice day session. That morning, Joss was acting like a teenager, giggling and prancing about. She dressed down, more down than normal for these practice sessions.

At the track it all changed. Joss kept looking around, spending little time watching the races like she normally did. At the race itself, Joss was Joss. Doing her thing, but Delta could tell she was distracted.

The same thing happened in Mexico. This time Joss was really disheartened. She kept up her personal appearances and actually enjoyed some parts of it. Joss really loved the Mexican people. The night after the race though. Delta caught her wiping a tear from an eye once they returned back to the hotel suite. Joss didn't want to talk about it. Once again no package or booze awaited them.

Instead of flying to the next race destination, Joss had them fly to the small Brownsville airport. Joss was quiet for the whole trip and during the ride to her mothers house in the car that Delta had arranged to meet them there.

Her mother knew her daughter well and saw she was upset. She banished Delta from the kitchen taking Joss by the hand and looking into her tear brimmed eyes.

"What's going on Joss?" Her mom asked.

"He didn't come mom," Joss whispered. Tears started to flow. "He always comes to the Austin and Mexico races. At least he used to send me stupid flowers or chocolate bars and a stupid note. This time, nothing."

"Come with me," her mother said. She took her by the hand to the oversized pantry in the kitchen and opened the door.

Inside was three cases of German schnapps, and a pallet of Canadian beer called Kokanee.

"Really?" Her mom asked. "This came with it."

She handed Joss an oversized card. Hand drawn inside was the map of Texas. Below that, a hand drawn map of some other place, beside that, an eye with a tear dropping out of it.

"When did that come?" Joss asked.

"The Schnapps after Austin. It came by DHL with a German address. The second today from Fed EX from someplace in Canada." Her mom said. "What's going on Joss?"

Just then Harriet, her moms live in assistant walked in, followed by a DHL delivery man pulling a pallet jack with a large box on it. He left the package in the kitchen.

Grabbing a large kitchen knife, Joss attacked the box. Inside were an assortment of German chocolate bars, some tacky plastic flowers and a very large teddy bear. There was no card this time. A large envelope instead.

Inside was a picture of her and the whole German family in the back yard in Germany. There was also a hand written letter. Joss had to keep wiping her eyes as she read the letter, then dashed off to the bath room, letting the letter fall to the floor.

Her mother picked it up.

Hey Texas

Everybody here misses you and sends their love.

He told me to tell you he was sorry for Texas and Mexico, but something came up. He was pretty upset about it Texas.

I told you if you played your cards right you could wrap him around your little finger.

Your bud

Anna

Joss came back from the washroom, blowing her nose loudly in a tissue. Just then, Delta walked in and saw the big carton.

"Not again," Delta said.

"You're just jealous," Joss said. She was all smiles now

"So, which one is he?" Her mother asked, Pointing at the picture.

"That's Anna, Heiner and Rosy her grand parents, Elka her mother, Jokin her uncle and Stef her dad." Joss said pointing each out. It was clear to all that Joss liked these people.

"Oh," her mom said.

"*He,*" Joss said. "Took the picture."

At that point, her two sisters rushed in and hugs were going all around. They liked Delta and hugged her too.

"Woa," Kat her older sister said. "Somebody has the hots for you sis." She was pointing at the large carton on the kitchen floor.

"You ain't seen nothing yet," mom said.

She opened the pantry door and pointed to the contents.

"Holy shit," Lin her younger sister said. "This guy sure knows the way to a girls heart. Chocolates, hard booze and beer."

She grabbed a bottle and tossed it to Kat, then one for herself.

"Oh God," Lin said. "Kokanee? That's very Canadian. But it's awesome!"

"Ok Del," Kat said. "Spill it. Who is this guy?"

Delta just shrugged her shoulders. She too grabbed a bottle of beer.

"Kinda thought there was a guy," Delta said. "But your sis, being your sis..."

"He a German or what?" Lin asked. "Those German guys are hunks."

Joss wagged a finger at them. She had a sly grin in her face and a twinkle in her eye. She would let them stew on it for a while. Then she changed the subject.

For the next three days, one of the five women would ask some subtle questions here and there trying to ferret out who Richard was. Joss didn't fall into their traps. she had a secret and she meant to keep it.

"I'm taking some time off," Joss told her mother the day before she was to leave for Russia. "At least a year, maybe more. The studio is just starting the script for the next movie mom. I'll do it, then probably retire."

"You sure about that Joss?" Her mother asked. "You gonna toss it all away for a man like I did?"

Her mom had tossed away a lucrative career as an advertising executive for her father, a minor executive at a mid sized oil company. Who turned out to be a bum, who tossed her aside for a younger model the first chance he got.

"No mom," Joss said. "It's time. I, we, have enough money mom. This fame stuff is getting old. I want to slow down and enjoy life mom, while I still can. Settle down, find a nice hunk, have a couple of kids. If not with this guy, well, there are plenty of them out there."

"Oh no honey," her mom said. "You've got it bad for this one. It won't be so easy to walk away from this time."

While Joss and her mother had been talking about this, Lin and Delta, who had been out shopping, walked in.

"Please tell me he's not that co-star of yours," her mother said.

"Ewwweee!" Lin, Delta and Joss all said at the same time.

"Really mom!" Joss said. "That guys a dweeb.. OK, gotta go get packed for Russia."

The next day, just before they were set to leave for the airport, a FedEx delivery came. It was a letter for Delta. She tore into the envelope and read it. She then sighed, looking exasperated.

"What is it?" Joss asked. "Everything okay?"

"It's literally nothing." Delta thrust the letter into Joss' hands. As Joss read it, a smirk appeared on her face.

Naughty, naughty girl, Delta. It began

Setting your hound Scotty on my scent, and even trying to hunt down my family in Germany?

It's a waste of time. If she hasn't told you yet, you don't need to know yet.

Leave it alone. The harder you look for me and the deeper you dig, the more she will resent you, Delta. And she really likes you. Keep that in mind, eh?

Joss showed the letter to her mother and laughed.

"We have been looking in the wrong place," Delta said. "He's Canadian."

"Good luck on that one Del," Joss said, dragging her large wheeled suit case to the front door.

After a last round of hugs and kisses, Joss and Delta were whisked way to the airport in the waiting limo and soon were jetting their way to Sochi Russia.

The only people on the plane were her gaggle. Joss made a point of sitting beside Delta in the private executive jet on the first leg to New York.

"Look Del," Joss said. "Yes, I really like this guy and I think he really likes me. I don't know what his story is. I think he is Canadian, but am not sure. He has two sons, that don't speak to him, and a bunch of in-laws the same. His wife died and they blame him for it. The Germans are her relatives, and they told me he was in no way responsible for it. There, now you know almost as much as I do about him.

"He's a nice guy. Looks like he has a couple of bucks. Owns his own airplane. Doesn't bug me about this fame shit. There you go."

"In fact," Joss said after a few minutes of silence. "He kept going out of his way to avoid me. I took the bull by the horns in Austria Del. I chased him down, not the other way around."

"You sure about this Joss?" Del asked. "Why all the big secrecy? What's he hiding?"

"Maybe he just likes his privacy. Have you thought about that?"

The two didn't exchange another word until the plane landed for a brief layover in New York. Scotty had asked them to stop over so he could give her the contract proposal for the new movie.

Scotty was waiting on the tarmac and entered the plane as soon as he was able. The two women updated him on the situation.

"Maybe he is just protecting himself Del," Scotty said. "Or, if what I suspect is true, protecting Joss. You know how hard the paperatzy can be at times Del. He might have a business concern he wants to protect from all that. I kind of like him already. He could just have easily used Joss for some fast and free publicity. But he didn't

"Looks like that German family is the same way. You have some good friends there Joss."

"I think so," Joss said. "After Russia, I'll see if I can get them out to the ranch for a month or so. Unlike you guys, I know how to get ahold of them."

"Ok Joss," Scotty said. He tossed a thick closed file on her lap. "These are the contracts for the next movie. No rush, by the end of the year would be nice. All right, I am busy and have to go. Toddles, have good holiday."

As fast as he had arrived. He was gone.

Chapter Five

Russia was also one of her favourite races. She had a lot of fans in Russia. Unlike other places, they were not pushy about it though. She did have to put up with the usual hassle from the big shots. But she had learned early in her career, that it didn't matter which country they came from, big shots always acted the same way.

Arrogant and full of self importance and themselves.

Unlike the vast majority of the Formula One circuit, the Russians actually came for the racing. All of it. The VIP suite was fuller than normal, even for the first practice sessions.

Joss saw right away that one small box was empty. Her heart skipped a beat and her hopes began to rise. While Joss was attentive to those around her, her eyes kept darting around the room. She would occasionally walk to the window and look down at the pit lane. Clearly she was looking for some one.

Then before the last preliminary race before the F1 Cars would go for qualifying runs, Joss spotted him and smiled.

"Come kiddies," Joss said. "Time for some fresh air."

She made her way down to pit lane. Nobody ever tried to stop her from going where she wanted to go. Once she arrived there, the Brits broadcasting company sent Clarissa and her crew chasing after Joss.

Joss made her way down the pit lane, at home amongst the noise of engines roaring as they were tested, air guns working as they spun on lug nuts to tires. She stopped here and there asking a question of some one and signing an autograph or a selfie from one of the crews. But her eyes were always focused on one car and its crew.

"A hundred Euros and diner on car 38," Joss said, walking up to Richard. He turned and looked at her over the top of his sunglasses.

"You're on," he said. "Your gonna loose your ass this time kiddo."

Delta just stood there, looking suspiciously at him.

"We shall see," Joss said.

And she was off to the next pit stall.

"Make sure you have the money this time Texas," Richard called out as they walked away.

Joss noticed that Delta kept glancing over her shoulder towards Richard and the crew.

Once they were alone in their hotel suite, Delta asked, "That was him wasn't it?"

"Who Del?" Joss said. She had been chipper all the rest of the day. Giddy almost.

"The guy you made the bet with," Del said. "He called you Texas."

"You must have miss heard him or something Del," Joss said. "Ok, off to bed, big day tomorrow."

That also was unusual for her. She usually made the rounds of the parties the night before the big race. She had only done gone to bed early once before.

In Austria!

"No you don't missy!" Del yelled and chased after Joss. "Not again!"

Joss looked back at her and smiled, a glint of mischief in her eyes. Then she playfully ushered Delta out into the hallway and shut the door.

Suspecting that Delta would be up early the next morning, Joss made sure to already be gone by the time she arrived at her room.

Joss was already sitting at his table when Richard arrived. She was watching the pit lane and the crews making ready for the GT race. It was their last race of the year and the team that Richard had been talking to was only one point behind car 38 in the overall point standings.

She gave him a quick peck on the cheek as he sat down.

"You think your guys have a chance?" She asked. "#38 is good at this track."

"We'll see." Richard said, taking a pull from the beer. "Car is almost perfect. Jochen wants it badly. Ya it will happen."

"Jochen?" Joss said.

"Ya, you met him in Germany," Richard said. "He owns the team."

"Anna's uncle?" Joss asked.

"Ya," Richard said. "Anna is the driver."

"What??"

"You ain't the only one with a secret life Texas. She does ok today, she'll be in F2 next year. Well, she'll already be in F2 next year, but if she wins, it will be at a better team."

"Does she need a sponsor?' Joss said. "I can help, or get some one to help."

"You'll have to ask her Joss," Richard said. "I kinda stay out of that part of it. Rosy handles all that for her."

"Here," Joss said. "Take the stupid hundred Euros. Bets off."

"Atta girl Texas," he said. He pulled a hat from under his jacket and handed it to her. It was in Annas team colours.

"You jerk!" Joss said, punching him on the arm. "You played me!"

"Such an easy mark too." Richard said. He bent over and gave her a quick kiss on the lips. She almost fainted, her heart was racing so fast.

Then the race started. While Richard quietly watched, sipping on his beer, Joss was at the edge of her seat. When Anna passed 38 for the lead, she jumped up and yelled. Then with a strength Richard didn't know she had, picked him out of his chair, hugged him and gave him a big kiss.

The race was over, Anna had won and with the win, had won the GT championship.

"Ut oh," Richard said. He pointed to the front entrance. Delta had just walked in and was scanning the crowd. "Your blood hound is on the scent."

"Let her look," Joss said. "Come on, I want to congratulate Anna."

"Is that wise?" Richard said.

They made their way toward the back entrance.

"Even if they recognize me," Joss said. "So what. It can't do anything but help her."

Anna was in the process of putting her helmet away and removing her driving suit when they arrived.

"Anna!" Joss screamed as she came up behind her. "You little sneak!"

"Texas!" Anna screamed. "You came! Did you see? I won!"

"Ja ja, niece," Jochen said. "Ja Ja. We all know. You won. Hello Texas. Where have you been?"

Before Joss could reply, they were surrounded by the British broadcasting crew. Joss put her arm around Anna, who did the same with Joss.

"Isn't she great?" Joss said beaming."This is my very special friend Anna. You watch, she'll be in the big show in a couple of years."

While the press gaggle turned their attention to Anna and away from Joss. Johnny the ex formula one driver stopped her. For a commentator Johnny was one of the better ones.

"I think you are right," he said. "Not only that, but I think it will not take to long. It's about time we had a female F1 driver and she's good. You endorsing her will make a big difference Joss. Thank you for that. I like the kid Joss."

"So do I Johnny, so do I," Joss said.

"Hey Richard," Johnny said. "Come to gloat did you? I told you I liked Anna. I just didn't think she would make it. You know..."

"Ya, I know," Richard said. "She was going to F2 anyway Johnny. We'll have to see where though. Rosy can be tough to handle sometimes."

"Don't I know that one," Johnny said. "Jochen, you need any help, you let me know hey?"

"Ya for sure Johnny," Jochen said.

"Be nice," Richard said as Johnny walked away. "He could just as easily turn on Anna."

"Ja Ja," Jochen said. "I'm going to have to find somebody like Delta for Anna soon. Rosy will piss to many people off. See ya Rickhart. Don't be a stranger Texas."

Jochen hurried over to the press gaggle around Anna.

"Speaking of blood hounds," Richard said, pointing his chin down to the end of the pit lane.

Delta and the rest of the gaggle were making their way down from the far end.

"Come on, I'll take you someplace they can't get at you from," Richard said, taking her hand.

The GT cars were hurriedly exiting the pit lane as the main Formula One crews began to set up for the main race. Most of the GT crews knew Richard and some Joss. Not so for the Hubba Bubba pit garage that Richard came to.

"Hey Richard, Joss," a man, clearly not a mechanic said, coming up with his hand outstretched. "Anna did good this year. I going to have a shot at her?"

"Depends on Rosy, you know that Gunther," Richard said. "I have any say in the matter, ya, you've got a shot. Up to Anna though."

"You want to watch the race from here Joss?" Gunther asked. "We have better network feeds and you will be right at the centre of all the action."

"Oh could I Richard?" Joss said. "Sure why not?"

Gunther handed her a set of headphones, Richard another. His name was on his.

Richard explained that she could hear all the communications between the team and the drivers as well as the television feed.

"Richard is usually down here with us. It just the North American ones he's up in the box," Gunther said.

"What!" Joss said and belted Richard on the arm. "You bum! Why did you do that and not let me know?"

"To be fair Joss," Gunther said, "Richard was not around the last month or so."

"Sorry Joss," Richard said. "Something else came up and I couldn't make it."

"Atta girl Texas, give him hell eh?" One of the drivers said as he walked up. "He needs a kick in the ass from time to time. So, Anna's gunning for my job eh? Good. I'm getting to old for this stuff."

Joss looked from man to man. This was one of the premier drivers on one of the premier teams that was always in the hunt for the world titles.

"Joss Lynn, George Hamilton," Richard said.

"Big fan of yours Texas," George said, shaking her hand.

"Same for me," Joss said.

"Come on, I'll show you the car." George said.

"Good for her," Gunther said. "If she doesn't thank you for it, I will."

"Ya, I don't know why her handlers hadn't thought of this," Richard said. "She's a big racing fan. Especially of your team and George."

"They just want her to make money for them Richard. You know that. Have fun today, make sure she does too eh? I gotta go to work now. Hey Anna, good job today kid."

"Why'd you take off so fast Richard?" Anna asked in German. "I wanted to share that moment with you."

"You know me Anna," he replied in the same language. "It was your moment, not mine. Yours and your uncles. Both of you worked hard for it."

"Joss! You're here!" Anna said. She grabbed Joss and gave her a big hug. "Did you meet George yet? I know you are a big fan."

Richard faded into the background letting them be. He did notice Delta lurking around though. There was to much security around the garage and she didn't have the correct pass to gain access though.

Richard grabbed another set of headphones and made his way over to where Delta was. Joss saw that they exchanged a few words before Richard brought her into the garage and where the personal guests were allowed to watch the race from.

"Look what the cat dragged in Texas," Anna said as Delta and Richard walked up. "You going to play nice Delta, or am I going to have to kick your ass."

"Anna!" Joss said. "Delta is like you. One of my few real friends. Even though she gets paid well for it."

Richard walked away, a grin on his face.

"He'll be hanging out with Gunther over there," Anna said, pointing to the booth by the pit wall. "I don't know what those guys do over there, but that's where he usually is. Unless he's with you Texas."

"So you're the famous Texas then?" A dressed to the nines female said as she walked up and sat down with them. "George is a big fan. So are the kids. Anna, you going after my man's job?"

"As if," Anna said. "Maybe as a back up and test driver. F2 is probably as high as I'll ever get."

"Not with me, Texas and especially him Anna," the woman said pointing down at Richard. "Your going to be in the big show Anna. What you do when you get there is up to you.

"Hello, I am Sandra Hamilton, George's wife, your are?" She stuck her hand out to Delta.

"Delta," she said. "I am Joss's personal assistant."

"Oh you're more than that and you know it," Joss said. "Joss, pleased to meet you Sandra."

"Ah so you do have a name Texas," Sandra said. Then she laughed. "Yes I know who you are. We just didn't know who this Texas was. It seems super hunk Canuck has taken a big shinning to you Texas."

"What?" Sandra said, looking at Anna shaking at finger at her. "I'm from the farm in Wyoming, you know that."

"Kids these days," she continued. She put her arm through Joss's. "Come, let's leave these low life wrong side of the tracks people behind Joss. I mean, really."

"Oh yes," Joss said. "All these small town hicks are all the same Sandy."

Delta stuck her tongue out at them as they walked away.

"You gonna be a problem for my cousin and Joss, Delta?" Anna said.

"Only if he hurts her Anna," Delta said. "Then the wrath of god will descend on him."

"Ya me too,"Anna said. "She loves him like crazy Delta. And he won't show it around us, but he loves her like crazy too."

"Up to us to make sure it stays that way then hey?" Delta said in German surprising Anna.

"My ancestors came from the same place hers did," Delta said. "We kept our traditions. Her people didn't."

"So did his," Anna said also in German "His people were originally from our part of Germany, like hers."

"Mine too," Delta said. "Somewhere around Karlsrue I think."

"Well then,"Anna said. "It's all good then."

"I hear you're thinking about retiring after your next movie," Sandra said. Her and Joss had moved to the upper deck of the garage complex. They had a better view of pit lane and the start straight from there. "Super Hunk have anything to do with that?"

"No, not really," Joss said. "I was on the fence about it long before I met him. It's getting old Sandy. I never really liked the life style anyway. I have enough, it is invested wisely, I'll do ok."

"Ya George too," Sandy said. "His contract is up at the end of this season. He wants to talk to Gunther and Richard first, then Anna. If she is serious and wants it, he will stay on for next year and the year after to show her the ropes. Otherwise? Back to backwoods Alberta for us."

"Alberta?" Joss asked. "Where's that?"

"Just across the border from Montana." Sandra said. "Lots of movies shot there. You do know where Montana is?"

"Hey!" Joss said. "I passed high school, barely."

"Me too," Sandra said. They both laughed. "Boys and parties for me."

"Boys and singing for me," Joss said.

"Don't sweat it," Sandra said. "I didn't know what Alberta was either. It's a lot like Texas but bigger, colder and closer to the mountains. They have more oil than Texas and more cows."

"That where Richard is from Sandra?" Joss asked. "I really don't know all that much about him."

Sandra shrugged her shoulders.

"Who knows anything about Richard? Maybe Anna and her family?"

Then the race was on. It was to noisy to talk anymore.

Joss did notice that the television cameras caught her, Sandy and Delta, more than once, cheering when George made a big move during the race. It was kind of hard not to. The four of them were plastered all over the monster screens posted all around the track. The last quarter of the race settled down. George and his team mate had things well in hand. If nothing drastic happened in the last few laps, they were going to win.

"Keep an eye on him Joss," Sandra said. "He's going to make a break for it pretty soon."

Just then, one of the back markers spun out hitting the wall. Joss looked back down to the pit lane. Richard was gone.

"Damn that man!" She said. "Now what?"

"Now what, what?" Richard said. He was standing behind them, but out of sight of the track and the cameras.

Joss flung herself out of her chair and into his arms.

"I thought you had run out on me again," she said.

"No fear of that," Richard said. "Besides, you lost the bet and owe me dinner."

"What bet?" Anna and Delta said almost at the same time.

"That car 38 would beat you Anna," Richard said.

"Wait wait," Joss said. "One, I didn't know you were driving Anna. Two, I canceled the bet as soon as I knew."

"To bad, so sad," Richard said. "Can't welch on a bet already made. Come on Texas, time to blow this taco stand. And you aint' taking me to no rotten Ronnies or Pizza Hut neither."

"Oh, to Elka's then?" Joss asked.

"Elka's," Delta said. "Wheres Elka's?"

"That's my mom's restaurant," Anna said. "That's where he brought her after Austria."

"Somehow I don't think so Delta," Sandra said. "I think Super Canuck has other plans. George says wont be around much, if at all for the rest of the season. Got something special planned Super Hunk?"

Chapter Six

A cab took them to the executive area of the airport in Sochi. Once again going past all the private jets and rich peoples toys, to the lonely little single engine plane by itself.

There was a little more hassle than they had faced in Germany and Austria. It was after all Russia and they did like their proper paperwork. As Joss dug into her handbag for her passport, Richard put his hand on her arm. He handed two blue coloured passports to the immigration official, who looked them over, then the people themselves, then he nodded his head and they were clear to go.

Richard handed her one of the blue passports. The one he kept had a Canadian Shield on it. Hers, an American one. While he made his way around the plane doing his inspection, Joss opened hers. It was new and had a Russian entry stamp in it. The only one. It was also under her real name. Not Joss Lynn like the one she always used.

"How'd you manage that?" Joss asked holding up the new passport.

"Kind of helps when the Russian President takes an interest in things," Richard said. "I dunno. Maybe the promoters said something about you wanting to go on holiday anonymously?"

"So where are we going?" Joss asked after they had levelled off.

"Ever seen Russia?" Richard asked. "Not just Sochi."

"No," Joss answered.

"Good, that's where we are going."

It was dark by the time they landed five hours later. It was a small airport on the outskirts of a small city. Richard surprised her by speaking Russian to everyone he met. Everyone seemed to like him and by extension her. Some of the people spoke rudimentary English and tried to include her. Richard spent a lot of time translating.

Other than these particular people drank a little more than the people back home, Joss had the feeling they were much the same as normal Americans.

Richard didn't drink anything that night and once again poured her to bed later on.

"Come on lazy bones!" He said, tossing a pillow at her. "It's lunch time and you have to go shopping."

"Hu wha?" Joss mumbled. Her head was not quite pounding, but close to it.

"For what?" Joss asked a little more coherently.

"Well my dear," he said. "You are for sure going to be a little ripe after a few days of wearing what you have with you."

"Argh!!," she said. "OK, Ok, lemme have a shower first."

The hotel was close to the shopping district and they walked there. While not up to the standards a small American city was, this town was a far cry from what the news channels back home showed about Russia. Most of the cars driving by were new, European or Japanese cars. Yes, there were a few junkers, but the same thing occurred in the States. While the styles were slightly different, the clothing was very western European in appearance. The women had a different way of doing their makeup than Joss was used to seeing. Again, a far cry from what was shown on American TV, which generally portrayed Russians as drab and dreary people.

A few people noticed her, but they didn't bother her. Taking the way Richard was dressed into account, she bought understated *normal people*, clothing. Richard paid for it with cash, not a credit card.

Then he bought her a sturdy duffle bag. Back at the hotel, he showed her how to roll her clothing so it would stow easily in the duffle bag and not get wrinkled.

It was late afternoon by the time she was finished and Richard took her to the local Cathedral. It was magnificent. All the polished brass on the domes and inside and the colourful paintings and frescos inside.

Then they walked to a local neighbourhood restaurant. Once again, she had a great time. The people all friendly. This time Richard stopped her from drinking to much. He didn't drink any booze at all.

Early next morning they were back at the plane. A fuel truck was waiting for them. In addition to his pre flight safety checks, Richard supervised and measured the fuel in the four wing tanks. He paid the man in cash and soon they were off.

She was a little queasy on this trip and missed many of the sights as they flew along. Once again stopping at a small airport outside another small town.

She, like Richard, didn't drink any booze that night. The locals seemed disappointed, but seemed to all understand. Richard must have said something to them.

"Joss," he said once they were back in the hotel room. "Alcohol affects the inner ear for up to twelve hours after your last drink. That's why you were a little queasy today and why we didn't fly the day before.

"Like the last town, there is not much to see here other than the cathedral. I'd like to make an early flight tomorrow if it's fine by you?"

"Ok," Joss said.

They had sex for the first time that night. It was not rushed and he was very gentle with her. Something else she had rarely experienced in her past relationships. Those had generally been rushed and frantic affairs. Not the slow intent one she had just experienced.

This day, Richard had her come with him as he made his preflight checks. Showing her what he was doing and why. Also when they did his start up routine. He did it slower and explained what he was doing and why. The same for the run up at the edge of the runway. He verbally called out the speeds and what he was doing as they sped down the runway. Once they had levelled off at their cruising altitude. He told her what the control column and the foot pedals did. What to look for at the nose of the plane.

"Want to give it a try?" Richard asked. "It's not all that hard and I won't let you do anything wrong."

He explained how fast they were going and showed her on the large Digital display to her left how to see the direction they were going. How fast they were going, if the wings were level and if they were climbing or descending. Then he gave her control of the airplane. Coaching her the whole time. He had her go up and down, turn right and left and make a circle.

Joss was actually flying! It was exciting and exhilarating and scary, all at the same time.

"Great job," Richard said. He took back control of the airplane, engaged the auto pilot and they resumed their original direction.

"You've got some natural talent there kiddo," Richard continued. "Probably what made you such a good stock car racer."

"How'd you know about that?" Joss asked.

"Not hard to find out Joss, it's in your bio," Richard said. "Also, ever heard of a thing called google?"

She punched him on the arm.

"Yes I know about google," she said. "I'm not just a pretty face you know. Speaking of which, how come I can't find out anything about you on Google?"

"Well miss nosy," Richard said. "Most of us normal type folks keep our digital footprint small. Not like you rich and famous types."

This time, when they came into land, he made all of his radio calls in English, not Russian, so she heard what he was saying.

Once they stopped and shut down. He had her follow him through his post flight inspection and showed her how to tie down and secure the aircraft. After he had written down some information in the two books he had with him at all times, he brought out a smaller, new one. Wrote something in it and handed it to her.

Lesson one and lesson two, were written in it, his name beside them and hers as pilot in command, for two hours.

The next day was more of the same. This time, he showed her how to adjust the throttle and the mixture controls and why. Then he had her slowly pull the nose of the plane upward while trying to keep the same altitude and stall the plane. And how to recover from it. She did it by herself twice. Then he took back over. This time when he landed, he told her what to look for, the speeds they were to come in at and when.

Once again he wrote in her log book.

The next day, he had her take off. Then during the trip, how to turn and hold the same altitude and what would happen if she didn't or did it wrong. He told her to put her feet and hands on the controls and follow what he was doing when they landed that afternoon.

All during their flights now, he would explain things to her and ask her questions after. Sometimes he asked her a question about what he had taught a few days before. Then he let her land.

The next day, she did everything but file the flight plan. That night in the hotel, he showed her how to do that. The next day he made her file the flight plan for that days travel. While he walked over to the control area to file it, she did the preflight and supervised the refuelling.

Once again, she took off, and this time, he operated the radios while she flew. She was also in the left seat this time not the right. Once she looked over at him and he was sound asleep. She whacked him on the arm then.

"Hey, You're supposed to be the pilot of this thing, not me!" She said.

"Why," he replied. "You're doing a great job."

"Some people," he continued, "no sense of ha, ha."

"You just wait until we get on the ground!" Joss said. "I'll ha ha you, you bum."

"Oh goody," Richard said. "Can't wait."

She stuck her tongue out at him but then was to busy making her final approach to land.

That night they landed at a small airstrip outside a small town. While she secured the plane, Richard went to the control tower and spoke briefly to the people there.

That morning after she had completed her preflight safety checks, he tossed the keys at her.

"Make two circuits of the field and two stop and goes, then come back here and shut it down." He said. He walked away.

"What?" Joss exclaimed. "Aren't you coming?"

"Hurry up then," he said, turning around and walking back wards. "The sooner you get that done the sooner we get out of here."

She was nervous at first. She noticed the plane had a little more power than with the both of them on board. Her first touch down, she floated a bit down the runway before the wheels hit. She was completely focused on what she was doing. How the plane felt, which way the wind was blowing her nose. Remembering what Richard had taught her and what she had to do and how to do it. The second touch down was much better, the fast take off after straight down the runway and when she landed for her final stop, it was almost perfect.

She taxied up to the tie down area and saw five more people standing beside Richard. They waited until she had finished her post flight, then, two of them, one a woman, rushed up, pulled her shirt out of her pants at the back and cut off the tail of the shirt with a big pair of sizers. Then the man splashed her with five gallons of water from a bucket over her head.

While she was spluttering her way through that, another man came forward and handed her a certificate written in Russian. Richard handed her another written in English. The Russian one had Joss Lynn written as the name on it. The English one her real name.

"Congratulations," the Russian who had handed her her Russian certificate said in good English. "You have just passed your first solo flight."

"Usually we have a big party to celebrate," the woman who had cut off her shirt tail said. "But Richard said you have a long way to go today. Next time, da?"

"Go get changed dummy," Richard said. "Your gonna make my seats all wet."

"He comes through here every year," the woman said. "Why he insists on flying that dinky thing all across Russia, I'll never know."

"What?" Joss said.

"Yes yes," the woman said. "Every year he fly across Canada in that thing, then down to Europe, back to Canada, then to Texas and Mexico. Then to Sochi. Now he will go back home for a while and maybe to Brazil. Who knows, sometimes he doesn't do the Brazil thing.

"You should be able to write your private licence by the time you get back home."

Like their new norm, Richard was in the right seat, Joss in the left. She was handling everything for this flight. It was a five hour run this time. She had to manage her altitude and fuel burn, or they would not make it to the next stop, a thousand kilometres away. Richard never made it obvious, but he was keeping an eye on the gauges.

They had been at cruise for an hour, not a word spoken between them.

"This is beautiful out here," Joss said finally.

"Ya," Richard said. "Not to shabby."

"The woman at the airport," Joss said. "She said I will be able to write my private licence by the time we get home. Is that true?"

"Pretty much," Richard said. "We have been doing your ground school up here and in the hotels. You will have to do a four hour cross country solo, which we don't have time for on this trip. I have been training you with the Canadian standard, but its pretty much the same as the American. You will just have to pass the final written with a seventy percent and the written radio exam. Plus a final check out with an FAA certified examiner."

"Oh," Joss said. She wasn't sure about this. Having only achieved a GED is school, she had never been all that good at exams.

"Piece of cake," he replied. "You've already got more flying hours than a lot of students and you are very good. Almost a natural."

"So you signing my log book is good then?"

"If you were going for your Canadian licence, yes," Richard said. "I am a certified flight instructor. The flight instruction hours is the same in both countries as is the training syllabus. But you still need an FAA check ride and have to pass their written exams."

"There is that much difference in the exams?" Joss asked.

"Not really," he replied. "Our exam puts a little more emphasis on icing conditions and remote flying conditions than yours does. It's a lot like what we are flying through right now where I come from Joss. But you need to know all the stuff, not just some of it. The Russians passed you."

"What?"

"Ya, thats not a solo certificate they gave you Joss, that's a Russian pilots licence."

"What? How?"

"The man you were talking to?" Richard said. "Sergei is the head of their general aviation department. It's his signature on the licence.

Being Joss Lynn is helpful sometimes. Just don't let it go to your head Joss. He knows me and knows I won't let you screw this up."

"The woman that was there said you do this trip every year?" Joss asked.

"Ya," he said. "This will be my fourth around the world trip. I think I'll do it the other way next time. Wind direction is different."

"In this thing?"

"Ya, what wrong with it? Its got plenty of legs, most of the time and I'm usually flying solo, that helps a bit on the fuel. I also have a hundred gallon ferry tank I can put in the back if I need it."

"It's kind of slow isn't it?" Joss said.

"So what," Richard said. "Who's in a hurry? Plus I get to see new places and meet new people."

"Can you afford all this?"

"It's not that big a deal," Richard said. "It costs eighteen grand to enter Russian airspace, even if it is only for an hour. If you notice, I generally land at small out of the way airports. The landing fees are very small, if there are landing fees. I use car gas not aviation fuel. And before you ask, this engine and fuel system has been modified for it. Don't try that at home kiddies."

"What the hell do you do Richard?" She asked. He just smiled at her.

"I don't ask you what you do," he said.

"That's because you already know what I do you bum!" Once again she smacked him on the arm. "Learning German I can see, that's your heritage. But Russian?"

"That also is my heritage," he said in flawless Spanish. "As it is yours. Ask your mother when you get back home. The Spanish? Well I know this cute girl that kind of speaks it, so I thought I'd impress her."

He moved his arm so that when she tried to smack him all she hit was air.

"All of us have to learn French until the second year of high school Joss. French, Spanish, Italian and some Portuguese, all have the same base language. Same with German, Dutch, Swedish etc. Russian, oh no, that's a whole different ball game."

'Why learn all those languages?" She asked.

"Comes in handy at times for work," he said. They were talking exclusively in Spanish now. "Plus it's kind of a hobby for me. I get lot of girls too."

This time he didn't move when she smacked him.

"No really," he said. "You know the Spanish speakers love you because you speak Spanish to them. I find it makes life easier. Especially here in Russia. If you have noticed, some of these Air Traffic Controllers English is not so great. Plus you meet lots of interesting people, who show you lots of interesting things."

"I never really thought about it that way." Joss said. "It makes sense. But don't the Russian officials hassle you?"

"Not as badly as your country does," Richard said. "I always have my paper work complete and up to date. I follow their laws and regulations. Same as I do in the States."

"But why..."

"Do Americans have so much hassle coming to Russia?" he finished for her. "Because they come with a superior attitude and don't want to follow the rules. A lot of your people do the same when they try and cross into Canada. Then get pissed because they can't. Canada is not the US Joss. We speak the same language, share the largest undefended border in the world and have many of the same values. But we have many different laws and regulations. Some better, some not so much.

"People though, well people are pretty much the same all over. They want a good safe life for themselves and their kids. Most people are good folks. Just like you once were Joss."

"What do you mean, once were?" she shot him a dirty glance.

"The more rich, famous and powerful people become Joss, the more they loose touch with normal people," Richard said.

"You didn't," she replied. "Neither did I."

"Who said I was rich, famous or powerful Joss? I just make the most of what I have. And yes you did Joss, and you know it. Or is this being with me just a simple distraction for you?"

"God damn you no!" She burst out.

"I have control of the plane Joss." He said. She was crying now.

"How can you say that to me!" She was working into a fine furry now. "I have told you how I feel about you!"

"Wouldn't be the first time a woman has pulled the wool over my eyes Joss."

She looked over at him. He was staring out the cockpit window, straight ahead. She knew the autopilot was still flying the plane. Then something Rosy had said about Richards in-laws hit her. She calmed down.

"Do you know how many times men have screwed me over Richard?" She asked. "I kept telling myself, this one will be different. Am I making the same mistake with you?"

He looked over at her. Then he shrugged his shoulders.

"Hell, I don't know," he said. "I don't think so."

"I don't think so too," Joss said. Now she kissed the shoulder she kept smacking. "Now can I please resume flying. My asshole flight instructor might flunk me if I don't get enough hours in."

He smiled, and all was right in her world again.

They took the next day off. Richard told her they were in a small town called Lavrentiya. Richard had hired a driver and they had driven to see the small local museum. The museum had an exhibit of winged shaped items that had been carved from Walrus ivory. Archaeologists had discovered them and it had been determined that they had been used to prototype harpoon tips. Other than the museum, the airport and the fact it was the administration hub of the district. There was not much to see. The town only had five hundred full time residents.

She asked Richard why there seemed to be many soldiers in the town. Richard told her that it was just across the Bering Striate from Alaska. They had a simple dinner in the restaurant attached to the small hotel and turned in early.

He had her up before dawn the next morning.

"This leg, like our others have been, will be around six hours, maybe a bit more," he said. "It is by far, the most dangerous one though. We will be crossing the Bering Sea and Alaska, then landing at Inuvik in the Northwest Territories."

"Why?' Joss asked. "It's almost four hundred kilometres farther. Why not land at Nome Alaska, then transit to Inuvik?"

"Don't have to clear customs twice and pay access and landing fees to those dastardly Yanks," Richard said. "They make us Canucks go through all kinds of hoops crossing over from Russia. It's not so bad in Canada. Plus I have a Canadian registered aircraft, pilots licence and passport. I have to be pilot in command when we land though. You get all the hard work, I just land us eh?"

At the plane, he handed her an inflatable life vest and showed her how to put it on.

"We won't be out of safe gliding distance to land at anytime, so we don't need the survival suits." He said.

He had her file the flight plan. The officials scrutinized her Russian pilots licence, saw the name on it, then couldn't be helpful enough after. Of course Richard had to take photos of Joss and everyone in the control tower, and the ground crew, and the immigration people.

"Anytime your highness is ready," Richard said once they were buttoned up in the airplane.

Joss stuck her tongue out at him, then she was all business. Soon they were out of sight of Russia, with nothing but the Bering Sea beneath them. She was nervous, but kept at it. Richard kept asking her questions about what to do if this or that happened. He also had her doing all of the radio calls.

She was given precise heading and altitude instructions she had to follow. The closer they came to the Alaska coast line, the more precise and terse it became. Then they were switched to a different frequency and things became more relaxed. The next two hours, they were flying high over rugged mountains and all to soon, were transferred over to Canadian controllers. That's when Richard took control.

Inuvik was 80 miles inland from the coastline of the Arctic Ocean, and Makenzie River. They flew out over the ocean a short way, then headed south inland. Richard told her that in the late eighteenth century, Alexander Makenzie had been the first European to reach the Arctic Ocean by land from Montreal, it had taken him several years and the river was named after him. Inuvik was a centre for mining and off shore drilling. As the town came into view, Joss saw that most of the houses and buildings were built on stilts and about the size of single wide trailers. This was because of the perma frost and the very long -40 degree winters Richard told her. In a short time they were on the ground and taxiing to where a waiting vehicle was parked. The exhaust coming out of the running vehicle with Canadian government plates on it told her it was cold.

"Hey Tim," Richard said as he left the plane. By the blue uniform he was wearing, Joss thought he must be a customs official.

Richard handed his passport and flying documents to Tim who gave them a quick glance, then with an exaggerated flourish, he stamped an empty page on Richards passport.

"Welcome home,." Tim said. "We were expecting you last week."

"Something came up," Richard said. Then proceeded by her long legs, Joss came out of the plane.

"Oh my..." Tim said. "She's not a Russki is she buddy?"

"Naw," Richard said. "Just a Yank."

"I'll Yank you you bum!" Joss said, made to whack him, saw the customs official and the pistol he wore, and thought better of it. She flashed on the charming smile.

"Here is my passport sir," she said with her Texas drawl.

Tim did a double take at Joss then the passport and back again.

"Welcome to Canada Miss Litzenburger," he said. He gently stamped her passport.

"That who I think it is," he said into Richards ear.

"Yes it is sir," Joss said.

"Umm,,,Sorry Miss Lynn..." Tim stammered out.

"So can I fly now that we have made our official landing in Canada or what?"

"Only for two hours," Richard said. "Then you are over your daily max time."

"Oh poo," She said.

"Speaking of which, another six hours to go kiddo." Richard said. "Bathrooms in the building there. Hurry up eh? You still have to fuel the plane and file the flight plan for the next leg."

Joss was muttering as she stomped away.

"What was that student pilot?"

"Nothing Mr. Flight Instructor sir. I'll be as fast as I can. Dear." She slashed her eye lashes at him and was gone.

By the time she returned, the fuel truck had pulled up.

"Hey boss," the fuel truck driver said. "Same old same old?"

"Ask the pilot Herman," Richard said. "I'm just the passenger this time."

Richard, and Tim, listened as Joss asked all the right questions about the fuel grade, then watched as the fuel was pumped in and she made her preflight. She caught Richard taking a photo of Tim with him pointing at her while she checked the wing flaps, and she wondered if cell phone cameras had been snapping shots of her the whole time.

"Ok,ok you bums," Joss said as she walked up. "At least Americans are up front about it. Richard, gather the gang."

Two people came running out of the control tower, joining the fuel guy, Herman, and Tim, and a couple of ramp people hustled over. Richard snapped several pictures of them on Tims phone. All of them standing beside Richards plane.

"Now, one of you guys take a picture of me and the hunk there hey?" She said.

"No time Joss," Richard said. "We gotta go. You're not night rated."

"Nice save buddy," Tim said.

"It won't matter Richard one, of those guys will have taken a picture of us standing by the plane together. It will be all over the internet tomorrow." Joss said.

"I doubt it," Richard said. Then had her begin the preflight checks. She was to busy soon and forgot all about it.

Six hours later they were landing at a large airport. It was pitch dark, the city street lights and runway lights shimmering made the scene fantastic. They had been flying the last four in the dark. Once in a while lights from a small town or isolated farm came into view. But it was mostly dark. From the radio calls Richard was making to the tower, Joss surmised they were in a place called Yellowknife. When she had filed the flight plan in Inuvik, Richard had told her to plan for CYZF the airport code, until now, she had not known the name.

He taxied to the hold down area and shut down. Both of them took a side and tied down a wing and placed a wheel chock. They both did a fast walk around, grabbed their duffle bags, grabbed a cab and headed for a hotel.

"I thought you didn't like landing at big airports?" Joss said. They had just come back from a late diner.

"Normally I don't," Richard said. "But both of us have had a long day. No sense in pushing it. One more flight tomorrow. Then you have a decision to make."

She raised her eyebrows.

"You do your four hours of solo. I watch you write your exams and you get your Canadian Pilots licence. Or, you do your four hours solo, I sign off that you passed your flight requirements. You wright your FAA exams, do an FAA flight check, and you get your American pilots licence. Your choice. You have a couple of days to make up your mind."

They were up early the next morning and headed to the attached restaurant the hotel had. This was more like the small town restaurants Joss was used to back home in Texas. Three rows of booths for four. One along each wall and one up the centre. Other than the collage aged waitress was not wearing a uniform like in the states, she was dressed much like anyone her age would have been. Richard ordered the breakfast special, three pancakes, ham and three eggs and a black coffee. The waitress told Joss there was a seniors special that had the same, except two pancakes and two eggs and that the ladies generally ordered that one. Joss agreed, adding a glass of orange juice to her black coffee.

Joss caught the waitress point their way to the cook and say something. The cook stuck his head out and had a look, then shrugged his shoulders. The waitress said something else and pointed again.this time, the cook waved his hand at the waitress and shook his head, the waitress came with their coffee and Joss' orange juice and Joss saw she was scrutinizing her more closely this time. She went back to the counter.

"Ya, your right," the waitress said loud enough that Joss could hear. The cook was in the back. "Close enough to be her twin, but it ain't her."

"Richard," Joss said. "Where exactly are we?"

"Yellowknife," Richard said. "You know that, you filed the flight plan."

"Ya I know, Yellowknife," Joss said. "But where in Canada is it? I only see the small maps we have, not the big picture.

Richard picked up her cell phone, had her unlock it for him and hit a few buttons. A few minutes later he handed it back to her. It had a map of Canada and Alaska on it. And there was a red line going across Alaska, to Inuvik, then down to Yellowknife.

"Yesterday," Richard said. "You flew across the Bering Sea, Alaska, the Arctic Ocean and landed in the North West Territories. Then we took off and landed in Yellowknife, the capital of the North West Territories.. Tomorrow, we will be in the Province of Alberta. And, you will have flown over the Great Slave Lake. One of the biggest fresh water lakes in the world."

Joss looked at the map for a bit and saw just how far they had really flown the day before. Then she looked down at the outline of Alberta and remembered a note he had sent her with that same outline on it.

"You're from Alberta right?" She asked.

He shrugged his shoulders and smiled.

"Anywhere near George and Sandra?"

He shrugged his shoulders again.

"You ever going to give me any straight answers? Don't bother, you're just going to shrug your shoulders again."

Richard got up and headed to the bathroom.

"Don't worry Joss," their waitress said when she came over and filled her coffee. "He does that all the time."

"He's brought other girls here?"

"Naw just you, you must be something special. He comes by now and then with some of his buddies. They ask him questions like you do and he just shrugs his shoulders."

At the airport, Richard made her plan and file the flight plan and to some airport called CEA3, all the weather briefings and the alternate landing fields to it. Then without any warning, he tossed the keys at her and started walking away.

"Where are you going?" She yelled after him trying to figure out what was going on.

"Sooner you get going, the sooner you get your last cross country solo done." Richard said.

"Oh, OK," Joss said. "But how are you going to get there?"

"You just worry about getting you there," Richard said. "And I'll worry about getting me there."

She did her preflight and nervously taxied to the edge of the active runway. She was given clearance and she was quickly in the air.

"Good flight Joss," the ground control controller said to her just before he gave her her frequency to change to.

"Jesus," she muttered to herself, "Damn Canucks."

She was quickly given her new altitude clearance and VFR squawk code. Then dialled in her flight plan on the GPS and let the auto pilot take over. She was paying attention as she flew, but her mind was going over everything that Richard had said to her at breakfast. Should she write the Canadian exam or wait and write the American one. Or both.

"Hey Xray Zulu, you do know you are crossing Great Slave Lake now and will soon be crossing the sixtieth parallel for the first time?"

This was being broadcast over the frequency that all the pilots monitored and would talk to each other in flight. Xray Zulu was the last two digits of the planes licence number.

"Ya where are you you bum!" Joss said.

"Now now Xray Zulu. Crappy radio protocol there eh? Your flight instructor might get pissed about that."

That was a different, but some what familiar voice and she could clearly hear laughter in the background.

"Well you tell Mr. Flight Instructor his student is going to kick his butt once she's on the ground."

"Atta girl Texas, you tell him eh?"

This was a female voice.

After what seemed an eternity, but was only five hours, Joss landed at a small one runway airport, taxied over to where some fuel tanks were located and shut down. She did a fast walk around the airplane then walked over to the fuel tank. Richard had shown her how to operate one, these were self serve. Making sure she had the correct fuel tank, Joss, first, unreeled the ground strap and attached it to one of the the tie down rings on the wing. Walking back to the pump, she plugged in her credit card waited for it to process. Once accepted, Joss unrealed the unwieldily and thick hose and dragged it to the left wing. It was a low wing airplane, so the fuel inlet was on the top of the wing and easy to get at. Once it was filled almost to overspill, Joss moved to the next wing and repeated the sequence. The final act was to replace the ground and fuel lines.

Richard had told her to park the airplane in front of the only dark blue hanger at the airport. At the time he had told her that, she was wondering how she would be able to find it at an airport with that vague of a description. Now though, it was much easier. There were only a couple of dozen hangers and only one was dark blue. She crawled back in the air[plane, fired it up and taxied to the hanger she had been told to park at, then shut down again. Now she wrote in her log book the time the flight had started and ended. Did the math for the number of hours, five and digging into the glove box, filled in the same on the airplanes log book.

Richard came out of the man door, and held his hand out for her log book. He quickly scanned it then wrote something in it. While the flight had been smooth, she still had not made up her mind about the exam. Then looking at Richard she did.

"So, you make up your mind yet?" He asked.

"Ya, I'll take your test," she said. "I was paying attention, I have a whole year to write the FAA one."

"Alright," Richard said. "In you go then."

He ushered her into an office at the rear of the hanger and pointed at a desk with a small pile of papers on it.

"You have three hours kiddo, Best be getting at it."

He walked out of the office and gently closed the door after him. The exam was one hundred fifty multiple choice questions. She needed to achieve a grade of seventy percent to pass. Richard had told her that if she came across any questions she had trouble with, she should put a star beside it and go to the next one, coming back once she had finished all the questions to try again. She was so engrossed in what she was doing, she didn't notice Richard open the big hanger door, bring the plane in and unload it.

By the time she finished and looked around, he had the cowling off the engine and was poking around on it.

She walked over and tapped him on the shoulder. Then handed him her exam papers.

"You sure?" He asked. "You still have an hour and a half left."

Joss breathed a sigh and shrugged her shoulders.

"I finished it," she said, "looked it over, and well, I did the best I could. I think I did ok, but who knows?"

"Ok," he said. "There is a bathroom with a shower over there if you want to change and have a shower. I'm going to be a while looking over your exam."

She was nervously pacing around his airplane when he came out of his office. At one point, she saw him pick up the telephone and call someone and laugh, the hang up again. What did that mean? Did she pass or fail? She hadn't felt this nervous about anything since her High-school exam days. To her, this was more important. She wanted it badly.

Richard turned on the computer on his desk, waited for it to boot up, then spent several minutes typing something into it. Then a few more clicks, more typing and a few more clicks. He reached over to a small printer beside the computer, pulled a piece of paper out of it, wrote on it and came out of the office headed her way. His face was blank as he walked up to her, so she couldn't tell from that if she had passed or not. She stopped her pacing and stoop rapidly tapping her left foot on the floor.

On the top of the papers was her flight log book. She flipped to the last entry. It said passed and Richards first name and his instructors licence number. Then she looked at the top sheet of paper on the pile in front of her. It was her pilots licence! A pen was thrust under her nose from behind and she quickly signed it. Then the pen was pulled away, she was spun around and Sandra was hugging her.

"Congratulations Texas!" Sandra said.

George was standing beside Sandra and he hugged and congratulated Joss as well.

"How did you guys all get here before me?" Joss asked. The four of them were sitting around a table in the hanger, bottles of beer from the fridge in hand.

"Well," Richard began.

"We just happened to be flying by and he asked us for a lift home," George finished for him.

"So, like the good neighbours we are," Sandra said. "We did."

"And my plane is a whole lot faster than your old bucket of bolts," George said.

Richard shrugged his shoulders.

"I gets me where I want to go," he said.

"Umm .. not that I'm complaining," Joss said. She tried to stifle a yawn. "Its been a long day. Can we go to the hotel now? Please?"

"Hotel hell," Sandra said."You're staying with us. We have plenty of room. You'll have your own bathroom and every thing. My kids would kill me if they couldn't meet you Texas."

"You guys go ahead," Richard said. "I'll catch up with you later."

Chapter Seven

J oss woke up and found herself alone in the bed. Not that this was strange. Up until recently, she always woke up alone. She heard a racket from what sounded like a kitchen, threw some clothing on and headed toward the sound. Sandra was busy making breakfast on a stove top located in a centre island in a large kitchen. A teenaged boy, with an empty plate and a large glass of milk was seated on a tall stool at the breakfast counter attached to the centre isle.

"Morning Texas," Sandra said. "Coffee in the pot, cups by the pot."

"Holy shit! You were't lying mom, that's Joss Lynn." The boy exclaimed.

"Language bubba language," Sandra said. "My son Charles."

"What really? She's here?" Then screaming and a younger teenaged girl barged in.

"My daughter Jess," Sandra said. "Ok ok, how do you like it when people act like that around your dad?"

"Oh," Charles said. "Sorry Miss Lynn."

"That's ok guys," Joss said. Joss laughed ."I get a little gaga around your dad myself sometimes."

"Hey hands off," Sandra said. "You got your own hunk. Leave mine alone."

"Ewe, mom!" Jess said.

"Ya, ya, off to school with you now," Sandra said.

"Don't worry Miss Lynn," Jess said. "We won't tell anybody you're here. We know what it's like to be bugged."

Breakfast was served, Sandra joined them with her own plate and they were soon all chatting about the hassles and some of the funny experiences with all the media they had run into over the years.

Breakfast finished, the kids gathered up the dishes putting them into the dishwasher and grabbed the school books laying on another near by kitchen counter. Charles grabbed a set of car keys from a hook hanging on the cupboard with other car keys beside on separate hooks and the kids were off.

"Speaking of the Hunk," Joss said. "Where is he?"

"Where he always is," Sandra said. "With his girl."

She saw the startled look on Joss's face.

"No, no, his plane Joss, his plane," Sandra said. "He actually lives in the hanger Joss. Well unless he's chasing around after you that is."

"Why? Does he have no money?"

Sandra snorted her coffee she had just sipped, threw her nostrils.

"OK look," she said a after a moment. "I don't know what he has told you or not told you. So best I say nothing. You want to know why he lives in the hanger, you ask him yourself."

"Every one leaves him alone there Joss," George said as he walked in the kitchen. "Well mostly anyway. His kids know where to find him if they want. Usually they just send a lawyer over to get more money from him when they need it."

"And he always gives it to them," Sandra said. "They both live in big fancy houses, drive fancy cars. Bla bla bla. They ask, he gives."

Joss was not sure how to react to this. She knew the boys were a sore point for Richard, but her own upbringing left her little prepared with how to react to it. George tossed a set of car keys at her.

"Go talk to him," he said. "Maybe he'll tell you. He won't tell us."

Walking toward the door George had pointed to, she opened it and saw it was an attached double car garage. There was a Mercedes E class and G-wagon parked inside. Hitting the key fob the horn beeped on the E Class. Hitting the garage door opener attached to the drivers sun visor, Joss careful backed out of the garage, then adjusted the mirrors and seat to suit herself. She had been to tired to notice when she had arrived, now she looked at the front of the house as she waited for the garage door to close. Unlike in the States, where houses in estates were generally two story, this one was a bungalow with a large foot print. A three car garage was on the other side of the house from where she was and what looked like another one off by itself toward the rear of the house.

All of this was located in the centre of what looked like a couple of acres of lawn bordered by rows of poplar, spruce and lilac trees and shrubs. The drive was paved and while there was a wrought iron tall gate at the entrance, it was open. The paved drive continued on for about half a mile, three wire bobbed wire along both sides of the drive. Looking left, Joss saw some cattle in a field. To the right, some kind of crops were growing. The drive lead to a narrow paved two lane highway. Remembering how they had come the night before, Joss turned right and onto the highway.

There was no traffic on the highway and Joss, with some squinting at the dual numbers on the speedometer, found the small numbers were miles and the large numbers kilometres per hour. Seeing that 80 kilometres per hour was the same as 50 miles an hour and figuring the laws would be similar to what she was used to, kept it at 50. This gave her chance to look around.

There were farm lands all around, most were grain farms, some had cattle in them and more than a few had oil pumps going up and down. The farm houses she drove by were well kept and large. Most with trees bordering them like the Hamilton's house was.

She came to a stop sign and now didn't which direction to go in. To her left in the distance, she saw a single engine airplane coming in for a landing and surmised that was where the airport was.. Turning left, she headed in that direction. As she drove she looked to her left. She saw a cut-off that led to a farm field, pulled into it and stopped.

She got out of the car and looked at the mountains. Even though it was late spring, they were still snow capped and the morning sun hitting them made them look outstanding. They appeared so close, she felt she could walk there easily in an afternoon..

Getting back in the car, she continued on and found the airport. She drove the low key Mercedes down to the hanger, tried the man door and found it open. And Joss found him. Sleeping on a couch beside the airplane. She walked over and crouched beside him, stroking his cheek.

"Hey," he said, opening his eyes.

"Hey yourself," Joss said. "You got a place to cook some breakfast and brew some coffee in this place?"

"Shit" he said. "I just sat down to take a rest. What time is it?"

"Ten in the morning," Joss said.

He stood and gave her the follow me signal. He walked to the other side of the office she had used to write her exam and opened a door in the wall there. It opened up to reveal a spacious living room and kitchen setup.

"Ill be right back," he said. "Need to scrub some of this grease off me."

Joss gave herself a tour. It didn't take long. There was a love seat with marble covered coffee table in front of it, a recliner with a small round marble topped table beside it and what looked like a folded up Murphy bed in one wall. Typical of a man, a large flat screen TV took up much of one wall facing the chairs. A small kitchen with cupboards and a small range cook top combo on one side of the cupboards and a built in dishwasher on the other side sat astride a single sink and faucet combo. A two place breakfast nook was to one side. All of the furniture and appliances were high quality. If she hadn't seen it herself, Joss would have thought she was in an expensive loft type apartment. Not the back end of a hanger.

"Why?" She asked him as Richard walked back in. She motioned her arm around the apartment.

"How much room does one guy need?" He said. "I like to work on my plane. I like to fly. So why not?"

"But Sandy says you give your kids cash like it's coming from a money tree," Joss said.

"Unlike somebody else I know," he said. "I let my money work for me, not the other way around."

He kissed her on the cheek and went to the kitchen counter and got the coffee maker working.

"I have my plane, my pickup, my nice little apartment and now a cute girlfriend. What else could a guy need?"

"Ah, to tell his girl friend where he lives, so she can come hang out with him from time to time?"

"Ya well, his girlfriend hasn't told him where she lives yet too," He said.

"Ok, you've got a point there," Joss said. "To be honest, I don't get much time to spend there."

"There an airport close by?" Richard asked.

"Ya, there is a landing strip right on the property and a hanger," Joss said. "The studio picks me up from there sometimes."

"Show me," Richard said. "It's in Texas right?"

He hit a button on a remote laying on the kitchen counter and the TV mounted on the wall came alive and after a few seconds, displayed an aerial map of Texas. She gave him a general location. There were three airports in the vicinity. He picked one and zoomed in on it. It was about forty miles from Brownsville.

"That yours?" He asked.

"To be honest, I'm not sure," Joss said.

"Ya that's it," Richard said. "Its registered to your holding company. Cool, now we can fly you home. Might take a couple of days though. Plus I have to finish doing some work on the old girl here."

"Plus, the new girl wants to play with her boy toy for a while," Joss said. "Without any nosy neighbours prying eyes around."

"Things just keep getting better and better," Richard said.

Joss used his landline telephone to call her cellphone answering service. She had taken the battery out of her cell phone and placed the phone and the battery, in a led lined bag so nobody could call her or track her.

"Shit," she said after hearing one message. "My lawyer is in a big panic. You have anyway we can call him?"

"Ya we can use my computer," Richard said. "I use a VPN network, so he won't be able to find us."

"Hey Joss," Scotty said when they finally got threw to him. "Where are you? Never mind. More importantly how fast can you get here? The studio is in a big panic about something and they need to see you right away."

Joss looked over at Richard and he flashed three fingers at her.

"Three days Scotty," she said. "At my house. Not their offices or yours. I'm on holidays, they know it, you know it and I haven't signed their stupid contract yet, so am under no obligation to them for any reason."

"Fine," Scotty said. "I'll let them know."

He cut the connection.

"Now where were we?" Joss said. She pulled him down on top of her.

With the both of them flying, it only took one day. She flew the first leg under daytime visual rules. He flew the last legs at night under instrument rules. Richard had looked up the airfield before they had left, found out it had a radio activated set of runway lights and had entered it into his on board flight system. When they reached ten miles from the airfield, Richard dialled in the radio frequency, keyed the microphone twice and hoped the lights would come on. Other wise he would have to overfly the runway at least once to make sure of where it was.

Thankfully, the marker lights came on, mostly. Some were non functional, but there was enough of them working that he could determine the shape and where the runway was.

"Wow", Joss said. "I didn't know I had those."

Turning the airplane around on the runway, Richard saw the hanger off by itself to the side of the runway in his landing lights and headed that direction. Joss being the passenger for this leg, got out of the airplane first and headed to the hanger. The door was locked.

Now what? She thought.

"Hey Del," she heard Richard say.

"Hey back," Delta said. She gave Richard a hug.

"I generally hang out here when Joss is off doing whatever," Delta said. "I saw the runway lights come on, heard the airplane coming and figured it was you guys. Scotty gave me a heads up you were coming. I told the security guys to back off, not to worry."

She walked toward Joss twirling a set of keys around her finger.

"No hug, no keys," Delta said.

Joss ran up, gave Delta a quick hug, grabbed the keys out of her hand, ran back to the hanger door and started trying keys in the lock. She was bouncing up and down and had a look of desperation on her face.

"There better be a bathroom in here!" She said as the door finally opened and she bolted inside after fumbling for a light switch.

"Pays to be a guy sometimes," Richard said. He laughed.

Delta looked over and saw Richard doing up the zipper of his pants and a large wet patch on the ground by the tail of the airplane.. Delta shook her head and smiled.

A few minutes later, with an electric whine and much clanking and squealing from unused wheels, the hanger door began to open.

Showing Delta where on the wings to push, Joss took the other wing. Richard grabbed the propeller and the three of them pulled the Cherokee into the hanger, then shut the hanger door.

The Cherokee now safely in bed, the tired couple put themselves to bed.

The morning of the meeting, Joss had woken at six am, had a shower, curled her hair, carefully applied her makeup and chosen the clothing she would wear for the meeting. After that, she had set her coffee maker on brew and began to pace. She was not quite sure whether she was upset, angry, or concerned about this meeting. Most likely a combination of all three. What she did know, was that she was getting extremely tired of people trying to take control of her life and planned to do something about it..

She quickly ducked her head in her bedroom and saw Richard still sleeping. Whatever happened today, she vowed to herself, that Richard would not be involved and that if anything interfered with her relationship with him, she would retire on the spot.

When she returned to the kitchen, Delta was sitting at the breakfast nook, coffee in hand and Joss's cup in front of the seat next to her. Like Joss, Delta had carefully done her hair and makeup and dressed in a professional manner.

"How's the Hunk?" Delta asked.

"Sleeping like a baby," Joss said. She sat down beside Delta and kissed her cheek. "God I love that man."

"I'm pretty sure the feeling is mutual Joss," Delta said. She patted Joss's arm and kissed her on the cheek as well. "You going to be ok today?"

"Ya, I'll be alright," Joss said. "This time with Richard, well, he has this way about him you know? He asks me questions. He never tells me what I should do. He just asks me questions. I mean, I pretty much knew already what I wanted to do, but he helped me sort through what is really important and what is not."

Joss took a sip of her coffee.

"If I don't hear what I want to hear today Delta," she said. "I am going to retire from this movie stuff. I might record an album again, but I am tired Delta, really, really tired."

"I know hon," Delta said. "And I haven't helped much either. It's just that I worry so much about you."

"You are worse than my mother sometimes Delta," Joss said. She smiled. "And I love you for it."

"Hey guys," Richard said, walking into the kitchen. "Is that coffee I smell?"

"Woa look at you two, all dolled up and ready for war eh?"

Unlike them, Richard was wearing jeans and a polo shirt and was barefoot.

"Get over here bum and give me a kiss," Joss said.

"No way," Richard said. "I was married long enough to know better."

He did come over and carefully gave her a hug. Just then, the air was disturbed by the sound of jet engines as a corporate business jet landed at the private airstrip and taxied as close to the house as it could. It shut down and four men descended and headed toward the house.

"Well," Richard said. "I'll leave you to it then."

He took his large coffee cup in hand and walked out the kitchen door to the large patio attached to it, sat down on a deck lounge chair, put his ear buds in and began to listen to music.

Delta and Joss gave each other a fast look over to make sure all was alright, stood and waited.

It wasn't long in coming. Carson, her co star and want to be boy friend, was yelling at her, demanding to know where she had been, what she had been doing and why she had not been answering his calls or texts as he stepped into the kitchen. The two studio executives were upset as well, and Scotty, well Scotty just stood there.

"Gentlemen," Delta said. "Perhaps we can sit down at the dining room table?"

While they all moved to the dining room, Carson did not stop complaining once.

Just as they were all seated and Delta made to get them all coffee, one of the studio men's cell phone rang, he looked down at the number and turned white.

"Good day sir," he said. He hadn't even asked for permission to take the call. Nor had either man introduced themselves yet. "Yes sir, right away sir."

He hit a button on his screen and laid the cell phone in the centre of the dining table.

"Sir, you are on speaker now sir," the exec said.

"Good morning everyone. My name is Black. I own the studio. First, I will not apologize for interjecting myself into this meeting. I will apologize to Miss Lynn for disturbing her well deserved holiday.

"First to my two executives. If it was important enough to bring Scotty from New York and your selves and Mr. Carson from LA, then fly in our corporate jet to Texas for a meeting with Miss Lynn, then it should have been important enough to inform myself. Which no one thought to do.

"Mr. Carson, what exactly do you do for us? You are an easily replaceable actor. We paid you an enormous amount of money to act and then to help promote the film. You did the absolute minimum you could do on both accounts."

Carson had lost all his bluster now and was becoming concerned.

"On the other hand, Miss Lynn has run herself ragged for the last two years on the studios behalf. Contrary to what you four men assume, what Miss Lynn has accomplished in the last month alone, has done more to promote the franchise, than your four efforts combined. Her trip across Russia and Northern Canada, has seen her social media presence explode. Her active promotion of a young up and coming future female Formula One driver, has tripled the female social media interest.

"That she is one of the very few people, let alone females, to fly across Russia, the Bering Sea and Arctic Ocean is giving us unprecedented media coverage. Her obtaining, not only a Russian private pilots licence, but a Canadian one, is astonishing. And once the studio releases footage of her stock car racing days, we expect more of the same.

"In fact gentlemen, Miss Lynn in real life, almost parallels the character she plays in the franchise.

"On the other hand Mr. Carson. You have never owned an automobile, or even obtained a drivers licence. You are in fact, the exact opposite of the character you portray. Your relentless harassment of Miss Lynn is well documented. As is her position on it.

"Therefore, your services are no longer required Mr. Carson. If Delta would please have Mr. Carson escorted out of the house? Our studio provided car and driver are waiting to take Mr. Carson to the nearest town and to drop him there."

Carson was almost shaking now as he watched his career go out the window.

"Next, I have it on good authority, that Miss Lynn is seriously considering not being involved in our next production. A production that has already had much time and money spent on it. Now you two so called executives have spent further hundreds of thousands of dollars scheduling this meeting. Money that would be better spent in production. This could easily have been handled in different manners.

"You will immediately leave and return to LA at the conclusion of this meeting. I expect a complete report concerning this matter to be on the President of Human Resources desk by tomorrow morning and a carbon copy to myself. I also want to know your reasons why, you should continue being our employees."

Now it was the studio executives turn to be concerned and they both thought maybe their careers were now over as well.

"Scotty. As Miss Lynn's personal negotiator, you should have handled this long before it reached this stage. In fact, it is my personal opinion, that you have been looking after your self interests and not Miss Lynns. I have contacted your firms principle and informed him of such. He is sending his own business aircraft to return you to New York. You have until that time, to come up with reasons why Miss Lynn should keep you on as her representative."

Scotty was looking at the floor. Not his usual self assured self at all.

"Delta. Of anyone in that room, you have been the one who has selflessly devoted yourself to Miss Lynn. Why you stay with her is beyond me. That being said, you as well, could have handled this situation better, and you know it."

Now it was Delta's turn to look at the floor. Joss patted her on the arm.

"Lastly, Miss Lynn. You should have been more forceful in your objections to your costar and the fact that you were burning out. Unlike everyone else in the room, I respect your decision to keep your relationship private and to shield your relationship partner from the stupid circus that follows this industry around.

"However, you should have at least told Delta that you were going to be out of touch. That would have solved a lot of anxiety for many people. The studio has not started writing the script yet, so replacing your co star will not be that big of an issue. In fact, I believe that you should have some say on who that should be. We will supply you with a short list of candidates, but at the end of the day, it is the studios decision.

"We need an answer from you Miss Lynn. We have to write the script, scout locations, hire cast and crew and possibly a replacement for you. As such, I will need an answer from you regarding your participation in this project, no later than two weeks from today.

"Now, all of you have much to do and much to think about and I am a very busy man that should not have to deal with these types of minor problems. Good day."

Joss was more embarrassed than angry, but she was also angry. Never in her life had she been spoken to like that from a person of authority. What made it worse, was that she knew he was right. She should have been more forceful about her feelings on the Carson debacle and her burning out. Like the others in the room, now she thought maybe her career was over.

One of Joss's security people came and escorted the stunned co star away. Both the studio men were visibly shaking as they stood and hurried out of the house to the corporate jet. Delta, Scotty and Joss, just sat in a state of shock.

"Delta, would you mind?" Joss said finally, breaking the silence. "Pour yourself a Scotch or something and take Richard a beer or two. Scotty and I have to talk."

When Delta came on the patio, Richard had removed his ear buds and was watching the jet take off. She placed his beer on the table beside him and sat down on the chair on the opposite side of it.

"How'd it go?" Richard asked.

"We all just got shit," Delta said. "God himself from the studio called and basically told all of us to get our shit together. Crap!"

Delta almost drained the glass she had in her hand, then poured another large portion into it from the bottle of vodka she had brought as well.

"That bad eh?" Richard said.

Delta nodded her head, taking another sip from the glass. She turned and looked at him.

"Look Richard, I like you, it's not personal between us," she said. "It's just that I have seen Joss go off the rails before and it always, always, ends badly."

"Ya, I get it," Richard said. "Me being me is tough on you guys. I get that too. I keep my personal life personal and my other life my other life. Do you understand? Just like Joss is doing for me, shielding me from her business life. I do the same Delta."

Both of them sat and looked out across the back of the property in silence.

"You know she loves you don't you Delta?" Richard said finally. "I think you are her only friend."

Tears started running down Delta's cheeks. She nodded her head.

"All the same," he continued. "You have a life too Delta. Not only that, but frankly, in my opinion, your are wasting your talent doing this job and Joss is being selfish holding you back."

"I know," Delta said. "But what can I do? I love her too and yes, she is about my only friend as well. If I left? What would happen then Richard? She can be to caring, to understanding. You know what I mean?"

"Ya, been there," Richard said. "And I'm looking at somebody that's exactly the same way."

Delta looked up at him and the concern in his eyes. She flung herself out of her chair and buried herself into his chest. That's how Joss found them when she walked onto the patio, a martini glass in hand. Delta fiercely hugging Richard, tears staining his shirt and he gently rubbing her back.

"Leave you two alone for two minutes and what do I find?" Joss said.

Delta jumped up.

"Sorry Joss..."

"Come here you," Joss said holding her arms wide. "It's ok Del, it's ok". She whispered into her ear as they hugged. Joss gently stroking Deltas hair.

"She tell you what happened?" Joss asked Richard.

"I got the picture," he said.

"Scotty and I hashed some things out," Joss said. "Mr. Black was right. I should have been more clear and assertive about Carson and that I was burning out."

She turned to Delta.

"Del, you did try to tell me, I just didn't listen. Mr. Black was right, you work tirelessly for me. I hope you know I love you and appreciate everything you do for me?"

Delta nodded, she was still composing herself.

"What do you think?" Joss asked Richard.

"Doesn't matter what I think Joss," he said. "What do you want? Is doing the picture good for you? Or Not? I'm not going anywhere."

"What about Delta?" Joss asked.

"What about her?" He said. "She's a big girl. Are you doing what is best for Delta, or what is best for you? Can the both of you come up with something that would benefit you both? I can't answer that for you two. You can bounce ideas off me. But at the end of the day, you have to do what is right for you. Joss, Delta may be your only true friend."

He grabbed the full bottle of beer still on the table and stood.

"I'll leave you at it," he said. "I should go check on my girl."

An hour later, Joss and Delta walked into the hanger. They saw Richards feet draped over the copilots chair and when they came near, saw his head and shoulders were under the dash.

"Something wrong?" Joss called up to him.

After a series of grunts and squiggles, Richard emerged onto the wing. He had dust smeared across his forehead.

"Altimeter has been acting a bit weird," he said. "Loose connection on the pitot tube tubing. No biggy. You guys ok?"

"Sort of," Joss said. "I saw Scotty come and talk to you before the plane came and picked him up. What was that all about?"

"Like Delta had done with me earlier," Richard said. "He wanted to clear the air between us. I also got his side of the story about what just happened.

"To be honest Joss, unless it affects our relationship, or my hopefully new friendship with Delta, I don't really care what the movie or entertainment industry thinks of me."

"Oh, ok," Joss said. "Del and I were just wondering if you could help us out with something."

Richard smiled at them.

"I know, I know," Joss said. "Hear us out ok?"

"Yes, you were right Richard, I have more talent than this job requires," Delta said. "Joss agrees. The problem is, I love the job."

"I have suggested and Delta agreed, to get her an assistant, so she can free up some personal time," Joss said.

Richard pursed his lips and nodded his head.

"And I am going to look around for opportunities," Delta said.

Once again, Richard pursed his lips and nodded his head.

"Well, it looks like you've got it all figured out," he said.

"Um...not really," Joss said. "I kind of need Delta around and she agrees."

"And I don't really know what else I want to do," Delta said.

"So," Richard began. "You both want what is best for each other, but don't want to leave the other one in the lurch, but still want to work with each other, but give each other a little more freedom. Correct?"

"Yes, I know, it sounds stupid, but yes," Joss said.

Richard smiled.

"Now I know neither of you have been married or had kids." He said. "Joss, you are always on the look out for a sound investment to grow your stash right? Delta, you need some help getting something going right?"

Both women looked a little confused.

"A record producer saw a back up singer that had a good voice," Richard said. "A young nieve girl from the boondocks. He hired her as a session vocalist, then when the main female singer got sick, he had the session vocalist take over. That led to a full time position, which led to a hit song, which led to a bit part in a movie, which led us here."

"An up and coming music and film star needed a personal assistant to handle her day to day affairs. Which led to a very immature and inexperienced girl being hired to take on the position. Which led to the two of them becoming friends which led us here."

"And it all started from a very professional and experienced record producer spotting someone with talent that needed a break. He didn't have to. In fact, I'll bet it was a pain in the butt for him at the beginning. But look what it led to."

"So what you are saying," Joss said. "Is that I should fund Delta on some kind of start up?"

"Am I?" Richard replied.

"But what can I do?" Delta asked.

Richard shrugged his shoulders.

"I like my job, heck I love my job, but I am only one person. I can't do this for someone else and work for Joss too," Delta said.

"Yup," Richard said.

"So I would have to find someone to do that kind of work...Ok..I get that..But who do I get for a client? Where do I start?"

"Didn't you say Anna is going to need someone soon Richard?" Joss said.

"Ya, Rosy is good at the hard core negotiations stuff, but she is a bit of a hard ass for the other stuff," Richard said.

"There you go Delta," Joss said. "Anna has met you. She told you she would kill to have someone like you. That's your foot in the door."

"Ya, you're right," Delta said. "I even know someone who would be perfect for the job."

Richard grabbed a screw driver and began to remove the pitot tube from the wing while the women forgot about him and chatted about their options. They then went out for a walk to talk some more, leaving him to his baby.

They returned hours later, after Richard had buttoned up the cowling and was trying to decide wether to go for a test flight now, or wait until the next day. Delta was carrying a small cooler full of beer. She handed one to Richard and Joss and opened one for herself.

"Thank you Richard," Delta said.

"For what?"

"For helping me," she said.

"Hey, all I did was make a statement and ask a couple of questions," he said.

"Joss told me that's what you do Richard," she said. "You actually know what we need to do, but you don't tell us."

"Give the girl a cookie," Richard said, winking at Joss, who stuck her tongue out at him. "If I tell you what I think you should do, that's my opinion, not yours. I ask you questions, you form your own opinion, make up your own mind and voila, it's your decision, not mine. Right or wrong, good or bad. Ultimately, all of us knows what we want Delta. We just want someone to validate it."

"You learn that from being a father and a husband?" Delta asked.

"Nope," he replied. "Long ago and far away, like yourselves, I had an old veteran take a young pup under his wing and show him the ropes."

Richard found a couple of chairs and dragged them over to the hanger door next to a chair he already had set up there. He sat down and looked out at the stars. Delta and Joss sat down beside him.

"What I did learn though," Richard said after some moments of silence. "Happy best friend, happy wife, happy life."

"What?" Delta said.

"If you are happy Delta, that makes Joss happy, which makes me happy," Richard said.

"Or in my case, happy airplane, happy hunk, happy me," Joss said after taking a sip of beer.

"Ah guys are easy to make happy," Richard said. "Girl crooks her finger and says come here hunk and whoops that's all she wrote folks."

He was smiling, but his eyes were sad.

"Well mission accomplished Super Canuck," Joss said. "Anna said yes. I gave Rosy a call while we were out walking, she's ok with it."

"I contacted someone I know who would be perfect for her," Delta said. "She seems to be on board. Anna and her are going to meet tomorrow."

"Got a lawyer yet?" Richard asked.

"What?" Both women said.

"Fastest way I know to ruin a friendship is to go into business together," Richard said. "Both of you should know that."

"Ya, I've got somebody that will fit," Delta said.

"I don't," Joss said. "And Scotty's firm makes enough money off me already. Not to worry, I'll have it all sorted out tomorrow."

"So," Richard said. "Did you notice that engineer that was scoping out Delta in Russia?"

"No," Joss said. "Do tell."

"Ya, Jochen smacked him upside the head a couple of times for paying more attention to Miss California here than the car."

Delta's ears were turning red.

"Ya right," she said.

"Oh doesn't she look cute turning all red like that?" Joss said.

"Almost as good as she looks stomping down pit lane in all her feminine furry," Richard said. "Her best features bounce ever so nice when she stomps around like that."

Joss burst out in laughter.

"Like yours don't Texas!" Delta said.

"Not as nice as yours do California," Joss said. "What do you think Super Canuck."

Richard put both hands up, palms forward at shoulder height.

"Hey keep me out of this one, it's a lose lose for me."

Joss smacked him on the shoulder.

"That's for noticing her bounces," she said.

Delta smacked him on the other shoulder.

"That's for not noticing Texas's bounces."

"And this is for everything you did for me today," Joss said.

She took his head between her hands and kissed him long and deep. Then she looked over at Delta.

"You find your own super hunk to kiss California." Joss said.

Chapter Eight

"I'm going to do the movie Richard," Joss said. "It will only be six months work. Three months prep and three months on location. The prep I can do anywhere. Here, or at your place or wherever. I'll make up my mind about another one after that."

"Good," Richard said. "You got that sorted out. Look this has been great, and for the most part I can handle what little business I have from anywhere. But I really do have something I have to handle in person. It won't take long, a couple of days. Then we can link up again later?"

"Sure," Joss said. "I have that studio meeting and some things to work out with Delta, but after that, I have at least four months before I have to start doing movie things."

"I also want to get my own plane," she continued. "Do you happen to know anyone who can help me with that?"

"Ya right," Richard said. "First. What do you want the plane for. Second, how many people are you realistically going to carry ninety percent of the time. Third how far, fast and high do you want to go. Fourth and most important, the cost of the plane and the maintenance for it."

"How do you mean?" Joss said.

"For me," Richard said. "Ninety percent of the time I fly alone. I fly long distances at a time, so I need lots of fuel capacity. Speed is generally not that big of an issue for me , but performance is. Hence my girl. If I need to go somewhere in a hurry far away, I still use the airlines Joss."

"Oh, lots to think over then," Joss said. "I enjoy flying Richard. While it might be slightly more inconvenient, flying my own airplane I can come and go pretty much when and where I want and not have to put up with all the media and public hassle at airports. Heck, I can even try some of those hundred dollar hamburgers I hear so much about in out of the way airports."

"Well at least you have your own runway and hanger," Richard said. "Better than I can say."

It was a long night that night and a long good bye early the next morning before Richard took off.

It was so early that morning, the dew was still on the grass when the dark blue Cherokee left the runway. Wrapping her arms around her chest, Joss watched the Cherokee dwindle into the distance. She had never felt so incomplete in her life as she did right now watching Richard go away.

Delta came beside Joss and put her arm around her.

"He'll be back Joss," Delta said.

"I know," Joss replied. "It's just hard sometimes. He is right though. We both have business lives we have to care for as well."

"Speaking of which," Delta said. "You have a contract to review, I have an assistant to interview and both of us need to finalize our own agreement."

It was a busy week. Joss had sent in her signed contract to the studio, accepted Delta's suggested assistant. Hired a lawyer, coordinated with Delta's new lawyer, signed an agreement for them both and transferred the start up costs for Delta's new venture.

Having a lot of time on her hands, between reading and studying the script that the studio had sent over, Joss found a competent local flight instructor, passed her check ride and exams and now had an American pilots licence under her legal name. Next, in quick succession, she trained and passed her over the top and night certifications and was trying to decide if she should start instrument training.

Richard was arriving tonight and while on a personal level she was anticipating his arrival, she wanted to talk to him about an airplane she had found.

Richard had arrived just before dark. It had been a long night, with not much sleep. Delta could be heard rummaging through the kitchen so they both decided it was time to get out of bed.

Delta gave both of them a bunch of static for sleeping in, then laughed at them. She had a busy day. The new assistant was starting today and she had to get her up to speed while things were still slow. She poured herself a cup of coffee, blew air kisses at them and left to her study room.

"Richard," Joss asked. "Can you fly me to Dallas today? I have an aircraft I would like to look at."

"No, but I will come along," he said. "Joss Lynn needs to bank some more hours towards her instrument licence."

She smacked him on the arm, then yelled down the hall to Delta to tell her they were going to Dallas and would be most of the day.

After the routine checks, Joss quickly settled into the familiar pilots seat and they were soon off the ground. She did a perfect landing at the smaller airport just outside Dallas and taxied over to a hanger and shut down. Jack, the sales man was waiting for her.

"Classic plane," he said. He began to walk around nodding his head. "In fantastic shape for an old girl." Climbing up on the wing he peered inside and saw a fully upgraded instrument panel with all the latest gauges.

"Don't see many of these with those," he said. "I can get you top dollar for it."

Then he noticed the prominent sticker in French and English posted by the entry that he had missed, stating it was an experimental aircraft. He looked back at them, Richard just shrugged his shoulders and grinned.

"I guess not then," the salesmen said. "What can I do for you folks today? Looking to upgrade? A twin maybe?"

"Don't look at me," Richard said. "I'm just providing transportation today. She's the one looking."

"Piper Archer," Joss said.

"Sure sure, got a few good ones here, low hours clean paint and interiors."

"Want a new one," Joss said.

That got Jack's attention.

"Only got one of those," he said. "It's a DLX and is fully loaded."

"Let's have a look then," Joss said.

She wasn't hiding her Texas drawl today and was wearing clothing that could have come from Target. Sure enough, inside the hanger was a shiny new Piper Archer, white with blue stripes. Any hope of having a nice easy sale went quickly out the window and Joss expertly made her way, not to the interior, but all along the out side of the airframe. Closely examining everything. She had the salesman remove the cowling and looked over, under and around the engine and all the equipment mounted there.

Once satisfied with that, then she went through the interior, having the salesman explain the avionics systems installed and the features the airplane had. While that was going on, Richard had made his own inspection. Satisfied for the moment, Joss and the salesman exited the airplane and with Richards help, the cowling was put back on and helped push it out of the hanger.

Then Joss, with Jack at the controls were off on a test flight.

"What do you think?" Joss asked Richard when they came back.

"How did it handle?" Richard asked.

"It needs some flap trim adjustment, the brakes were a bit spongy and the rudder sluggish," she said.

Richard nodded his head, then pointed his chin at the salesman.

"How much?" Joss asked.

"Five fifty," the salesman said. "Like I said it is fully loaded with every option."

"Not enough to justify an extra hundred grand worth though," Joss said.

"Five and a quarter," the salesman countered. "Best I can do. Got plenty of interest in this plane."

"If there was plenty of interest it would be gone already," Joss said. "Its already got 50 hours on it."

"Sorry, best I can do," he said sticking to his price.

"Ok then," Joss said. "If that's best you can do, that's the best you can do." She waved her hand at Richard

" Come on Richard, let's check out the dealer in San Antonio."

"Wait, wait," the salesman said. "Let me ask the boss. What's your offer?"

"Four seventy five," Joss said. "Tax included."

"No way he's going to go for that mam," Jack said shaking his head. "I'm not even going to ask."

"Bring him out here and let him tell me that then," Joss said.

"Look mam," the man, clearly the owner of the deanship said. "That is way to low a price for a new aircraft."

"For one thing, it's not a new aircraft," Joss said. "It's got fifty hours on it. For another, it has ailerons and flap damage, the rudder cables are misadjusted and the trim needs adjusting. Now I am willing to have a wire transfer of four hundred seventy five, right here right now and fly out of here. Or, we go to San Antonio and see what they have to offer."

The owner mulled it over for less than a minute, then stuck out his hand.

"Deal," he said. "You can pick it up Friday, I'll have my mechanics fix it all up for you."

"I think not," Joss said. "If your mechanics were any good they would have spotted all this and had it fixed already."

She pointed at Richard who was standing beside his own plane.

"I have some one more than qualified to fix these minor details, he rebuilt that whole plane himself."

"Would you like a check ride mam," the salesman said. "No charge."

"I flew that Cherokee all across Russia and down from Canada," Joss said. "I don't think they have changed that much over the years, do you?"

Once the salesman saw the name she put down on the registration forms, his whole attitude changed.

"You fly this hunk of crap back home Richard," she said tossing the keys at him. "That way you'll know what you have to fix."

Joss quickly did a pre flight and was soon taxing away, followed by Richard.

"Ten percent under blue book," Richard said to her over the radio. "Remind me never to negotiate with you."

"What did you think?" She asked.

"Just a couple of minor tweaks," Richard said. "I could handle it tonight, but I'd rather celebrate with you tonight and fix tomorrow."

"You can get about four thousand feet higher than me." Richard said. "I'm not allowed a turbo charger. Or a variable pitch prop. Other than that, I can keep up with you no problem. Jet fuel is easier to get than what I run, so another bonus in your favour."

"So I did good?" Joss asked.

"Hell ya," Richard said. "Miss Texas Money bags."

Joss and Richard were sitting on the love seat in the living room. Richard with his normal bottle of Coors, Joss with a glass of red wine in hand.

"What did Joss blow money on now?" Delta said as she walked in, Clary, her new assistant beside her. "A bunch of new shoes? Or, I know, a new Porsche."

"No," Joss said. "A new airplane. I have this nice landing strip and hanger on the property, why not?"

"Ya I was wondering why the Piper PR people were calling. They want to have a meeting with you to discuss some promotional thing."

"When do I have some free time?" Joss asked.

"All day Tuesday," Clary said.

"Ok, set it up then," Joss said.

"They're going to offer you one of those new pressurized models Joss." Richard said.

"No doubt," she said. "And only for five years or something. Not interested. I like my Archer and I own it outright."

All that weekend, Richard tweaked Joss' airplane, then she would go for a test flight and he would tweak it some more. Finally satisfied with how it handled, Joss broke some news on Richard.

"Richard," Joss began. "Some time ago, the Institute of American Indian Arts asked me to give a lecture to their visual arts students. Up until now, I have been far to busy. They have been doing good work over there. Last week I had Clary contact them to see if they were still interested. They said they were and I am scheduled to go there for Monday.

"I think this is really important Richard and I would like you to come along."

Joss knew how he disliked being around to much publicity and expected him to decline.

"Sure why not?" Richard said surprising her. "They have great food in Santa Fe, but..."

Joss was learning about the buts.

"We take your plane, you fly and I ain't buying diner. You invited me, you pay," Richard said. He tensed up waiting for the smack on the shoulder. He received a kiss on the cheek instead.

They took off just after dawn and were parking the Archer at the FOB, forward operating base, at the Santa Fe Regional Airport three hours later. The FOB's around the States were where private pilots could park their planes temporarily, get food, fuel and do flight planning. Some had loaner cars they would rent out by the day. It looked like renting a vehicle would not be required. A newer model Yukon with IAIA on the front doors was waiting for them. A tall dark skinned girl in her twenties was standing by the Yukon and came toward them.

"Welcome to Santa Fe Miss Lynn," she said. "I am Chooli Bitsilly from IAIA and I am to be your guide during your visit with us."

Joss shook her hand.

"Joss," she said. "The hunk here is Richard."

Chooli stretched her hand to Richard who shook it, then placed his right hand on his heart and said something in a native language.

Chooli also placed her hand on her heart and replied. Then rapidly spoke some more.

Richard put his hands to his sides palms out stretched.

"Sorry," Richard said. "I have a buddy who is Deni and thought I might say hello like he had taught me. That's all I know though."

"My people originally came from Northern Canada" Chooli said. "You pronunciation is not all that good, but better than most. Are you from up there?"

"No, I'm a bit further south," Richard said. "Mostly Blackfoot by me."

Joss gave him a whack on the shoulder.

"Quit flirting you," she said. But she was smiling.

Not waiting, Joss hurried to the front passenger seat and jumped in.

"Shot gun!" She yelled through the still open door. "You snooze you loose."

Chooli thought she heard Richard mumble something about spoiled Texan actresses.

"Ya ya," Richard said. "Yak it up. Just for that I'm having seconds tonight at diner. And you're still buying."

"What are you studying?" Joss asked as Chooli began to drive.

"Singing, song writing and music production," Chooli said. "My voice is not as good as yours Joss, but maybe some day..."

"That's what Joni Mitchel, Buffy Sainte Marie and Jan Arden thought too Chooli," Richard said. "Look where they are now."

Chooli looked in the rear view mirror at Richard. Joss turned around to look at him.

"Joni Mitchel I have heard of," Joss said. "I think Buffy Sainte Marie too. Jan Arden?"

"All three are Canadians," Chooli said. "Buffy and Jan are Canadian Indians."

"Joni and Jan are from just down the road from me in Alberta," Richard said. "Buffy just across the border in Saskatchewan. Jan is about your age Joss, she sings contemporary stuff mostly and is not that well known outside Canada."

Richard began to hum a song vaguely familiar to Joss and Chooli began to sing it.

It was one of the anti Vietnam era theme songs made famous by Donavan called the Universal Soldier. Choolli had a good voice and the way she sang it pulled on Joss's heart. Joss looked back at Richard. He was staring out the window and looked like he had just brushed a tear away.

"Buffy Sainte Marie wrote and composed that song Joss," Chooli said after she had finished singing. "Not Donovan or Glen Campbell like everyone thinks. Joni Mitchel credits her with her inspiration to be a song writer. Jan Arden is admired among the Indian people. Excuse me, First Nations People as you Canadians say."

"You have a great voice," Joss said. "If you have some time after the seminar, maybe you can come for diner with us and maybe show me some of your songs."

"What? Me?" Chooli said. "A Navajo Indian from the back and beyond. Ya right."

"A small time young back up singer from the wrong side of the tracks in Brownsville Texas," Richard said. "Going no where fast. Sound familiar Chooli? It should, you're sitting right beside her."

"Long ago and far away," Joss said. Now it was she who was looking out the window. Her left foot was lightly tapping the floor.

The campus was a twenty minute drive from Santa Fe. While the buildings had a native appearance, they were new. Chooli pulled up to a building and stopped. A number of older people were waiting. Most of them dressed as most academics dressed. Clothing and hair mussed. This turned out to be the faculty of the Arts department and the head Dean of the Institute. As normal, right after the introductions, Richard was forgotten, which was fine by him. He tagged along looking at the buildings and the kids he saw. Everything was neat and tidy, like most collage campuses. Students were rushing to class or gathered in small groups.talking. One group of boys was tossing a football around, others frisbees.

They were hustled into a building and down some corridors to what was described as the Green Room. Young make up artists were waiting and they began to work on Joss. Seeing he was only in the way. Richard went out to the hallway. He followed some students and soon found himself in front of a door which had a placard on it with Joss' name. Walking inside, he saw it was a performance hall, not a lecture hall and it was already half full of excited students. Richard found himself an empty chair in the last row and sat down, and like the students waited.

The hall was packed. Students were standing at the back wall, sitting in the isles and on the floor in front of the stage. The crowd hushed as the lights went down and the stage lit.

The dean came on stage and began the normal speech about how lucky they were to have such a celebrity come and talk with them. Then he introduced Joss and everyone leaped to their feet and clapped and cheered.

Joss came on stage with her patented smile and acknowledged the crowd. She put her hands up palms forward and motion the crowd to sit.

"Thank you so much," Joss began. "I so rarely have the opportunity to give back. This is truly an honour for me and I am touched by your reception of lil' ol' me from Back Water Texas."

Joss turned to the side and motioned off stage. Chooli walked out with a guitar across her shoulders. The crowd rose and cheered again. Joss motioned them to sit again after a few moments.

"Well," she said. "I guess no introductions are need hey Chooli? Seems you're just as famous here about as I am.

"On our way here, Chooli sang a song for me. I am going to try and sing it as well as she did. I want all of you to listen to the words."

Joss started to sing Universal Soldier with Chooli accompanying her with the Guitar. She put everything she had into her singing. She didn't prance around the stage like she did at her concerts, she just stood and sang. She didn't use a microphone, the acoustics in the room were perfect and every word could be clearly heard. She was breathless when she had finished and the crowd silent.

Joss grabbed the microphone from the podium set up for to speak from.

"Thanks Chooli," Joss said. "This! This is what a song can do! It can have such an impact to quiet a room this size! It inspires thought and emotions. It can change the world. I only wish I had half the talent that song writer had.

"That song and many others like it, were written by Buffy Sainte Marie a member of the Blackfoot Nation in Saskatchewan. It was she that inspired the great Joni Mitchel to be what she became. Both of those women changed North American history. Just by singing and song writing.

"Another member of the Blackfoot nation, Jan Arden, sings about social issues and the troubles her people face daily. All of those women humble me. I just sing and act. They are the true artists, not me.

"I do not have a collage education. I barely made my GED in high school. But I could sing. I was in the right place at the right time.

"Each of us in this room have the same opportunity to change lives. Some of us by singing or acting. Others by writing or producing or directing. Lighting, camera operating, stage design, wardrobe design, makeup artists, the list goes on and on.

"My mother told me, whatever you do in life, do it the best you can do. Then teach others to do it better.

"Recently, a man called Richard taught me to fly airplanes. He didn't ask to be paid for it, he just did it. I'm not sure, but I don't think he has a PHD either. Yet he is wise and a great mentor.

"If you came here just to hear me sing or talk about how great I am, you are going to be disappointed. Underneath all the glamour and glitz, I am just like all of you.

"I like to read a good book, ride horses out in the wild, once in a while drive a fast car and go for a beer.

"When I was growing up, it was just me, my two sisters and my mom who worked two jobs to keep us fed, clothed and a roof over our heads."

Joss stretched out her hand and pointed at the crowd.

"Bring up the house lights,' she said. She started to pace around the stage pointing at the crowd as she did and the house lights came up. She came back to the centre of the stage dropped the mic on the floor and in a voice loud enough all could hear she opened her arms wide.

"You have all of this! You have each other! You have these great professors and a fantastic institution. Make the most of it.

"Then give it back! That is when the true learning begins, when we give back. Just like Chooli did on the ride over here. The student teaching the teacher."

Joss picked up the mic again.

"Now," she said. "Some Canadian Hunk told me he is taking me for something to eat and I'm taking him up on it. Never been out with a Canadian before. Might be interesting.

"Thanks for having me."

Joss walked off the stage. Once off, she leaned up against the nearest wall and put her head against it taking deep breaths. She saw Chooli looking at her and noticed no sound was coming from the crowd.

"Well," Joss said. "I guess that didn't go over all that well then."

Chooli took her by the arm and led her to the edge of the stage. Few of the students had even stood let alone leave yet. Some were staring at the ceiling in contemplation, others were quietly talking among themselves.

"Yes it did Miss Lynn," Chooli said. "Most of the time at a seminar like this we can't wait to get out of here. You had an impact Joss, where it counts. Here and in here."

Chooli touched her forehead and her heart.

"Short, sweet and impactful Miss Lynn. We usually get long winded dissertations that mean little to us. Thank you Miss Lynn."

Joss began to feel emotions she rarely felt. That one simple thank you and the quiet concert hall meaning more to her than all her sold-out concerts put together.

"Get me out of here, before I start bawling all over the place," she said.

When they came to the car, she sat in the back seat. Richard was already there. Joss spent the whole ride back to Santa Fe looking out the side window trying to get control of her emotions.

"Ok," Joss said as they came to a stop outside a restaurant in downtown Santa Fe. "Enough 'Poor me'. You better have brought your songs along like I asked Chooli or I'm gonna whack you upside your head and not let you have any desert."

"Ah don't mind her Chooli," Richard said. "her bark is worse than her bite. Ow, that hurt. Take the damn ring off next time you hit me eh."

Richard began rubbing his shoulder.

Joss kissed the shoulder and looked at him with that twinkle in her eye.

"Sorry," she said. "Eh."

"Ya ya," Richard said. "Yack it up Ya'all."

Joss muttered something in Spanish, Chooli laughed.

"Come Chooli," Joss continued in Spanish taking Chooli by the arm. "These unsophisticated Canadian men. I mean really."

"Speak for yourself your Holiness," Richard said also in Spanish. "I at least have my high school diploma."

Chooli wasn't sure if they were joking or not. Then Joss kissed Richard on the neck and they both looked deep into each others eyes. Chooli could see the love there, in both of them. The restaurant was busy, but not full and they were easily able to find an empty table. The atmosphere was light. It was called Tomasita's and was one of the more popular restaurants in Santa Fe located, in the historic Rail Station district. The building had originally served as a station for a long defunct rail line.

The interior walls were bare brick, with open large wood beams. Wood panels were prevalent throughout the interior, chairs and tables made from wood. Someone must have called ahead, as the owner was waiting for them as they entered and they were escorted to a large corner booth with a round table. Asked if they wanted a libation, Richard ordered a coke.

"Go ahead," Richard said. "I'll fly back."

Joss ordered a Sangria for herself and Chooli.

The place was filling up quickly and soon happy customers were chatting away. Richard ordered the steak lunch special, Joss and Chooli the Tamale Monday special. Joss was more herself now, the conversation light and cheerful. She asked Chooli about herself, what she was studying besides music. Joss did not notice Richards eyes darting all over the interior especially when new customers walked in.

The conversation shifted easily back and forth between Spanish and English. Their waiter knew Chooli and told Richard and Joss that Chooli was one of their regular performers on Friday night. As they finished and were waiting for desert, the owner came by and asked how everything was. It seemed as though he did that with every table, not just for them, although he did sit down with them for a few minutes which he did not do with the other guests.

He spent most of the time teasing Chooli, who teased him right back.

"Would it be possible for me to have a tour of the kitchen?" Joss asked. "I used to be a line cook in Brownsville. I'd like to see your setup."

The owner jumped up and beamed.

"Of course Miss Lynn, follow me," he said.

That was the first time since they had walked in that anyone had acknowledged who Joss was. Richard stayed put at the booth, while Chooli and Joss made their way to the kitchen. It was well appointed and spotless. The staff were busy preparing the lunch menus. George, the owner, proudly told Joss that all the ingredients were local, the recipes handed down traditional family recipes. Everything was made on site, not brought in frozen and reheated. The tour took over an hour, with Joss asking many questions about how things were done and why. Not only of George, but the staff doing the work.

"Chooli," Joss said. "Would you mind? Ask Richard to join us?"

She turned to George.

"Do you have a camera handy?" She asked.

George hustled away to his office coming back with a 35mm camera just as Chooli and Richard appeared in the kitchen.

"Give the camera to Richard George," Joss said. "You stand on my right, Chooli the left."

Richard took a couple of shots of the trio, then Joss told the rest of the kitchen staff to join. Richard took some fast shots.

"Now the front staff," Joss said.

George hastened to the front and the front staff appeared and another set of photos with Joss in the centre flanked by George and Chooli with the staff ranged around them was taken.

George came to Richard and outstretched his hand for the camera.

"Your turn," George told Richard.

Joss saved the day.

"Richard is camera shy," Joss said. "Well, we have to be going. Big day for me tomorrow. I told the Hunk and Chooli I was buying. Time to settle up."

"No no," George said. "It's on the house, I insist. As long as I can put these pictures up on the wall that is."

"Sure make your day," Joss said. "Make sure everybody in the pictures has a copy."

They made their way back to the institutes Yukon with George escorting them and they were off to the airport.

"Next time we come Richard," Joss said. "I want to check out the market. I hear they have some talented artists on display."

Chooli began to speak of all the art work, tapestries, pottery, silver and leather work, all by local artists. As well as traditional and contemporary paintings, drawings and photographs.

The ride was quickly over and Richard was busy checking the airplane over.

"I haven't forgotten you Chooli," Joss said. "I said I would have a look at your work and I will. If you don't mind, I'd like to take them with me. You have copies right?"

Chooli nodded and rushed back to the car, coming back with a vinyl portfolio, full of papers. Joss took them and then hugged Chooli.

"Thanks for everything Chooli," she said. "Especially the briefing in the green room about Jan Arden and the lyrics to the Universal Soldier. It meant a lot to me."

His walk around complete, Richard removed the tie downs and chocks, placing them in the baggage compartment and crawled into the pilots seat beginning his checks in the cockpit.

"Take care Chooli," Joss said.

In a flurry, she was up in the cockpit, the door shut, engine started and they were off.

Once in the air, Joss, once again, let the emotions of the day in. How she, a nobody from no where had silenced a packed auditorium of students and faculty, with one song and an impromptu speech of less than five minutes. Her words finally hitting home to her and she was almost overwhelmed by it.

On schedule, a Piper M350 landed on Tuesday Morning and taxied out to the hanger where Joss, Delta and Clary were waiting. Joss was wearing what everyone expected a female celebrity to wear, designer slumming clothing. The other two women wearing up scale business attire. The executives were dressed in business casual. All men in their mid forties. One an advertising executive, the other two, factory representative.

After the introductions, Joss was given a tour of the airplane. It was a large six passenger airplane. Unlike most small single engine airplanes, this one was pressurized, not unlike a commercial jet was. The four passenger seating was side by side and facing each other. The seats were high end leather, the carpeting plush. The cockpit was loaded with all the latest avionics and radios. Joss was impressed with how roomy it was compared to her smaller Archer.

It would require her to upgrade her pilots licence though. The M350 had a large engine and collapsable landing gear, which put it in the high performance and complex aircraft category, which Joss did not have a type rating for. While it was fast and could fly high, it guzzled fuel at double the rate her Archer did and the maintenance costs were much higher.

Joss escorted the three executive types to the house, Sam, the pilot stayed behind, doing his post inspection and doing a preliminary return flight plan to the factory in Florida. He occasionally looked over at Richard through an open door of the hangar, where he was tinkering with Joss' plane.

Sam walked in just as Richard was adjusting the flaps on the new Archer.

"The dealer should have done that for you." Sam said.

"Ya, the dealer should have done a lot of things," Richard said. "But he didn't. Which explains why he doesn't sell many aircraft for you guys. We got this one for ten percent under bluebook and I'll have it up to spec in about two more hours."

"Wow, is that a '63? A Cherokee 235?" Sam asked. He walked up to Richards plane and started walking around it. The cowling was off revealing the engine. The pilot whistled.

"How'd you get the FAA to approve that mod? That's one of those Corvair marine V8 conversions isn't it."

"Transport Canada didn't have a problem at all with it," Richard said.

That's when the Sam saw the Canadian registration number on the tail, the sticker beside the door in French and English advising the plane was an experimental aircraft.

"I am limited to a normal aspirated engine, fixed tricycle gear, a fixed pitch prop and under two hundred and fifty knot maximum speed. " Richard continued. "There are a few other minor details, but basically I can do almost anything someone who builds an experimental aircraft can do. Except for the fuselage assembly, I have basically replaced everything else, with as built or better parts from non certified suppliers for about a third of the cost of taking it for repair and using certified parts."

"Ya it would be nice if the FAA would let us do that here," the pilot said. "I do most of the work myself and pay a certified mechanic to sign off on the work. But I still have to buy certified parts, which are double or more in price."

"If I have any major work on the engine, I'll probably get a mechanic to do it," Richard said. "I'm not an engine guy. I do check and calibrate my avionics though. The equipment to do it is not all that expensive, it's easy to do and these new devices either work or they don't.

"I think Corvair is working with the FAA to have this engine certified for especially this model and its retractable brothers. It will be like mine, two hundred and ten horsepower, so it will fit with your regs. I burn anything that you can get at your local gas station, just like your car. Or avgas if I have to. They call for a recommended two thousand for overhaul, but I have almost three thousand on this one and absolutely no issues."

"Which, I am sorry to say, I can't say the same for the Archer there, or your M350. And I don't think either one of them are worth the asking price. But Joss has the money and for what she needs, the Archer is perfect."

"They want to give her one of these," Sam said. "But only for five years. And they want her doing personal appearances and like that with it."

"Up to her," Richard said. "But five years, she can have this thing registered in Canada under the owner/pilot designation like mine is and really trick it out. I think the FAA will be forced to do something similar soon."

"I hope so," Sam said, "It's getting to damn expensive to fly anymore."

The main door to the hanger opened and the women trailed by the three execs walked in. So much for my nice quiet day, Richard thought'

"That's my Archer," Joss said. "And that's the Cherokee I flew across Russia and down to here in."

"What?" Sam said looking at Richard.

"Ya, and she didn't even know how to fly when we took off in Sochi," Richard said. "It's no big deal. I've done the northern world crossing three times, with the standard tanks. We made it from Central Alberta to here with one stop in what, twelve hours or so?"

"Next month we plan on going to São Polo for the F1 race," Joss said. "I might take my new toy. We'll have to see if I can put enough hours in her to be confidant in the engine or not. If not, we take Richard's instead."

"That's a '63 Cherokee 235 isn't it?" Carl, the senior VP of Piper's marketing division said. "How about you take them both? On our dime?"

"Nope," Richard said. "I do not need nor want the publicity. Plus, this is hardly a stock certified 63 Cherokee."

"Your a certified flight instructor right?" Carl said. "Couldn't you do for one of these young ladies the same thing you did for Joss?"

"Probably not," Richard said. "Joss being who she is, allows her certain....privileges, that others do not."

"Oh somehow I think that if Piper wants something to happen, we can make it happen," Carl said. "So which one of you ladies would like to become a pilot?"

Delta and Clary looked at each other, then both shot up their hands. The exec laughed.

"Ok," Carl said. "Same deal as I offered Joss, but with Archers, matching Archers."

"As long as it doesn't interfere with their work," Joss said. "And as long as the training takes place here. I can't afford to loose both of them for the time it will take to get them certified."

"We've got two and a half months to the Brazil race," the exec said. "That enough time?"

"Should be," the pilot said. "They need to get their medicals done this week though."

"Make it happen," the exec said. "And you sir, I would really like your airplane to be part of this as well. How about this, no mention of you or pictures of you. Just the Cherokee. So what if it's highly modified. It's time the FAA got off their butts and made the same thing happen here anyway. All expenses and any repairs included plus a hundred grand."

"Hell, I don't get out of bed for less than a hundred and fifty," Richard said.

The exec laughed.

"Ok, two hundred," he said.

"Send the paperwork," Richard said. "And I train the California bobble head there." He winked at Delta.

After a little prompting some weeks later, Clary admitted to being from Boise Idaho. A few days after that, two graphic artists from the Piper factory showed up. A few days after that, the tail numbers were relocated to the tail fins, up high and as small as legally permitted. Below them, the outlines of Idaho on Clary's, California on on Delta's and Texas on Joss's. Otherwise they were identical. Richard forbade them to touch his baby, but he did relent to them touching it up some and waxing and polishing it.

A few weeks after that, the PR people showed up and a series of pictures were taken of all four aircraft together, then with the three women standing beside them, then individually, both in the cockpit and posing at various places around the planes.

It took all day. Sam and Richard spent the day in the shade of the hanger drinking beer and swapping flying stories. When a brake was called for the photo team and the women to change clothing, Richard took Sam over to his baby and showed him where and how he had mounted his de icing equipment and how much less it was than then manufacturers of the product wanted.

The crew and women returned and the men retreated back to the hanger. Then Sam was called and he had to put on his Piper flight suit and pose for some shots with Clary and Delta.

The day came for Delta and Clary to solo. Joss begged the two instructors and they agreed. They sent Clary up first. Then as she taxied up, they sent Delta up. While Richard kept an eye on Delta, Joss came up and first high fives, then hugged Clary. She spun her around, pulled the back of her shirt out of her pants and cut the tail off. Then ran while Sam dumped a pail of water on her.

Clary was still wringing the water off her shirt when Delta arrived and received the same treatment. Richard was no where to be found as the pictures were being taken. Once they PR team was gone, Richard came out of hiding and one by one handed the first solo certificates to each woman.

Joss shoved Richard out of the way and hugged both Clary and Delta, telling them how proud she was of them.

The next day, Sam gave Joss her Instrument Flying check out. When she came back down and he congratulated her on passing, the PR people were busy snapping away again. Then Delta and Clary burst onto the scene and plastered Joss with whipped cream from the can. This too was captured on camera.

For the next ten minutes or so, Delta and Clary were running in all directions staying away from Joss who had to finally resort to just yelling names at them as she could not catch them. Everyone, including Joss was laughing.

Joss looked over at the hanger. Richard was laughing so hard he had crouched down, almost unable to stand. Joss shook her fist at him, then stomped into the house in fake anger to have a shower and change of clothing.

They had a week to go until they had to leave for Brazil.

The small airfield was packed. Including the three girls and Richards airplanes, there were two corporate Piper aircraft for the execs and the PR team. Two twin engine Senecas, that would be taking the flight pictures the whole way. These had a pilot each, a camera operator and a sound tech in each. All packed in and around an airstrip that had been designed to hold one or possibly two corporate aircraft at most. Airplanes were parked on grass beside the paved runway and on the grass on both sides of the hanger.

Go Pro cameras were fixed in several places on all four aircraft, inside and out. Richard made sure the cameras in his cockpit would be unable to show his face. All the footage and sound would be edited by editors after each day.

The flight briefing for the flight to the Piper factory, the first leg of the journey was intense. This is when everyone found out exactly how expert Richard was. Each plane was assigned a specific spot to fly in the loose formation. It was a similar formation that the airforce used, but much wider. Richard would be the leader, to his right and slightly behind would be Clary. To his left and behind Clary, would be Joss, with Delta to her left.

The Senecas and their camera crews would take off first and form up on them later. Once at altitude and clear of any traffic they would begin maneuvering around the four plane formation. Joss was nervously tapping her left foot on the ground. While she was confident in her piloting abilities, this flight was going to be on a whole different level. She was, in addition to making sure she was flying correctly, making sure she was in the proper position and match every motion that Richard and especially Clary did. She also had to be aware of Delta's airplane and the continually changing positions of the camera aircraft. Clary and Delta, once they had formed up, had been instructed to match whatever Joss and Richard did.

The time came. The preflights were made. The twins took off and Richard made his way to all three women, hugging them and giving them words of encouragement. They would be on their own up there. Two women with less than one hundred hours of flying time, another with just over, were about to start an epic journey from Texas to Brazil. Yes, they had a lot of support on the way. But in the air, they were alone in that cockpit.

"San Antonio control, Cherokee 235, Charley Gulf Foxtrot Xray Zulu and formation of four requesting clearance for take off and flight to Florida, VFR," Richard said on the radio.

"Charley Gulf Foxtrot Xray Zulu and flight of four cleared for take off and VFR to Florida. God speed Xray Zulu and flight."

They took off in a very staggered two plane formation, then linked up with each other.

"Ok girls not to bad, it'll get better every time we do that." Richard said.

"Ya right," Joss thought. She was working hard, matching Clay's somewhat erratic plane movements, making sure Delta didn't come to close and keeping in control of her own airplane. All at the same time.

"Xray Zulu flight, Miami control, squawk 2699, ident."

Joss quickly dialled 2699 on their transponders and hit the ident button. She could tell on her flight display that the others had done the same, as one by one their aircraft became visible on her display, along with the two Senecas. The two corporate aircraft being much faster were out of range now. Now the controllers would see all four of them.

Again, there was a heavy PR and press presence at the Piper factory hanger. Richard had his Piper hoody and ball cap on, with dark sunglasses, so even if he showed up in a picture, nobody would know who he was. They were more interested in the girls anyway.

The four planes were quickly pushed into the hanger and teams of mechanics were soon swarming all over them. Not Richards girl though. The team assigned to him were allowed to look but not touch.

The next days trip was to Nassau in the Bahamas. Over breakfast, Delta and Clary told Joss they were extremely nervous about todays flight..

"Just more of the same," Joss said. "Just water instead of hard ground under us.."

Both girls listened intently to the briefing the chief Piper flight instructor gave. Joss and the Seneca pilots were paying attention. Richard was sleeping.

He was all business at the weather briefing the next morning though. This time he took each woman aside and asked them pointed questions about the upcoming flight, what they would do in certain situations, then clapped them on the shoulder.

"Piece of Cake," he said.

Joss had been going over the weather carefully as well.

"Going to be a little bumpy in spots," she said. "But otherwise we are golden,"

"Piece of cake," she said as Richard came up to her. "At least if we ditch we won't freeze to death."

She gave Richard a quick kiss, then everyone headed to their aircraft and started their preflight inspections.

When the airplanes were pulled out of the hanger, Richard was already in his plane all closed up when they pushed it onto the apron in front of the hanger. He had arranged it so he was the last one rolled out after all the picture taking of the women doing their walk arounds preflight checks were complete and they entered and shut their doors. Then he was rolled out. Even so, he was getting a little warm in the ninety degree heat by the time they were given the ok to start engines.

Joss gingerly scooted her way across the passenger seat and gingerly sat down on her pilots seat. The seats were already becoming almost uncomfortably hot to the touch.

"Hey Xray Zulu, aren't you a little cooked in that old crate all buttoned up?"

One of the Piper pilots in a Seneca asked on the frequency they had chosen to communicate with each other.

"Nope," Richard said. "Another benefit of the V8 boys, General Motors AC unit bolts right up to it. It's actually a little chilly in here."

"I'll chilly you when we get back on the ground," Joss said. "I'm boiling in here and I have the vents wide open."

"Well Texas," Richard said. "Take your right hand and slide that nice sliding lever on the dash to the full blue mark from the full red mark."

"Geez Texas even I figured that one out," Clary said.

"Nobody likes smart ass Idaho," Joss said. "Oh crap, now I'm freezing in here."

Nobody said anything, mostly because they were laughing to hard.

The flight was a little easier this time for Joss. The two girls were keeping in better position today. Flying over the ocean was not as bumpy as flying over the land was. Joss even had a few moments to look at the ocean and see the seemingly tiny ships sailing by. She calmed down and started to enjoy it. Then, all to soon for her, they were breaking their formation and lining up to land. They would come in one minute apart. Richard first, then Clary, Joss and finally Delta.

Joss saw a fairly large crowd of people standing around one hanger and as she taxied toward it. Bright flashes from still cameras and hand held telephones began going off.

Clearing customs was easier for Richard than it normally was. The customs guys were more interested in the girls. And because of his low key markings and that fact that he was the first one to taxi to their designated hanger, nobody paid attention to him there either. Every one was to busy taking pictures of the girls as they taxied in.

The next day was the hardest leg. They had to swing out into the Atlantic Ocean first. Then negotiate some high terrain and then land. Flying in and around mountains was old hat for Richard. He did show up for the briefing but hardly paid attention. He could see the girls were nervous. He flashed them an ok sign.

After the briefing was finished and the coffee and doughnuts came out. He motioned the girls to follow him and took them to a table by the back wall. Then he took out his binder, went to a clear page and began to draw pictures and diagrams.

Joss saw he was all business now, no joking around. Richard First, he told them he flew in mountains all the time, then, explained what they could face and how to respond to it. He was very clear and concise in his explanations, then asked each of them questions and answered theirs when they asked. Now they were much calmer and more confident.

"That was an interesting way of teaching that," the head Piper training instructor said.

"I've got a couple of thousand hours of mountain flying under my belt," Richard said. "Most in the Rockies, but some in the Urals as well. As far as mountain flying goes, this is no big deal for me. They have some tricky air currents, but nothing the girls can't handle. I just teach how I was taught. That's usually the first thing any of us gets where I'm from. Our mountain endorsements. I go from three thousand feet ground elevation to about ten thousand in about ten minutes from where I live. Rising all the way. Can be fun on a hot June afternoon."

"I'll bet," the head instructor said. "How many hours do you have?"

"On my girl there, coming up on thirty five hundred." Richard said. "Over all, I dunno eight ten thousand? Got my licence at seventeen. I like to fly, what can I say."

"Every couple of years, he flies the circle route into Europe, then across to Russia, across Russia and Alaska then home." Joss said.

"This trip here?' Richard said. "I've done this route once before. I usually follow the Rockies down through Mexico and South America and come in cross the Amazon. Usually nicer scenery. But this time..." he nodded his head toward the three girls.

"Plus," He continued, "All expenses paid and I get paid to do it. Bonus. I was coming anyway."

The trip to Brazil was uneventful and not overly long. Most of the flight was over water. They flew a little higher this time in order to clear the mountains and possible air currents around them. The seas was clear, the islands they flew over deep green, fishing boats and large ships plying their trade. Joss saw a few large yachts headed the same was they were.

The coast of Brazil came into view. The lush green Foliage a contrast to the blue of the ocean. While they were clear of the mountains, they still had to be aware of the downdraft coming from them. Soon, the brown haze from the air pollution of Sao Polo began to stain the horizon and the vast city of fifteen million began to take up most of the windshield.

Joss was glad that Richard was the flight leader now. It was his responsibility to make all the radio calls. Due to the large amount of air traffic the sprawling city had, there was much commercial traffic.

The airwaves were full and Joss had to change frequencies twice to new ones so she could hear the traffic and orders given by controllers.

In addition to the main International airport which catered to airline traffic, there was also a domestic airport which handled the local Brazilian commercial traffic. Both of these airports were busy with large jests. They would be landing at the Campo de Marte airpot which was reserved for General Aviation aircraft. It was also home to many heliports and helicopter hangers. These were used as air taxis to and from Sao Paulo.

Once their flight had reached the busy air corridors, the two Seneca's had left them behind and now the four Pipers single engines, once again broke formation to form line astern. This airport was also busy, especially with the traffic for the Formula 1 race.

As Joss came in to make her final approach, she saw the even bigger crowd waiting for them at their hanger. In addition to the print media, there were three large vans with large communications dishes coming from their roofs.

The customs routine was much much shorter than normal for Richard. But the girls had to put up with a lot more of the media this time. It being an international sporting event.

As she knew would happen, Richard disappeared. He wasn't even at the hotel. Nor was he at his normal box seat for the preliminary test runs. But Joss knew where she could find him. The team was waiting for them. Handed them their headsets and pointed to the roof.

"Texas!" Sandra yelled. She ran up and gave Joss a big hug. "California, nice to see you not all grumpy for once," she gave Delta a hug too.

"Clary," Clary said.

"Ah, so this is the new Idaho then?" Sandra said. "Let me have a look at you."

Sandra took Clary's shoulders and slowly spun her around.

"Not to shabby," Sandra said. "And this is Baden, Annas girl."

"Nice to meet you in person Hilda," Delta said. "I am Delta, this is Clary and that is Joss."

"Joss, this is the assistant I arranged for Anna."

"Yes yes," Sandra said. "All so formal. Texas, California, Idaho and Baden. So much easier."

"So where is Super Canuck?" Joss asked after shaking Hilda's hand.

"Well mine is getting his normal work out," Sandra said. "Yours is down there on the wall. Anna is taking her first run as the test driver for the F2 team today. It's only for today though. The normal driver will do the rest and the race."

"Already?" Joss said. "She just finished the GT series."

Sandra shrugged her shoulders and the five women walked over to where Anna had just come out of her race car and was undoing all the zippers of her racing suit.

"Well look at you Texas," Anna said after she had changed out of her driving suit and joined them on the roof. "All fancy in that official Piper get up."

"I can get you one too if you want one," Joss said.

"Ah no, sorry," Anna said. "My sponsors would flip out."

"Ok, how about Hilda then?"

"Nope," Hilda said. "Same deal with me."

"Hey, I'll take one," Sandra said. "I don't have any sponsor ship deals and I fly a Piper 600."

"What?" Joss said. Joss had not known that Sandra knew how to fly. "Delta..."

"Already on it boss," Delta said, she was already talking on her cell phone.

"George won't get in trouble?" Joss asked.

"Oh poo poo," Sandra said. "Nobody signed any contracts with me Texas, just George."

"They want to meet with you tonight over diner Sandra." Delta said.

"Give me a sec California," Sandra said.

She pulled out her phone and hit a predial number.

"Hey Chris, I've got a meeting with the Piper Aircraft people for a sponsorship deal for diner tonight. You free? Cool see you then kiddo."

"Ya me and Chris will be there," Sandra said.

"Who's Chris?" Joss asked.

"Georges agent," Sandra replied.

"Oh shit, they are not going to know what hit them." Joss said.

"Ya, the bobble head Formula 1 show wife and one of the best sports agents in the business," Sandra said.

Joss, Sandra and Anna laughed. Delta, Clary and Hilda just smiled not sure what was going on.

"Whats so funny?" Richard asked as he reached the roof.

"Piper wants to make a deal with Sandra," Delta said. "And she's bringing Georges agent with her."

"Good," Richard said. "He's just a barracuda. Sandra, well Sandra is more like a Great White shark. She'd eat them alive."

"Hey, it costs a lot of money to own that thing," Sandra said, talking about her and George's airplane.

"You coming to the hotel tonight?" Joss asked while everyone else was busy talking among themselves or watching the goings on in the pits. Knowing and dreading what his answer would be, Joss looked into his eyes.

"I'd love to, but I better steer clear," he answered. "The paperatzie are going to be all over you guys for a while."

"Do you know where he spends his nights at these things?" Joss asked Anna the next day.

"Not really," Anna said. "Ive heard rumours , but nobody knows for sure. If you can make a break for it. Go check out the hanger tonight."

That's where she found him.

"So that's the reason you can take out the back seats?" She said looking in the passenger door.

He had a sleeping bag and air mattress laid out behind the pilots seats.

"I'm not even going to ask," she said as she clambered in. "I'm joining you."

"It's nice here," Joss said cuddled close. "Not exactly quiet with all the air traffic noise, but nice. Nobody hassling me for interviews or snapping pictures."

Richard gave his patented shoulder shrug.

"One of the reasons I sleep out here," he said. "Helps me clear my mind for the racing."

"And away from prying eyes with the latest hotty too," Joss said.

She felt him stiffen up, just slightly. She looked up at him, he was staring blankly at the ceiling. She gently kissed him on the neck.

"I'm sorry Richard," she said. God, that Matti really did a number on him she thought.

Richard took a deep breath and sighed, he looked into Joss' eyes and she felt her heart rate jump. He ran his hand up and down her back, sending shivers down her spine.

"No Joss, nothing to be sorry about," he said. "I just come here to be by my self. Well, I did latch onto some Hollywood bobble head recently. I wonder if I should ask her to come see my airplane? What do you think?"

He tensed up waiting for the punch on the arm. Instead Joss flipped on top of him.

"I think she just said yes," Joss said. And they were to busy to talk anymore.

"Can I join you after the race tomorrow Richard?" Anna asked the next morning at the track. "I don't want to go home. This is my last function for the year and I need some me time."

"Ya sure kid," Richard said. "Now that Piper has Sandra, they don't want me and the old girl around anymore."

"Super, I really need someone to talk to Richard." She said.

"Well, a couple of days with me in the air might clear you of that right quick," Richard said. They both laughed.

"I'd like your opinion on some things Richard," Anna said. "Ja, Ja, I know your thoughts on that. I didn't say advice. I just want to bounce some thoughts off you."

Richard nodded his head and looked over at Sandra.

"Hey Sandra, anyway Heidi can catch a lift back with you? Anna wants to to hang with me on the trip back home."

"Sure no problem," Sandra said. "Beats being cooped up in the back seat of that bucket of bolts of yours for two days."

"Great," Richard said. "You can cart all of lard ass here's excess baggage too then. Shit that hurt." Anna had smacked him hard on the arm.

"Ha," Anna said. "Joss just gives you love taps."

As was normal for him, Richard and Anna were gone before the race ended. In fact they were in the air when it ended. The race was never in doubt. George and his team mate were one two from start to finish.

"Ok Anna, what's up?" Richard asked once they had reached their cruising altitude.

"I'm not so sure I want to do this Richard," Anna said. "All the press, all the pressure. I just want to race."

"All Joss ever wanted to do was sing," Richard said. "She wanted to make a living at it, yes. But she didn't want all the fame and glory."

"What about you Richard? How are you able to cope?"

"Different for me kid," he said. "What I do, does not need publicity. In fact it might cost me more. It actually did. I lost my family because of it, remember? I can handle what happens to me Anna, I've been doing it a long time. Me, your uncle and Sandra."

"No Richard, she was gone anyway," Anna said. "Don't forget that. She pushed you to be who you were, then tried to make the best of both worlds and got burnt for it. Your kids are just being asses."

Anna made herself comfortable after that and fell asleep. Allowing Richard to be alone with his thoughts. He knew his kids were caught in the middle. That they had been influenced by his in-laws. He also knew he had to keep his distance to protect them. Not from himself, but from what he did, who he was.

Richard allowed Anna to take off and fly at Mexico. She had her licence, just never had the chance to fly much. Especially internationally.

"Have you told Joss what you do yet?" Anna asked once they were in cruise.

"No" he said.

"Do you think that is wise?"

"Oh pulling my BS on me eh?" He said. They both laughed.

"No," he answered. "But necessary right now. I'll talk to her about it for sure after the movie shoot is over. I'll give her a little bit before if she pushes me about it. So far she hasn't even mentioned it."

"She must be in love then," Anna said. "Good. Do you love her?"

"Ya I think so," he said, then he looked over at her frowning at him. "Ok, Ok, yes alright."

"Good, I really like her," Anna said.

"Look Anna, I'd like to help you, offer you some advice, but I can't. You know my business, it is completely different than yours. Joss would be the better one to talk to, or Sandy, or your uncle."

"Ya, Sandy can give me advice from a drivers point of view," Anna said. "Joss from a female dealing with fame point of view."

"There you go," Richard said. "I don't know how long Sandra will stay with us in Texas. She'll be missing her kids. But Joss and I are going up to my place next week for a while. You can fly up with her then if you want. And once we get to my place, take all the time you want with Sandra. The season will be over by then. She won't have to go anyplace."

Then like Anna had done on the previous leg, he leaned his head back on the headrest. Anna was one of the best new talents in the racing scene. He really hoped she would pursue it. He also knew the pressure would be on her hard from the media. Her being the first female Formula 1 driver. He also knew, that no matter how much he wanted to help her make her choice, he was not qualified to do so. His eyes started to droop and he was soon asleep, only waking once they started to loose altitude and land to clear customs. An hour later they were pushing the plane into Joss's hanger.

"Whoo shit," Delta said coming into the kitchen a couple of days later. Joss was already draped on Richards lap, Anna smirking on another kitchen chair. "Now I know what it's like to put up with all the bullshit you guys have to put up with all the time. No thanks, you can have it."

"He give you flight lessons on the way Anna?" Joss asked.

"No, I'm already IFR certified," Anna said. "The bum there slept almost the whole way."

Richard shrugged his shoulders.

Hilda and Clary walked in next, dragging luggage behind them, computer bags and purses over shoulders.

"So, you catch the flying bug Hildi?" Richard asked.

"No thank you, to much work for my liking."

"Ya those high performance puppies can be a handful sometimes," Anna said. "Uncle Jochen has one, his is a Cessna though."

"Thems fighten words round here kiddo," Sandra said as she walked in, also dragging her suitcases behind her. "Where's the booze?"

Joss pointed to a side board with bottles on it.

"Cessna, phtt, phtt," Joss said. "Argh I wanna barf just saying the word." Then she laughed. "What do I know? I've never flown in one. I like the hunks plane and bought one like it."

"Thank Christ that's over with," she continued. "That was worse than the studio crap I do, and paid less."

Except for the brief moments alone with Richard when she could sneak away, when Joss wasn't doing Piper appearances, she was being constantly harassed and followed by all kinds of media types. From Formula 1 media, to Brazilian television, to various aviation media types. At least the aviation types asked Clary to schedule time for interviews and treated her with respect and not a bobble head. Unlike the majority of the other media types.

"Speak for your self," Sandra said. "I get free maintenance and repairs for the next five years. Free fuel for three and made a cool five hundred Grand. Euros, not dollars. Paid to my account in the Bahamas."

"Spoil sport," Joss said. "Got the same deal with the airplane, but five hundred US."

"What did you get Low Risc?" Sandra asked Richard.

"All expenses and two hundred Canuck." He answered. "Easy money for me, I was gong anyway."

After diner, the whole gang had moved to the fire pit behind the house. Richard, being the only male, was delegated to start the fire and was harassed by all the women as they drank their beverages. He just smiled, knowing he was in a lose, lose situation if he tried some comebacks.

The sun had gone down, an hour after that, the other women left. It had been a long few days for them all. The only people left around the fire pit were Sandra, Joss and Richard. The others had all gone to bed.

"Whats up with Anna," Joss asked. "I noticed she has been a bit distracted lately."

"She wants to talk with both of you," Richard said. "I can't really help her. My business is totally different from the entertainment business. Publicity is actually a bad thing for me. She's having a tough time with the lime light thing."

"Ya it's a big adjustment for sure," Joss said. "She'll be ok. Ok, it's a little chilly out here for me. Don't stay up to late hey? I'm tired and I hear my bed calling my name."

She kissed Richard, hugged Sandra and grabbing her empty glass, headed toward the house.

"You tell her what you do yet?" Sandra said.

"No, and don't you spill the beans," Richard said. "Anna asked me the same thing. Joss hasn't bugged me about it yet. I'll tell her what I sort of do after her picture shoot is over. She doesn't need to know about the other things we do Sandra. It's to dangerous for her to know."

"She's not Matti Richard," Sandra said.

"I know that. She takes me for who I am and doesn't want to change me. Yet. You women kinda do that sometimes."

"Not me" Sandra said. "But then I'm a different cat right? It's going to be tough for Anna. F1 Is a tough game even for the guys. She is going to be the ice breaker. The first really good female F1 Driver. She is going to be under the microscope for a long, long time Richard."

"And that's why she needs friends like you and George," Richard said. "Jochen try's, but he's her uncle. Me, I can listen, but what the hell do I know?"

"Ya, you're the typical he man Hunk type for sure," Sandra said. "Not the touchy feely type at all."

"Ya, like you're a typical female Sandra."

"At home I am Richard. At home I am."

Richard leaned back in his chair and Sandra leaned her head against the back of hers. He was looking at the fire, she at the stars. Neither seeing what they were staring at, thoughts lost in the far away and times past. Times when things had been much much, more intense and dangerous than they were now.

Joss found the both of them sleeping in their chairs by the fire pit the next morning. The fire was just embers now. Both hands were holding untouched bottles of open beer in their hands.

"Hey bums!" Joss yelled waking them both.

They startled Joss by both dropping the bottles and jumping up, turning sideways to her and reaching for something that was not there on their right sides. Both heads were sweeping back and forth, eyes darting. Just as quickly, both Sandra and Richard changed stances and expressions to their normal ones.

"Almost gave me a heart attack there Texas," Sandra said. She took a swig of her beer and made a face, before pouring in the fire pit.

"Ug," she said, "beers flat. Sure hope somebody has coffee and breakfast going on in the house."

Joss was wrapped up in Richard. Sandra sighed, knowing she would not be missed and headed toward the house and breakfast.

As had been predicted, Sandra took off for home that afternoon. Heidi and Delta were closeted all day. Delta explaining how she did things for Joss, Heidi explaining what was happening for Anna. Joss was busy wrapping up the Piper tour interviews and talking with the movie people regarding the new movie and Clary was running between both groups handing off messages and doing whatever else needed doing, like coffee and snacks.

Richard was, as usual for him, in the hanger tinkering with something on his plane. Anna came by, still in her jogging suit, after a couple of laps around the airstrip. She did a round of sit ups, leg lifts, pushups and found a doorsill to do some pull ups. After that, she walked over to the ever present coffee maker, found a clean cup, poured herself one and walked over to where Richard was tinkering.

"Something amiss?" She asked. Richard noticed her English was getting better.

"No," Richard said. "Just routing the cooling line from the radiator a little. I'm just doing keep busy things right now."

"Nothing pressing at work then?" Anna said.

"Dunno, probably not," Richard said. "That's what I have minions for eh?"

"We going to the hanger, or the other place?" Anna asked.

"I dunno," Richard said. "You think I should?"

"Might be good to ease her into things a little," Anna said. "She's pretty easy going, but most women don't like surprises sprung on them. Especially the money and housing type things. But Joss might be different. She is an independent self made woman."

"So, any guys kicking around the bushes?" Richard asked.

"Ya right," Anna said. "Who has time?"

She walked over to the baggage door, opened it up and brought out her overstuffed computer bag. Walking over to the table they normally did their flight planning from, she dug out a laptop, found the correct North American adapter for it, plugged it in, then found a thick manual, plunked it down on the table, sat down and began to work.

Richard had found a deck lounge chair and was sitting on it, back reclined, feet outstretched before him, beer in hand. His new, almost bent to suit him Piper ball cap down low on his eyebrows. He was awake, as from time to time he would take a sip of the now luke warm beer he had in his right hand.

He was looking out across the runway at the land beyond. It was a nice view, but he had found over the years, if he spent to much time away from his mountains, he began to miss them. And he hadn't been back for a couple of months now. In fact, it had been almost a year since he had been back to the other place. What he considered his real home. How his cattle and horses were doing. Maybe it was time to let Joss know a little more about him. He loved her, that was true, but was not sure about how far he should let her into his real life.

Joss sneaked up on Richard, who at least appeared to be sleeping, and crouched beside him, kissing his cheek.

"Wow, that's a big book Anna has there," Joss said.

"Those are just the regulations," Richard said. He pushed the cap back to the crown of his head and kissed her on the lips.

"The stuff on the laptop is even bigger," he continued. "Come on, I haven't seen the back side of your property yet."

Richard stood and held out his hand to her.

"Yes you have," she said. "Last night."

He patted her rear with his free hand as they started to walk across the runway.

"And a very nice view it was indeed," he said.

The further they walked from the runway, the less luscious the grass was. Soon it was thin, but tall, almost to their knees. Scrub brush started popping up here and there. The farther they walked from the house and yard, the quieter it became. The distant screech of a hawk and the crickets, the only sounds. At one point, Richard stopped, dug the toe of his right sneaker in the ground a couple of times, bent over and picked up some dirt, feeling it's texture in his fingers and letting it sift out to fall back on the ground.

"It's a little to dry for most crops," Joss said. "And I don't have time to farm anyway. But who knows? Maybe after I retire."

"How much land do you have?" Richard said.

"Just about eight hundred acres," Joss said. "Nobody has farmed this place for ages. Some oil guy owned it before me. It was his play palace for the latest girl friend. I picked it up for a good deal from his wife after he died."

They walked on in silence a little longer. It was quiet out here and they could hear birds chirping and insects buzzing. The wind was softly rustling the grass and sub brush. The weather not yet as hot as it would be later in the day.

Joss became quiet, reflecting on days past. They walked on hand in hand in silence. Richard respecting Joss's quiet moment.

"You ever miss your old life Joss?" Richard asked.

"Some," she said. "Like now, walking through this field. We just had one hundred sixty acres and my dad spent most of what little money we made on booze, horses and women."

"Well, at least you had horses," Richard said.

Joss laughed.

"Ya we had a couple of old nags at home," she said. "I was talking about the track Richard. That's why mom left him. He lost the farm a year or so later. Mom worked two jobs in order to cloth, feed and house us. When we got older, we all got part time jobs to help out. My father was no where to be found."

Joss walked along a bit in silence once again after that. Reflecting, mostly, on the hard times the, her sisters and mother had experienced in those dark days.

"Until I got my big break," she said at last. "Oh ya, my dad was all over me then. I punted him about two months after he started leaching from me. He made out pretty good using my name for a while. Last I heard, he was in Seattle drinking his life away."

"If people don't want to change Joss," Richard said. "There is not much we can do about it."

Joss looked over at him. She was learning when he used that soft tone in his voice, he was hurting. Unlike most people she knew, he didn't look at the ground when he was upset. Instead, he was always looking out into the horizon his eyes not seeing what was there. She felt so helpless, seeing him hurt so deeply about things he would not share with her. When would he trust her enough to share it.

"Do you want to talk about it?" Joss asked.

They had come to an old boundary fence that split the land into one hundred sixty acer parcels. The wire was rusty, some of the posts were rotted at the ground and in places, the wires had come off the staples that held it to the posts letting it sag to the ground.

"You could rent the land out Joss," Richard said. Trying to change the subject.

She stopped him, turned him to her and held his arms in her hands.

"You can talk to me Richard," she said softly.

"I know," he said. "Just not now. I'm not ready. I enjoy what we have together Joss. I don't want to ruin it. Soon you will be back to work and I have things I need to make happen. I just want to enjoy the time I have left with you."

They both stood and looked out across the fence in silence. Other than the wind picking up and rustling through the grass and bushes, or a high flying jet airliner. It was quiet. While she was upset, because he was upset, she hid it well. She was a very good actress. She would let him be, for the time being.

"You are right," Joss said. "Not often, but this time I think you might be right. It's an awful waste to let this land go back to nature. I'll have to figure out how to make that happen."

Richard chuckled.

"Like I said to Anna this morning," Richard said. "That's what I have minions for."

"What?" Joss said.

"I don't have a need for a personal assistant like you do Joss," Richard said. "But I do have people that run things for me. What? You think all I do out in that hanger is play with my girl? You've got a fantastic WiFi signal out there."

"You bum!" Joss said and smoked him on the arm. "And here I thought you were the lost puppy without me."

"Well that too," he said pulling her to him.

Sometime later they were walking back into the hanger. The sun was starting to go down and as they entered the hanger, Anna was just packing away her laptop. At least Richard was slowly opening up with her Joss thought. The big thick wall he had built around himself was slowly crumbling. At least with her.

"I see you had a nice walk," Anna said walking up to Joss and pulling some dried grass out of her hair. "I hope you didn't scare the wild life to much with your rolling around in the grass."

"Oh shut up you!"

Joss walked off to the house pulling grass from her hair and brushing down her clothing.

Richard laughed, Joss heard him, turned around and flashed her famous smile at him. He thought her smile out shone the sun.

"So?" Anna said.

"Ya, file a flight plan for home tomorrow Anna," Richard said. "We'll do customs at Lethbridge. You go with Joss, I'll take Clary"

"Heidi with Delta then?"

"Ya, Delta is a better pilot than Clary," Richard said. "You guys stick together. I'm going to run a little harder and longer this time."

"You're the boss Richard," Anna said.

"No, we are still on holidays Anna," he said. "Right now I'm just your cousin."

Richard had already filed his flight plan the night before, but he made Clary make one up anyway. It was good experience for her. Most pilots never flew the long legs they were about to fly. They did at most, four or five hours a week. This trip, they would do that per leg. The girls didn't have quite the range or the speed that Richard had and Heidi not being a pilot, they had to limit their time in the air to eight hours a day. Richard and Clary didn't have that problem.

They would do the fifteen hour flight in one shot with two fuel stops only. No layover.

Richard would fly the last leg. It would be dark and Clary didn't have her night rating yet.

"Good to go?" Richard asked Clary. They pulled the aircraft out onto the apron in front of the hanger and Richard watched Clary do the preflight on it. Soon the other two planes were dragged out and Richard shut the big hanger door. By that time Clary was in the pilots seat doing her pre start checks. Anna was doing the same on Joss's bird. Joss was watching her and came up to Richard.

"See you in a couple of days love," Richard said. They kissed long.

"I'm pushing straight through." He said.

"I would too if I could," Joss said. "It's going to be a long two days without you."

They kissed again.

"Get a room hey!" Delta yelled over at them.

"Get a boy toy California!" Joss yelled back. She then gave Richard another quick kiss. "I'm going to really enjoy the delights of your little apartment. I can't wait."

"Ok, gotta go," Richard said.

Clary soon had them in the air and at cruising altitude. This early in the day on a weekday, it wasn't busy on the airways except for the commercial traffic. The further away from the big population centres they went, the quieter the radio became.

"This thing has a lot better get up and go than mine does," Clary said. "With your fixed pitch prop, the climb rate is a bit slower. You sure you want to keep at seventy percent power? It's going to use more fuel and be harder on the engine."

"Hours per gallon of fuel will be higher," Richard said. "But time in the air will be less, so it works out about the same. Also, my engine is not like the one you have Clary. Yours is based on nineteen forties technology, mine, the latest technology. There is a big difference."

"Could I change mine to match yours?" Clary asked.

"Right now, no." Richard said. "And I wouldn't advice it anyway. It would cost you about forty thousand dollars to do the conversion, about two months of FAA paper work and you would be without your plane for about a month while they did the work it. Fly for a while with what you have Clary. Piper is going to pay for everything for the next five years. After that?"

"Ya, you're right," she said. "I might find a boy toy who will end up taking up all my time."

He asked her how she was liking working with Joss. She told him Joss was a lot less demanding than her previous boss had been. He had been a real jerk, a full of himself new recording star. The work for Joss was more demanding, but Clary had the freedom to handle it her own way. Within reason. She would most likely have a couple of hundred messages and emails waiting for her when they landed for the last time.

They were just lining up for take off at their first fuel stop, when Joss' and Delta's Archers were on final approach for landing. Having been given clearance to take off in between Delta's landing and another approaching aircraft, Richard did not even have enough time to wave as the girls swung into the taxiway after landing. He lined the plane up on the centre line, pushed the throttle all the way forward and they were off. This would be the last time they saw them until the final landing.

"I see what you were saying back in Nassau," Clary said. "These mountains are a lot higher and the air more bumpy."

They had been following the rail and road passes at first, now they were climbing out over them. They were still able to use visual flight rules. The clouds were high and scattered. Richard plugged the oxygen system in for first Clary, then himself and showed her how to use it. They were just reaching ten thousand feet in altitude and he had been cleared to twelve thousand. Oxygen was required after ten thousand feet.

"We're cutting the corner of your state pretty soon Clary," Richard said. "Then into Utah and Montana."

"I've seen this from the air before," she said, "but not this low. It's more breath taking down here."

"Do you get home much?" Richard asked.

"Not for the last couple of years," she said. "My kid brother is graduating High School this year. Joss told me if I don't take a couple of weeks off then to go home, she'd fire me."

They both laughed.

"Sounds like her," Richard said. "She means well, just has a hard time expressing it sometimes."

"Like somebody else I know," Clary said patting Richard on his left forearm.

"I get every second Friday off," Clary continued. "With Idaho, I can fly up Thursday evening and fly back Sunday. It'll all work out."

Richard pulled out his cell phone and called Canada Customs as they hit Montana. They had to give an hour notice to have an agent meet them. The agent and the fuel attendant were waiting for them at the fuel bunkers in the FOB at the Lethbridge Airport.

"Welcome home," the agent said to Richard, quickly scanning his document visually, then scanning the passport electronically.

"Anything to declare, firearms, more than ten thousand in cash, bla, bla, bla," the agent said with a grin on his face.

"Ya ya Bruce," Richard said. "Yak it up."

He was a little more thorough with Clary's paper work and a little more professional in his questioning.

"Welcome to Canada mam," he said and handed her back her paper work. "Don't let this yahoo lead you around by the nose eh? I hear his girlfriend is the jealous type."

He jumped into his government vehicle and was gone.

"What..." Clary said, her ears turning pink. "No way Richard. You're a nice guy and all.."

"Don't worry about it Clary," Richard said. "Canuck sense of humour. It takes a bit of getting used to."

Soon they were taxing to the runway once again. The engine sounding a little differently. Richard explained that it would take a few minutes for the electronics to adjust to the higher octane the leaded fuel had, but that it would smooth out soon.

As the sun was going down anyway, Richard had chosen to file an Instrument Flight Rules flight plan. He would have to once it got dark anyway. It was just easier this way. Once they had reached cruise, Richard began to show and teach Clary how to fly by instruments alone.

An hour later, Richard changed his second radio to a different frequency and keyed his push to talk button twice. In the distance, runway lights came on.

"Chinook traffic, Gulf Foxtrot Xray Zulu on ten mile final, straight in approach the field is in site."

Then he touched a key on the main display that switched the radio back to the main frequency.

"Edmonton control, Gulf Foxtrot Xray Zulu has the field insight, ten mile final. Cancel IFR for final approach and touch down."

"Xray Zulu, Edmonton control, confirm cancel IFR."

"Chinook traffic, Xray Zulu on three mile final, full stop." Richard said.

He was busy now, adjusting his speed to the conditions and slowing the aircraft down to landing speed, adjusting his elevator trim and lowering flaps. The runway rushing up at them and then a gentle bump and chirp from the tires and tire rumbling, confirming they were on the ground.

"Edmonton Control, Gulf Foxtrot Xray Zulu is on the ground, 19:45 and please close the flight plan."

"Xray Zulu Edmonton control, confirm on the ground at 19:45 local and close the flight plan. Welcome home."

"Xray Zulu, have a great evening." Richard had rolled and elongated the rrs in great when he had said it.

He tuned to another frequency as he taxied and again keyed the push to talk button three times. A hanger door started to open. Once they arrived, Richard expertly spun the plane around so the tail was facing the hanger door and shut down.

"Back right," Richard said. Pointing to the washroom in the corner of the hanger.

Clary hurried to where he was pointing, he walked over to a corner of the hanger and relieved himself. It had been a long flight and a long day. Clary arrived in time for her to help push the plane back into the hanger. Then she began to unload their few bags from the baggage compartment. Richard closed the big hanger door.

"So," Clary said. "You guys have an uber or taxi service or something out here in the sticks?" She said.

"Nope," Richard said, picking up his duffle bag.

"Well there is no way in hell I'm sharing your bed in that dinky apartment Joss told me you had in the back of this hanger. And there is no way in hell I'm sleeping on the coach."

"Oh ye of little faith" Richard said. "Come on slow poke grab your stuff."

They walked out the man door and Richard started walking up the still lit at intervals apron. There was enough light from the runway lights to show Clary, they were now walking on a paved road. Then, as the lights started to become to dim to see any more, a series of low light landscaping lights came on. Even spaced along a now concrete walk way. The runway lights shut off then.

They walked up a slight incline and wham. A whole series of spot lamps came on revealing a large house. What Clary could see of it anyway in the almost pitch darkness. Richard took her to the impressive front door, it had two interlocking doors, both dark blue, with side lights on both sides and a half moon shaped stain glass window on top. Richard punched in some numbers into a keypad there and opened the door. Once inside, he hit a light switch, then hurried away to where an alarm system was beeping away. After disarming it. He walked around to where the kitchen was and turned the lights on.

Clary looked around her as she followed Richard into the kitchen. The wide foyer led directly into a large living, sitting room with a large fireplace taking up the far wall. Expensive leather furniture, marble topped oak coffee tables and the ever present in a man's house, large flat screen TV and stereo system.

Attached to this was an equally large dinning room. It had expensive solid wood furniture and a filled large china cabinet above a large hutch, also in solid wood.

The kitchen itself was almost as large as Clary's apartment was. It had a large wrap around kitchen counter with a lot of prep area, with cupboards all along them. A large four place cook top was placed on one side of a centre set of cupboards.

All the appliances were large, stainless steel clad and expensive.

"Wow, nice place," Clary said.

She heard a forced air furnace kick in. Then Richard turning a tap on in the kitchen.

"Coffee or beer?" He asked. "That's all I have here right now."

"Beer works," she said.

"Any room but the one at the back on the right side," Richard said. "Your pick."

Clary spent some time choosing a bedroom. There were five, not including the master suite. Again, the furniture in the bedrooms was high end solid wood. By the time she had unpacked her things and come back to the kitchen, Richard was boiling some water, a box of spaghetti beside the stove and a couple of cans of chilli were being opened and put in a pot.

"I've got some burgers and other things in the freezer if you want," Richard said. "But I'm kinda hungry and don't want to wait for them to thaw out. Sorry, no fresh veggies. Got some canned stuff in the pantry there if you want."

"No, I'm good," Clary said.

She gave herself a tour of the house, but Richard didn't mind. She looked at a couple of photos of his two sons and their wives. One small one of a blond woman on a horse. But other than that, a typical man's home. Little of the nick knacks that a woman would have scattered about. But other than the large TV hung on the wall, none of the garish posters and trophies or sports memorabilia that men usually had on display. While not austere, it was definitely something that showed women were rarely here.

"That the ex?" Clary said pointing at the picture of the blond on the horse.

"Ya," Richard said.

"I take it Joss doesn't know about this place?" Clary said.

"Nope," He answered. "She'll find out tomorrow afternoon. Surprise! It's ok, I still run faster scared than she runs mad."

Both of them laughed. Joss did have a quick temper at times, especially when she was tired. Richard had learned her bark was far worse than her bite and he had survived much, much worse in his past. He also knew it was always a fast outburst followed by a very intimate apology after.

"How long have you owned this place?" Clary asked.

"I dunno, five, ten years," he said. "Haven't been here for what, a year or so? What with Joss and you guys' tour and all. If I'm only going to be around for a few days, I usually stay down at the hanger in town."

His cell phone rang at that time and he answered it, putting it on speaker to keep his hands free for cooking.

"Hey bum," Sandra said. "You made it home ok."

"Ya, was no big deal," Richard said. "Clary flew the first half. Say high Clary."

"Hi Sandra. How are the kids?"

"Hey Idaho, argh, my daughter's getting to be the wrong age you know? Getting boy crazy. My son, like his dad, car crazy."

"I've got a couple of younger sisters," Clary said. "You want I have a talk with your daughter?"

"Wouldn't hurt," Sandra said. "Joss and especially Anna will be a big deal for her. But some one wth a saner wiser head would be better."

"Super Hero back home yet?" Richard asked.

"Ya, early this morning," Sandra said. "He's beat from the awards party and the jet lag. Not to worry, he for sure wants to be there tomorrow for the barbecue."

"Barbecue?" Clary said. "What barbecue?"

"Ut oh," Sandra said.

"Surprise!" Richard said, followed by a grunt, as Clary smacked him in the arm.

"That shoulder of yours is going to be awfully sore tomorrow Super Hunk," Sandra said then laughed.

"Nah, she hits like a girl, oh damn. Hit the left shoulder next time eh? Joss is going to make the right one sore enough as it is."

Sandra was howling with laughter on the other end of the telephone.

"Ok boss, I'll catch ya tomorrow," Sandra said, and hung up.

"She ever take anything serious?" Clary asked.

"Oh ya, all to often," Richard said.

The spaghetti was done, he put a large portion on her plate and put the pot of steaming chilli down beside it with a large spoon sticking in the middle of it. Then heaped a pile of spaghetti on his own plate, sliced a chunk of thawing out butter on the top, shook some powdered garlic over it all, the layered chilli on top of all that.

If anything, Clary put more of each on her pile. Richard complimented Clary on her progression as a pilot and how she was helping Joss a lot at work. while they ate. Then Richard piled everything into the fridge or the dishwasher and they went to bed.

Clary went looking for him the next morning. He didn't appear to be in the house, but the coffee was made and still hot. She pored herself a cup and walked out onto the attached deck. Being fall and in the mountains it was a little chilly. They were in a two acre cleared area almost surrounded by spruce trees. She heard a vehicle arrive and Richard talking with some one. Then a small engine started with a roar and soon a man driving a riding lawn mower was making his rounds, cutting the long grass.

Clary went back inside. Richards head appeared climbing up some stairs by the front door. He had what turned out to be an empty travel mug in his hand as he went to the coffee maker and refilled it.

"Got some bread for toast in the fridge thawed out if you need it," he said. "Sandy is hitting the grocery store for me this afternoon. Back to work for me I'm afraid. Won't be getting much done once Joss gets here."

He jogged back down the stairs and a short time later she could hear he was talking on the telephone to someone.

Clary made another plate of spaghetti and chilli from the left overs from super, placed it in the microwave, then retrieved her laptop from her bedroom. She found a handy spot with a plug in close to the breakfast nook beside the built in cooking range and fired up the laptop. By then, the microwave had finished with her plate of food. She plunked it down beside the laptop and rummaged through drawers until she found a fork. First plugging in her headset and microphone combo into the laptop, then her head, she took a bite of food and opened her emails and was soon engrossed in her work.

"That's not the airport we landed at the last time I was here," Joss said as she saw Anna's flight plan being displayed on the digital display.

They had just taken off from the Lethbridge customs stop and were now lazily gaining altitude waiting for California to join up on them. The formation flying was becoming easier the more times they did it.

"The boss said go there," Anna said. "So I go there. I still can't get over how well you handle all that attention stuff Joss."

"I have learned to split myself Anna," Joss said. "Right now, I am Joslyn, back there, I was Joss Lynn. The fans are important Anna, without them, we are just normal folks. They are the ones that pay our bills. But they don't need to know about Joslyn or her life. That is totally different. I play the media game when I have to, not because I have to. There is a big difference. That co star of mine had to play it. He was not a great actor with a lot of followers, so he needed the attention. I don't and neither do you."

Joss explained that the media would be chasing Anna. She was unique, a new story. She didn't have to do outrageous things to get media attention. The challenge would be not to let it go to her head.

"No fear of that," Anna said. "Grandma will clue me in right quick."

Her English was getting better all the time. She still had an accent, but it wasn't a hinderance. Joss went on to explain. She never lost sight of who she was or where she came from. And that, while she was an actress and a singer, those were jobs, not who she was. Anna would understand that with time. Right now she was a racing driver, it defined who she was. Everyone was like that at the beginning, no matter what job they did. But at the end of the day, they were just people, nothing more, nothing less.

November 2684 Tango flight, Edmonton Control, decent to eight thousand.

Edmonton Control Tago flight decent to eight thousand copy.

Joss was working the radios today as Anna was doing the flying.

"I have the field in sight Joss," Anna said.

"Ya ok, me too" Joss said.

Edmonton control, Tango Flight, we have YPZ in site, ten miles.

Chinook traffic November 2684 Tango, flight of two on ten mile downwind approach.

Delta slowed down and moved behind to the proper spacing, then they turned to line up the runway and landed. The runway was bordered by two large hangers. A large bungalow style house was within easy walking distance of the hangers situated in what looked like two acres of yard surrounded by tall spruce trees. A paved driveway led to the front of an attached triple car garage.

"Wow nice place," Joss said. "You know the owner?"

"Ya," was all Anna said.

She taxied to one of two large hangers and spun the plane around before shutting it down. The big hanger door started to open. Richard and Clary were standing there. After carefully exiting the plane, Joss rushed Richard. He grabbed her and swung her around. Delta parked beside Joss's plane and it was to loud to talk until she shut it down. Joss saw Richards plane in the hanger.

"You come here often, it's beautiful," Joss said.

"Not as beautiful as you are," he said and kissed her.

"Ah Geez, my own personal porn show." Delta said. She came up and hugged first Clary ,then Richard.

"We going to meet the owner?" Joss asked. "Anything I have to worry about?"

"Nope," Richard said. "I own this place."

He was tensing up waiting for the smack on the shoulder.

"You have good taste," Joss said kissing the shoulder instead. "For a man."

"Ya ya," Richard said. "Clary? Take the three yahoos up to the house. Anna and I will put the birds to rest."

Joss, Delta and Heidi grabbed their luggage and followed Clary to the house.

"Flight ok?" Richard asked.

"Ya the usual hassle with Joss stuff aside, it was all good," Anna said.

"A little birdie tells me Piper wants to put a little patch on your uniform Anna," Richard said.

"Well it had better be a lot better deal than the one Diamond just offered us," Anna said.

"Really," Richard said.

"What, Rosy not tell you yet?" Anna said. She laughed.

"Anything pressing Clary?" Joss asked once they had reached the house.

"Studio sent over some costars they want you to look over and some plot scenes. Nothing that can't wait. Delta has a couple of things she should handle today. Sorry Heidi, I have nothing for you.
"

"Anna has a sponsorship offer to go over and approve or not and the team manager wants to talk with her, but that will be for early this morning." Heidi said. What? Satellite technology, I have a bigger budget than you guys and don't have to do pilot things when we are flying. I can actually get some work done."

"Ok, I'll tell you the same thing Richard told me," Clary said. "Any room but the one I'm using and the big one down on the right and at the end. That's for Joss."

"Jeez," Delta said when they linked back up in the kitchen. "This place is bigger than yours Joss."

"No kidding," Joss said. "Some how I think Super Hunk has been holding out on me. He does have good taste in furniture, but little of anything else."

"I haven't seen the down stairs yet," Clary said. "But I think he has an office down there."

Joss's cell phone rang.

"Hey Sandra, ya we just got into the house. Nice place he has here. Umm. Lemme think, vodka for me, ladies? Ok, more vodka, light rum, some schnapps and some decent wine. Ok, see you soon."

Joss hung up, then said, "Sandra is making a booze run for us, says all Super Hunk has on hand is beer and not much of that."

Anna and Richard walked in at that point, Anna had her laptop bag on a shoulder and took the duffle bag out of Richards hand. Then she went downstairs with the duffle bag on one shoulder, her computer bag on the other.

"Wow not to shabby buddy," Joss said, snuggling up to Richard in the kitchen. "Nice surprise. You had this long?" I could get used to this place in a hurry, Joss thought.

Richard shrugged his shoulders, "Five, Ten years? Lose track sometimes."

Delta, Clary and Heidi had taken their laptop bags to the dining room, found placemats and putting the computers on them, began to boot them up.

"Go play with your girls Joss," Richard said. "Anna and I have something to discuss."

"Don't take to long hey?" Joss said kissing him and giving him a squeeze.

The women made a tour of the house and Richard went downstairs. It felt nice to have a full house once again.

He went into his office and scrolled down to Rosy's email. Read the document attached to it and printed it up. Anna watched him standing by the door.

"Well," Anna said. "It worth it?"

"Doesn't look to bad, especially access to the wind tunnel. Not a bad deal from the teams side of things." Richard said. "But having access to you is the hinge of the deal Anna. So you have to be happy with your part of it. The commercial shoot should only be a week or so and they only want you for the year end stock holders meeting for a meet and greet."

"Five year deal on their new DA50," Anna said. "Service, repairs and parts, plus fuel. One million Euros. I guess I can live with that."

"You missed the performance clauses Anna," Richard said. "Top five in F2 an extra 200 thousand, fifty thousand for a win, thirty for second, ten for third. Two hundred K for making F1 and they add a zero to the other numbers. Per year."

"Um....wow," she said.

"There are a few other things you will want to make sure of Anna," Richard said. "They have some personal conduct things in there. Nothing to outrageous. I don't think they are that bad. It looks like a good deal to me. But I'm not you."

"Leave me with it Richard," she said.

Richard came upstairs to get more coffee from the kitchen and saw Heidi was looking for Anna.

"She's looking over that sponsorship offer from Diamond," Richard said. "I guess Rosy sent it to her instead of you."

"No, I got it first," Heidi said. "That's what I want to talk to her about."

"She's down in my office," Richard said.

"I think the team owner should take it," Heidi said. "It's a good deal for the team and Anna Richard. Can I count on you to help if we need it?"

"Sure," he said. "But between you, Rosy and Anna, you won't need me."

"Hey bums a little help here!" Sandra said, flinging the front door open and plunking a box of groceries on the floor.

It wasn't one vehicle in the drive, but two. One a Mercedes G wagon, the other a Ford pickup. Both fully loaded with boxes of food and booze. George and the kids each with a box in hand were making their way to the house. Soon a relay system was in action. The four girls bringing the stuff into the kitchen, the five out side carting them in.

"Where's the kid?" George asked.

Both men were staying out the way, pouring drinks in the dining room. It never paid to get in the way of motivated women at work. The kids had Richards PlayStation going.

"Downstairs deciding on whether she wants to be a rich twenty year old, instead of a famous twenty year old," Richard said. "Diamond aircraft just gave her a fantastic sponsorship offer. It's good for the team too."

"Hey," Sandra yelled from the kitchen. "A little vodka for the hard working women around her would be nice."

"What's up dear," Sandra said coming up to them for her vodka.

Richard told her about the deal for Anna.

"Holy Cow!" Sandra said.

"Not to worry Sandra," Richard said. "We have something in the works for George to, but not with Diamond. They aren't the only European aircraft manufacturer."

"No way!" Sandra said. "I'll punt that Piper into the ditch and set it on fire if I can get one like yours Richard."

"Shh, not so loud eh?"

"Oops, sorry boss," Sandra said.

"What's all the excitement over here?' Joss asked as she joined them from the kitchen having finished putting things where she wanted them, making her own little mark on the house. She put her arm around Richards waist.

"I dunno for sure," Richard said. "But I think my cousin is about to become a very rich little girl. Diamond has just made her a sweet sponsorship deal."

"OO, diamonds," Joss said. "Always a good deal for girls. Oach! That hurt!"

Sandra had just punched her on the arm.

"Diamond Aircraft, not diamonds," Sandra said. "Texans always this dumb, or just this one? Hey! Watch it Texas I punch back."

"I'm getting outta here before they both gang up on me," Richard said and headed for the deck, George on his heels.

"Cowards," Joss said. "Both of you."

She and Sandra both laughed.

"So what's a Diamond then?" Joss asked.

"The one they are offering Anna is like my Piper, but with modern styling and made out of composite materials," Sandra said. "A little heavier on the controls than Piper, but they handle better. They also run on diesel or jet fuel. Made in Austria. So that fits for Anna as well."

"Ya, jet set Hollywood for Piper, jet set F1 star for Diamond," Joss said.

Anna and Heidi walked up the stairs, they both had huge grins on them.

"I take it you signed then?" Sandra said.

Anna screamed and rushed into Sandra's out stretched arms. Then to Joss'. Joss told Anna how happy she was for her.

"This calls for some bubbly," Joss said and headed to the kitchen.

"How'd she do?" Delta asked Heidi.

"Ten million this year, minimum," Heidi said. "She makes F1, twenty every year, plus bonuses. A DA50 for five years, parts, labour, service, fuel included. It's like your airplane on steroids. A commercial or two a year, one personal appearance a year, some personal conduct stuff. It's a good deal. The team makes out ok too. I hear the boss is happy."

"Happy driver, happy team, happy owner," Sandra said coming up to them. "Now it's up to you, to make sure she stays happy eh? You too California, your part of her team too."

"Hey," Delta said. "How come you don't have a nick name?"

"Cause Badden has to prove to me she is as bad ass as her name." Sandra said over her shoulder headed to the deck where the men were standing beside a smoking barbecue.

After the barbecue, the two couples had split off from the single women and were sitting on the deck snuggled up in their pairs. The girls had gone back into the house and the laughter coming from the dining room proved they were having a good time. Georges son had his drivers licence and had driven his sister home, letting the adults do what adults did.

It was a nice clear night, the constellations very clear tonight.

Joss and the others sipped their drinks in quiet contemplation, Joss' thoughts went to comments she had heard the others say from time to time.

"There a reason why Anna and you guys call Richard Boss all the time?" Joss asked.

The other couple looked at Richard.

"Seriously," Joss said. "You don't do it all the time, but enough for me to want to ask."

"You don't tell her," Sandra said. "I'm going to."

"I own the racing team Joss," Richard said. "The F1 team, the F2 team and the team Anna just finished on. Jochen asked me if I could help with Anna. Had my people run the numbers and said what the heck. I can help a relative out and make a couple of bucks too. Plus, I like racing."

She pushed back from Richard and looked at him. No way he could afford this place and a large racing team. There had to be more. Was she maybe making a mistake?

"Is that how you can afford this place?" Joss asked.

"Gee thanks for all the help Sandra," Richard said. He wasn't exactly happy.

"No, I've been wondering for a while, I just kept forgetting to ask," Joss said.

"More like he kept steering you away from it if I know Richard," George said. "He funds a few things for me and Sandra as well. Smart guy your Richard."

"Something like Midas," Sandra said. "Everything he touches turns a profit."

Richard sighed and stood. Joss was not sure if he was happy, or unhappy or what.

"The racing thing and what I do for Sandra and George are sidelines for me, helping friends out," Richard said. "Ok come with me I'll show you a bit of what I do."

He took Joss down the wide and large stairway to his office downstairs. The downstairs was the same size as the up stairs, about four thousand square feet and his office took up about a quarter of it. There were at least five computer monitors around it, three of which were on. They had four or five graphs each on them. Richard pointed at the monitors.

In addition to the monitors, there were two other large main frame type computers and a bookshelf full of what looked like economics books along one wall. a large filing cabinet was along another. The desk was large, but not opulent, the chair behind it looked comfortable and well used.

"Those are the stocks I am playing with, own and deciding what I want to do with, buying or selling," Richard said. "I make most of my money doing that."

"Oh, day trading." Joss said. Hmm a gambler? She didn't know all that much about stock trading.

"Some, not much," Richard said. "Usually, I find something that interests me, keep an eye on it for while, see which way the market is going and buy, sell or hold on to it. It might take five years sometimes."

"You ever do any movie things?" Joss said.

"A little not much," he said. "They usually loose money. Not good investment stuff. This usually doesn't take up much of my time. It frees me up to do other things like chase famous women all over the world."

"Who was chasing who?" Joss said. "I seem to remember it a little differently."

"Nice set up you have here. I'm watching a couple of those too." Delta said. She pointed at the monitors.

"Ah, not a normal Hollywood bobblehead then," Richard said.

"Hey a girl has to look out for her future," Delta said. "You never know when you're gonna get fired with these temperamental artist types."

Chapter Nine

Joss and Richard had the kitchen to themselves. The others were in their rooms working. Anna and Heidi were out jogging. Joss took her coffee and walked around the living room.

"Good looking boys," she said. Looking at a picture of two boys who shared many of Richard's features.

"John, the eldest on the left, Don the right," Richard said. "My boys."

"Who's the blond?" Joss asked, she thought she already knew the answer.

"Matti," Richard said. "I can get rid of the picture if you want."

Joss had picked up the picture to get a better look. She put it back where it had been.

"No, that's ok, only if you want to," Joss said.

She never pushed him about his past relationship or his kids. He would share with her or not. It didn't change her feelings for him.

She asked him how much land he had. He told her two thousand acres out right and another thousand he leased from the government. He overwintered five hundred head of cattle, right now he had about a thousand. There was six hundred acres in crops or hay. The rest pasture for the cows. He had two separate companies set up. One for the crops, one for the cattle, that in turn leased the land from a third company that he owned.

"I have the whole enchilada," Joss said. "Brains and Hunk rolled into one. Why Matti let you slip through her fingers is beyond me. Her loss, my gain."

"Ya well..." Richard said.

Joss kissed him on the cheek.

"You have any ponies on this here ranch?" She asked.

"Ya, someplace," Richard said. "I'll get one of the guys to bring a couple in for us. When do want to go ride?"

"Now to soon?"

Richard laughed and made a phone call.

There were two men by the corral with two horses ready to go. The corral was beside a barn that looked like it could hold ten or more horses. There were four three bedroom houses down the gravelled lane. Other out buildings, steel granaries, large five ton trucks and other machinery, told Joss this was a working farm.

Richard quickly went over his horse and made to go help Joss with hers. She already was adjusting her stirrups and setting things up, so he let her be. Then she smoothly rose into the saddle and stood looking at him.

"Lead the way good sir," she said after he had mounted.

He gave her a quick tour of the yard, explaining what the different buildings were for and the type of machinery they held., then down to where he thought the cattle would be. It was a warm fall day, but Richard had insisted she bring a lined jacket along. Again proving she was no novice, she shrugged off the jacket once it got to warm, rolled it up and tied it to the saddle using the tie strings mounted there.

"You don't ride bad," Richard said. "For a back wood Texan."

Joss shook her fist at him, but she was smiling. After about an hour of riding, some of it in single file down trails that winded through trees, they came on the cattle in an open field by a mountain stream. The cattle knew they were there but were not overly concerned. Two large mule deer were quietly grazing on the other side of the stream from the cattle.

"Those deer are much bigger than ours," Joss said. "You ever go hunting?"

Richard shrugged his shoulders, which Joss was quickly learning meant he had, but he didn't know how she felt about it and didn't want to upset her.

"I used to go with my dad before he became a complete idiot," Joss said. "But our deer are a lot smaller than yours."

"It's a little to early yet," Richard said. "I like late November better. The Elk come out of the national park then."

"I gotta get down for a bit," Joss said. "Been a couple of years since I been on a horse."

West Texas was coming out now when she spoke. Again proving she was no novice, she just let the reins drop on the ground, but she stood on one. Richard got down and just let both reins go to the ground. Seeing that, Joss took her foot off hers.

"Cheerist," she said. "It's even quieter out here than my place. Them big black birds some kinda eagle?"

"No, those are Ravens," Richard said.

"Shoott, they're big," she said. "A gal could get used to hanging out around here."

"You won't be saying that come January," Richard said and laughed.

"Come Janury, I expect to be someplace in sunny Africa," Joss said. "Damn studio can't make up it's damn mind where though."

"Kinda dangerous down there in some places right now Joss," Richard said.

"Ah heck," Joss said. "Dangerous in a lotta places in the States 'bout now too."

She was full on Texas now.

"Well, we'all had best be head'n back afore Californy calls out the state troopers or some stuff."

Richard starting laughing

"What the heck ya-all laughing it?" She said.

"You'll be spitting put a wad of chewing tobacco next," Richard said.

There were more than a few people hanging around the yard and corral when they came back in. Men and women, teenagers and older.

"Well ifn ya-all are like the folks back home you ain't gonna say nothin," Joss said, "Common over, bring ur cameras or cell phones or whatever the heck."

After Joss had dismounted, Richard took both horses over to the corral and started unsaddling. The foreman came over and gave him a hand.

"Thanks for that boss," the foreman said.

"Don't thank me," Richard said. "Thank Joss. I had nothing to do with it."

Joss had the small crowd around her laughing at something she had said.

"Whut's so darn funny," he heard her say. "Ya-all don't understand Texican or sumtin"

"Oh now she's just playing with them," Richard said. "Look Jim, just tell everybody not to say where she is. Otherwise we'll have all kinds of city folk and stuff all over us."

"You got it boss," Jim said.

"I better get her out of there," Richard said.

"Come on Texas," Richard said as he came up. "You promised to cook tonight."

"OK" she said. "See ya-all later."

They were holding hands walking back to the house. The people she had just met were nice and a bit shy, not like the people she ran into usually.

"Good bunch a folks ya got back there bubba," she said.

"Ya most people are pretty decent out here," Richard said.

"Hey Ya-all," Joss said. All the girls were sitting around the deck relaxing and talking. They were drinking their favourite beverage. Joss grabbed a beer and tossed one over to Richard. She popped off the top and took a big gulp.

"Bubba there has some decent horse flesh," she said "Ya-all wanna come riding tomorah?"

"I'm game," Clary said.

"Not me," Delta said. "I know what Joss gets like when her Texas starts showing up."

"Sure I'll come along," Heidi said. "I used to ride at pony club back home."

"Too much stuff to do," Anna said.

"Give Sandra a call," Richard said. "I'll bet she'll come along."

"Hey ya'll," Joss said into her cell phone. "Were going riding tommorah. Ya-all wanna join us?"

"What?" Joss said. All the girls on the deck were laughing. They could hear Sandra laughing on the phone too. "Why is everbody always laughin at me lately? Ya-all coming tommoah or wha?"

"Ok, she's in," Joss said hanging up the phone. "She said she done trust your stupid nags Ricardo, she done gonna bring her own pony down heah."

She gave everyone a dirty look, as they were staring at her with smirks on their faces. "What y'all starin' at?"

"She get like that often?" Richard asked Delta.

"No thank god," Delta said. "It's usually just at home and when she gets drunk. She keeps this up for to long and the studio's going to have fits."

"Hey now!" Joss said.

"Ah let her be," Richard said. "It's telling us she is comfortable with us."

Joss gave him a hug. "Thanks for sticking up for me. You're right, I am comfortable here, it's like home for me. But ya, I'm kinda laying it on a little thick, ain't I?"

Everyone laughed.

"Ya think?" Richard said.

When the women arrived back home the next afternoon from their ride, they were all reverting back to their native accents. Except Heidi, who already had a German accent. Clary's Idaho accent was not all that pronounced, and nobody but Richard could figure out Sandra's. Richard knew, but he didn't say anything.

Even Delta was letting the California slip out every once in a while.

Richard had started talking in German to Anna and Heidi when they were alone. Then it was time for Anna and Heidi to go home to Germany. A last farewell party and tearful goodbye in the morning and they were off to the Calgary International Airport for the flight to Frankfurt.

Things quickly settled into a routine after that. Joss handling her commitments given her by Clary or Delta in the morning, then studying the lines of script the studio had sent her in the afternoon.

Clary and Delta handling things most of the day. Answering emails and phone calls for Joss, handling items they could themselves and passing the others off to Joss. Richard was generally down in his office, doing what he did. Sometimes on the phone or video conferencing for most of the day. The evenings were spent watching movies or just talking. Weekends were for exploring and flying.

"I like this," Joss said one night after the sun had gone down.

They had a fire going in the fireplace and she was curled up beside him.

"I think I'm going to half to pass on the hunting thing," Joss said. "The studio wants me in LA to shoot some action shots on green screen."

"Ya cool," Richard said. "We can link up when you're done."

"It'll have to be in Texas Richard," she said. "I'll only have a week or so, then I have to go to the UAE for the location shots, then back to LA for the final scenes."

"Ya no big deal," Richard said. "I have a lot going on then as well."

They sat quietly looking at the fire. Joss wondering how she would manage with out hum by her side, especially at night.

"Um...Joss?" Richard said.

She looked up at him. He was not looking at her, but out the window, his eyes far away.

"My kids asked if they could meet you," he said.

"Sure why not?" She said.

"I know this great steak house in Calgary," Richard said. "Serves the best Prime Rib anywhere."

"What? In public?" Joss asked. "Not very personal, especially for a first meeting Richard. I am potentially replacing their mother after all Richard. First impressions and all that. Plus, not having the hassle of me in public."

She sat up and turned him so he was looking at her.

"Here, in this house, or not at all."

"Um...I dunno about that," Richard said. "I don't think they'll go for it. Things being the way they are with us..."

"Well tough shit," Joss said. "They don't come here they can kiss my ass."

"Give me your phone! Come on! Right now! What's John's wife's name?"

"Jenny," he said.

Joss punched in the number and let it ring, mumbling men under her breath.

"Hello, is Jenny there? HI Jenny, it's Joss Lynn calling. Ya hi. Look, we would love to have you guys come over for diner. Sure, up at the farm, heck I'll even help cook. Great! See you then."

She did the same with Don's wife.

"There," she said tossing the phone back at him. "That's done. It takes a woman to figure out how to manipulate another woman. Tell Sandy she better get her and Georges butts out here for diner too. Might as well make it a twofer."

The night of the diner, Delta and Clary thought they would give Joss and Richard privacy and headed to the Cattle Baron restaurant in Calgary that Richard had wanted to take Joss to for diner. George and Sandra were the first to arrive. Joss saw Sandra look over at Richard more than once while he and George were talking cars. Unlike Sandra normally did, she barely touched her first drink, she normally tossed the first one back and sipped the next. She was also fidgety and distracted, again, unlike her. When the door bell rang a half hour later, Sandra flinched and shot a glance at Richard who was looking at her. The living room went quiet. Nobody said anything or made a move.

"Oh for the love of God!" Joss said.

She jumped out of her spot in the love seat next to Richard and walked to the door. She composed herself, running her hands through her hair and smoothing down her blouse, then flung the door open with her patented smile on her face.

"Hey guys!" Joss excitedly said. "Come in, come in. I am so excited to finally meet you all."

The two couples were dressed in high end designer clothing. The wives clothing, hair and makeup not over done, but a little more than would be normal. Joss took one of the wives in each arm and escorted them into the living room where everyone was now standing and waiting for them. George was the only one smiling, Sandra and Richards faces were neutral.

"Jenny, Pat, long time no see," George said coming forward and giving each woman a hug. "John, Don, looking debonaire as ever" he shook each mans hand.

"Hey," was all Sandra said, she just nodded her head at them.

Each of the wives made a point of going to Richard and hugging him. The boys and he just nodded at each other.

The attention was clearly focused on Joss, as she knew and was used to happening. She acknowledged their compliments of her and her accomplishments and was carrying more of her load of the conversation.

"Well, if I don't get back in the kitchen, my world famous TexMex is gonna burn," Joss said.

She started toward the kitchen, Pat and Jenny rose from the seats on the couch and made to follow.

"No, no," Joss said. "You are my guests, you just sit yourselves back down. Richard, maybe. A glass of wine for the ladies?"

Nothing put Sandra off. She was right behind Joss and went right to the refrigerator, grabbed a beer, popped the top and chugged the first half down. Plunking it down on the kitchen counter, she started in on getting plates ready and running them into the dining room and setting the table.

In the living room, George was carrying on all the conversation. Richard just quietly sitting, occasional laughing at some remark, or replying to something George asked him.

Joss and Sandra made several trips from kitchen to dining room bringing in the food, then Joss called them all to sit. The boys and their wives sitting as far away from Richard as they could get away with.

While she was putting her best face forward, Joss was finding it harder and harder to do so. The attitude from sons to father was not hostile, it was non existent, like he was not even there. She reached the boiling point and the pretences went out the window.

She slammed the table top, hard, shoved her chair back and stood. She had shocked even Richard and Sandra by those actions.

"Come here you two idiots!" She said pointing at the two boys. She took them to the living room and showed them their pictures. Then handed them the small one of their mother on the horse.

"He looks at that picture all the time," Joss said. Her voice was firm. "And when he thinks I'm not watching, a tear runs down his cheeks. You think he didn't care about her. Hell, he still does. And you two. I don't know what went on with your mom and him or you guys. He hasn't told me and honestly it's none of my damn business. But you keep hurting the man I love with my whole heart and soul and I tell you what, You're gonna wish you were dead."

She stomped her way out of the living room, grabbed a beer and her coat on her way outside to the deck.

"Oh she's pissed, big time," Joss heard George say. "Best stay the heck out her way right now."

"Ya, you stupid asses piss me off too," Sandra said. "And I do know what went on. I was there remember. Common George, time to go home."

As Joss paced back and forth on the deck, she saw Sandra grab her purse and drag George out the door. She also saw Richard looking back and forth between his boys at the dining room table and her outside. Finally he made up his mind and came to her on the deck. As soon as Joss saw him coming, she started to calm down, then get upset for a different reason. How hurt she knew Richard was about his son's, how much he loved her and didn't want to see her hurt.

"You ok Texas?" Richard asked. He didn't often call her that.

She flung herself on him, pulling him tight. And soon her shoulders were shaking as she was crying. Richard had his head on top of hers looking up at the stars.

The shaking started to subside. And soon the two of them were just standing holding each other. He was gently stroking her back. Then a knock was heard on the patio door and it opened.

"Sorry," John said. "Dad, can we talk?"

"You gonna be ok Joss?" Richard asked.

"Ya go," she said, wiping her eyes on her coat sleeve.

Richard went into the house, grabbed a coat and motioned the boys to follow him. Joss knew he would be taking them to the hanger. She walked into the house, grabbed a glass and poured a big shot of vodka in it.

"Fucking men," Joss mumbled not carrying if she was heard or not.

"Can't live with them", Jenny said.

"Can't live without them," Pat said.

"Shit," Joss said. "Used to hear my grandad say that about women."

"Ya so do our dads. Jenny," she, said holding out her hand.

"Pat," she said holding out her hand.

"Joslyn, Josyln Litzenburger," Joss said shaking each woman's hand.

"Now that we're all friends, care to join me?" Holding up her glass.

Both women filled theirs up.

"To fucking men," Joss said and they clinked their glasses together.

"And oh god how we love to do that!" Pat said.

"Pat!" Jenny said.

"What?" Joss said. "It's true isn't it?"

"Touché," Joss said and laughed.

Then the conversation changed to other topics. Jenny asked Joss about what happened with Carson. Both Pat and Jenny expressed their agreement with Joss, saying the guy was a jerk. They even included some of the same experiences they had experienced with men over the years. Which of course led to the dumb things most men did, including how they let their stupid pride get in the way all the time. Joss thought she might like these two young women.

"Thanks for doing that Joss," Pat said. "We've been trying to get them back together with Richard for years. We don't know what went on, they haven't told us. But from what we have been able to work out, it wasn't Richards fault."

"That's all we have been able to find out too." Joss said. "Anna and her family know, but won't say anything. If Sandra doesn't tell me pretty soon I'm gonna kick the crap out of her."

"Good luck on that one Joss," Richard said. He and the boys had just walked in and were taking off their jackets. "She'd hand you your ass, no problem. Any beer left?"

"You guys?"

"It's ok, Pop, I'll pop my own, you'd like to give me alcohol poisoning the way you pore drinks," the John said.

"Ya, I'll grab a beer," the Don said.

"Addressing the elephant in the room," Richard said. "Over the years, things have been said, others, unsaid. Circumstances, all on my part, led to this point. I apologize to Jenny and Pat for all of that. Joss, I know how hard you worked tonight, trying to patch everything up between us. And...well it worked."

"Joss, I'm really sorry we upset you," John said. "I don't know why we were fighting anymore in the first place. I'm John, people call me pipsqeek, I dunno why."

"I don't either," Joss said "Christ, what are you six five?"

"Played centre in basketball," Richard said. "He was pretty good too."

"What?" John said. "You came to the games?"

"Didn't miss one," Richard said. He shrugged his shoulders. "You know, your grand ma and aunts..."

"Ya," Don said. "And that stupid no contact judgment the court gave. What a crock."

"Came to all your wrestling matches too Don," Richard said. "Ruling only said no contact, not no seeing."

"Sorry Miss Lynn," Don said. "I loved mom a lot, still do and it hurts sometimes you know. Pop is easy to take things out on. He never says anything, so we think he doesn't care. Seeing you out on that deck crying, holding him so tight. You love him so much."

Tears started running down his cheeks and Pat rushed to him.

"Pop used to comfort Mom like that all the time too," John said. "Ya, we really know what happened that night Joss. We just chose not to see it, to blame him for it instead. Thanks for pointing that out Joss. It's going to take some time. Guys are guys you know? But it'll work out."

"Come here you big piece of shit," Jenny said. Opening her arms. She gave him a long hug

"Ah crap," John said "She's pissed. How much booze you 'been swilling?"

"Jus' a lil' wee bit," Jenny slurred.

"So, who is this Anna and her family Joss?' Pat asked.

"Your husbands cousin," Joss said. "From Germany."

"You met Anna?" John said.

"Yes, first in Germany at her home, then in Sochi Russia, then in Brazil, that was fun, then here for a week."

"Ah shit," Don said. "Serves us right for being assholes. I really like Anna, she's good people. It would have been nice to hook up with her."

"Season opener is in Australia in March," Richard said. "I'm sure you guys can mooch a ride off the teams corporate jet with George and Sandy. It'll be her first start in F2. I'm planning on showing up."

"Ya like that little puddle jumper of yours will make it to Brisbane," Delta said.

"Ah yee of little faith," Richard said.

"Ok, who the hell is this Anna!" Jenny said.

"Anna Kneble, the racing driver," Joss said.

"She's your cousin and you didn't say anything!" Jenny whacked her husband on the left shoulder.

"I can tell your wife loves you John," Richard said.

"Why's that," he was rubbing his shoulder.

"Cause she hit you on the left shoulder not the right one," Richard said. He and Don laughed.

"What, you saying I don't love you?" Joss said and whacked him.

Don looked at Pat and raised his hands to shoulder height palms outward.

"Good boy," Pat said and pulled his head down to kiss him.

"See," Don said. "see what happens when you treat a woman right?"

"Owww, that hurt!" Pat had whacked him on the right shoulder.

"Not it at all Pop," John said between laughs. "Jenny is left handed or I'd be getting it on the right shoulder too. Omfff!"

Richard looked down at Joss, she kissed his shoulder instead.

The ice now broken, the three couples moved to the living room and sat. While not exactly chatty, chatty, joy, joy, the conversations were pleasant. Don began telling Richard how well their business was doing and thanking him for the money to fund their startup 3D printing business. That the company was now, after three years, starting to generate profits.

They now had ten employees and were experimenting with making car parts out of carbon fibre.

Joss saw Richards interest really pick up on that remark. He began to ask first Don, then John after being told that John was the design guy, questions.

"Mind if I get one of my engineers to get in touch with you John?" Richard asked. "Maybe just at first, to make prototypes for wind tunnel testing for us."

Joss watched the interaction between father and sons and could't stop her smile. All three of them now fully engrossed on the new project possibility.

John looked at his watch.

"Shoot, we had better be going," John said. "I didn't realize how late it was getting. I'll email you the quarterly results tomorrow Pop."

"Sure no problem." Richard said.

He escorted his sons to the door.

"Thanks Joss," Richard said after everyone had left. "We worked some stuff out."

"Sometimes it takes a third party to smack some sense into peoples heads," Joss said. "A wise man named Richard told me that once."

Chapter Ten

It had been their last night together in Texas. It had been an emotional week. Both Richard and Joss dreading the departure time. Yet, knowing it must happen.

The studio had sent the charter plane to pick up Joss, Delta and Clary. They were off to LA, then to the UAE. Richard was flying his Cherokee home. Giving Richard a fast goodbye hug, Clary and Delta entered the jet, leaving Joss and Richard to their goodbyes.

"It's only three months Joss," Richard said. "Once you're working you'll be ok."

"Ya I know," she said. "And they are letting me go to Australia and you will be in Abu Dhabi, then we can go home together after the race."

"Yup," he said. "You better get going Joss. They'll be waiting for you."

One last kiss and she was gone. Richard watched until they were dots in the sky. He walked over to his plane and retrieved his cell phone from the duffle bag in the baggage hold. Locked the hold once again and twenty minutes later had set the auto pilot and dialled a number in his cell phone.

"Warsaw."

"Hey Boss," Warsaw replied. Richard admired the familiarity of her thick Polish accent. "She on her way then?"

"Ya, got anything interesting?" Richard said.

"Some rumblings but nothing concrete yet," she said.

"Ok, keep me posted," Richard said. Then ended the call.

Now he turned on the laptop he had put on the copilots position, made sure he had a satellite feed and slaved it to one of his dash monitors. They were touch sensitive, so he was soon where he wanted to be.

"Hey Boss," Gunther said. They were video conferencing. "That Diamond wind tunnel is already making results for us. We were able to spot some flaws in the aero package on the car and tweak them. Nobody is going to see this one coming. We'll be doing the F2 cars tomorrow, and Cuthburt is sending your sons some preliminary designs to make for us."

"Good stuff," Richard said. "Anything else I need to know?"

"Nope all good so far."

"Alright then, keep me posted."

Sandra was next.

"Hey Boss what's happening?'" she said.

"Girls are bye bye, I'm headed home for bit. Warsaw says there are some grumblings but nothing concrete. Race team is happy," Richard said.

"Same as Warsaw for me Boss. Nothing solid."

"Ok, you get my list?"

"Ya working on it boss. Where do you want it?"

"I dunno, Abu Dhabi for now. I think something is going to go down around there someplace. It's pretty central."

"No problem boss."

Now, in between watching his flight status and making radio reports, he was watching one particular stock. It was prime and he had been waiting five years for it. Finally, two hours after the market opened it did a dip, as it did every year at this time. He hit enter and started a fire storm. The little dribble of sell orders grew, then grew some more. The market noticed, sell orders started piling up, the company tried to stem the run by buying. It only made it worse. By noon the stock was in free fall, panic was setting in. With two hours left to go until the market closed, Richard hit enter again. By the time the market closed, he had control of the company and had made a thirty million dollar profit doing it. He had no doubt he would own over fifty percent of the company soon. The company had leveraged itself to the brink trying to stem the panic. Now they couldn't pay for the margin call. He had them, they knew it but didn't know who had done it.

One of his people would be calling the CEO tomorrow with the good news. One of his people, all of whom called themselves his minions. All of whom he had made extremely wealthy.

JOSS WAS UP IN FIRST class along with all the A list actors, writers, the director and a couple of producers. Delta and Clary the only PA's in sight. The other ones were in back with all the other worker bees. Once the seat belt sign came off, the three of them and Karen, her female co star were sitting on the floor between the rows of seats playing poker.

It was a sixteen hour flight and a person could only drink so much booze, sleep so much and watch so many old movies.

"So how's the boy toy?" Karen her co star asked.

Karen had been one of the costar suggestions the studio had provided Joss with. Joss had run into her on two of the Bond movies she had done previous to when the Jan Fields movies began. Both of them were about the same age and somewhat similar back grounds.

Karen was from the western part of South Dakota and had grown up on a ranch to the west of Spearfish. Her parents were still married and she had a brother two years older than her. Her father also was a heavy duty mechanic and made most of his money repairing farm equipment and highway tractor units for the locals.

Her brother, Sean, had been bitten by the racing bug in high school. Her father being a mechanic was extremely helpful. They would find a suitable car in one of the many auto grave yards in the area and convert it into a rally car. Karens dad had all the required tools and equipment to make roll cages, gut the interiors and rebuild engines etc. Karen would help out and admitted to being, in her words, not to shabby a welder. She was to young to have a drivers licence and became Seans navigator. She found she really enjoyed it and soon, they were touring the Mid West in the family motorhome with the car in a trailer pulled behind it and doing well.

One of her teachers had asked her in her high school Junior year to try out for a roll in the schools annual Spring play. She had agreed and thought the project would be fun, which it was. This had led her to be asked to play a part in Spearfish's annual Passion Play. That play was always well attended over the three days it ran. She was asked the following two years as well. During her last two years at high school, she had played the lead actress in all the schools productions. Not only did she like doing them, but, she was well received by the audiences.

Karen had asked her parents if she could enrol in the Theatre Program at Black Hills State University in Spearfish. They had agreed and Karen had enrolled in the Theatre Program. She had also enrolled in the Modern Languages Program, Majoring in Spanish and minoring in Lakota, German and Russian.

Living at home and commuting back and forth to Spearfish had been not only convenient, but easier on her education budget as she didn't have to pay for her housing. Directly anyway. To pay for her programs, Karen had worked in her fathers truck shop. At first doing what ever needed doing, then more and more in rebuilding engines and transmissions. To add to her academic load, her father had made her his apprentice and while she had to take courses and exams every year in mechanics, she was able to do the courses on line remotely and write her exams at the university.

As she had told Joss once over some beers after a days shooting on the Bond film, a girl had to have options in case this acting thing didn't work out. Her youthful good looks, great body tone from working on the ranch and the mechanic shop and her language skills had seen her quickly obtain rolls in movies and television series. At first as a walk on girl friend, then more and more into more demanding rolls, usually as the bad guy. She had even been on a Mexican Action Series where she played a female resistance leader from America.

She had several major parts in Westerns and World War epics, on any side. She could leverage her language skills to suit most rolls she was cast in. This had led to the Bond audition, where she played one of the supporting roles for Joss's CIA character.

While she and Joss had not exactly been close, they did hang around together on location shoots and after the studio shoots. Like Joss, she didn't much like the media circus, but put up with it. Until her roll in the first Jan Fields movie, the media had not really paid all that much attention to her anyway.

When Joss had called her personally, for an audition on her first Jan Fields movie, Karen had jumped at the opportunity. They got along well together and liked each others company, a rarity in their business. What Karen had thought was an audition for a small part had become a shock when Joss called her the next day to congratulate her on getting the part as her co star.

"Probably spending all my hard earned money," Joss said. She laughed. "Nah, he's probably made the whole production cost of this movie already today," she said. "If not today, by the end of the week."

"The guy is amazing Karen," Delta said. "He just sits and watches. Some times days or weeks, sometimes years. Then wham, bam, thank you mam, just like that he makes ten, fifteen million. Then he'll turn off the computer and go play with his other girl."

"You put up with him and another girl?" Karen said. "Or, wait, you're the other woman right?"

Joss laughed.

"No he has an airplane he plays with," Joss said. "Something like mine but much older. He's flown it around the world several times. He taught me how to fly in it."

"And me," Clary said. "Well just my night and over the top endorsements, but hey."

"Tell me he's at least a little cute Delta," Karen said. So far she was the big winner at the poker hands. "Not some old worn out geezer."

"Oh who," Delta said. "Canuck Super Hunk? No where near as cute as the one I'm going to grab."

"Ya right," Clary said. "You run the other way every time a cute guy comes around. Me, I've got my eye on a Super Texican Hunk."

"Damn women are as bad as we are," Hal, the director said to Jorden, the producer sitting next to him. Who's cell phone went off.

"Oh shit, it's the boss," Jorden said. "Yes Mr. Black how are you today sir? Yes its all good sir. Miss Lynn? Why yes sir, right now I believe she is loosing big at a poker game she, her two PA's and Karen are having sitting on the floor sir. Yes sir, thank you sir, I'll tell her sir."

"Miss Lynn?" Jorden called, looking behind his seat. "Mr. Black said he's not paying you to lose all your money playing poker mam. But if it makes you happy, it makes him happy."

"That Mr. Black sounds a lot like Super Hunk doesn't he?" Clary said.

Delta looked up at Joss, who was looking at her.

"You don't think?" They both said at the same time.

"Nah, no way," Joss said. "He said the movie business is a money loser."

Six hours later, their butts were sore from sitting on the floor and they were hungry. By the end, Karen was up twenty dollars. They had been playing for quarters.

"More fun flying than riding in one of these things," Delta said.

"Ya, but it would take us a week to get where we are going," Joss said. "Even Super Hunk says he takes passenger service at times."

"Super Hunk have a name? Karen asked.

Karen was sitting on the right side, outer seat. Joss was sitting in the centre aisle across from Karen. Clary was on Joss's left sound asleep. Delta was on Karen's right watching a movie.

"Yes," Joss said. She picked up the book she had brought along to read.

"You must really be in love then," Karen said. "He doesn't like the limelight I take it."

"He says drawing attention to himself is bad for business." Joss said. "He was the pilot in the old plane that was leading our formation flight down to Brazil."

"Ya everyone was wondering who that was," Karen said. "Got any tips. I could use a guy like that. All of mine end up being jerks."

"Kind of tough in our business Karen," Joss said. "I've had my share of jerks too. Or the guys who can't handle the pressure, or guys that get jealous.

"I slummed down one day and chased him down. He had been avoiding me like crazy for about six months."

"Oh, I never thought of that," Karen said.

"I think you are like me Karen," Joss said. "But I will tell you this. It won't work if you're a publicity hound. Guys like Super Hunk run like heck the other way if you are."

"I do what I have to," Karen said. "I don't need the nonsense that goes with it all. Two more shows and I'm done."

"Kind of sad hey," Joss said. "We starve and freeze and sleep in cars in back alleys, waiting for our shot. Sometimes for years. We get it, five, ten years max and we're done."

"And the smart ones like you and me, milk it for those five, ten years and salt our money away." Karen said. "I have my own Delta, Joss. He's not quite as good, but close."

"Delta is one of kind Karen," Joss said. "Clary actually works for her not me. Heidi, Anna Kneble's girl? She's one of Delta's girls too."

"Who gave her that idea?" Karen asked."Don't tell me, Super Hunk right."

"Ya," Joss said. "He's kind of like Midas. Everything he touches turns to gold."

RICHARD HAD PUNCHED in 7765 on his transponder and simply flew over the border and continued on this time. He normally did when he was alone. No one ever questioned it, on either side of it. An hour and a half later, he was landing at the ranch.

He was at his computer downstairs with his diner on the desk sifting through data. He couldn't put his finger on it, but something bad was going to happen soon, some where in the Middle East.

It was their third month on location. So far the shoots were going well. It was cool, for the UAE, in fact, down right cold some nights considering the day time temperatures. There had been delays a couple of times, when the wind whipped up the sand to much to shoot. But not to often.

It was an Islamic country, so no booze in public and definitely no drugs allowed. But there was an active night life. Of course Joss and Karen and all the other stars were in big demand all the time. But, they needed time off from time to time.

Today, Delta and Joss were heading to Dubai to go shopping and site seeing. They had four body guards, but they kept their distance and let the two women do their own thing for the most part. Having a headscarf was actually a good thing for Joss. She didn't stand out as much that way and they had a much better shopping experience than they normally did. If anyone did come to close, the body guards just came closer. That was enough to put other people away. This was their third trip to the same mall.

The mall was the second largest mall in the world and had over 1200 shops in total. With so many shops, there was only so much shopping they could do. This time they went to fashion street which had the designer fashions. Both women picked up things from the Ralph Lauren shop, some elegant lingerie from Women's Secret and what shopping trip would be complete with out a pair of shoes. This time from Santoni.

They had arrive early at the huge mall. It served over ten million shoppers per year and was always busy. The mall had arranged to give Joss and Delta a tour of the famous aquarium and underwater zoo before it opened to the public at ten in the morning. It held over 33000 fish and was a lot to take in, in the two hours they only had to tour it.

Getting to be late afternoon, Joss and Delta stopped to have some of the Peri-Peri chicken they had heard so much about from others at Nando's. Both of the women enjoying the garlic flavoured dish.

"Two weeks Delta, two weeks," Joss said.

"Ya I know already," Delta said. "You have been giving me a day by day count down for the last week already."

In two weeks they would be heading to Australia for the Grand Prix race. And Joss was becoming more distracted by the day. She had only spoken, texted or the odd video conference with Richard in the past three months. He would be with the race team at the race. She was so very much looking forward to her first meeting with him, she had so much to share with him about her experiences in this wonderful country.

They had finished their shopping for the day and were headed for the mall exit and their waiting car. This was the main mall entrance and like much of the mall was lavishly decorated. As there was so much traffic, it had been arranged to have the car pick them up right at the entrance. Shots rang out just as they went out side. In seconds, shots were being fired everywhere. Men, their guards as well as others caught in the crossfire, were falling, Joss and Delta, having grown up on the wrong side of town, both dropped to the ground as the first shots rang out. Now they were trying to find where they were coming from to get out of the crossfire.

Rough hands picked them up, four men each carried them to a van and tossed them inside. Joss squirmed, trying to break free, but there were to many of them. Gun fire, lots of it, going on all around them, sometimes explosions. The van accelerated away with squealing tires.

At first they thought some security forces had rescued them. Then the zip ties came out. Both Joss and Delta began to fight back then. Both of them had some martial arts training. They received many hard and rough punches to heads and ribs for their troubles. Their arms were roughly pulled behind their backs and wrists tightly zip tied together. Followed by their ankles being zip tied together and finally rough hoods pulled over their heads. They had just been kidnapped.

Chapter Eleven

Richard was up in the kitchen grabbing a beer. Nothing much was going on and he was about to head to the hanger and tinker for a bit. Then his cellphone alarm went off, followed by his computer alarming.

He took the steps down to his office in one step and in a flash was at his keyboard.

"Fuck!" He said.

He hit a couple of keys and the phone began to ring.

"Wyoming, Black, condition green. Texas and California have been kidnapped. Half an hour."

"Warsaw, Black, condition green. Texas and California have just been kidnapped. Helsinki in six."

"Worms, Black, condition green. Texas and California have just been kidnapped. Baden in ten."

He hit another button and everything began to shut down. Then he was charging up the stairs and out the door heading to the hangers.

He didn't stop at the one that held the Pipers. The big doors to the hanger next door began to open. It held two airplanes. One a Pilatus PC-12 single engine turbo prop. The other a Pilatus PC-24 twin jet. He hooked the tugger up to the PC-24 and dragged it over to the fuel tanks.

He had just finished parking the tugger back in the hanger and was beginning the preflight inspection, when a Mercedes G-Wagon came flying up his driveway and with a squealing of tires, braked inside the hanger. Sandra came flying out of it, slamming the door behind her. She was quickly up in the co-pilots seat, turning things on and beginning check lists.

Richard came on board making sure the air stairs were closed and locked then crawled into the pilots seat and began his check list.

"Greenland first," he said. "Then Helsinki, then Baden. We'll figure out the next one after. Starting one."

"One is green," Sandra said.

"Starting two," Richard said.

"Two green," Sandra said. "Edmonton control, Black Two"

"Black Two, Edmonton Tower, over."

"Edmonton control, Black Two condition green, Greenland direct, angles forty."

"Copy Black Two, condition green. Cleared for take off your discretion. Squawk seven seven six, six, copy."

"Cleared for take off our discretion, squawk seven seven six six, copy."

"Black Two, cleared to ten thousand at 27, cleared to angels fifteen, right turn fifteen, cleared angels forty. Speed at your discretion."

As Richard was entering the information on the instrument panels, Sandra was reading back the information to Edmonton. They were taxing to the runway now.

Less than forty minutes after receiving the call, they were in the air, and now he was Black and Sandra was Wyoming.

Three and a half hours later they were refuelling in Greenland. Nobody but the fuel handlers came near the airplane. Half an hour later they were cleared priority to Helsinki. Richard was working hard to keep his emotions in check. He well knew how badly these types of things could go. He had to be cool, calm and professional. Not only the girls lives, but his teams were at stake.

Just as they crossed Iceland at forty thousand feet, Richard's cell phone went off.

"Hey John what's up?" Richard said.

"You on Joss's deal Pop ," John said.

"Ya, me and Wyoming are on the way. We're picking up the rest of the team next."

"You think it's the same type of deal as with Mom?"

"Nah," Richard said. "Sounds like an extortion kidnapping. Not political. I've been real careful son."

"Ya I know Pop," John said. "Give em hell Pop, Wyoming."

"Oh ya," Sandra said. "Those assholes picked the wrong girls this time."

The call disconnected, and Sandra looked over at Richard. She took his right hand in her left and gave it a squeeze. He looked in her eyes and she in his. He kissed her knuckles. She smiled. Then they became what they really were. Cold hearted assassins.

Warsaw came on board in Helsinki. She had two very long hard cases with her. She handed a thumb drive to Richard, now in the co pilots seat. Then stowed her cases in the baggage compartment at the back and took her seat facing the bulkhead between the cockpit and the rest of the cabin and fired up her monitors.

Sandra came on board and shut and latched the air stairs. She gaveWarsaw a quick hug.

"You going to be ok, Black?" Warsaw asked, concern on her face.

"Oh ya, he is definitely in Black mode, though," Sandra said when Richard didn't respond. "So am I. I really like Texas and California. I am some pissed."

"Da, me too," Warsaw said.

Two hours later they were on the ground in Baden. Jochen, code name Worms came aboard at that point. Like Warsaw, he had two long hard cases with him. He gave Sandra a glance and lifted an eye brow. Sandra looked at the cockpit where Richard was then back at Jochen. She could tell he was not only concerned about the girls, but Richard as well. Sandra flashed him the ok sign, Jochen nodded, took his cases to the baggage compartment and like Warsaw, strapped himself into the other bulkhead seat and fired up the monitors before pulling on his headset.

Sandra went back to the cockpit and strapped herself back in. Soon the engines fired up, they taxied to the runway and were airborne.

"Next stop, Turkey gang. Then me and Wyoming for sure need some sack time." Richard said. "We've got some good intel on who and where these yahoos are right now. They have already contacted the studio in LA. who have handed it off to their insurance company, who have handed it off to their hostage negotiating team. CIA and the State department are all over it. They have been told a special negotiating team has been assigned and to give them any info they have and stay out of their way, for now."

"Knowing the Yanks," Jochen said, "They've got all kinds of Seal and Delta types in the air already."

"We are at least forty eight to seventy two hours ahead of them," Warsaw said. "Typical governments, lots of hurry up, then wait for the politicos to make up their minds what to do. Russia will be doing the same. I could have finished making my award winning cabbage rolls and pirogies. Now I will have to toss them out when I get home."

"Which is why they have us eh?" Richard said.

"Oo, cooking for someone special Olga?" Sandra asked.

"For me to know and you to try and figure out Sandra," Olga said.

"Ok, enough chit chat." Richard said. "Back to work."

Sandra took them off and when she wasn't watching the gauges, she was busy sifting through data like the others were.

Then they were on the ground at a small military airport in Northern Turkey. This time Richard left the plane and supervised the refuelling. He grabbed four square boxes and placed them two at a time in the airplane. All the time he had his balaclava covering his face and had black gloves on his hands. No one but the fuel handler had come close the plane. Once he was inside, they taxied to the far end of the taxiway and shut down everything but the small auxiliary power unit that had its own eight hour fuel supply. All of them were asleep in minutes.

Sixteen hours had passed since the girls had been kidnapped.

Joss didn't know where she was or what time it was. They had been driven for a very long time, then transferred into some kind of airplane. After an eternity, they had been carried out of the airplane, tossed into another vehicle and driven for some time. Then had been carried and dumped where they were now.

She had tried to call for Delta and had received a kick in the ribs for her troubles and told to be quiet. The voice had an Arabic accent. The whole time she had been restrained hand and foot and her head covered. At some point, she had asked to go to the bathroom and had once again been kicked in the ribs, at which point, her bladder had let go. Eventually it had dried. Now, she was hungry, and thirsty and had to relieve herself again.

Joss had never lost consciousness and other than being roughed up. She had otherwise not been molested or abused. She didn't think they had been abducted for political reasons, or there would have been much more abuse involved. having received instruction on how to behave in situations like this, she vowed not to be her normal confrontational self and appear meek.

She heard footsteps approaching. They stopped in front of her. She was jerked up right and the hood was ripped off her head. The lights were so bright she had to squint, because they were hurting her eyes.

"There," a mans Arabic accented voice said. "You wanted proof of life? There it is. Two more days. Then we kill the other one."

The bright light snapped off and Joss's vision began to focus. The zip ties on her feet were cut. Then the ones on her hands.

"I apologize for your rough treatment Miss Lynn," a new voice said. It had an Eastern European accent. "But speed was essential and I fear my colleagues were a bit insensitive."

Now Joss's eyes were clear enough she could see the man standing in front of her. She could also see two other men, one on either side of the man, pointing assault rifles at her. None of the men were tall. The Arab speakers dressed in middle eastern garb, the man in the centre wore European clothing. While the Arab speakers appeared hostile, the European appeared non comital and professional. While the one's with the rifles were concerning, this man was a business man. He would and could be violent, but not out of choice.

"We brought the clothing you and your assistant had purchased at the mall." The man said. "In a moment, you will be taken to have a shower and to change into these new cloths. The ones you are wearing will be cleaned. After you and your companion have cleaned up and changed cloths, we will give you food. Then let you alone to rest. If you decide, ether one of you, to try and escape, we will shoot the other one, is that absolutely clear?"

Joss looked across the room to where two more men with assault rifles were standing. Delta was on her knees in front of them. Her face was a mass of bruises and she was holding her side.

"Can Delta please have some medical attention?" Joss asked.

"Delta has already been cared for Miss Lynn." The man said. "She does not have a concussion and her ribs are bruised only. Nothing is broken."

"Then please let her clean up first," Joss said.

The man said something in a Slavic language and Delta was gently lifted up and escorted out.

"And you Miss Lynn? I hear you have taken some blows to your stomach and ribs?"

"I'll be ok," Joss said. "My dad hit me worse than those guys did."

"You must believe me Miss Lynn, it is not in our best interest to harm you. But we will if we have to."

He left, leaving the two men with the rifles behind. Joss looked around her. She was in some kind of large bedroom type room. A small window was up high, so it must have been in a basement. It also looked like it had been cobbled together recently. The sheetrock lined walls were not painted, the ceiling light was encapsulated by a thick metal grid, to keep them from trying to tamper with it Joss thought. She knew from her safety briefings that these type of things were generally over in a week, two at the most. She wondered if Richard would be informed. Clary for sure would let him know. Knowing Richard, he would use every contact and every means at his disposal to find her. What he could do about it was something else again.

A short while later Delta walked back in with her guards. She was wearing new clothing and her hair still wet from the shower.

"Your turn Miss Lynn," she was told.

She stood on her own and was escorted to a bathroom with a shower stall. Her clothing bags on the bathroom counter. Stripping off her soiled clothing, she first relieved herself, then scrubbed herself down in the shower, chose the most comfortable clothing she had purchased to wear and put them on. They were definitely not the type of clothing for this situation, being more for a classy diner out type clothing. One did, what one did though. She left her soiled clothing where they had fallen on the floor. Her little act of defiance.

Joss was escorted back to the room. While not leaving the basement, the shower and bathroom had also been of hurried construction, Joss felt they were in a house of some sort. The lack of traffic noise convinced Joss they were in the countryside. A table, two chairs and two cots with blankets and pillows had been brought in. Delta was seated at the table. Joss sat across from her. Soon food and apple juice and coffee were brought in for them. At all times, men with rifles were standing away from them covering them with the rifles.

Once they had finished eating, everything was cleared off the table and they were left alone. Joss grabbed Deltas hands across the table. She winced a bit as she did so.

"You gonna be ok Del?" Joss asked.

"Christ I feel like you look Texas," Delta said, she tried to laugh but her ribs hurt.

Joss had looked at herself in the mirror in the bath room. Her left eye was black and she had bruises on other areas of her face. Her whole left side was one massive bruise.

"I dunno," Joss said. "I kinda like our new look. Makes us look bad ass. At lest you can smile. My face hurts to much for that."

"You think they are going to kill me in two days Joss?' Delta said. "I'm the logical one. You're the big money."

"Nah," Joss said. "They might cut off a finger to make a point. But what the heck, one less nail to worry about hey?"

Joss was also worried. She had to keep upbeat for not only Delta, but her own sake. The kidnappers were more likely to cut off her finger or an ear, than Delta's.

. The team members walked up and down the aisle a few times moving arms and shoulder getting the kinks out from sleeping in the comfortable but still airplane seats. They were still parked by themselves at the edge of the main taxiway leading to the main runway. If they had not known already, powerful jet engines roaring for take off in pairs would have let them know it was a military airfield and the days sorties were beginning.

"Our stuff has arrived Black," Sandra said. "They are going to drop it outside. Worms and I will retrieve it when it gets here."

"We've isolated the sat phone they are using Black," Olga said. "Next time they use it we will have them."

One by one, boxes of gear were being handed into the plane and taken to the back of the cabin. Now the four of them relaxed in the comfortable cabin chairs sipping coffee and waiting. There was no sense in making any type of rescue plan until they knew what they were going to face and where they would be going. While all of them were still aware that some very violent actions would soon happen, they carried on as normal as they could. Richard and Jochen spent most of the time talking about the up coming season opener in Australia and what they thought their competitors were going to throw at them.

Sandra trying, without any success what so ever, to ferret out who Olga was cooking the special diner for.

"Bingo!" Olga said. "Sat phone is dialling."

Everyone gathered around her monitor. They got everything, the whole message. Joss was squinting into the camera light, her face a mass of bruises.

"Well she's still alive anyway," Richard said.

"I dunno," Sandra said. "I think she looks kinda bad ass."

"You would," Jochen said.

"Got them pinpointed?" Richard asked.

"Close enough," Olga replied. "Armenia."

A map came up on her display showing the location. It was a remote farmstead in Syunik Province, deep in the countryside of the southern part of the country.

"Perfect," Black said.

"Sat coverage and drone coverage right away please," Olga said on her comm unit.

"German and Russian boss," she said. "Yanks are to far away."

"Got Sat coverage now Boss,' Jochen said.

As requested, it was a wide angle shot that took in a five mile radius. What they were looking for was not near the farm house.

"Got four drones Boss, vectoring each to a possible landing zone first. Then for intel at the target."

"Call in for some fuel for the onboard generator Wyoming." Richard said. "I'll do the preflight. I want us wheels up ten minutes after we know what we're looking at."

Twenty one hours after the girls kidnapping.

"Hello???" Delta called out.

The door opened and two guards walked in, a third was still outside.

"Any chance we can get a deck of cards in here?" Delta asked. "We're kinda bored."

Something was said by one of the men with the rifles in the Slavic language. A fourth guard who had not been seen outside, walked down a hallway. A couple of minutes later he was back. He handed a deck of cards to one of the men in the room, who tossed it on the table. They made to leave.

"We wouldn't say no to some beer," Joss said. "Or coffee, or whatever."

Another couple of minutes and two bottles of beer were plunked on the table. The guard lifted his eyebrows.

"We're all good now, thanks," Delta said. And they were left alone again.

"Five card stud, one draw," Delta said and she began to shuffle the cards.

"Well we're not in a Muslim country," Joss said taking a sip of her beer, she looked at the label on the bottle.

"And it doesn't look like we are in Russia or Ukraine," she pointed at the label on the bottle. It was not in Cyrillic.

That piece of detective work done. They got down to some serious poker playing.

Twenty two hours after the kidnapping.

"Ten in the house, four of them at all times in front of this door," Olga said. They had an infra red image of the farm house on the data screen. "The other six look to be lounging in the kitchen or the living room. The two Charleys are in the room guarded by the four Tangos. Looks like they are playing cards."

Charley was their code word for friendly, Tango, the bad guys.

"That's my girls," Sandra said.

"We've got four Tangos outside," Olga continued. "One at the front door, one at the back. The other two are up by the gate."

"Ok piece of cake," Richard said. "Gear up people, it's time."

The four went to the back of the passenger compartment and grabbed a duffle bag each. Then began removing clothing and donning black tactical uniforms. Each team member had a Sig Suaer automatic pistol in a holster on their chest. Richard and Sandra in .45 caliber, Olga and Jochen in 9mm. Each had an H&K 416 with 5.62 Nato rounds, with a grenade launcher mounted under the rifle barrel. The rifles had long silencers mounted on them.

Four long barrel high caliber rifles were laid by the door. Each of these were 338 Norma chambered. Everyone but Richard had semi-automatics, Richards was bolt action. Each rifle had a long silencer attached and a high power scope mounted on them. Clips of ammunition for all types of the weapons they were carrying were loaded and stuffed into the weapons or in pouches on their pants and built in vests on their chests.

Five minutes after that, they were airborne.

Twenty three hours after the kidnaping.

"You hear that jet engine pass over head just now," Joss asked.

"Ya" Delta said. "Probably just some airliner coming in for a landing down the way bit."

Twenty five hours after the kidnapping.

The sat phone rang twice before the leader of the kidnaping operation answered. "Yes?"

"Good day," Richard said. "I'm your new negotiator. I am just calling to ensure that everything is alright and to let you know the money is ready to leave for the drop off area."

"Very good," the leader said. "Call me when it has left." He ended the call.

Richard and Sandra had chosen to leave the long guns behind. They had come in across the back fence and had made their way to the side of the house. Now they were twenty yards from the doors. Richard had the rear, Sandra the front.

"Anytime guys," Richard said.

Two loud puffs were heard and the two guards at the gate were down. Another two puffs and the door guards were down. Richard and Sandra were sprinting for their doors. Eight large holes in rapid succession appeared in the wall where the guards were. Then the grenades went off in the kitchen and living room.

"Get us some fucking wheels Worms!" Richard yelled into his com unit.

Joss heard loud noises hitting the outside walls and loud thumps outside their door. Both Joss and Delta looked at the door. Then explosions rocked the building and windows blew out. Both of them hit the floor. They heard some loud puffs outside the door, then it was kicked in. Two figures, dressed head to toe in black, bodies loaded with weapons and clips of ammo, burst into the room, scanned around and two voices, one male and one female each yelled out, "Clear!"

"Have no fear California and Texas, Wyoming is here," the woman said. "Come on girls your freedom ride awaits."

Joss thought she recognized the woman's voice from somewhere but things were happening much to fast for her to get a grasp on the situation.

They were escorted down a hallway littered with dead bodies. One very tall figure in the lead, the woman behind walking backward scanning the rear. Both of them had weapons ready. The tall man saw a body on the floor move and he shot it twice, then carried on.

A van with another black clad person in the drivers seat was idling in front of what was the front door of the house. Joss and Delta were hustled into the side door. The black-clad woman stayed crouched by it. The man went to the rear, flung open that door and crouched, pointing his weapon out the rear. Then with tires spitting gravel from the rear tires, the van headed out the gate, turned right, drove a hundred yards and stopped. Another dark clad person ran up from the right side of the road, tossed her long rifle in the back of the van and jumped in the front passenger seat, her assault rifle pointing out the door window.

Once again, gravel was spitting out from under the rear tires and they were rocketing down the road. A short time later, they pulled off the road, sliding to a stop.

"Come on move it move it!" The tall man yelled. "Worms, get the women in the plane! We're not in the clear yet!"

His voice sounded familiar to Joss. But again, she had no time to processes it as she was roughly hustled toward an airplane by the larger black clad women who had been in the front seat of the van.

They were pushed to what turned out to be a small executive jet aircraft. Shoved into two seats in the cabin. The airstair was closed and latched, the engines were spooling up and they were soon accelerating down the road and airborne. A few minutes later, they clearly heard on a set of head phones laying by their seats.

"Frankfurt tower Black Two, Eta one hour."

"Control, Warsaw, Charley is clear, Tangos are down, and the bill is in the mail. Warsaw out."

Chapter Twelve

The woman who had been talking took her head phones off, followed by the balaclava. She unclipped her seat belts, grabbed two weapons from the floor and headed to the rear of the cabin. A few minutes later she was back in her chair, minus weapons and ammunition. Then the man who had driven the van stood, grabbed two more weapons from the floor and headed to the back.

"You're the woman who was in Russia when I soloed," Joss said.

Olga looked back, smiled and saluted.

The man came back.

"Jochen, is that you? Joss asked.

He too looked back, smiled and nodded his head.

Then the tall man came out of the cockpit with two Assault rifles, also headed to the rear of the cabin.

A short time later, the other woman came out of the cockpit, she had already removed her balaclava and was shaking out her hair.

"Well Texas," she said. "Your gonna need a hell of a lot of makeup on your face to cover up all that shit on your face."

Joss flung off her seat belt and rushed Sandra, grabbing her in a hug.

"Sandra thank you, thank you, thank you!" Joss said

Delta was just beginning to stand when a gentle hand gripped her shoulder and pushed her back down.

"You give those ribs a chance eh California." Richard said.

Joss spun around at the sound of his voice and found her self staring into his deep blue eyes.

"No shit Wyoming," he said. "I don't think the whole world has enough makeup to cover that shit on her face."

She was in his arms squeezing him tight.

"Thank you Richard" she kept whispering.

"For the moment, my name is Black, Joss, just Black. The last one of these I went on didn't work out so well."

"Hey!" Delta said. "Who's flying the plane?"

"What this thing?" Sandra said. "It pretty much fly's itself. Pilots are just accessories."

"Ok, settle down," Richard said. "Over by the door is Warsaw, ex Polish special forces, on the other side is Worms, ex German special forces, Wyoming, ex American special forces. I am Black, ex Canadian special forces. We are team Black. Part of a very special and very covert multi national organization. This team is private. I think the others are as well, but I don't know for sure, nor how many other teams there are.

"Now, we are headed to Frankfurt. We have special clearance and first priority. Do you ladies need medical attention? Were you sexually assaulted? Do you need to have that checked just in case? If so, I would recommend that happen right away. Don't be heroes or martyrs about it."

"I'm ok Black," Delta said.

"Me too Ri...Black," Joss said. "I never lost consciousness or was drugged." Joss was still coming to terms with who and what Richard, Sandra and Jochen were. Especially Richard.

"Me too," Delta said.

"In that case," Black said. "I can have you back at my place in about twelve hours. Your choice"

"I'd like that," Joss said. Delta nodded her head in agreement.

Richard looked at Olga.

"Already done boss," she said. "And boss, I have a craving for Canadian beef steak."

"Drop me off at Frankfurt boss," Jochen said. "I still have a lot of prep to do on the car. Then have to get it ready to ship."

Richard looked over at Joss and saw how big her eyes were, especially when she looked at Sandra who was still fully decked out in her weapons and weapons harness

"Wyoming, will you get all that shit off your uniform. You're even scaring then heck out of me." Richard said.

"Love you too Boss," Sandra said.

Two hours later, they had just reached cruising altitude after refuelling and letting Jochen off in Frankfurt. The Atlantic Ocean was all that could be seen. Delta was asleep and try as she might, Joss was nodding off.

"Ah boss," Olga said. "We might have a problem here."

The video screens came alive by each seat and the audio was set up to high. Delta woke up halfway through what was about to happen.

A CNN talking head was excitedly chatting away and the red banner depicting breaking news was running along the bottom. Their Audio feeds kicked in just as the picture changed to the devastated farm house in Armenia. There was a high police presence and more than a few fire trucks and ambulances were on the scene.

Thank you Wolf, CNN has been granted unprecedented access to this crime scene Wolf. This morning an hour before dawn, a dramatic shoot out occurred here at this farm house in a remote area of Armenia. At this point, the Arminian officials are not releasing much information Wolf, but unofficial sources are telling me that in the pre dawn darkness this morning, a special forces team conducted a successful rescue mission of international actress and singer Joss Lynn and her assistant. Who as you know Wolf, were kidnapped in a bloody shoot out in Dubai just over twenty four hours ago.

My sources are telling me that this was a very professional and sophisticated attack Wolf. Something only a highly trained government special forces team could manage. My sources also tell me Wolf, that the

Armenian government had been consulted and informed of this rescue mission and approved it.

As we know Wolf, the United States is renowned for doing these kinds of missions at short notice.

Yes Candice we have been informed by the White House, that the Press Secretary has scheduled a Press conference to be held shortly to discuss this matter. Are there any reports of casualties and the condition of Miss Lynn and her assistant?

At this time Wolf, my sources tell me that they have ten bodies inside the building and another four outside. There is no information on the condition of Miss Lynn and her assistant or of the rescue team. Indeed we are unsure of the exact number in the extraction team Wolf.

Stand by Candice, we are just receiving some drone coverage of the rescue it self.

What was shown was an overhead shot of the two men at the gate going down, seconds later the men at the two doors going down, then two figures rushing the house, bright flashes from the grenades exploding inside the house, then more flashes from rifles on the inside. Several seconds later a van sliding to a stop, followed by a tall man, rifle in hand scanning the area with his rifle, then two women, one supporting the other, then another soldier walking back ward scanning the area, the two women being shoved in to the van and it scratching away.

Richard made the cut it signal to Olga. Joss was holding Delta's hand across the small table separating their two chairs, both women had the other hand across their mouths. Only now, was the impact of what had occurred hit them.

"Well Fuck!" He said.

"Boss, priority call boss," Olga said pointing to her monitor.

"Ya, had to know that was coming," Richard said. "Patch it back here."

"Good day ma-am," Richard said in Spanish. "Thank you ma-am...It appears that California has some bruised ribs ma-am, both of them are banged up a bit and a bit shaken up, but otherwise in good shape ma-am. They have requested to be taken home ma-am. Very well ma-am."

Richard stood, switched the call to the girls headphone sets, and disappeared into the cockpit.

"Miss Texas, Miss California," a woman speaking Spanish said. "We are glad that your injuries are not severe and we trust our team are treating you well. A team was waiting at the ransom drop off point and those sent to retrieve it have been taken prisoner and being interrogated by our people. We have already handled the other Tangos we know about and we will have more in the future as our prisoners. Unfortunately, your government is insisting that you be returned to Frankfurt and that you be given a complete medical examination at their very well equipped hospital.

"I hope you understand that our organization has to comply with this request. In order for us to provide the high level of service that we provide, we require a large amount of cooperation from all governments around the world. So I am afraid we have no option ladies."

The plane began a steep bank to the left and they were soon headed back the same direction they had just come from.

"I understand ma-am," Joss said in her Texican accented Spanish.

"Would you be so kind as to translate what I just said to Miss California?"

"Unlike Texas here," Delta said. "I actually speak proper Spanish ma-am," Delta said.

"Oh, and with a Catalonian accent as well. Very good."

"Pleased ma-am," Delta said. "We have already thanked the rescue team. Would you please pass on my gratitude and Texas's, shit Texas take it easy hey, my ribs hurt. Would you please pass Texas' and my gratitude to all the people of your organization for all the hard work they have done on our behalf?"

"On behalf of everyone here and myself, I say you're welcome. And the American government is going to be short a very substantial amount of money very soon I can assure you, for the stunt they just pulled. Very well, I wish you the best and tell Black he needs to take you out for a fancy diner to celebrate once you get home. And not to Pizza Hut or a barbecue in his ratty back yard!"

There were two military ambulances waiting at the apron when they shut down with four armed and armoured Humvee's stationed around them. Joss and Delta chose to enter the same ambulance and soon they were being whisked away.

Olga had joked that Pizza Hut actually sounded good, so they decided to order take out.. Once the pizza arrived, being dropped in the doorway of the airplane so the team could not be seen, Richard began to debrief the team. What had gone right, or wrong. What they could have done differently. And, what their support teams did right or could have done differently. Richard had recorded all of that to transmit later to each of them for their own written reports and to send to the woman who was in charge of the teams.

Three hours later, finishing up the last of their pizzas and soft drinks, Richard, Sandra, and Olga were watching as CNN was broadcasting live, Joss and Delta coming out of the hospital amid a barrage of camera flashes. The two women approached a set of micro phones set up and waited while the US Ambassador to Germany spoke. Then he held his hand out to them and they came forward. Delta, gingerly holding her side came to the micro phones. The tv shots going close up to highlight the massive bruising on each woman's face.

"On behalf of Miss Lynn and myself, we would like to thank the United States Government, the wonderful staff of this hospital, all the men and women who were involved in this rescue event and especially, the brave men and women who put their very lives at risk coming to our aide.

"Miss Lynn has personally thanked each member of that team. For myself, I am humbled and deeply grateful for everything they have done for me."

She had to stop for a moment to compose herself. Joss rubbing her back.

"Everyday, our soldiers put themselves in harms way to keep us safe. I am deeply grateful. We will be answering no questions and we hope you will respect our and our families privacy as we recover form this traumatic event in the coming days."

The last shots were of Joss hugging Delta, then the both of them walking arm and arm to a waiting large SUV and being whisked away.

"Well, back to work for us I guess," Sandra said.

When the motorcade arrived, Joss and Delta shook hands with everyone and they were quickly in the airplane and taxiing to the runway. Joss breathed a large sigh of relief and saw the empty pizza boxes and drink containers in the trash by the galley.

"You bums had better left us some Pizza and beer!" Joss yelled out as they accelerated to take off speed.

"What a shit show!" Joss said.

"Ya, total commitment from the Yanks? CNN news coverage," Sandra said. "What? I'm a Yank. I can say that. Well I used to be a Yank anyway. Fucking SEAL and Delta teams had not even reached their bases yet and we had you in the air."

Olga pressed a button on her console.

"I'll see if she is available sir," Olga said after listening for a moment.

"Somebody from the White House," Olga said. "President wants to talk with you Texas,"

"Ah hell, it'll be a never ending shit show now," Joss said.

"I could tell him you are resting Texas." Olga said.

"No I'll handle this, patch the yahoo threw. Like I need all this right now."

Joss handled herself well, with dignity and poise for the one minute interview with the president. Of course, minutes later, it was broadcast in its entirety on CNN. Only Joss's voice was heard, no video and you could hear they were in the air as she had to speak loudly to make herself heard over the aircraft noise.

"You guys can watch that nonsense if you want to," Joss said. "I'm tired of it already. Got any booze in this bucket of bolts?"

"We'll get you some in Greenland Texas," Olga said. "Unfortunately we are still working."

The pain killer kicking in and the excitement had seen Delta drift off to sleep, leaving Joss alone with her thoughts. What else had Richard not told her? Could she live with what he was? What she had just seen him do? Just outright killing a wounded man laying on the floor and not even thinking about it.

Sandra was on her way back to the cargo area to make sure all the equipment was still secure, she saw the look on Joss's face and sat in the chair across the aisle from her, spinning it to look at Joss.

"You ok Joss? Really. This is Sandra speaking here, not Wyoming. Wyoming would crack some stupid ass remark. Sandra is really concerned."

"Ya I'm ok Sandra, really." Joss said. "He said the last mission he was on like this one didn't turn out to well. What did he mean by that Sandra?"

"Not up to me," Sandra said.

Joss glanced over at Olga.

"Don't bother asking Olga there, Joss, she was no where around. Go talk to him, he might talk to you about it now."

Joss thought about it for a while. Did she really want to know? Would he even tell her? More importantly, how would she react to what he said. Joss got up and walked to the cockpit, poking her head inside. Richard was leaned back in his seat, both hands behind his neck. She bent over and kissed him on the neck.

"Hey You," she said. "Mind if I join you?"

He nodded and took his hands from his head. Joss climbed into the copilots seat and looked over the instrument panel. It wasn't much different than hers was.

"Wow, we're really zipping along here aren't we?" She said.

"You would like some answers," he said.

Joss nodded her head.

"My name has not always been Richard..."

Richard explained how he had been a soldier in the Canadian army and had been a member of a very secret special forces group. So secret, that even the government officials didn't know it existed. It was decided by certain people in high places, that forming a special group made up of individuals from the Five Eyes, countries would be made up. So the top soldiers from Australia, Canada, Great Britain, New Zealand and the United States would team up. Germany and Poland, had asked to be a part of it and agreed upon. So the group grew from ten members to twelve. Which was perfect as it made up three complete teams.

To make it logistically easier, it was decided to bace the team in Belgium, which was where the Headquarters of NATO was. This would provided easier access to intelligence and support requirements. It worked out well for them.

There was always one team on ready status, one in backup status and one team, basically on holiday, but subject to recall at anytime. The rotation was a month at a time.

Matti and Sandra had hit it off right away, both being party animals and they would often be out clubbing together. Sandra had been one of the members of the team Richard was assigned to.

It was the start of their second and last year of service. Richards team had been the on call team and as such could not leave the base for that month. As was her habit, Matti picked up with her latest boy friend and took off to Amsterdam with him for the month.

Richards team had been dispatched to Spain, because it was thought that a terrorist threat existed. The standby team had been activated to hold in base and the one on leave had been recalled. It was thought the threat was credible.

"Unfortunately," Richard said. "Matti picked the wrong guy, at the wrong club, in the wrong city, at the wrong time."

As it turned out, the terrorist target was that club in Amsterdam. There were almost a hundred of them, well armed and trained. The Dutch had contained the scene quickly, but not without civilian and police casualties. The standby team was activated and dispatched to the scene, the holiday team was geared up and sent and Richards team was on the scene four hours later.

They were just in time to see not only the Dutch SWAT team, but both of theirs basically wiped out. But Richards team had been able to use that as a distraction and gain access to the club, from the building next door. Once inside, they're superior training, weapons and skill set turned the tide.

Out of the five hundred people who had been in the club that night, only twenty had survived. Matti had not been one of them. His sons had watched the whole thing on television, including the sight of their dead mother being carried out, uncovered, on a stretcher.

"So," Richard said. "I lost my wife and found out she was cheating on me, lost six good friends and both of my kids all in the same night."

"Oh my God" Joss whispered. She so much wanted to hug Richard, but did not want to disturb his train of thought.

The high profile disaster had seen the disbandment of the project. Richards wife being at the club that night and further investigation proving she had multiple affairs going on, saw Richards clearance stripped from him and he being reassigned to a supply unit.

His in laws had petitioned the courts and been granted custody of his boys. And he basically self destructed for a while.

A year later, using Sandra as a contact, the CIA had approached him with a contract offer. He had nothing to lose, and the money was good, so he took it. That led to other jobs with other countries and he became rather wealthy.

Sandra had met George by then and gotten out of the army. Jochen had left the German military right after the club fiasco. And they all kind of ended up back together. The six surviving team members. They formed their own company and all became very wealthy doing dirty little jobs for governments or corporations, that didn't want it to be known they were a part of it.

All of them liked racing, so they pooled their money and corporate contacts together and formed the racing team.

"So," Richard said. "There you go. You are in love with a highly trained, skilled and motivated killer Joss."

"Why do they all call you the boss?" Joss asked.

Richard shrugged his shoulders.

"Somebody has to be," he said. "And I have a certain talent for making them money and finding them new people for their projects."

"For example?" Joss said.

"A record producer contacted one of my friends. He had found a female singer who had a lot of potential, but because of her back ground and no mentors, was never going to make it. The producer called my friend, but he was fully involved in another project, so he called me. I had a look and a listen, contacted another associate in a law firm that specialized in those kinds of things, signed her on as a client and there ya go."

"So you already knew who I was then?" Joss said.

Joss did not know how she felt now. Had Richard been using her?

"Yes," Richard said. "That is why I kept ducking you at the races Joss. Well and the fact that I was still a little gun shy about women at the time. Still am in fact. And honestly, can you see why I don't need the publicity?"

But she had persisted, so, more to put her off the scent more than anything, he had taken her to Elka's restaurant in Baden and introduced her to his wife's German relatives. Who of course already knew of her and how she had gotten her start. She seemed to fit right in and actually like being a normal person. So he had taken a chance.

"And so...here we are," Richard said.

"Ya, so here we are," Joss said. "Thank you for telling me all this Richard."

She got up and walked back into the cabin taking the vacant seat next to Sandra.

"So?' Sandra asked.

"He told me," Joss said.

"And so?" Sandra repeated.

"Did you know about his involvement with my career?" Joss said.

"Duh ya," Sandra said. "I was one of the investors."

Sandra was just about to fall asleep because Joss hadn't said anything for a while. Joss was muling over everything Richard had told her. Not about her career, he had explained all that well enough, but the things about his wife.

"You were close to his wife?" She asked.

"Ya, I liked her," Sandra said. "She was fun to be around and a really good person deep down. She really wasn't cut out to be a wife. If she had been a guy, she would have been one of the cool guys with all the babes. We hung out a bit, but she was a little to wild and loose for me. Plus, I liked my job and needed my security clearance."

"You never talked to Richard about her?"

"What? No," Sandra said. "I thought he knew about it and was cool with it. Everybody on the teams knew about it Joss. We never spoke about it though."

"Everybody but Richard it seems," Joss said. "Nice bunch of friends you all were."

"Hey! Wait a minute!" Sandra said.

"No, you wait a moment!" Joss said. "A true friend would have found a way to talk to him about it! A true friend would not have let a woman do that to him! A true friend would have stood up for him in court, so he wouldn't loose his kids!"

Joss fell silent when she saw Richard coming out from the cockpit.

"Sandra did try Joss," he said crouching down beside her. "You were yelling loud enough I could hear you up front. Sandra tried to tell me, but I wouldn't listen. She tried to testify on my behalf, my whole team did, but because of what we do, our governments forbade it. I do not, nor ever will, blame Sandra for that part of my life."

"Go watch the plane for a while Wyoming, take California with you. Texas and I need some us time."

He sat down in Sandra's vacated seat.

Joss glanced over at Olga again.

"Don't worry about Warsaw," He said. "She don't understand English all that well."

Olga stuck her right hand over the seat, middle finger extended.

"Thank you for trying to stick up for me," Richard said. "You have just been asked to absorb a whole lot of information thrown at you in a very short period of time, while recovering from a very traumatic event that you have never been trained to handle. If you want, I can have some one meet us in Greenland to take you and Delta home Joss. So both of you can have time to absorb and heal from all this."

Joss grabbed his hand and squeezed it so hard he thought she might break it.

"I don't want to," Joss managed to get out. "But I think I have to."

"Right choice Texas," he said softly and he gently removed her hand from his. "Right choice."

He stood and gave her a kiss then made his way to Olga and spoke briefly to her. The last Joss saw of him was entering the cockpit. Delta came back in the cabin then. He didn't even come out to see her off at Greenland. None of them did.

"Shit" she said to Delta as they were winging their way back to Texas in a US government Learjet. "I think I just lost him."

Delta let Joss rest her head on her shoulder.

"And the sad part of it is," Joss continued, "I don't know if it's a good thing or a bad thing."

Chapter Thirteen

The studio had told Joss they had decided to shoot the final ten minutes of the film on a sound stage in LA using a green screen and her double. It was mostly filler action sequences.

Of course, they had missed the Australian and Abu Dhabi Grand Prix races. Joss and Delta were pronounced fit medically to attend the next race, in Portugal. They had to spend a lot of time in makeup rooms to render the still visible bruising on their faces acceptable for television. What could be seen was dull. To those who saw them in person however, they were still dark.

Joss had hoped, but didn't expect to see Richard and she didn't. She also couldn't use Georges team's garage to watch the race from. The studio and Piper, had upped her appearance fees for the races. Other aviation product companies had approached her to represent them. Now she had to rotate around the various VIP venues and saw little of the racing.

She had managed to ensure that she was allowed to attend Georges victory party and although Sandra and Jochen had avoided her like the plague, Anna had not. They had decided that during the off weeks when there were no races Anna, Clary, Delta and Joss would all link up and fly somewhere together.

Anna had conned Sandra into attending the second of these trips. Then Anna had arranged it so Joss and Sandra had to meet face to face somewhere that Sandra could not run the other way. After several awkward minutes, both woman had embraced. Now the three smaller airplanes had two big sisters joining them. Both Piper and Diamond took advantage of that, filming the flights using on board cameras on and in the aircraft. These videos became very popular.

They were never released until the month following the flights to allow the five women to enjoy themselves. Nor did they have camera crews following them around.

At the race in France before the Montreal race, Conetica, one of the teams in the bottom end of the F1 field, had experienced a bad wreck, that had not only totalled the car, but severely injured Jackson, the driver. The team used the engines and transmissions produced by Georges team and had hired Anna to replace the injured driver for the rest of the season.

Joss had really expected Richard to show up for that race. But, he was a no show. Anna had finished the race, but well down, last actually, but four cars including her team mate had not finished.

Another American race, this one in Detroit had been added to the schedule that year. It was held after the Montreal race. Anna had managed to battle her way to fourteenth position. Her teammate finished seventeenth.

There was a two week break between races then. So Anna was able to join the other four and they flew to Joss's Texas ranch for the week.

One day, Anna saw Joss slowly walk across the runway and toward the back of her property. She was walking with her arms crossed on her chest and her head down low. Not at all like Joss. Anna had hurriedly chased after her. When she caught up to her, Joss was standing, leaning her arms on top of a newly installed fence post watching the cattle graze in the pasture on the other side of the fence.

Anna thought she hadn't been noticed.

"We came out here about this time last year," Joss said.

"Ya, I remember that," Anna said.

"He gave me the idea to rent the land out," Joss said. "Then he told me he loved me and I told him the same."

Anyone who didn't know Joss, would think she was just talking. She was a very good actress after all. Anna knew better and knew what to look for. Joss bounced her right foot when she was angry, her left when she was upset. Her left was working like a trip hammer. Almost drumming the ground.

Joss noticed Anna looking at her feet and stopped bouncing her foot. Anna spun Joss around and hugged her. She could feel the tears begin to fall and soon the sobs began. Joss had never been a woman who indulged in prolonged emotional out bursts. This time was no different. She squeezed Anna, then gently broke away from her.

"Thanks, I needed that," Joss said. She wiped her jean jacket sleeve across her eyes and cheeks.

"Super star, man heart stealer, Joss Lynn loosing her shit over a man," she said. She had a sad smile on her face.

"We had sex just over there," Joss said pointing.

"Ah, that's when you frightened all the wild life out here" Anna said.

"What?"

"You had grass stuck in your hair," Anna said. "So did he. Don't even try to whack me on the arm you meany!"

Anna deftly spun away from the punch. Then was busy twisting and dodging as Joss chased her around the field, both women finally collapsing on the ground laughing. Joss suddenly stopped and her left foot started taping again but slowly. Joss was thinking about Richard and how much she missed him. Anna stood and reached a hand down to help Joss up.

"I should have gone with him instead of coming home," Joss said as they began to walk back to the house. "He gave me the choice. I thought at the time and it looks like I was right. I have lost him."

Anna stopped.

"What makes you think that?" She said.

"Well, he has been avoiding me," Joss said. Stopping and turning to look at Anna.

Anna said something in German and stomped her foot.

"Look," Anna said pointing a finger at Joss. "He was married for over ten years Joss. If anyone understands how a woman thinks it's him. Matti and her three sisters were borderline psycho. Sandra told me what he told you Joss and he was right, you made the right choice. You were an emotional wreck then, but didn't know it. Plus, he had a ton of things to do."

"Oh," Joss said.

"After a mission like that one, those teams have to do all kinds of reports Joss. A high profile one like yours is even worse. All traces of the teams involvement have to be erased. That takes a lot of effort and time.

"He also has a big business empire to oversee Joss. It mostly runs itself, but after a big mission like yours, he has to be more vigilant for a while. Go ask Sandra how many times he has asked her how you are."

Anna said some more words in German and started walking again. Joss following her trying to figure out what to do next.

Anna said something in German when they arrived at the patio where the other women were having afternoon cocktails. Anna stormed into the house and was chased by Heidi.

"Ah, what the hell did you do now Texas?" Sandra said. "She just called you a pigheaded self centred, dumb American."

"Give us the room hey ladies," Sandra said to Delta and Clary.

Joss walked to the sideboard and poured her self a glass of straight bourbon.

"I had a moment today Sandra," Joss said.

Then she related what had happened by the fence and the walk back.

"Well," Sandra said. "I'll add bonehead and overprivileged white woman to Anna's comments. Richard is nuts about you Joss. He is giving you time to figure your stuff out. Seeing you carrying on like everything is normal and having a good time without him. Knowing now what you know of his marriage. What the heck do you think is going on in his head right now?"

Sandra took a deep draft of her beer and let that comment sink in for a while. Joss was only just now realizing what she was getting herself into.

"We are soldiers Joss," Sandra said. "Good ones, veteran ones like he and I, have lost good friends before. They are still with us Joss, but we move on. We are survivors and that is what survivors do. He will bury his hurt and carry on Joss. You wanna keep him? You made a choice, not him."

Joss saw that Sandra had noticed her rapidly working her left foot. Sandra reached over and stroked her right hand.

"You're going to have to go to him Texas," Sandra said. "He's not going to come to you. You are used to guys chasing after you. Just twitching your finger and having them do your bidding. That's not going to work on him."

Sandra took another other pull of her beer. She smiled.

"This time anyway," Sandra said. "Men are so easy to manipulate. Bar Keep! We need some whiskey out here and none of that crap you Yanks call whisky!"

Richard had just stopped working for the day. He had not faired to badly on the latest market correction. His losses would not total more than a couple of hundred thousand or so. It was a nice night and he was sitting out on his deck having a beer.

The runway lights came on at that point. This was a rare occurrence, but not unknown to happen from time to time. The local pilots sometimes did touch and go night practice on his field. Sure enough, he heard an aircraft approaching, then saw the marker lights and as it came closer, the landing lights came on. It was a single engine propeller aircraft and the pilot was skilled. It touched down with just a slight chirp of the tires and instead of accelerating away as would normally happen for a touch and go landing, this one slowed down, deftly did a u turn and headed back down the runway to the taxiway leading to his hangers. As it went by his view, he saw it was a fairly new Piper Archer and it had the map of Texas drawn under the rear window.

Joss had just finished pushing her plane into the hanger and setting the parking brake. She was in the process of removing her duffle bag from the backseat.

"Good flight?" He asked.

She was in his arms kissing him everywhere instantly. He was barely able to hit the button to close the big hanger door. It wasn't until noon the next day until the duffle bag was finally retrieved from the backseat.

The two lovers had spent the next week reconnecting. Joss coming to terms with who Richard really was, Richard, being Richard. They had taken long drives in the country side, long flights along the rigid Rocky Mountains and across the vast empty spaces of the Canadian hinterlands in the north.

Today, as dusk was turning to night, they were walking back to the house from the stables after a full days ride. A ride that had shown Joss some spectacular water falls and deep ravens with rivers on the bottom. They walked hand in hand, swinging their linked hands like they didn't have a care in the world.

"Richard," Joss said, once the had entered the kitchen. "I hate to say this. I promised you and everyone else I would stay in touch so they wouldn't worry. It's been over a week now, I think I should check in."

As was his habit, Richard shrugged his shoulders. Then went to the coffee maker and started a pot of coffee. While he was doing that, Joss retrieved her cell phone from the bed room and while it was booting up, came back to the kitchen, tossed it on the table, embraced Richard and kissed him.

The phone began to emit almost continues beeps as messages, voice mails and emails began to download.

"Ah shoot," Joss said. "So much for the rest of the week."

She didn't even look at any of the messages, she just hit a predial number, activated the speaker mode on the phone and poured herself a cup of coffee.

"Where the hell have you been Joss!" Delta did not appear to be happy.

"You know exactly where I have been Delta," Joss said. "What's up?"

"God damn it! The Silverstone race! You've missed the first two days already for the week. Everyone has been understanding so far, but if you're not here, at the track tomorrow, people are going to be upset. I think I can stall them, it's only the first practice day. But I can't possibly see how you can be here any earlier than Friday night."

Richard was looking at his watch, then put his head down for a few seconds, while the two women were bouncing various ways to have Joss arrive at the British Grand Prix in Northamptonshire from the ranch by Friday.

"We'll be there by noon tomorrow," Richard said. "At the latest. I'll know for sure in an hour. Hang up now Delta, Joss has to get her stuff together."

"No way are we going to make it by noon tomorrow Richard," Joss said. "Even if you fly at max cruise and we both fly."

Richard just smiled at her.

"Shove your stuff in your duffle bag love," he said. "Pack light. You can have your kiddies pick you up any clothing and such you need. I'll meet you at the hanger."

Joss just tossed a deodorant stick, a brush and a clean set of underwear, jeans and a blouse in her duffle bag. As Richard had said, she would have Clary or Delta pick some things up for her, or have some one else do it for them. She didn't know if Richard would call a friend with a business jet to help them out or what. Only that he was sure she would be there in time.

As Joss ran around the corner of the hanger she had never seen open before, there was a large single engine turbo prop executive aircraft parked in front of it. It was a Pilatus PC-12. The cabin door was open and a small set of stairs led from the ground to the airplane. As she jogged to the cabin door, she glanced over as the hanger doors started to close and saw a similar aircraft, but with two jet engines at its rear parked inside.

Just as Joss entered the cabin of the PC-12, the runway lights came on, lighting the now, almost full dark, area. The lights in the cabin itself were on, but dim. She saw the first row of seats facing the bulk head separating the door from the cabin. Then two more rows of seats, arranged so the seats faced each other.

"Leave your duffle on the floor," Richard said from the cockpit. "Then strap your self into the copilots chair."

The cockpit overhead lights were on, but dim. The whole dash board lit up from three large digital screens and a number of other digital gauges and led lights. The dash was very similar to the one Richard had flown her back to Greenland in. While her Archer had similar type glass cockpit gauges and instruments, these were larger and there were more of them, including switches on the roof.

As Joss sat down, Richard rose and went into the cabin area. He picked up her duffle bag and went to the rear of the cabin and secured it in the baggage compartment located there. He came back forward and closed the combination stairs and cabin door, securely locking it. Then, sat back down in the pilots seat. He showed Joss where the seat belts were and how to put them on. They were not the typical type she was used to which were like the ones found in automobiles. These had two straps that came down, one across each shoulder, that attached to a single release catch on the lap belt. They were also much wider.

While she had been doing that, Richard had been entering data into a digital display, using a small keyboard located underneath it. Once done with that, he buckled himself in. He pointed out an exit point in the cockpit, in case of an emergency. A tone came onto his data display, and he put on his headset and motioned Joss to put on the one laying across the her steering yoke.

"Ok Joss," Richard said, his voice clear on the headset. "Our flight plan has just been approved. I'll handle everything this time. Once we are in cruise climb, I will show you how to operate the radios and things and explain other things to you."

"Edmonton Control, Pilatus PC-12, Charley Gulf Romeo Echo at YXQR with Xray requesting IFR clearance to Greenland, copy."

Edmonton Control rattled off some coordinates that Richard punched into his little keyboard, then gave them a squawk code to enter and cleared them for take off at their discretion. Richard repeated everything back to Edmonton Control, then hit a button and with a whine, the engine started to slowly turn the large five bladed propellor. It soon started and almost immediately, Richard released the brakes and started to taxi to the runway.

After announcing his intention to take off on the general frequency, he turned onto the runway, pushed the throttle all the way in and they were trundling down the runway. He was calling out the speed numbers as they quickly accelerated and...they were airborne.

Joss had watched everything. This large aircraft had taken off in the same distance her much smaller aircraft did, and it was climbing at almost double the rate hers did. As they were climbing, they made a slow turn to the right, then the wings levelled, the nose dropped a little and the airspeed continued to rise, as did the altitude.

"OK Joss," Richard said. "The auto pilot is working now. The cabin is pressurized so don't sweat it once we reach 10000 ok? If we have a decompression event, a mask will drop down in front of you.

Put it on the best you can. I'll help you when I can. So far we are cleared to 18000. I'll have to see what the weather is in about an hour or so, hopefully we can get up to 25000.

"In a bit, I would like you to make your way back threw the cabin and make sure nothing has come loose during take off and to check the luggage compartment in the back for the same thing. You will notice a few boxes back there. Don't concern yourself to much with them. Just know that should something stupid happen and I have to put this thing down, there is a survival kit and gear back there. Ok, go do that now please."

Joss took off her head set and made her way back through the cabin looking for any loose items and verified that everything was still tied down in the baggage area. She noticed that there was a fairly large empty area behind the last row of seats, big enough for another row and that there was a slightly smaller door located just before the baggage area. She ran her hands down one of the seats in the cabin area as she walked back forward. They were soft leather and had plush padding. She also wondered if other, more sinister items were in the large boxes in the baggage area. Then she was climbing back into the copilots chair and buckling back in.

Richard hit a button and the dim lights in the cabin shut off. The cockpit ones were already off. The cockpit only lit by the gauges and they were turned down low.

Once the city lights of Edmonton were behind them, they were cleared for 25000 feet altitude and given a new frequency to use. Richard hit enter on his display and the aircraft began to climb and the radio switched frequency.

"I usually stop at Iqaluit when I do these flights for fuel. Then overfly Greenland and land in Iceland. Unfortunately, Iqaluit is closed in an hour, and Greenland will be just open when we get there."

"You have enough fuel for that?" Joss said.

"Ya," Richard said. "This baby has an extended belly fuel tank. No problem. This thing fly's itself Joss, mostly. It's a little heavier on the controls than my girl, but not all that much and it's a heck of lot faster. I can also get into places that normally only a high wing piston aircraft can get into. Nice plane, expensive, but nice."

"What about that jet?" Joss asked."Wouldn't that have been faster?"

"Yes, and no Joss," Richard said. "It doesn't have the fuel capacity this one has and is only slightly faster. Plus, it's still a little hot to use right now. Unless I have to, I'll wait another couple of months before I use it. That's the one we used to get you Joss."

"Oh," she said.

"It can do almost the same things as this one can. It flys higher and faster, but like I said doesn't have the range. Nor the short take off and landings this one can do. Almost though. It can land on almost anything that is flat and long and straight, like this one can. Has the same cockpit layout and cabin configuration and like this one, is single pilot certified."

Soon the lights from the far between towns and villages became fewer and fewer. The odd glint of moonlight on the surface, betrayed they were flying over water at times. Joss found herself yawning and she looked over at Richard.

"Go ahead Joss," he said. "Have a snooze. There is a small bathroom to your left when you leave the cockpit if you need it. There should still be a couple of cans of soda in the fridge. I'll load it up and get some junk food delivered in Greenland."

Joss took him up on the offer and used the toilet. It was small, but functional. She leaned over and kissed his cheek before she buckled herself back into her seat and was soon asleep.

She awoke to a voice in her headset. Her ears were popping and she noticed the engine had slowed. Opening her eyes, she saw the nose was now slightly lower. Richard reached a hand over, it was holding a stick of chewing gum. Joss quickly unwrapped it and began chewing. The pressure on her ear drums lessened.

It was not yet daylight, the sun was just hinting at breaking the horizon. She could see the glacier clad mountains of Greenland in the distance and looking down, saw the North Atlantic below them. Ten minutes later, they were on the ground and taxiing to the refuelling area. Joss dug into her pocket for her passport. Richard put his hand on hers and shook his head.

Once he had shut the airplane down, he went out side and supervised the refuelling. Joss could feel the cold outside air coming in the cabin door and shivered. As Richard signed the fuel mans papers, a small airport pickup truck arrived. A woman got out and handed Richard a large paper bag. She could see him thank her, then she drove away and he was soon back inside, closing and locking the cabin door behind him. Joss heard a cupboard door close, then Richard was back in the pilots seat and buckling himself back in. He quickly went through his check list, asked for permission to start engines and soon, they were back in the air.

"Breakfast is in the galley Joss," Richard said. "Coffee in the overhead cabinet, coffee maker is on the counter."

Four hours later, they were making landfall and shortly after that, were on the ground, taxiing to the refuelling point. A luxury Range Rover was waiting there, Delta standing beside the rear doors.

"Se ya Texas," Richard said. "I have to refuel this thing, then do my post flight and tie her down. Get outta here. I'll catch up with you later."

Joss gave him a kiss, gathered up her duffle bag and headed over to the Range Rover. Delta gave her a quick hug, then basically shoved her into the back seat slammed the door, she ran around to the other side and the vehicle sped away as soon as Delta was inside.

After securing the aircraft, Richard made his way out to the front of the executive air service building to the always waiting cabs lined up there. He jumped in the first one and told the driver to take him to the race track. Approaching the track and the long line up of cars to get in, Richard directed the cab driver to take a diverging which ended up having only a few vehicles in it. It was the service entrance. They were stopped at the security checkpoint, which is where Richard paid the cabby and got out. He showed his pass to the security guard and headed to the track on foot.

After a few minutes of walking, Richard arrived at the check in point, once again showing his pass and was let through. He could hear race cars on the track now and after another long walk, come to the entrance to the tunnel that led under the track and to the pit area. This side of the tunnel had another control area, which he passed through and an additional one at the other end. After that was a fenced in walkway which led lastly to another check point, this one manned by F1 officials, who all knew him and he was quickly through.

Richard made his way down to the actual pit lane and walked by the team garages that Anna raced for. Other than he knew Anna and his company supplied engines and transmissions to the team, Richard had no involvement with that team. He glanced in Anna's garage as he walked by. She had her helmet on and was in an animated conversation with a mechanic, pointing at the front wing of the car. Richard smiled.

At last he came to the organized confusion of his own teams garages, looked quickly both ways to make sure he would not be run over by a race car and ran across to the booth set up by the wall on the other side of the pit lane. Sets of tires were stacked ready to be changed at the garage entrance, mechanics were sitting waiting in the garage. His head phone set was waiting for him. And engineers were poring over data coming in the screens before them. Donning the headset, he sat down.

"How we doing?" He asked.

"Right on target," Gunther the head engineer said. "We're just about to start race pace testing."

"How's the kid doing?" Richard asked.

"Top fifteen in qualifying testing," Gunther said. "They don't have the long term pace though."

"Don't count on it," Richard said. "She was giving her engineer shit when I walked by."

Things became to busy, as both of their cars hit the track. Data was being analyzed and different things were being tried. It was their teams week to be the featured team on the Sky Sports television network and several times Gunther was answering questions from the broadcasting team, mostly about their apparent lack of performance this week so far.

Richard smiled as Gunther told them how difficult the track was for their cars and how hard it was on tires for them. It was after all, the British Grand Prix and it was a British broadcasting company that had the broadcasting rights. Their team was not British based and did not have a British driver. Just then, something happened on the track and the broadcaster flipped away from them.

"Barkley, the Red Bull driver just set the fastest time," Richard said.

Gunter looked over at him, shrugged his shoulders and smiled.

"Oh well," he said. "Can't win every time."

They both chuckled. They knew they had the engines turned down to produce less power and that they were driving with a wet track set up. Just in case it rained on Sunday. Even with those handicaps, Barkley was just barely faster than they were.

"What do you think?" Gunter asked.

"Leave the engine modes the same," Richard said. "Then after qualifying, switch from the wet setup to heavy dry."

"Ya good," Gunther said. "Those guys have maxed out everything and will have to change the engine for the next race. We won't.

"How'd the time off go?"

"We hashed out some things," Richard said. "Joss has a lot on her plate right now. She needed the time off. She's in a little trouble right now, but I don't think she really cares."

"Well, whatever Anna said to her engineer seems to be paying off," Gunther said. "She's running twelfth in race mode."

"We'll see this afternoon," Richard said. "Here's what I think we should do..."

Excitement at the track after qualifying was high. Barkley had qualified fastest, his Red Bull team mate second. Then a Ferrari had snuck into third, with George and his team mate, Chico, fourth and fifth. Chico was very unhappy. George knew better.

For the first time ever, not only had Anna taken her teams car out of the first knock out round, but had made it through into the final round, qualifying tenth. Allen, her team mate had scratched his way to seventeenth.

"Ok," Richard said. "Now we see what Chico is made of."

"He's used to running up front.," Gunther said. "We'll see how he operates in traffic tomorrow."

"Anna finishes in the top fifteen," Richard said. "We contact her agent and setup negations for the end of the year to sign her for next year. You know and I know, Chico is going to blow this tomorrow. Hopefully he won't wreck the car. Gotta go Gunther. I need to pick up some cloths. I only have what I'm wearing."

"Cars waiting for you out back," Gunther said.

Richard saw there was a driver in the car, so went to the passenger seat. The driver was Delta.

"Hey Del, what's happening?" Richard said.

"You jerk!" Delta said as she put the car in gear and started off. "Do you know how much trouble she's in?"

Richard shrugged his shoulders and grinned.

"Sure, laugh it up!" Delta said.

She drove on in silence until they got on the motorway. Richard was looking out the window watching the scenery go by. Then she let out and audible sigh.

"I am fine Richard, how are you?" She said.

"Tired, not as cranky as you and can use something to eat and a shower," Richard said. "But other than that, all is good."

"Your team seems to have missed the boat this weekend Richard," Delta said.

"Those things tend to happen this time of year," Richard said. "The other teams start to catch up to us after mid season. How'd it go for you guys today?"

"Oh Joss could charm anyone anytime Richard," Delta said. "You know that. She had everyone eating out of the palm of her hand. I should have known."

"No," Richard said. "I'll talk to her tomorrow night. I was checking in with my minions daily Delta. I thought she was checking in with you guys every day too."

"Don't sweat it Richard," Delta said. "Joss is who Joss is. I should know better by now. She was with you, not who knows where. Where'd the plane come from?"

"Corporate plane of a buddies," Richard said. "Probably cost me a mint by the time I get back home."

"Did she give you any idea of what her plans are Richard?" Delta asked.

"Not for sure Delta," Richard said. "She likes this F1 stuff. I think as long as Anna is involved, she will be doing something. Other than that? Your guess is as good as mine. Clary with her?"

"Yes," Delta said. "And two studio people, two studio body guards, two F1 security people, that blond Sky Sports tv person and her crew."

"Real shit show," Richard said.

"Insurance companies are insisting on all the security Richard," Delta said.

They had driven up to the hotel Richard and the Hubba Bubba team would be staying in.

"Well," Delta said, "at least you're not sleeping in the plane this time. Make sure Joss gets to work on time tomorrow Richard. Please."

"As far as I know," Richard said. "Joss doesn't know where I am staying and if you were smart, you won't tell her. Take care California."

Like all the beautiful people, Joss was walking the pit lane, meeting and greeting others like her, or hangers on. Beyonce spent a good half hour talking with her in the Red Bull VIP suite. David Beckem, the soccer star and his wife, a famous singer from the Spice Girls group, spent another half hour talking in the Ferrari VIP suite and ran into Karen on the way to speak with Anna. they made a vow to link up in the States and Joss was off again.

She made sure she stopped in at Anna's garage, had a quick word with her, just before Anna had to hurry forward for the national anthem. She and Sandra were standing together when it was played. They would only have a few seconds to talk after. Joss had to go the VIP suites this time and could not watch from the pit garage roof.

It was noisy enough, with the crowd noise, engines starting, people rushing about, that Joss had to put her mouth right up to Sandra's ear to be heard.

"Have you seen him?" Joss asked.

Sandra turned her around. Richard was seated at his bank of monitors on the pit wall with the other engineers. Both his legs bouncing on the foot bar. All of them were very nervous, not just Richard.

"That's not normal," Joss yelled.

"No," Sandra said. "They are very worried. They're hoping they can salvage at least a podium today, but it's not looking good Joss."

Joss gave Sandra a quick squeeze, then she was hustled away. They were minutes away from the race start.

"Ok George," Richard said. Unlike most transmissions, this one was scrambled. "Try and stay out of trouble at the first corner, it's a long race. Then start pushing the Ferrari and push hard."

"What about the tires boss?" George said. "They won't last much longer than ten laps if I do that."

"We have it covered George," Richard said. "Don't sweat it."

George let the Ferrari get ahead of him, then stayed on his tail. Chico had a slow start and found himself back in the seventh place. He was not happy at all. Complaining like crazy. Anna had been passed by Fernando Alonso, a former world champion and was in eleventh.

After ten laps, Georges soft compound tires were worn out and they pulled him into the pits to change tires. He was pissed. He was more pissed when they put the hardest compound tires on the car. To make matters worse, one of the lug nut guns failed. It took thirty seconds to do a 2 second tire change. It normally took twenty four seconds to drive the length of the pit lane. In all, they had lost almost a full minute. George was in last place and in danger of being lapped on his slower hard compound tires.

Other than still bouncing his feet on the seat bar, Richard was trying to be neutral. While he knew they had a superior car and George was a fantastic driver, this was proving to be a tough test today.

"Sorry George," Gunther said. "Race your race, mode four."

"I'll try," George said.

Mode four meant he was to match the leaders pace.

Chico was having all kinds of issues and becoming more upset all the time. He finally made a mistake and spun, by the time he got back on the track, he was fourteenth. They called him in and put the medium compound tires on the car. The only car behind him, George and he was less than a second behind. The medium tires were faster than the hards and he quickly pulled away from George, both of them coming up to pass Allen, Anna's team mate.

"Where's the blue flags!!!" Chico yelled on the radio.

"You are racing for position Chico. No blue flags," Craig, his engineer said. Blue flags were displayed to the slower drivers to pull over and let the faster cars lap them. In this case, Chico and George were not lapping cars, but passing them.

Chico finally passed and took off after the next car. George had no trouble passing the much slower car. Both of them had passed the four slowest cars and were now in a ten second gap between the slowest cars and the mid field cars.

The third place Ferrari car had been slowly loosing pace each lap and they brought Carlos in to change tires. He came out of the pits five seconds behind George. And one lap down from the leader.

Sebastian the leader could not get closer than two seconds away from George. He sped up, George sped up, he slowed down, George slowed down. Meanwhile, Chico was steadily making his way up through the field, having trouble, but passing eventually. On the other hand, George picked his spots and passed quickly.

One by one, the other teams pitted to change to the medium tires. Anna had Alonso as his tires wore, now she found herself in third place as only her car and the two leaders cars had not pitted yet.

Then, at the last second, she peeled off and pitted. Like George, she put the hard compound tires on.

"Mode three George," Gunther said on the radio.

George picked up the pace and he was soon right behind Chico and after three laps, had almost enough time on Sebastian to negate a pit stop. They saw the leaders team come out of the garage with new medium compound tires after he had flashed by.

"Punch it George!" Gunther called.

By the next corner, George had passed Chico and was pulling away. He had a good twenty seconds of clear track ahead of him.

Joss had been talking to last years female Best Actress Oscar winner, Melanie about whether Joss was going to attend this years Oscar awards, when a roar went through the stands outside.

"What's going on?" Joss asked.

"George just passed Chico," Jane the Sky Sports telecaster said. "He is pulling away and already has gained three seconds on the leader. Not only that, Anna just put in the fastest lap of the race."

"What?" Joss said. "On hard tires!!"

Joss was no longer paying attention to the beautiful people. Her eyes firmly glued to the TV monitors all around the VIP suite.

Sebastian pulled into the pit, changed his tires and as he exited the pit lane, watched George blast by him. Then to add insult to injury, George set the fastest lap of the race on the second last lap and carried on, to finish a full two seconds ahead of second place. Anna finished fifth, the highest her team had ever finished. Chico ended up ninth.

Elated at how well Anna had finished the race, Joss rushed down to Annas garage. The team was high fiving and hugging each other. Joss elbowed her way through the crowd around her, Anna saw her coming and met her. Both women embracing. Joss spent the after race party with Anna and her crew in their pit garage. It was an epic party, the first time they had ever scored points. She knew Richard would have disappeared.

"Sign her Gunther," Richard said. They were huddled in the back of the Hubba Bubba garage, Gunther towling off the champagne George had poured on his head on the podium. "Now! Tonight! If Rosy gives you any grief, you call me right away! And make sure that little shit Chico doesn't find out!"

Richards cell phone rang at that point.

"Hey Rosy," Richard said in German. Gunthers eyebrows rose. Richard smiled. "Your ears ringing or something?"

"Ya ya, stupid Canuck," Rosy said. "You have this one phone call. Anna wants to drive for you, I want Anna to drive for you. Do you want Anna to drive for you?"

"Duh ya," Richard said.

"Done!" Rosy said. "We talk terms after the season good? And tell Gunther to keep his mouth shut! That stupid Chico is going to cost you enough points as it is. Anna does not need to know."

She hung up.

"We have a driver," Richard said.

"That fast?" Gunther said. "How much is she going to gouge us?"

"We'll talk after the season is over and she is not going to tell Anna. Oh, she said to keep your mouth shut Gunther."

"Ah give me a break you two!" Gunther said. "As if. Chico is costing us points as it is. Can you imagine what would happen if he found out we are not going to give him a ride next year?"

"Do what you can at the press conference Gunther," Richard said. "But let them know it was Chicos choice not to go on the hard compound tires. Which it was, he was very vocal about it on the radio."

Sandra came up then, looked at Richard and raised her eye brows. Richard smiled and shrugged his shoulders.

"Hey, the races have been boring lately," Richard said. "We just livened it up a bit."

"Oh," Sandra said. "And a little bird just happened to whisper into Annas ear too?"

"No Sandra," Richard said. "That was all Anna. I have a strict hands off policy."

"Jesus," Sandra said. "Poor George next year."

"Ya," Richard said. "Poor us if she signs with those other guys. Rosy won't even talk to us."

At the post race interview sessions, Chico was not outright blaming the team for his result, but close. He was even more miffed that Anna was getting much more attention than he was. As everyone knew would happen, Ferrari protested Anna's car. She had finished ahead of both of their cars and they needed the points.

The following weekend, the race was at the famous Spa Circuit in Belgium. As the drivers and their teams were walking the track the morning before the first practice session, Anna was approached by Richard, which surprised her. He took off her team cap from his head and handed it to her. She signed it and they walked together alone for a few seconds.

"Good job cuz," Richard said. "Got my eye on you kid. Good call on the wing and the tires."

"I had a good teacher," She said. "Plus I saw what George was doing on the hards. You're sneaky Richard. But not that sneaky."

"Like I said, good job kid," Richard said. "Don't worry about the protest. Ferrari always does that. Watch, they'll be making noises next about how we are giving your car special information. They might want to be careful on that one."

Richard moved off and Sophia, Anna's physical technician, came up beside her.

"Who was that?" Sophia asked. "He's kinda cute."

"Just a distant cousin from America," Anna said. "You know what it's like. Get famous and all of a sudden you discover all kinds of relatives you never knew you had."

The race in Belgium was historically hard on the cars. It was the longest track on the circuit, with the most high speed sections. Generally, all the teams put the last of their new engine yearly allotment, in the cars for this race. The remaining races had lower speeds.

Not so for the Hubba Bubba team. They kept the old engines in their cars, opting to replace them later. The media was having a hay day with it. Predicting that not only the second place team, but that the two Ferrari cars would beat the team. In fact, it was also broadly believed that the team could drop well down the order, as, all the mid field teams had not only put new engines in, but had put their last allowed body upgrades.

Richard had been a part of the decision making process and knew exactly what was going on and why.

All of the pundits agreed, the team had made a grave tactical error, that would cost them the constructors championship. George's lead on the drivers championship was secure. He only had to place fifth in this race, or, a combination of points over the next four races to equal that, and it was his.

Chico was already making noises about the team ruining his chances for a decent point finish. Richard and Gunther both knew, Chico had to go, even if they had not already made an unofficial agreement to sing Anna.

Richard had video conferenced with Jochen the night before. They both agreed, without Anna, the F2 team was destined to finish third at best. Sainz, the driver that had stayed, was good, just not that good. Bordane, the driver that had taken Anna's place, was young and had a little talent.

"Two things I need you to do," Richard had said. "First, get the scouts out looking for another Anna. They don't necessarily need to have funding. Diamond has agreed to keep sponsoring the team. Send me videos and backgrounds, I'll let you know who I like, then you guys check into them. Pick the one that will do the best for us. As a driver.

"Second. Find and train your replacement. Rosy is going to insist that you be Anna's team manager no matter where she ends up. The bidding is going to be high Jochen and Rosy for sure is going to do what she thinks is right for Anna."

The strategy for this race had been mapped out weeks earlier. While many things could and would come into play. In the teams mind, the issue was never in doubt. George would be the world champion by the end of this race.

It for sure, did not look like it during the first two practice sessions. Chico had hit the wall during the first session, his team frantically repairing the damage to the car. The Saturday qualifying session had confirmed it. George had qualified fifth, Chico ninth, Anna twelfth.

The smarter of the F1 pundits, warned the others that George and Chico had qualified on the medium compound tires, while the others in the top ten had used the soft tires. This would allow them to run later in the race to change tires. One thing was certain among all the commentators, instead of the normal one tire change, this circuit was hard on tires and there would have to be two tire changes.

Every other team had opted to start with the soft tires, except for Anna and her team. The die was set. The cars made their way to the starting grid, the start lights came on, and in a roar, twenty cars took off towards turn one.

By the end of the first lap, George was running eighth, contrary to the pre race briefing, Chico had blasted past George and was pressing the fourth place Ferrari. Anna had elbowed her way into tenth, the last points paying position. Again, the commentators were gushing over the British driver Mansel and Red Bull in first place and then Anna, who raced for Conetica also a British based team. George was quickly forgotten.

What everyone failed to see, but that Richard had planned for and now saw it paying results, was that George had kept ahead of the ninth place car, equalling his lap times and that he was consistently running two seconds a lap slower than the leaders. Once the seventh place car was ten seconds in front and the leader fifteen, George began to pull away from the ninth place car. Then he started to match the times of the leaders and kept it there.

Anna managed to pass when Alonso, the car in front of her, made a mistake as his tires were wearing out. She quickly drove away from him, but could not match Georges pace. Her car just did not have the aerodynamics to do it. No matter her, at times, super human efforts.

When the drivers using the soft tires all pitted on lap twenty five, Chico found himself in first place with a ten second lead on George. Anna was five seconds behind George in third. The other teams pushing hard to catch them.

Richard had predicted that the medium tires would last until lap 35. But despite being warned about it, Chico had pushed to hard, to fast and had to come in on lap 30. His tires completely worn out. That put him right down to Sixth place in the thick of the worst traffic, with few opportunities to pass and loosing time to George and Anna all the time. Anna came in on lap 36, as the fast Red Bull team came within a second of her. That put her in ninth, chasing Chico.

Remarkably, George, despite at times begging to come in to change tires, kept the trailing teams down to only gaining on him at most by half a second per lap. Anna was pushing Chico hard, forcing him to pass for seventh. Then sixth as she had passed the car Chico had just passed right behind him.

George was coming up on the slower cars to lap them on lap 45. Red Bull was now only one second behind him. At the last second, they called George in to pit for tires. The order was now what it had been at the start. Red Bull one two, the Ferraris three four and Chico sixth, with Anna right on his tail.

George came out of the pits in eighth place, with a five second gap between him and seventh and twelve seconds back from the leaders, who were now having to slow down to pass the slower lapped cars. George, with new, faster soft compound tires, began cutting into their lead by at least one second a lap. Then even when they had cleared the lapped traffic, he was cutting the lead to two seconds per lap as their tires became more worn.

Then, as it so often happened, Mansel, the leader pitted for new tires, followed by everyone else. George was back in the lead, no one around him to slow him down. Anna was still in sixth place, pushing Chico hard, who was having trouble with the Ferrari ahead of him, finally, with a risky move, passing him, but not opening up much of a gap. He kept calling for the team to give him more power, the team kept telling him that he had all they could give him. Although he didn't show it, Richard was becoming annoyed with Chico and his constant whining.

Anna started slowly loosing ground to the leaders, her car just could not keep up. Then disaster struck. In a large cloud of blue smoke, the engine in Chico's car had a catastrophic failure. He was out of the race. Richard slammed his hand on the consul before him, The race commentators were all in a an excited frenzy. Surely Georges car would suffer the same fate. Or his now aging tires would give up on him. Yet he soldiered on, keeping the gap between him and the second place car.

Ten laps from the end of the race an unfamiliar voice came over the radio.

"Crazy Canuck," was all Richard said.

To the shock, amazement and eventual excitement of the commentators, George not only increased his lead, but made fastest lap of the race for the next two laps, before cruising in on the last lap, five seconds ahead of the second place finisher. Anna once again finishing fifth. George had just won the world drivers championship!

Not so for the team. With both their closest rivals cars, Red Bull and Ferrari, scoring big points for second and third and with Chico not making any points for the team, their lead was cut substantially.

In fact, with the final three races held on tracks that did not favour their car, it was doubtful they would win.

There was a two week lull in the racing action now as the teams began the transport of the cars to Texas. The Texan and Mexican races were back to back, then another week off for the last race of the season in Brazil. Everyone in the Hubba Bubba team needed a break, especially Richard.

Richard had flown alone back to his ranch. Joss had post race commitments. It had been a lonely flight for Richard. He had come to enjoy Joss being in the cockpit with him. Life was what life was for them at the moment. The only time he and Joss had enjoyed to themselves was the week she had spent at his ranch and the flight to Britain. After that, Joss had been far to busy with her F1 commitments. While it seemed to Richard that they were closer now, he was still unsure if she had fully come to grips with her abduction, or his own role in it.

The following day, Richard had half heartedly played the market. The market was bad, but he still ended up clearing two hundred thousand dollars by the end of the day. The first money of his own that he had made this year to this point. Not that he was hurting. His dividends and wages from his other concerns alone kept him well heeled.

Even so, he decided to celebrate with drinking Alberta Springs Canadian whisky tonight, instead of his usual beer. He was just getting a glow on, when he heard an aircraft approaching from the south. It entered the pattern for his airfield and landed. As it came past his spot on the deck of his house, he saw it was a Piper twin engined Seneca and that it had the map of Alberta painted under the rear window of the airplane.

It made a u turn on the runway, taxied back to his end, and stopped. Two women got out of it, duffle bags in hand and started to walk toward the house. The Seneca went back to the runway, lined up and took off.

After the Belgian race, Sandra had asked Joss if she would like a ride back to Richards. George had to stay a few days at the factory in Britain to debrief the Belgian race and would fly home by charter later. Joss had agreed. Once Anna had found out, she asked to tag along. Delta and Clary would fly back to Texas in first class commercial. The three women had shared flying duties and except for stopping for fuel twice, did not make a layover. It had only taken a day and a half to make it to Richards, instead of the more normal three days.

Joss had never flown a twin engined aircraft before. It was much faster than her Archer was, noisier because the engines were on both sides of the cockpit instead of out front. It flew higher and there were more things to worry about. Such as having retractable landing gear and what would happen if one engine cut out suddenly. Joss thought she would stick with her smaller Archer. It suited her needs.

On the first leg, the women had chatted away on various topics. How well Anna was doing with her racing, what they thought of the Hubba Bubba teams chances for a team championship. Anna had flown that leg to Greenland. Joss would fly the next to Churchill Manitoba in Canada. And Sandra the last to home. It was dark when they left Greenland. As dark as it got for the limited nights of the summer in the higher latitudes. More of a, light dusk, followed by dawn. Anna had fallen asleep right after take off in the back seat. After seeing that Joss was handling the Seneca just fine, Sandra followed suit in the copilots chair, leaving Joss to her thoughts. And she had many.

She had already told the studio, she would do no more Jan Fields movies. At the Belgian race, Piper had felt her out about doing a promotion for them regarding the release of their newest airplane. Finally, Joss wanted to discuss with Richard their relationship and where it was going. Her biological clock was ticking and she would like to have some children at some point in the near future.

At Churchill, Joss had climbed into the back seat and like the other two women had done earlier, she fell rapidly to sleep. She woke up when her ears began to pop from the pressure change as they lost altitude and gathering her thoughts, she looked around, saw it was late afternoon and that Richards airstrip was in view. A few minutes later, they were on the ground. Sandra left the left engine running and stopped the right so Joss and Anna could deplane. After they were far enough away, she restarted the right engine and took off, headed for her hanger in Olds.

"Oh," Joss said minutes later from the kitchen. "The girl friend is away and the boy friend goes out to play."

She hadn't spotted Richard on the deck yet.

Joss started to rummage through the refrigerator while Anna walked out onto the deck and saw Richard there, she went back into the kitchen and came back with an empty glass in her hand. She kissed him on the cheek, poured herself a healthy portion and took a deep sip.

"Mmm, good stuff" she said.

"What you doing here," Richard slurred.

"Having a drink with my slightly pissed cousin," she said. Then laughed. "I think that's a heck of a good idea and will join him."

"Well the bum is no where to be found!" Joss called out from the kitchen. "Ladies night, woo hoo! Oh my, he has some excellent wine here, I'll think I'll drink it for him. You want a glass?"

"No thanks," Anna said. "I already have a drink."

"Well you really have to have just a little taste," Joss said walking onto the deck. She had a bottle in one hand and two wine glasses intertwined in the fingers of the other hand.

"This stuff is eighty bucks a bottle easy," Joss said.

She hadn't spotted Richard yet in his lounge chair. Joss poured two glasses of the wine, handing one to Anna and taking a sip of the other one.

"Good stuff," Joss said. She backed up to sit and then jumped up as she hit Richards legs on the chair, spilling the wine in the process.

"You jerk!" She said, then flung herself on him.

"Wha?" Richard slurred. "Anna found me right off. Not hiding here."

"Turn my back for five minutes and you're replacing me with a new model blond!" Joss teased.

"No chance of that," Richard said. "She's got to many brains for me."

Joss kissed him tenderly, then her eyes went wide and she pushed back from him.

"Are you saying I'm not smart?"

Richard shrugged his shoulders and grinned.

"Can't be that smart," he said. "Your choice in men sux."

Richard tensed himself for the slug to the shoulder. Anna could't stand it anymore and burst out laughing.

"Whats suh garsh darn funny!" Joss burst out. Her Texas coming out.

Anna rose from her chair, gave Joss a hug and kissed her cheek.

"I'll leave you two alone," she said. She walked back into the house.

"Now where we?" Richard said, pulling Joss close, his hands roaming. She resisted him for a mili second, the her hands were roaming too.

"Piper wants the four of us on display in Austin," Joss said the next afternoon. After the night of frantic love making and the long trip, she had slept most of the morning away.

"So, I need to pick up Texas and fly her home."

"Makes sense," Richard said. "Rub Textron's nose in it."

Textron was the company that owned Cessna and Beechcraft airplane factories and they were based in Texas.

"They want your girl too," Joss said. "They want to show everyone what can be possible with an older airframe."

"Not going to happen," Richard said. "Sandra has done the trans Atlantic run several times. Alone and with the kids. They would be better off using her."

"I'll have Clary let them know." Joss said.

"Richard," she said softly her left leg bouncing. "I have to leave in the morning. The studio has a promo video they want to shoot for the picture. Can you meet me at the ranch after? Please?"

"You know I'll be there Joss," he was looking her right in the eyes and she felt herself melting into them.

It was another night of passionate love making and Joss was reluctant to leave, but knew she must. With a heavy heart, she kissed him good by and had the Archer in the air, headed to California.

Anna and Richard watched Joss' Piper dwindle into a spec as it gained altitude and distance. Then slowly walked back to the house. Both respecting each others silence. Richard coming to grips with what he should do next with his relationship with Joss.

They walked into the kitchen, Richard pulled two beer from the refrigerator and tossed one to Anna.

"Ok kid," he said. "Back to the books for you and the computer for me. See ya in the morning."

Deciding to take a brake, Anna had checked in on him at one point, handing him a beer. He was on a video call with the two F1 team managers. He had his head set on so she couldn't hear what was being said, but Chico's manager was not happy.

Richard saw Anna go back up stairs to the kitchen which she had claimed to work from and make a call.

"Hi grandma," she said. "Richard is having a video conference call with his team managers. They don't seem happy. Anything I should know about?"

"Nothing that I know of," Rosy said. "How did Richard seem?"

"His typical non comital self grandma," Anna said.

"I do now Chico has been stirring the pot again," Rosy said. "A lot. Now he's saying if he is not signed by the Brazil race, he will jump to another team."

"Ya that would piss them off," Anna said.

"Oh shit," Rosy said, "my other line is ringing. That stupid American team is bugging me to meet with you Anna."

"Listen to what they have to say grandma," Anna said. "But let them know, I will talk with no one until the season is finished."

Two days later, they were passing over the mountains of Colorado at ten thousand feet headed to Joss' Texas ranch.. Anna was in the left seat. She couldn't tell if Richard was sleeping or not.

"Richard," she said. "Are you awake?"

"Huh?" He said. "Ya Anna, just star gazing. It's really nice here."

"Can we talk?" She asked.

"Guy problems?" Richard asked.

"I wish," Anna said. "I need your advice and I value your opinion."

"Ok shoot," Richard said.

"I have offers from Red Bull, Ferrari and the American team Richard. Who should I go with?"

"I can't answer that for you Anna," Richard said. "For one thing it's a conflict of interest, for another, I love you to much. Why don't you list the pros and cons of each team for me?"

"Red Bull has a good program and lots of funding, I think they will be pushing you harder next year than they did this year."

Richard smiled.

"Both of their drivers have a year left on their contracts, so they want me down on the junior team. Maybe sixth place tops.

"Ferrari wants a five year deal. I will be the number two driver and they want me to drop Diamond as a sponsor. Plus, well they are Italians and you know what Italians believe as far as women go."

Again, Richard smiled. He knew she was fishing, that she had already made up her mind, but he would say nothing yet.

"Aston Martin Racing is offering the most money. I will be their number one driver. They want a two year deal with an option for two more. I can keep Diamond as a sponsor, and they have incentive packages based on not only points. They are also lining up a big American Oil company to sponsor me. The same oil company is going to sink a lot of money into the team. I think they will also be pushing you next year."

Richard sighed. None of those teams were supposed to be approaching other drivers until the end of the season.

"Look Anna," Richard said. "You know this business. They will all promise you the sun the moon and the stars. What matters the most, is what is in here and in here Anna."

He touched her heart and her temple.

"If Anna is happy," he said softly, "Richard is happy."

"Sometimes I have a hard time understanding him Joss," Anna said later that night on the Texas ranch patio.

Richard was where he usually was after a long flight, with his other girl.

Joss had only arrived a couple of hours before they had from California. The promotional shoot for the studio had only taken a day. Now both women were relaxing on the patio, wineglasses in hand.

"Welcome to the club," Joss said and laughed. "I have a hard time understanding men at the best of times. And he is more, much more confusing than most."

"Even though it is against the rules," Anna said. "I have received offers from every single team on the circuit. But his. I asked his advice and he refused to give it."

"Let me guess," Joss said. "He asked you a bunch of questions instead."

Anna nodded her head.

"Richard and I rarely talk business together Anna. We keep that part of our lives separate as much as possible.

"I do know, that at a party at his house at the end of the season last year. George told him that he would stay on and mentor you for however long it took Anna. Richard had not asked him, he volunteered it. I also know that you have been groomed for an F1 seat for a very, very long time."

She walked up to Anna's chair and squared down in front of her taking her head in both hands.

"He loves you very much Anna and he wants nothing but the best for you. Yes of course he wants you on his team Anna. But he refuses to pressure you or Rosy. He will also not approach you until after the season is over, just to stop any interference talk or conflict of interest charges. Against you as well as the team Anna.

"He will be absolutely fine with what ever decision you make Anna. If I know him, he might even enjoy the challenge of you racing against them. It's early days yet Anna. Play them along like the beautiful woman you are. You do know how to string guys around yes?"

Annas ears turned red.

Joss caught Richard walking up to the deck out of the corner of her eye as she finished the last comment.

"What have you been saying to my young innocent German cousin?" Richard said, he made to give Joss a hug and a kiss. She shoved him away.

"Not with those oily greasy hands you don't!" She said.

"I'll have you know, your young innocent German cousin was just telling me how she could wrap an elusive fish like you around her little finger and what she does to them when that happens."

"Good, it's about time you learned some new tricks," Richard said over his shoulder as he walked toward the shower. Joss hooked an ice cube from her drink and bounced it off his back.

Both women laughed and referred back to silence. Joss thought the same as Richard did. That Anna had already made up her mind who she would drive for. Joss was just about to pick up her novel.

"You're right Joss," Anna said. "I see Richard doing it all the time. String them along, then blind side them with the decision he has probably made months before."

She smiled a little smile.

"Him and my grand mother." Anna said.

Chapter Fourteen

It had started the week of the Austin race. Anna was headed for this team or that. The pundits were analyzing everything, every little look or gesture. Chico was fanning the flames at Richards team. He wasn't helping his cause any, he kept blowing engines or spinning out. They were forced to use an old engine on his car now or get penalized for putting a new one in. Richard and both cars team managers said nothing. Richard and they had agreed to let him hang himself and not add to the controversy at all.

During the Mexico race, Chico's home race, he had poured gasoline on the fire and promptly wrecked the car on the fourth lap. George kept doing enough to keep the team in first place, barely. It would all come down to the last race, in Brazil.

Now even the team sponsors were getting on the bandwagon about Anna. For their part, Richards team didn't add to the controversy, nor did they respond. They expressed their confidence in Chico and how good a driver he was. Again, Richard had advised the team to do so, but to keep working on the car as normal, they needed the points.

All the team ever said was that they never discussed driver lineups or contracts with the drivers until the season was over.

Behind closed doors, the team did little to Chicos car but tweak it for the Brazilian track. The whole team was upset with Chico. None of his engineers or mechanics said anything and in fact, said little at all to him.

For his part, George was toiling away hard during practice, trying valiantly to keep within a second of Ferrari and Red Bull during the practice sessions. Anna working just as hard in her car.

George had to win the race now for the team to win. If Chico received any points at all, it would help, but Anna was consistently out pacing him. She was now in seventh place in the drivers championship, her team in tenth. Her team mate had even scored a point for coming in tenth in Mexico.

At one point after the third practice session, she had come unglued at one very persistent member of the press who had barely allowed her to get out of the car and remove her helmet. He started yelling sexually charged questions at her. Anna shoved him hard, then went after him throwing punches. So much so, her mechanics had to drag her away.

As one of the coolest heads in the sport, Sky Sports had asked Gunther his opinion of Anna's out burst.

"Look" Gunther said. "He was asking inappropriate questions right at the end of the practice session to a highly adrenaline charged driver. Frankly, if he had asked those same questions to me in that situation, I would have knocked him on his ass and he would be drinking his meals from a straw for the next month or so."

That set off a fire storm and soon Anna's actions were being justified and Conerbrook, a social media gossip columnist, banned from F1 for life.

Richard was wandering down pit lane, just like everyone else with an unlimited pit access pass was doing. The other teams had seen him around, just didn't know who he really was. Looking into Anna's garage he saw that Anna was at the back of the garage nervously getting ready for the qualifying session. He walked quietly behind her.

"Give 'em hell kid," Richard said.

Anna spun around, but all she saw was his back walking out the door.

George was working hard, but could only manage fifth in the first round of qualifying. The team switched to the medium tires for the second round. Everyone knew the car liked those tires better. The fastest time the cars made during the second session was the tire they would have to use for the start of the race. George was once again fifth as all the other teams also used the medium tire.

Now everyone switched to the soft tires for the last session. They were the fastest tires. With an apparent Herculean effort, George was fourth. Two corners from the start of the last run, Richard's voice was on the radio again.

"Crazy Canuck," he said.

George finished the lap in first place, half a second ahead of Mansel driving the fastest Red Bull car. Chico only managed seventh. Anna sixth, her teammate tenth. The first time that team had both cars in the last qualifying session.

"Oh shit," the Red Bulls team manager was overheard saying. "Did those bastards pull something over on us again or was that a fluke?"

At the beginning of the race, the teams were slowly making their way around the track on their warm up lap. Teams were giving last minute instructions to their drivers or words of encouragement, except for Georges team. They were strangely quiet. In Chico's case, nothing would be said except to answer questions or to tell him when to pit. It was by design for George.

The cars were slowly making their way up the start straight to their positions when Richard's voice was on the team radio once again.

"Do I have to say it?" Richard asked.

The car was lined up, it was in gear, the start lights were all lit, George had the engine at the rev limiter.

"Nope," he said. "Crazy Canuck!" He yelled as the lights went out.

By the end of the race , George had lapped everyone but Anna in fourth and was fifteen seconds ahead of the second place Red Bull team. They had won the drivers championship and in convincing fashion. Anna was trying to pass Nico, driving the third place Red Bull car down the finish straight, but her car just didn't have the legs and she finished, her front tire beside the car's drivers cockpit.

An hour after the race, Richards cell phone rang. He was still at the track, although, getting ready to make a break for it.

"Ready to sign?" Rosy said.

"As long as it is not to outrageous, yes," Richard said.

"Don't have a bird," Rosy said. "It's less than the Aston Martin offer, but she has more say on her own personal deals."

"Ya done, send it over," Richard said.

"Ok, she is on her way, have her uniform jacket ready." Rosy said. "Oh yes, Jokin is on his way too."

Everyone in the Hubba Bubba garage was in party mode, having just won the drivers championship. Finally getting his attention, Richard beaconed Gunther over.

"Our new driver and her team manager are on the way over," Richard said. "Make sure her and his jackets are ready eh?"

"Oh you sweet Crazy Canuck," Gunther said and kissed Richard. Then he jumped high in the air.

"We have Anna! We have Anna!" He yelled. The whole garage erupted, everyone was hugging and jumping up and down. Except for Chico, who forgotten, dejectedly walked away.

Joss, Delta and Clary were standing beside Jokin in Anna's garage. From the Hubba Bubba teams point of view, it had not been an epic race, just more of the same. Not so for Anna's team and Joss wanted to be a part of it.

It wasn't an epic party yet, but it was getting there. The team had finished the highest it ever had. Everyone knew it was Anna, her skill as a driver and attention to detail that had been responsible. There were a few members of the press still hanging around, but most had left to cover the other teams.

Jochen's cell phone rang.

He said a few words in German, smiled and hung up.

"Come," he said to the three women. "You are just as much a part of this, come."

Jochen made his way to his niece and spoke into her ear. She said something in German to him. He shook his head and pointed at the door. Joss began to smile.

"Here we go," Joss told Delta and Clary. "Stick close, this is going to be wild."

"Well I guess that's it then," Hal, Anna's team owner said. "Rosy has made her decision. No hard feelings Anna, without you we would be still on the bottom."

He held his arms out and Anna hugged him. She hugged every member of her team, then tears in her eyes, she was reluctantly dragged out onto the abandoned and now lonely pit lane.

"Who did we sign with Uncle Jochen?" Anna asked in German.

"You'll see," he said as they kept walking.

People in each garage they came to looked at her expectantly as she came by. But they kept walking to a very noisy and loud Hubba Bubba garage. Jochen pushed her back hard so she stumbled inside. The place erupted.

"Are you kidding me?" Delta said. "Richard said Rosy hadn't even called him."

"She didn't have to," Jochen said. He walked in to more cheers.

Constance, the Sky Sports journalist, knowing of Anna and Joss's close relationship had shadowed them to the garage and the crew were filming. Constance began to talk rapidly into her head phone set.

A pair of gentle hands placed a jacket around her shoulders.

"Welcome to the team," Richard yelled into her ear in German. She looked around and he was walking away.

Anna took the jacket off and looked at it. Then she quickly put it on and zipped it tight. Jochen already had his on.

"Texas! Look!!" She yelled. Then she jumped high and screamed. Both women rushed each other and were soon hugging. Joss had tears in her eyes.

Alerted by Sky Sports, the garage was soon under attack from the media. Finally, Gunther found a bull horn and let loose with a loud blast from it.

He waved Anna, Jochen and George over. He made sure Anna was standing on one side of him, George on the other.

"It is with great pleasure," Gunther began "that the Hubba Bubba racing team announces the signing of George to a three year extension to his contract, the signing of Jochen Kneble as team manager and...his niece, Anna Kneble as our new driver!"

Once again the garage erupted as the teams started cheering.

Constance made sure her crew got a shot of the three Piper girls, their arms around each other, beaming at Anna in pride. Then Anna jumping into their arms for a group hug.

"I don't know how you pulled that one off," Hal the Red Bull team manager said to Gunther. "Rosy was listening but not committing to anything. I'm not sure she even talked to Anna about it."

"Of course, we had internal discussions about the possibility," Gunther said. "But the boss is adamant about the wait until after the season rule we have. We hadn't even talked with her or Rosy. Honest Hal. A little bird did tell me Anna was not pleased she would have to go to your farm team though."

"Ya well, that one was out of my hands," Hal said. "You know how my boss, Berger can be."

"Ya, it would be good for you guys if he was to slowly fade away," Gunther said. "You might be beating us if he stayed out of things.

Seriously, an hour after the race, Rosy called the boss, made an offer and..."

"I ever going to meet this boss of yours?" Hal asked.

"I doubt it," Gunther said. "He's not called Crazy Canuck for no reason."

"What? I thought that was some kind of code," Hal said.

"Ya it was. Good luck next year Hal, you'er going to need it."

It had been several months since Joss and Richard had been afforded some time alone. They made the best of it, flying in Richards plane up through central America from Brazil and over to Trinidad for a leisurely week there. Next up to Oklahoma and on up to the Dakotas where they spent two days with Karen on her father's ranch..

Cal, Karen's father, had a paved runway and hanger down from the house. He had built an RV 10, low wing, fast experimental airplane and he and Richard spent all their free time talking and tinkering with their planes.

The studio had asked Karen to do a Netflix series. A spin off of her Jan Fields movie character and Karen had agreed. Both women discussed that together. While intrigued, Joss declined on appearing in the pilot show. She had decided acting was over for her.

On the third day, Joss and Richard were back in the air. Even though it was fall, the flights so far, had been nice and the Great Plains a change from the more normal mountains and foothills of the Rockies Routes they normally flew.

They garnered some attention from the local aviation crowds at the small airports and towns they landed at. This was more due to the Canadian registration marks on Richards airplane than who Joss was. In fact, dressed in normal people clothing and affecting her Texas drawl, nobody even recognized her.

Most owners of small aircraft, rarely fly more than two or three hours per week, so seeing a Canadian registered aircraft at their small airports on the prairies and finding out they had originated their flight in Brazil was something special for these people. They were always treated warmly and many times were shown local attractions. Attractions that went under the radar, because they were not on the *must visit* tourist lists.

Some days Joss was in the left seat piloting the airplane, some days Richard. At one point, near Bismarck North Dakota, the engine began to run a little rough, so they landed, refuelled as normal and obtained a tie down spot. It was still a warm part of fall, so Richard removed the cowling and began to poke around.

It did not take long to find the problem. A spark plug wire had come loose and shorted itself out, causing damage to the lead and to the electronic ignition module that was operating at the time. Having a backup ignition module, they had switched to it in flight and of course, now that ignition module was damaged as well.

The local Forward Operating Base operator had come over to see what the issue was. Saw the exotic engine installed in the Piper and asked if he could help.

"Ya" Richard said. "Is there a NAPA parts store close by? I have to pick up a couple of ignition models, new plugs and wires."

Richard was given directions and a courtesy car. Off he and Joss went. The first stop was of course for some breakfast at a local diner in Bismarck, they had left early from the last town. Then to the auto parts store, which Joss had little interest in. Joss wanted to check out the local mall, so of course an hour or so was spent doing that, which Richard was little interested in. And a stop at the local Pizza Hut for some pizza and soda take out.

They dropped off the loaner car and headed back to the airplane, shopping bags and pizza boxes in hand. Richard dug out his always present small tool bag from the baggage compartment and with a little help from Joss, started removing and replacing parts.

"I sure hope one of you folks is a certificated aircraft mechanic," a voice behind them said.

Standing there was the FOB manager, a couple of guys in coveralls, and a guy in business casual dress. The man who spoke had a dark blue blazer with FAA written on it.

"Is there some kind of problem?" Richard asked.

"There is if you don't have a mechanics certification," the FAA man said. He introduced himself as Bob to Richard and showed him his credentials. "Plus, I need to see your pilots licence, your aircraft registry and insurance papers and your log books."

"Sure no problem," Richard said. He went to the airplane cockpit and pulled out the small file folder that held all that information, handing it to Bob.

"When was the last time this engine was overhauled and how many hours are on it?" The Bob asked.

"Um...at a guess, about thirty six hundred," Richard said.

"What is the suggested TBO of this engine?"

"They weren't sure, but initially said twenty five hundred for both the engine and the geared reduction unit." Richard answered.

"So you are well over then," Bob said. Now he began to go in-depth into Richards repair log book. Noting that all the annual inspections had been done on or beforetime. All the periodic maintenance intervals had been completed. A list of each and every adjustment, no matter how minor had been logged.

"Each of these entries are signed by you as owner/pilot, is that correct?" The Bob said.

Now the FOB man, the men in the coveralls and the business dressed man were nudging each other and smiling.

Bob looked over Richards pilot licence carefully and the ownership documents and insurance forms. There were some more documents with prominent Transport Canada markings on them, that were inspected. Then the US travel and entry permit was gone over.

"Mind if I have a look at the aircraft?" Bob asked.

"Make your day," Richard answered.

Followed by the gaggle of others and now a growing crowd of interested local pilots, Bob made a tour of the outside of the plane. He basically did a preflight examination of the control surfaces and noted what notice stickers were in place. Bringing out a tape measure, he measured the small identification numbers and jotted down the results of that, again eliciting a round of elbow poking.

Joss began to wonder if maybe Richard had broken some rule and that they would be unable to continue their journey home.

Most American aircraft had large identification numbers that would take up half of the side of the aircraft. These were small and located high on the tail. All of the marker and landing lights were inspected.

"Nice," Bob said. "LEDs. That must have set you back a wad of cash."

"Nah," Richard said. "Couple of hundred bucks from Amazon."

The inspector ran his hand along the side of the aircraft.

"Nice paint." He said.

"Ya..did it myself," Richard said. "Took a weekend and five gallons of high gloss enamel house paint. All in, about a thousand dollars."

Now there were murmurings coming from the pilots in the crowd. It normally cost sixteen or more thousand to paint an airplane and at least a month to accomplish it. Joss herself was learning things from these exchanges.

Climbing up on the wing, the inspector noted the rather large sticker in French and English mounted beside the cockpit entry stating the airplane was an experimental aircraft and sat in the copilots seat.

"Nice interior," he said.

"Ya, I got a local gal to reupholster everything for me, she did a pretty good job eh?" Richard said. "Im happy with it anyway. Set me back five grand."

It was twenty thousand to do that normally. This was another cost that Joss had not known about.

"Nice glass panel," the inspector said. "Full IFR panel, auto pilot, twin radios, an HF radio, ADSB in and out. Sweet. Let me guess, you installed it yourself?" Bob was smiling now.

"Yup," Richard said. "All the latest and greatest gismos, for a fraction of the cost. Nice when you can install experimental equipment, less money and more features."

Coming back out, Bob opened the baggage compartment and looked inside. He saw a five gallon container with fluid in it and tubes running out of it.

"Ok," he said. "That one has me stumped."

"Deicer," Richard said. "I don't look to fly into icing situations, but things happen sometimes right?"

He took Bob around showing him how the deicer was distributed to the propeller blades, leading edges of the wings and the tail surfaces. He explained how the system works and for how long it would work.

"Came in handy that one day over the Greenland ice pack hey hun?" Joss said. "Was a night flight too, could have ended up being a bad night in a hurry."

She had said it loud enough so the onlookers could hear.

Bob whistled.

"I'll bet," he said. "That's a forty grand upgrade."

"Nah," Richard said. "About five, maybe. Took longer to figure out how to run all the lines than to install it. Works pretty good, but still, wouldn't want to fly into known icing conditions."

Now they were back at the engine. Bob asked a bunch of questions about it and after inquiring into the cost, whistled again. Richard explained that to replace the engine that normally came with this airplane would cost around forty thousand dollars but that this one had come in at around twelve. Joss was rapidly beginning to understand now why Richard had done what he had done to the Cherokee.

"I notice you have an advanced pilots certificate," Bob said. "Which would explain the two hundred fifty horse power engine, but why a fixed pitch prop and not a constant speed?"

"I have an advanced licence because I fly other complex aircraft," Richard said. "Not for this one. We are regulated by speed, retractible landing gear and constant speed propellers in Canada, not horse power and the others. No way this thing will ever get above two hundred and fifty miles an hour, it has fixed landing gear and a fixed prop, so Texas there with her non complex aircraft licence is legal to fly it. Add tricycle landing gear to the equation and the plane is eligible for the Pilot/Owner category."

"So, what's the issue with the engine then?" Bob asked.

Richard showed him the faulty plug wire and that while the electronic ignition modules, spark plugs and other wires would most likely be fine, he would change them all just in case.

"We have about a thousand miles to go before we are home," Richard said. "No sense in pushing it."

"What parts are you using?" The inspector asked.

"Normal General Motors stuff," Richard said. "It's a GM manufactured motor after all. Can get parts anyplace just about."

"Ok, well you carry on then while I finish up my paperwork." Bob said.

In less than an hour, Richard had replaced the spark plugs, ignition wires and ignition modules. He received a nod from Bob when Richard asked him if he could test the engine. It fired up, much faster than a normal aircraft engine would, and was purring like a lion right way. He revved it up some, then taxied at slow speed to the run up area and tested it some more there, received permission to do a high speed taxi test, then came back and shut it down.

Bob gave him permission to reinstall the cowling and to make a test flight. An hour later Richard was back on the ground. In front of Bob, he filled out the log book documenting the work done and the results of the test flight and signed it.

Bob signed off on it.

"So," Bob said turning to the crowd of onlookers. "Basically, what Richard has done to the old girl here, is except for the basic airframe, totally rebuilt and upgraded her for what about sixty grand? He only spent thirty grand to buy it. So for around ninety grand, he has basically a supped up new airplane. To do that normally here, would have set him back two hundred grand easy.

"You guys should get off your asses and start lobbying my bosses to allow the same thing here. Maybe you will be able to fly more than a couple of hours a month then. See you Richard, ma-am, have a good flight home."

The FOB and maintenance people surrounded Bob as he walked away, demanding answers. A few of the pilots who were watching everything came up to Richard and asked him more about his plane.

"In Canada, the government realized that there were many very good older airplanes just sitting around," Richard said. "Sure, in major population centres, there are many certified aircraft mechanics. But what about the out of the way places, which are many in Canada, in fact, for much of the part of the year, the only access to and from some remote areas is by air. You guys all know how expensive it is to properly maintain the airplanes and how much time it takes to do it.

"So, they came up with a solution. If the aircraft is a single engine, non complex airplane more than five years old, the owner of the aircraft, if a certified and current pilot, can maintain and repair their own aircraft. We have to apply for it and put a sticker on it proclaiming it and we take full responsibility for the work.

"At times, I do have an aircraft mechanic look into something for me, but rarely. Essentially, we have the same rights as an operator and builder of an experimental aircraft, except we can't modify the airframe itself. We can install non certified equipment, like I have with my avionics and engine. With the engine though I had to obtain a sign off from Transport Canada, our FAA, though, as well as the de icing equipment I designed and installed.

"Oh ya, I also use what ever kind of gasoline I can find. This is a flex fuel engine, like your car engines. I prefer high test car gas, as long as the alcohol content is around ten percent. Unfortunately here, I'll probably use the leaded av gas on site."

"Hell how many gallons you need?" One of the pilots asked. "I've got an empty one hundred gallon slip tank in my pickup. I'll run ya into town to pick some up."

Joss volunteered to do the fuel run, leaving Richard to show off his plane and answer more questions.

"You guys really fly to Greenland or was he shitting us," the man asked as they drove to town. He was a local farmer named Will Brandt. He was about Richards age and the large slip tank in the truck bed and the items in the cab, told Joss he was a farmer.

"Richard has made several cross Atlantic crossings in that airplane," Joss said. "I was with him when we used the Russia route to do an across the world flight. In fact, he is a certified flight instructor and he taught me to fly on that trip."

They arrived back at the plane and Richard and Will began to fuel it up. An impromptu party had been organized and everyone was soon headed to a local barbecue hall, that was quickly filling up as news of the visitors spread.

Soon the food and booze was flowing, Joss looked over at Richard and he nodded his head. She went to the bar and grabbed some beer bringing it back to the table. Richard kept drinking cola. Richard asked Will about the Americanized German being spoken around them.

"Ya," he said. "Most of our families came from Russia back in the old days."

"Really," Richard said. "So did mine."

"What part?" Will asked him in German.

"My family, from about halfway between Kieve and Oddesa," Richard said.

"Mine were from the Volga."

"Richard Rosenbaum," Richard said. The men shook hands.

"Joslyn Litzenberger," Joss said in passable German. "I think my folks came from around Odessa some place. We ended up in Texas."

"Small world hey?" Will said.

"Ya, I always say, if you have a German last name and come from Southern Saskatchewan, chances are I'm related to you," Richard said.

Will laughed. "We say the same thing here, but for North Dakota."

A band was setting up on stage now. There were four members of the band. A drummer, a bass guitarist and two guitarists. One of the guitar players and the bass player looked to be brothers. Joss thought she might recognize them as a country group that had done quite good until dropping out of sight.

"My moms mother was actually born in North Dakota," Richard said. "Along the border some place."

"Know what her maiden name was?" Will asked.

"Kline I think, ya Kline," Richard said.

Will called a woman over, it was Janet, his wife.

"You have any people married into a Canuck family?" Will asked.

"Hmm....Ya, my grandmothers sister married a guy named George back in the late twenties." Janet said.

The band started to play, drawing Joss's attention. Now she knew who they were.

"Hey, that's the Kline Brothers isn't it," Joss said. "They could have been huge if they had stayed with it."

"Ya, my brothers did all right," Janet said. "Made a lot of money, but got tired of being on the road all the time."

"Don't I know that one," Joss said, then caught what she had just said. "I was a back up singer back when I was young and dumb. Was fun for a couple of years but.."

"Ya," Richard said. "She met some crazy Canadian and packed it in."

Joss pulled him tight and kissed him.

"Nice save," she whispered into his ear.

"Well, it would appear we are cousins then," Richard said. "My mom always said the Kline Brothers were her cousins."

"My grand dad used to ship booze, horses and gasoline across the border with your grandad," Janet said.

"Ya, I heard about that too," Richard said.

"Hey," Will said, "My dad's sister married a Rosenbaum, from Regina."

Richard smiled and shrugged his shoulders.

"Ya, I know big families, pretty soon everyone is related to everyone," Will said.

The band had stopped playing for a quick beer break. Joss saw how well the band played together and how professional they sounded. Janet stood and walked up to the band and talked to one of them.

"Hey Joslyn, come on up here, we could use a female voice tonight," one of the band members said. The crowd began to look around. It being a local crowd who basically knew each other, Joss stuck out and they began to clap, encouraging her to go.

Joss looked at Richard, her eyes pleading. It had been a long time since she had sung just for the sake of singing.

"You sure Joss?" He asked.

"I'll be low key, it's been a while since I was on stage live." She said.

She let Janet drag her by the arm and made like she was reluctantly being coerced into coming to sing. Joss conferred with the guitar player and they started with "Jolene," an easy and well known Dolly Parton song. Then testing her knowledge, he began the starting notes of "Heart of Glass" by Blondie, and Joss was able to pick up on it right away.

The crowd noticed how well Joss sang and cheered loudly. Joss bowed and smiled.

Joss then for the next song sang "Crazy" by Patsy Kline, and her talent really started to come forth. Now warmed up, she didn't wait for the band to start, she started right in on "Harper Valley P.T.A." It took the band a couple of bars before they caught up to her, and by then she was strutting her stuff around the stage. The crowd was loving it.

The band was picking up on her energy and she was soon singing duets with the guitar player. The crowd was having a great time.

The band took a break, and Joss rushed over and gave Richard a big hug and a kiss.

"Oh this is so much fun!" She said. "The guys are great aren't they?"

"Shit, you're pretty good," Will said. "You said you were just a backup singer?"

"It was just some rock band I think. I didn't do any country stuff with them," Joss said.

"Yeah," Richard said. "She had pretty much packed it in by the time I met her. She hasn't sung on stage with a band for a long time."

Janet came back to the table.

"You're pretty good for a backup singer Joslyn," she said. "You should have stayed with it."

"Ah, that scene was getting old ya know?" Joss said. "I much prefer hanging around boring Super Canuck here."

Joss had a beer and the band was back on stage. She had her head on Richards shoulder and a smile on her face.

"What do think folks?" The guitar player said. "Should Joslyn from Texas come back up here or what?"

The crowd started to cheer and Joss headed back to the stage. Janet hurried up and spoke to her brother quickly.

The band broke into "Roxanne" by the Police, and Joss swung right into it. She was having fun and so was the band. As soon as the first two notes of the next song were played, it was like a switch had gone off inside Joss and Richard muttered *"Oh shit"*. It was Gloria

She could sing it in her sleep, and she was right into her performance mode now. At this point, she saw how the members of the band all grinned at each other knowingly. The crowd was becoming quiet. Joss turned her back on the crowd and began to sing, acapello, her cover of *The Power of Love*. The band softly joined in, letting her high powered vocals come to the fore. During portions of the chorus, she pointed her arms to Richard and the love she felt could be seen by all. She put her heart and soul into the whole song.

At the end of the song, Joss was breathless, the crowd was silent.

"Well folks," the guitar player said. "Is that anyway to greet our guest? Academy Award and multiple Grammy winner Joss Lynn!"

The crowd erupted. Flashes from cell phone cameras were going off all over.

"Woa, woa up there ya-all," Joss said in her Texas drawl. "Ya-all know the Kline Brothers is as good as I am! In fact, I'd say they're better!"

To distract everyone from their star-struck state, she started singing "Truckers Heaven" one of their most popular songs and the band followed her. All of them grooving to it. What followed was epic. A mix of Kline Brothers country and Joss Lynn rock and contemporary. The assembled crowd received a free two hour epic concert from two world class acts. The very walls were shaking. The beer was flowing, the crowd howling for more.

Finally their voices and bodies tired, they had to stop. Joss came back to the table and chugged a whole bottle of beer down, sweat was pouring down her face, her shirt soaked. But she was happier than Richard had ever seen her.

Putting two tables together the band and their wives joined them.

"Wow, that was fun," Joss said. "I forgot how much fun performing can be."

"Ya," the guitar player said. "It's some different from a crowd of thirty thousand in an arena in some city someplace in the middle of a two hundred day tour."

"Ya," Joss said. "That's a job, not a passion. This was playing for the sake of playing. Totally different."

She had her head on Richards shoulder and was stroking his arm. Taking in the crowd, the surroundings, joining in on the horror and stupid stories from touring days with the band members, all the while laughing at how dumb they had been.

It was well past midnight when they left. It wasn't all that far to the hotel and it was a warm night. Richard and Joss chose to walk. They had the street to them selves. It was a typical small prairie town that rolled up the sidewalks after midnight most nights. The sky was clear and the stars were shinning brightly.

"Do you miss it?" Richard asked.

"Sometimes," Joss said. "Like tonight. Tonight was fun. Most of the time it's not though. I go through the motions...."

Richard gave her a quick squeeze. They took off the next afternoon, nobody noticed.

Returning to Canada and landing in Regina, Richard rented a car. They drove to where his ancestors had begun life in Canada, a half hour drive east of Regina. It was flat and dry. The only trees anywhere, the ones planted around the farm houses themselves. Joss looked around her. She could just barely see the tops of the tallest buildings of Regina in the distance. A Little over two miles to the south was a town of around two thousand people. It had three of the classic wooden grain elevators common throughout the prairies on both sides of the border. There was a community hall and a combination gas station convenience store and not much else. Joss noticed the town had the same name as the town in Germany that Anna was from.

"Shit," Joss said. "I thought West Texas was dry and desolate. This is on a whole different level."

"Winter blows in late November," Richard said. "And stays until late April, sometimes the middle of May. The blizzards can last for days and thirty below is the norm, not the exception. Imagine what it was like for them back in the eighteen nineties. No electricity, no natural gas or even wood to burn at times. Cut off for weeks sometimes. Lots of people went crazy Joss. Whole families would die after a bad storm. The summer would hit around a hundred degrees some days."

Joss was taking in her surroundings. It was laid out like a typical eastern European settlement. Ten houses on one side of a large wide street, ten houses on the other, a church and a small school at the back end and in the centre of the street. The church had a round dome on it instead of the more common steeple. Each house had a barn or quonset hut behind them. One hundred yards away and down a hill, Richard took her to a grotto, an out door church, that had been cut out of the side of the hill side. A large statue of the Virgin Mary was prominent on a ledge on the hill. Another fifty yards to the north, a small creek meandered and on the hill opposite, a large metal cross made out of steel railroad rails dominated the skyline.

Richard showed her a memorial plaque that had the names of the founders of settlement listed on it. That it had been established in 1892 by settlers who had come from the Beresan district in what is now Ukraine.

"They had so little back then," Joss said. "Even my people. They had it tough Richard."

Joss had grown up hearing stories of her own ancestors when they first came to Texas around that same time. How they had struggled to grow crops even to just feed themselves the first years. At least there were plenty of scrub trees they could use to keep warm in the much milder winters of Texas. Richard told her that the first year, his people had lived in canvas tents and that his ancestor had dug into the side of the hill some ten feet, then made front walls of sod for their first house. They collected cow dung to burn.

So very different than today, with television, internet, running water, indoor plumbing, central heating and cooling, that everyone took for granted today, non existent in those days. Even something as simple as a refrigerator to keep food cold in the summer, or electricity, was not available.

"Ya, they didn't have all the things we do now Joss," Richard said. "They made it all happen though. They started it all. And really, they were just as rich as we are Joss, maybe more. They had what is really important. They had each other."

Now Joss began to understand how not only the people of Texas and the western USA were so tough and self reliant but Canadians as well. They had to be or Mother Nature would kill them. Why they were so religious. Not only to commune with God, but to gather and socialize.

Flying home west along the Trans-Canada Highway the next day, they had good WiFi coverage. Richard now knew Joss and Delta had been working on something as far back as Brazil, and now that she had good wifi, Joss had initiated a video conference call with Delta and Clary.

"We'll missy, you sure made the headlines," Delta said, holding up the front page of a gossip column. There, taking up the whole front page, was Joss performing with the Kline Brothers.

"Oh give me a break!" Joss said. "It was fun, the Kline Brothers are pros, we had a blast."

"Ya ok, the promoters and sponsors are not all that pissed off," Delta said.

"Hey," Joss said. "They need me, I don't need them."

"I've run the numbers and the time commitment," Clary said. "It all looks good Joss, just what we wanted."

Joss took a quick look at the instrument panel.

"We should be home in a couple of hours," she said. "I'll look it all over then ok? But if you guys say it's ok, it'll be ok."

She signed off, then spent some time looking out the side window. She took a deep breath. Not sure how Richard would react to what she was about to tell him.

"So, this is what is going to happen," she began.

She explained how Piper was going to launch a turboprop aircraft to compete with Cessnas. They planned to launch it at the annual Sun and Fun fly in near their factory complex in Florida. They wanted Joss and the girls to film a commercial and for Joss to sing for it. They were going to give the girls outright ownership and the usual freebies for five years of one airplane each. They had made the same offer to Joss.

"I have access to a very nice PC-12," Joss said. She was smiling. "That is a much better airplane and besides, I like my little Archer better anyway. It can go more places. Anyway, they are paying me very well, it's a one time deal and I really want to do it Richard."

He nodded his head. Joss felt he was uncertain if this was a good idea or not.

"Really Richard," she said. "This will be my swan song. I owe the girls for everything they do for me. After this, I want to have a couple of brats with a hunk I ran into on my travels and disappear."

"That might be kind of hard to do Joss," Richard said. "What with my F1 commitments."

"Oh faster than you might think lover boy," Joss said. "Some new hotty will come along that wants and needs the attention. I will soon be yesterdays headlines."

"Well," he said. "I guess we should get married then."

"Not unless you really want to," Joss said. Although her heart was pounding so hard she thought it might burst out of her chest, she didn't let on. "It's not a big deal for me at least. I know you love me. I also know you are good with kids. Maybe our kids can have sort of a normal life. What do you think?"

Richard shrugged his shoulders and smiled. Joss slugged him, much harder than she normally did.

"No, you are not getting away that easy this time," Joss said. "You say it, not shrug your shoulders and smile."

Richard looked over at her. Both her right and her left foot were bouncing, hard.

"Yes Joslyn Litzenberger," he said. "I will be a father for your children and will love you and them. And be a royal pain in the ass for you until I die."

She reached over, hugged him hard and kissed him tenderly.

"Good thing I have a good autopilot on this thing," he said.

As he expected, she slugged him again, this time just a tap.

Chapter Fifteen

Joss was a half hour out from her airstrip. She wished the three days she had spent with Richard had just been for them alone. That was not to be however. There were last minute details she had to handle and Richard had some trends he had been watching for years start to turn his way.

He had told her to take his girl and fly to Texas, he would find a way to meet her in Florida. As Joss taxied to her hanger after landing, she saw four of the new Piper turbo props parked beside it. One had an outline map of Idaho painted on the side, the other, California.

There were also half a dozen semi trailers parked in the yard. Some had cables coming out of them, others, loaded with equipment. Four airstream travel trailers and three busses converted to RV's. There were lighting stands and cameras, boom mikes and about a hundred people doing various things.

A camera was following her taxi progress to the hanger. It filmed the shut down, Joss climbing out and doing a quick check of the outside, then push it into the hanger, unaided. She came back out with her duffle bag over one shoulder, her purse over the other. She casually walked by the turbo props, pulling her aviator sunglasses down to gaze at them as she went by, then casually walked into the house.

"All we are missing is the lions, tigers and elephants out on the yard," Joss said.

She tossed her duffle bag on the floor by the kitchen table, her purse on top of it. She hugged Delta, then Clary and made to head for the refrigerator, but Clary handed her a glass of vodka.

"I was watching you walk in Joss," Clary said. "The director looked like he was happy with the shots they took of you landing and looking at the planes."

Joss shrugged her shoulders.

"So," she said after taking a sip. "What else is going on besides the zoo out there?"

"Well," Delta said. "We are both now certified to fly the turbo props."

"And we have been practicing the Sun and Fun demonstration routine," Clary said. "It's going to be awesome!"

"Can't wait to see it," Joss said. "But I suppose, like normal, I'm going to hate it by the end of the week."

Clary came up and kissed Joss tenderly on the cheek.

"What the hell was that for?" Joss said.

Clary pulled out her cell phone and hit play, showing Joss singing The Power of Love with the Kline Brothers.

"What's the big deal," Joss said. "You've seen me sing that song a couple of hundred times."

"Not like that Joss," Clary said. "So much passion. I could almost see your heart coming out of your chest. The real Joss, the Joss I have come to love like my sister."

"Nor I Joss," Delta said. "That whole impromptu set. I have never seen you perform like that Joss. Never."

Joss sat down at the table looking at her drink. Both her legs still. Her emotions running high remembering the night, the joy she had felt.

"Because I wasn't working," she finally said. Her voice just over a whisper. "I was with some truly remarkable musicians, who were just playing because they wanted to..."

"And because I was with the man I love with every fibre of my body, in a public place together without him disappearing," she said.

Joss tossed back the glass of vodka, grabbed her purse and duffle bag and headed to her bedroom.

It was early the next morning, the sun was up, but still cool. Joss walked out of the house, her hair pulled into a pony tail that came out of the back of her Piper ball cap. Her Piper blazer open just enough to show some cleavage and putting her aviator glasses on.

"Alright Ya-all!" She said. "Show me what ya got."

Cory, the director, hurried over and escorted her to a small row of chairs with a video monitor. She watched the footage of the planes doing their routine. She made them rewind and start again, this time her right toe started to tap out a beat. The third time she made them run it, her head started to move.

"Ok," she said. "Get those planes in the air," she said. "I need to see it and feel it."

She made the girls do it twice.

"Ok, tell them to rotate for a bit," Joss said to the director. "Get the camera planes in the air. Have your crew ready to go."

"Ok, full rehearsal," Joss said.

The director rushed around getting everything ready. He asked Joss if she was ready, she began singing Retribution, her spy thriller song. In time to the aircrafts maneuvers, Joss began to move. It was a five minute routine and when it ended, she was spent.

"Ok if I have a half hour or so before the next take?" Joss said.

"Um...Ya sure," Cory said.

The girls landed and, waiting for them, Joss walked with them to the house to cool off and change their clothing. After they had grabbed something to drink, they put on clean new uniforms, did their hair and makeup, and made their way back outside. The director looked up from his monitor, his editor watching beside him.

"Did we get enough aerial footage?" Joss asked.

Cory asked his editor about it, and they spent a moment jogging through the footage on the monitor. "Can you also dub the music in?"

"Shouldn't be an issue," the editor said.

"Um... Miss Lynn?" Cory said, looking up finally.

"Ya ok," Joss said. "I know it was crap. But that is what rehearsals are for right?"

"Um...Well...If you really want to Miss Lynn, we can do another one. But it's fine right now," the director said. "We have to edit in the music and a little bit of footage integration between the aerial shots and your on the ground footage. But other than that. I am happy."

"Oh, ok then," Joss said. She started walking toward the hanger.

"Hey!" She yelled to the two Piper pilots standing there. "I want to try out one of those puppies. And not one of the girl's planes."

"Um...Miss Lynn?" Johnson one of the Piper pilots said. "These aircraft are much more powerful than your Archer ma-am."

"Oh cut the crap," Joss said. "I'm certified to fly a PC-12, if anything, this thing will be easier to fly."

"Yum, nice view," Richard said. Four cameras had been rolling when Joss sang her song, they caught every side of her, all of her movements, the song coordinated with the fly bye of the airplanes.

The song was the climax of the five minute promotional video. Piper had sent it to all the aviation television shows, internet influencers and Piper clubs all around the world. The final shot was of Joss her head held high, her right fist pushed in the air as both planes streaked by at low level and high speed. The Piper logo taking up the whole screen for the last thirty seconds.

"That for sure is going to be tough to match live," Joss said. "Oh well, the acoustics are going to be shit anyway."

They were sitting in their hotel room in Lakeland Florida. Richard had flown in with Sandra. She was there with her PC-12 to showcase for Pilatus. Anna was there with her Diamond for the same reason. Of course, the venue would also provide for the unveiling of the new F1 and F2 cars in the new colour schemes and the names of the aircraft companies promptly displayed on the large rear wings of the cars.

"We may not have the video," Richard said. "But we have the race cars."

The couple had made the most of the week. No body knew who Richard was, and Joss dressed like a normal farm girl, so no one paid attention to them. There were a lot of exhibits to see and an almost constant air show occurring overhead.

Richard spent some time looking over the newest avionics and radio products. The annual event drew over a hundred thousand visitors for the week it was on. It was a must attend visit for many in the General Aviation crowd. From Cirrus, Cessna, Piper and Bonanza, to, Pilatus, embrasure and Bombardier, almost all the major business and general aviation manufactures had product on display.

War birds from WW1 Fockers and Spads, WW2 Spitfires, Hurricanes, P51 Mustangs, Corvairs, P38 Lightnings, a B17 and B25 bomber. Rare FW 190 and Meshersmit 109's from Germany and one each of the last flying Lancaster and Mosquito bombers. Each flew demonstration flights over head. Saber and Phantom jets from Korea and Vietnam eras made an appearance. The Royal Canadian Airforce Snow Birds did an acrobatic routine.

Delta, Clary, Anna and Sandra had to be at their companies exhibits for most of the day. But at night, the six of them would link up in one of their hotel rooms. Richard would even come for an hour or so.

Piper had paid a hefty price to be placed in the last airshow slot Friday. This would be followed by the official unveiling of the planes with Joss doing her thing. After that, Joss and Richard were off to places unknown for a while.

Friday, Richard had the day to himself. Anna and Sandra would be at their display most of the day. Delta and Clary going over last minute details of their demonstration flight and Joss? She was capable of doing her own disappearing act when she wanted to. Especially just before a big performance, which this was turning out to be.

A stage had been set up in front of the main taxiway about mid point of the runway. It had tarps enclosing it completely and a barricaded area in front. At intervals through out the day, the band could be heard doing sound checks and instrument checks.

The sun was starting to go down and the air show announcer, announced a one hour break, before the Piper demonstration and Joss's performance. Richard collected Sandra and Anna and they found a spot on the left side of the stage, that would provide them with a good view of both the air show and the stage.

A crowd of around fifty thousand began to gather. Anticipation was rising. Two turbine engines were heard to be starting in the distance.

"And now ladies and gentlemen," the announcer said. "Sun and Fun in conjunction with Piper Aircraft are pleased to announce, Joss Lynn and Texas!"

The tarps were flung apart, the band began to play. Joss' plane, Texas, was on stage broad side to the crowd. Joss came out and deftly climbed down the wing. As her foot hit the stage, she began to sing Flyin' High, the cover song for her new album of the same name.

She was classic Joss, except she had a Piper ball cap on her head and a Piper jacket unzipped down to her navel. She was all over the stage, interacting with the band and the crowd. It was loud, it was fast and the crowd was loving it. The stage manager got Joss's attention by coming on the stage and waving his arms.

The drummer started to tap a little tap on his snare. The rest of the band was silent.

"And now Ladies and gentlemen!" The air show announcer said. "California and Idaho!"

Both the airplanes flashed by side by side just above the runway at high speed. One carried on straight while the other did a high rate climbing turn to head the other way. The band broke out with the song from the video commercial, it started a little slower than normal. Both planes came by and did some of the classical air show maneuvers like wing overs and high over shoots, then as they disappeared once more, Joss started in on the explosive and emotional ending to the song.

At its crescendo, Both planes crossed each other at high speed right above the runway, wings sideways to show off the full fuselage, then quickly levelled out and rose straight up in the air. Fireworks went off and the song was over.

"Whew eee!!" Joss belted out. Her much more powerful sound system drowning out the airshow announcer. "Wasn't that more fun than chasin' a Hogg in the pen?

"Why California and Idaho make Texas look like a country bumpkin. Now Piper asked me to join them in this little show of theirs. I flew one and wooeee, it is some nice bird. Fast, maneuverable, mmm, mmm, just what a girl wants. Sometimes.

"Nope, for us country girls, we like slow, easy and reliable, hey girls? Those are the keepers. Fast and smooth, well they are just for fun. Am I right girls?"

The women in the crowd started cheering.

"Now, I'm sure ya-all 'member the formation flight we made two years back from Texas to Brazil? Ya-all 'member that beautiful navy blue '63 Cherokee 235 that was in the lead right? Well, the powers that be decided us girls needed an experienced pilot to shepherd us. And well, to be honest, he was a major hunk ladies, let me tell you what hey? Wink wink nudge nudge.

"On the way back, we had a different lead, a Piper Seneca, whose pilot has over two thousand hours of flight time, most of it in the Seneca and most of it long distance commutes, sometimes to and from Europe.

"Come on up here Alberta. Come on, don't ya-ll be shy now. Ladies and gentlemen, Sandra Hamilton, the pilot of Alberta and the wife of four time and current formula one world champion, George Hamilton!"

Sandra came up on the stage, Joss warmly hugged her.

"Now, I have a confession to make folks," Joss said, keeping her left arm around Sandra's waist. "On the trip back to Texas, I was not flying alone. I had a pilot with almost two thousand hours flying with me. A pilot who has made several cross Atlantic trips solo, shared the flying duties with me. George Hamiltons' new team mate, and rising star, Anna Kneble! Come on up here Anna!"

"Wow, what a fantastic crowd!" Anna said after hugging both Joss and Sandra. They each had an arm around the others waists. "I am truly humbled, to be here, a young, little back woods German girl, with two women, super star women. It is truly an honour for me."

Joss noticed Sandra being reserved and knew Sandra wasn't used to the media attention like the other two were, so stayed quiet.

"Just to put it into the ball park for ya-all," Joss said. "Not only does Sandra function as Georges wife, she is his agent, his travel agent, his head personal assistant and the mother of his two teenaged children! Plus she is a fantastic pilot. Now, that folks, that humbles even me."

An suv pulled up next to the the stage then.

"And here they are!" Joss said. "California and Idaho, Delta and Clary. My two best friends!"

There were hugs all around, and the crowd was eating up how much the five women liked each other.

The girls formed a line, with Delta and Clary in the centre, Sandra and Anna on the sides. Joss strode forward and lowered her head. The lights on the stage dimmed.

"A while ago" Joss said. "I was searching for just the right song for the opening credits for Stardust, my new movie. I ran into an outstanding young singer songwriter in New Mexico. Chooli Bitsilly of the Navajo Nation. She wrote this song and agreed to let me record it."

Starting first with the drummer, then the guitars, after the first few notes. It was the opening credit song to Joss's soon to be released spy thriller movie Stardust.

It was all about the struggles, the passion and the power of women. Joss sung it with every bit of her that she could give. At the end, she turned and sung the last words facing the girls, her arms outstretched and they ran to her. The lights went out. The crowd exploded in cheering.

And then it happened.

Shots, multiple shots from multiple directions rang out. At the first shot, Sandra had Anna by the arm and had flung her beneath Joss' plane. Joss and the two others were already face down and scrambling the same direction.

"Stay there and stay down!" Sandra ordered.

She dashed off the stage heading for the sound of the gun fire. On her way, she elbowed a state trooper who had his pistol drawn and stripped him of it, then looking across the crowd, headed to the left edge of it. The crowd didn't know where to go or what to do, people were being shot on all sides from multiple directions. The smart people among the crowd dropped to their faces on the ground, while the rest, the majority of them, ran amok.

Joss took a risk and peaked out from beneath the belly of her plane. She saw Sandra level her pistol in a two handed grip and fire two quick shots, then run over and strip the assault rifle from the man she had just shot.

Looking in the other direction, her hand flew to her mouth. Richard was calmly walking behind another shooter, un armed, he violently grabbed the man around the neck with his left fore arm and stabbed a pen into the shooters right ear. As the shooter went down, Richard pulled the assault rifle from his hands and shot him twice in the head.

Scanning around, Richard spotted another shooter on his side and fired two rapid shots putting the man down. Sandra did the same to another shooter on the other side. Joss nearly panicked when she saw a state trooper armed with a shotgun advancing on Richard. The trooper looked about to fire at him but then saw Richard had his rifle trained on him.

"Get on your radio!" Richard ordered. "Tell who ever is in charge, there are two special forces people here and that they have the situation under control and to stay out of our way. We will, I repeat will, shoot anything or anyone with a weapon. Is that understood!"

He didn't wait for an answer, and he turned and dropped to one knee. He raised the rifle and tapped the trigger twice. A figure holding a rifle fell from a lighting tower. Richard spotted the other high shooter on the opposite side and took him out. Then he bent down, pulled a full clip from the tactical vest of the first man he had killed and replaced the one that was in the rifle. He grabbed two more, shoving them into his back pants pockets.

The state trooper was beside him.

"US Marines, Recon sir!" The trooper said.

"Ok," Richard said. "Watch my six, but stay out of my way Marine. You ain't trained on how we operate."

Richard took out another shooter on the fringes of the crowd as did Sandra from the other side.

"That female in the white flight jacket?"" Richard said. "She's one of mine. I will be most unpleased if one of you yahoos shoot her."

Joss could hear the ex Marine relay that through his radio before he moved into the crowd. The people scrambled away as best they could, clearing a path for him and the trooper. To Joss, everything looked to be in slow motion, she could see the flames coming out of the rifle barrels and the empty shells coming out after the rifle had been fired. Richard and Sandra and now the ex Marine, pivoting and searching the crowd almost like a slow dance. Richard shot another of the shooters, the ex Marine grabbed the mans rifle as they went by. Sandra had picked off two more. There was just one left. He had a woman with one arm around her neck, the free hand holding an automatic pistol at her head. Richard calmly walked forward, his rifle trained on the pair.

"You come any closer and I'll shoot her!" The gunman yelled.

"Go ahead," Richard said. "It'll give me a clear shot at you later."

The man looked between Richard advancing on him and the state trooper nearby, both with their rifles trained on him.

"And if he doesn't get you," Sandra said from behind the man. "I will."

The man raised the pistol to his forehead, but Richard fired once, hitting the man in the elbow, severing it and the hand it was attached to from the arm, the pistol flying from the now limp hand.

The man went down, the woman scrambled away. Richard walked up and put his right foot on the screaming mans throat.

The ex-Marine kept his rifle at the ready.

"We clear Wyoming?" Richard said.

"Looks like it Black." She said.

All three of them were scanning around looking for threats.

"Ok Marine, cuff this guy and call for medical for him," Richard said. "We need him alive."

Richard roughly jerked the injured mans belt off of him and fashioned a tourniquet around the arm to stop most of the bleeding.

"We gotta go boss," Sandra said. She had retrieved the mans pistol and disarmed it, now she did the same with her weapons dropping them to the ground. Richard did the same with his.

"Good job Marine." Richard said.

Then he and Sandra started making their way through the panicked crowd towards the stage.

"Who are you guys!" The trooper called after them.

"Just tell your bosses, Wyoming and Black were here." Sandra said. "Semper fi Marine."

Surrounded by state troopers, Richard and Sandra hustled Joss, Anna, Delta, and Clary out of harms way to a nearby secure hanger. Sandra saw them safely into the hangar, while Richard performed another one of his disappearing acts.

"You guys ok?" Sandra asked.

"Ya," Delta said. "We're all inner city kids. We've seen this kind of thing before."

Joss walked over to a table where some bottled water and paper towels were. She grabbed a roll of the towels and four bottles then walked back. She wet down a piece of the towling and began to gently rub the blood stain from under Sandras chin behind her ear.

Sandra took another bottle of water and took a deep drink.

"I don't suppose you guys have anything stronger around here eh?" She said.

"Thanx Texas," Sandra said.

"No," Joss said. "Thank you Wyoming, again. Is he going to be ok?"

"Who Super Hunk?" Sandra laughed. "Piece of cake kid. We were more worried about getting shot from our own side. Good thing this didn't happen in Texas eh? I'd be leaking like a sieve right now."

"What was this all about?" Joss asked.

"They didn't want you guys," Sandra said. "We know the MO of these creeps. They wanted to make a statement. About whatever waco cause they believe in. Get in, do as much damage as you can, then go. Gets them noticed. Would have worked too. But we were here. Still a bunch of innocent people just got killed."

Sandra took a deep breath.

"Ok, scared mom routine now eh?" She said. She sat on the floor, her elbows on her knees, head in her hands and started to cry. She wasn't acting.

Joss had been pacing the hotel room for an hour, where was Richard? Was he wounded, arrested or? Then Richard walked in. She rushed into his arms. He held her, but that was all. She looked up at him, his eyes were distant, he had blood on the left side of his face, his right shirt sleeve and hand were dark red.

"Sorry Joss," he said finally. "I have to take back my proposal to you. I can't expose you to this kind of danger."

He gently pried her away from him, made his way to the closet and started packing his duffle bag. She came behind him, gripped him hard and spun him around. She was not going to let him get away this time. She looked right into his eyes, hers on fire.

"You came into my life," she said. "You accepted all of my stuff. What makes you think I won't accept yours? That thing that happened today would have happened if you were there or not. If we were together or not. Now get out of that clothing and have a shower hey. Git now!"

Richard had just finished rinsing the shampoo out of his hair, when Joss wrapped her arms around him.

"And exactly how are you going to get home hey?" She said, kissing his neck. "I'm the only one with a plane here."

Chapter Sixteen

The attack had been plastered all over the world. Not only all the major news networks, all the bloggers and social media types were all over it. Curiously, there was no video of the take downs of the attackers. It was mostly surmised that everyone had been to busy trying to figure out what was going on, or simply trying to stay alive, to take cell phone videos. From the start of the attack to the finish, it had taken just under ten minutes.

Most of the scenes had shown the panic and Joss and the girls scrambling for cover on stage. The aftermath of the attack showing multitudes of ambulances, fire rescue teams and police from every local, state and federal agencies, descending on the area. The Florida National Guard had been called out and were providing assistance where ever it was required.

Other than giving law enforcement agencies their statements, Joss and the other women had nothing further to say. It appeared that a pilot had been contracted to ferry Joss's airplane home and she flew back with Clary. Sandra and her Pilatis had disappeared. Anna, with the help of Florida Sate Troopers, took off in her Diamond, where, nobody knew. She had not filed a flight plan.

None of them had their cell phones on and had rendered them untraceable.

Sandra, having the fastest plane, arrived first at Joss's ranch, Next were Delta and Clary with Joss. Anna right behind them. Richard arrived a couple of hours later in Joss's Archer. Richards plane had already been in the hanger, and with a little jockeying around, they were able to put Sandra, Anna's and Joss's airplanes in with it. Clary's and Delta's, they left tied down outside.

After that, the six of them made their way into the kitchen and the libations it held.

Joss wanted to say something, but didn't know how to go about it. Delta had told her before they had left she would say nothing. Clary had not even noticed that Sandra had disappeared during the attack. She had been hugging the ground under the Archer on stage.

Anna was looking at Richard, waiting for a sign of some sort.

Richard and Sandra were drinking their normal beer from the bottle. Both with non committal expressions.

At that point, the beating of helicopter blades coming from the distance was heard. Joss walked over to the patio window and looking out, saw three helicopters arriving. All had a major news outlets logos on them. One from ABC, one from CBS and of course, CNN.

Joss walked over to the radio transceiver she had on a kitchen counter and turned it on. It was already tuned to the frequency that was published for her airport traffic.

"Don't any of y'all even think about landing here," Joss said, keying the handheld mic. "This is private property and this is Texas. You land here, y'all are gonna find out how many holes I can put in your pretty lil birds right quick like."

To make their point, Richard walked over to the large emergency kit located under the centre kitchen island and withdrew a flare gun. Walking to the patio door, he pulled the door open enough for him to point it out of, aimed it the CNN helicopter that was just flaring to land and pulled the trigger.

The flare hit right in front of the passenger in the cockpit, the pilot quickly pulled up and away. To help things along, Clary had run into her bedroom and come back loading shells into her pump Remington Defender shot gun. She was loading buck shot into it. Unlike Richard had done, Clary walked right out onto the patio and let loose, firing at the now retreating helicopter.

She loaded five more shells into it quickly and pointed at the ABC helicopter that was coming in range. She fired at it and it swerved away. The CBS helicopter just circled the area. Clary was laughing as she came back inside.

"I doubt if I even came close to hitting them with this thing," Clary said. "They're lucky I left my AR15 back home on dad's farm."

"Don't pay to mess with a back woods woman from Idaho," Joss said. She had just returned from her bedroom with a Glock 9mm automatic pistol in her hand. "Or a backwoods Texas woman."

"Put the toys away," Richard said. He was placing the flare gun back in its spot in the emergency kit. He held his hand out to Joss and gave her the fork it over gesture. She gave the pistol to him and Richard expertly removed the clip and the round chambered in the barrel. Then looked the pistol over.

"You even know how to use this thing?" Richard asked.

Joss made a fist to smack him in the shoulder then saw the cold look in his eyes. She left the fist at her shoulder.

"I mean for real Joss," Richard said. "Like Sandra and I can. Are you ready to face how it feels to kill some one?"

Sandra had done what Richard had done with Clary's shot gun, emptying the magazine and leaving the beach open, she returned it to Clary. Richard took a quick look out side and saw the news helicopters had flown away.

"Get the box out of the plane Wyoming," Richard said.

Sandra walked out headed for the hanger. Five minutes later, she was back in the kitchen with a long and thick hard covered box. She plunked it on the floor and opened it. Clary made an audible gasp as she saw what was inside. A large caliber long rifle, an assault style rifle, grenade launcher underneath the barrel, and a kevlar tactical vest

Sandra picked up a pump action shot gun from the case and jammed a large banana shaped clip into it.

"Now this is a shot gun kid," Sandra said. Her face lit up ear to ear with a smile. Richard pulled out another large clip, removed a round and tossed it at Clary.

"Norma 338," Richard said. "It's for the big stick. I can blow the engine almost right off one of those choppers a kilometre away. That Mossberg Wyoming has, holds twenty five twelve gauge tactical rounds in it. Each round has five .30 caliber pellets in it. She also could blow one of those choppers out of the air with it."

Sandra tossed a black automatic pistol at Joss.

"That's a Sig Sauer in .45 caliber," Sandra said. "It, like all the other weapons in this case have threaded barrels to accept silencers. Most bad guys coming after you Joss, will have an armoured vest on. That 9mm of yours will hardly slow them down. Right Black?"

Richard shrugged his shoulders.

"Might maybe make a bruise Wyoming," Richard said.

"Those are weapons Special Forces use!" Clary said. "My dad was a Green Beret in Iraq. "How'd you guys get those weapons, especially in Canada. And I thought your nickname was Alberta, Sandra."

"Everyone in this room knows but you Clary," Richard said. "I am Nato code name Black, Sandra, Wyoming, Jochen is Worms and we have a another team member, Warsaw, who you have not met.

"Sandra is ex American Special Forces, Jochen, ex- German, Olga, ex Polish and I'm ex Canadian."

"We are members of a highly specialized private enterprise Clary," Sandra said. "Governments from all around the world hire us to do jobs they do not want known they were involved in."

"They were the ones that rescued Delta and I last year Clary," Joss said. Now she had her arm around Richards waist. "And the ones that took down those bad guys yesterday."

"But Sandra was with us under Joss's plane," Clary said.

"Or was she?" Anna said. "I saw her shoot at least three."

Sandra was putting the weapons back in the box on the kitchen floor. She shrugged her shoulders.

"Peace of cake. Right boss?" Sandra said.

"Walk in the park," Richard said. He walked to the refrigerator and pulled two more beer from it. He chuckled.

"You should have seen that Force Recon guy Wyoming, I thought sure he was gonna shit his pants when I drew down on him. Good man. I checked up on him, he's still in the active reserve and they call him up all the time."

"Thinking about hiring him boss?" Sandra asked.

"Maybe," Richard said. "I've got Birgitta looking into him."

"Is Birgitta the Spanish women I talked to after Frankfurt?" Joss asked. "I thought she was the boss."

"No Joss," Sandra said after giving Richard a dirty look. "It was Richard's idea, Richards funding started it. At first it was just us and the one's that were wounded in Amsterdam Joss. Brigitta lost a leg and a hand in that operation. She's ex Australian special forces, not Spanish. She does most of our research for us. Two of the other survivors handle the IT stuff and two more the admin stuff."

"But you told me you didn't know how many teams there were and who they were Richard." Joss said.

"I don't," Richard said. "That's all handled by some one else Joss. That way, if we get captured, we honestly can't tell any one anything. Because we don't know anything."

"Speaking of which," Sandra said pointing at Richard's watch which was blinking red.

Richard punched a pre-dialled number into his cell phone, put it on speaker and laid it on the counter top while he opened a beer for himself and tossed the other one to Sandra.

"Hey Seville," Richard said. "What's new?"

A fast stream of Spanish expletives came from the other end. Richard laughed.

"Sure laugh it up," a female said in Australian accented English. "Are we going to get paid for that?"

"We can try," Richard said. "The authorities know two special ops people, named Black and Wyoming did all the work. Not a big deal anyway. Used the bad guys weapons and ammo and we were most likely saving ourselves anyway. But getting paid for it would be nice."

"I'll see what I can do," Brigitta said. "Joss, Anna, Delta and the new girl Clary? They are all un hurt?"

"Ya, a little shook up, but ok," Richard said. "Joss told me if I disappeared on her she'd hunt me down and shoot me with the Glock 9mm pop gun she has."

"I did not!" Joss said. "Besides, I would have sicked Clary on you with that shot gun of hers."

"That's the spirit Texas," Brigitta said. "I take it Clary knows then?"

"Ya we just told her," Richard said. "Say hello Idaho."

"Um..Hi?" Clary stammered. Brigitta laughed.

"Idaho there," Sandra said. "Just finished charging out of the house and started blasting away at a couple of choppers with her Remington Defender."

"Takes after her dad she does," Brigitta said.

"You know may dad?" Clary said.

"Did two tours in Afghanistan with him," Brigitta answered.

"Afghanistan?" Clary said. "Dad was never in Afghanistan."

"Ya hey Bosie, Long time. Wyoming here," Sandra said into her cell phone. Sandra held the phone away from her ear and some barley audible expletives were heard coming from it.

"Hey! Be nice now," Sandra said. "Got your munchkin standing beside me. I'm putting you on speaker."

"What do you mean Clary is standing beside you," they heard a man say. "She's in Texas working for Joss Lynn. I'm waiting to hear from her. Her mom's worried about her after that Florida deal."

"Peace of cake," Sandra said. "Black and I handled it. No muss no fuss."

"You I knew was there, saw the vid, Black too? Those yahoos had no chance.

"Clary you Ok? Your mom and especially me are worried."

"A little shook up pop," Clary said. "Sandra made sure I was safe before she took after the bad dudes."

"Idaho there, just finished charging out on the patio and blasted away at a couple of choppers," Sandra said. "Seville says she takes after her old man."

"Seville is there too?" Bob, Clary's dad asked.

"Not physically Bosie," Brigitta said. "Like you, on speaker phone."

"Seville says she did two tours with you in Afghanistan dad," Clary said. "Is that true?"

"Yes," Bob said after a couple of seconds of silence. His voice was quivering. "We can't always tell everything we do Clary. Our last job together was a bad one. I was wounded, three of our guys were dead and Seville was running out of ammo. A Canuck Special Ops guy was popping the Tallies as fast as he could with that big rifle of his, then a Canuck deep recon gang code named Wind Riders showed up and saved our asses."

"Was able to link up with the Wind Riders after and buy a round of beer," Bob said after a few seconds of silence. "I never did find out who the special ops guy was."

Joss had been so engrossed in the conversation, she had not noticed Richard disappear. Looking around she saw him on the patio. His elbows on the railing, looking into the distance.

"His name is Black, Bob," Joss said. "He, Sandra and the other members of his team saved Delta and I last year and again yesterday. If he was standing here right now with us, he would shrug his shoulders and say it's all in a days work. He's standing on the patio right now looking off in the distance. He doesn't do that often Bob.

"I have to go to him. Nice talking to you Bob, Seville."

Joss walked out on the patio beside Richard and like him laid her arms on the railing and looked into the distance. She knew he knew she was there.

"They were surrounded," Richard said finally. "No way they were getting out of there. I was tasked as over watch for them, but the Tallies had laid a perfect ambush. I had only seen ten of them and didn't think it would be a big deal. Was over two hundred of them hidden in under ground bunkers. I only had one hundred rounds for my big stick and about two hundred for my assault rifle. I was to far away for the assault rifle, so started in on them with the big stick and screamed bloody murder for help.

"Luckily, the Wind Riders were in the next valley tasked to look for this same group of bad guys. Was over pretty quick when they showed up. They helped patch up Bob and when they heard the choppers coming with the help, the jumped in that ratty G-wagon of theirs and took off. So did I.

"Canucks don't like anybody knowing what their Social Ops people do."

Joss put her head on Richards shoulder.

"Seville is part of your company but Bob is not?" She asked.

Richard kissed her on the forehead and smiled.

Joss stood away from him and looking at his face saw the smile.

"Does Clary know?" She said. "Of course not. Does he know who you are?"

Richard shrugged his shoulders.

"Doubt it," he said.

Richard put his right arm around her waist and gave her a squeeze, then he dragged her back into the kitchen.

"Whatcha think Bosie," Richard said. "Should we give Idaho a job or what? She's pretty good with that pop gun of hers. Hit the second chopper with two rounds she did. Hey! Take it easy Texas, that shoulder ain't healed up from the last five times you belted it."

"She should be better than pretty good," Bob said. "She's been coming hunting with me since she was ten. Was that really you up there with that big stick that day Black?"

"Well some one has to look out for you stupid yanks Bosie," Richard said. "Jeez Wyoming! Hit the other arm eh?"

"Give the bum one for me too?" Brigitta yelled into the phone. "And use the same arm! I didn't know it was him up there either!"

"Owe! Shit!" Richard said as Clary, Delta and Anna all slugged him, on the left arm though.

Everyone in the kitchen could hear laughter coming from both cell phones.

"I need to talk with Clary," Bob said. "In private."

Clary picked up Sandra's cell phone took it off speaker and headed off to her bedroom, listening as her father talked.

"On another topic," Brigitta said. "I've got Melbourne looking into that State trooper. I think he is a good fit. Make him an offer?"

"Won't hurt," Richard said. "Black Team is going dark Seville. We are all to busy doing other shit right now."

"Yes, yes," Brigitta said. "Now with Anna driving for you as well. Yes, all of you will be far to busy. As am I. Take care all."

"Clary gets a job offer, but I don't?" Delta said.

Joss could see Delta was upset. She looked up into Richards blue eyes. He was looking but not seeing, eyes almost glazed over. She felt him take a deep breath and come back to the here and now.

"You should think long and hard about that Delta," Richard said. "You think you know what we do, but you really do not."

Richard walked to the refrigerator, pulled out another beer and headed out of the kitchen door toward the fire pit. A few minutes later Joss could hear him splitting wood. Sandra, like Richard had done, grabbed another beer and a full bottle of vodka and headed to the fire pit herself. Delta made to go after them, but Joss grabbed her arm and stopped her.

"Let them be for a while Delta," Joss said. "For the most part they are like us Delta, normal people. But they can and will kill anyone at anytime. I watched Richard kill the first attacker yesterday with a pen Delta. A pen."

"They can do the same thing with their hands," Anna said. "My uncle has been training me for years. If I had to, I could do the same. My father started training me kick boxing at eight. He was an officer in the army at the time."

Clary walked back in the kitchen at that point and laid the cell phone on the table.

"Where are they?" Clary asked.

Joss pointed down at the fire pit. Sandra and Richard were sitting beside a now working fire in it. Both looking at the fire, holding their beer. Not drinking, or seeing the fire.

"My dad does the same thing once in a while," Clary said. "He never talks about things he did in the war. Never."

"They do," Anna said. "But not to us. Even though they are not saying anything, they are both talking to each other right now. Watch."

Joss saw Richard put his head on Sandras shoulder and she, her head on his.

"I have seen my uncle do the same," Anna said. "They have a bond stronger than they will have with any other, including you Joss. He loves you Joss, he always will and your children. But they? They will always be closer Joss. I have to go study now."

Anna walked to where her bedroom was in the large house.

"My dad says," Clary began. "Those that talk the most about it were never there. When he and his buddies get together at a reunion, they wander off by themselves, just like those two are doing right now. They will sit at a table by themselves and just look at their drinks. I grew up with this Joss, Delta. I know my dad loves me and will do anything for me. I also know, I will never have all of him. So does my mother.

"Some veterans become hard and callous. The good ones, like those two and my dad? Their spouses don't leave them because they are mean or abusive. They leave them because they will never own them completely."

Joss gave Clary a quick squeeze.

"I know Clary, I know," Joss said. "I am the same with Clary and Delta. With those I have shared something special with. Who I have been on stage on tour with, or like Karen, have forged a special bond with.

"I think that's why Richard and I have bonded so well together. We both know, that at some point, part of us will always belong to some one, or something else."

The three of them sat at the kitchen breakfast nook for some time silent. Joss could see that Delta was still troubled.

"Clary," Joss said finally. "Delta and I need to talk. I know you want to talk to Sandra and Richard. Why don't you go down to the fire? They have started swilling that god awful vodka now, so it should be all good."

As soon as Clary had left the kitchen headed to the fire pit, Joss took both of Delta's hands in hers and looked her in the eyes.

"What you and I have," Joss said. "Is the same Delta. We have shared and been through so much together. Richard knows that Delta, he is not worried about it. Why has he not offered you a job? He, and I, know, you would be a great asset for him. I am learning to become comfortable with what he is Delta. Like he said earlier,

I know how to use that Glock and I have killed animals hunting, but never a human being. Have you even fired a gun, let alone killed anything with one?"

Delta shook her head.

"Did you really see what happened in Arminia and yesterday Delta? Or did you block it all out like I did in Arminia?"

"I saw it!" Delta said. "How can you ask me that!"

"I didn't in Arminia Delta," Joss said. "I heard the gun fire, I saw the bodies. That's it. Yesterday. Yesterday, I watched Richard shove a pen in a man's ear and twist it. Blood was spraying all over Richards arm and face. I saw people being thrown off their feet, some of them losing parts of their bodies as they were hit by the bullets. I heard them scream in pain or just fall down in a heap silent. I saw one that Sandra had shot in the head, fall to the ground and go into convulsions before his body knew it was dead.

"That's what I mean about seeing Delta. Richard and Sandra, not only did they see those things, hear those things, but they know, they were the ones that caused it Delta. Did you know Richard and I have agreed to spend the rest of our lives together Delta? To have kids and raise them together? He asked me three weeks ago. I said yes."

"I thought so," Delta said.

"Last night," Joss said. "Richard came into our hotel room. His clothing and arms covered in dry blood. He told me he had to take back the proposal Delta. That he had no right to ask me to share all the killing.

"I think that is why he hasn't asked you Delta. Not because he does not care about you. Because he cares to much about you."

It had gotten dark now. Joss could make out that three people were sitting by the fire, but not much else. She rose, took a bottle of wine from the refrigerator and two wine glasses. Then beaconed Delta to follow. They walked to the group around the fire.

"Hey!" Joss said. "What's the big idea. Swilling all my booze and not asking me to join you."

"Speaking of which," Richard said, making to pull Joss on his lap. "We are about running out of your lousy booze."

Joss slapped his hands away and pointed at the hanger.

"Plenty in the hanger," Joss said. "Take California with you. The rest of us girls will stay here and celebrate the hunk and my's getting hitched."

"What?" Clary said. "You're getting married!"

She jumped up and hugged Joss.

"Now, now," Joss said. "Nobody said anything about getting married. Just getting hitched. Far as I know, according to Canuck law it means the same anyhow."

"Aw shit," Richard said, as he and Delta headed into the dark toward the hanger. "Thanks for reminding me. Have to get you to sign that prenup."

"I'll prenup you, you bum!" Joss yelled after him. "I'm probably worth more money than you are anyway!"

"Won't matter anyway," Sandra said. "He owns half of your shit, you half his, after tonight anyway, now that it's public and all. But just the earnings after tonight and if you can find all his."

Sandra laughed, then they all did.

"Me too," Joss said. "My mom didn't raise no dummy."

Anna, finished with her studying and seeing everyone around the fire pit, came and joined them. Clary told Anna about Richard and Joss and the hen party started. Delta walked up with a case of beer and two bottles of wine.

"The Hunk said to much estrogen around here," Delta said. "Clogging his sinuses. He'd rather smell gasoline and oil in the hanger I guess."

Chapter Seventeen

The women had discussed among themselves the night before, that going to Richard's ranch in Canada was the best option right now. As none of the media outlets knew about Richard's ranch, it was the best option to lay low in for a while. Richard had left right at daybreak in his Cherokee, it was by far the slowest of all the airplanes.

The Formula 1 season opener was in a month and there would be a week of testing at the track in Bahrain before the opening race of the season, also at that track. Anna told Joss that while she really wanted to stay with the rest of them, she couldn't. She would fly, more or less directly to Germany, pick up Heidi, then fly to the Hubba Bubba factory in Britain for simulator work.

Clary had decided and Joss had not only agreed but strongly encouraged her, to go home in Idaho and spend time with her family. Joss had decided to ride in Delta's new airplane. It was faster than her Archer and Sandy would take her PC-12 and meet them at Richard's place. The PC-12 was the fastest of the airplanes.

All four women's airplanes took off at the same time. Anna heading east, the others north west. Clary and Delta formed a two airplane formation, Sandra took off last and stayed with them until they reached twenty five thousand feet. That was when Sandra began to pull away from them with her higher cruise speed.

After reaching cruise speed and altitude, Joss fell asleep in the copilots position, leaving Delta alone with her thoughts. Joss kept reliving the attack in her dreams for a while, sometimes making a comment that Delta could hear. Mostly, they were about Richard and an attacker he had as yet not noticed.

Delta was about to wake her up, when she saw Joss smile and her face relax.

"I love you so much Richard," Joss murmured. "We are going to make beautiful children together."

While Delta was happy for Joss, she was still troubled by what she had experienced. As the airplane was on auto pilot, her mind drifted back to the attack. How she had been so very frightened. The sound of gun fire, the screams coming from the crowd. While she had not witnessed Richard and Sandra's actions or seen much of the carnage in the crowd, she did remember seeing Joss clean Sandra's face from blood stains, hearing Sandra make one of her wise cracks, then devolving into a quivering wreck for a couple of minutes. After that, it was like a switch had turned off and Sandra was Sandra once again. Almost. Sandra made sure each of them was ok, did they want to talk about it, how they were managing, could she do anything for them.

At that point, state and federal officials had showed up and Sandra, like Richard had done earlier, disappeared.

Delta was in the lead of their little two plane formation and she looked over her right shoulder at Clary and keyed her mic.

"All good over there?" Delta asked.

"All good Delta," Clary answered.

The frequency they had agreed on to communicate with each other was on one of the two radios they had. The other was tuned to the air traffic control frequency.

"I was on auto pilot for the first while," Clary continued. "But my mind was wondering somewhere it should not be. So now I'm manually flying. At least you and Joss can talk to each other."

"Ya right," Delta said. "Her Holiness, Bridezilla, is snoozing. I'm getting almost a play by play semi porn broadcast over here."

"Hu...what?" Clary heard Joss say. Delta still had her mic keyed.

"Oh Richard, you make me so hot," Delta mimicked. "Oomph!" As Joss whacked her shoulder.

"I do not talk in my sleep," Joss said.

"If you say so your Texasness," Clary radioed back.

"Your lucky you're to far away," Joss said. "Or I'd whack you in the arm too. You going to be ok over there. You should be splitting away from us in a few minutes."

"Ya, I'm ok," Clary said.

They had been in the air for two hours now. They had just been cleared by Denver control and would be out of Colorado soon. Sandra was not even a dot on the windshield anymore. That didn't mean she couldn't still hear them though.

"Say high to your pop for me Idaho," Sandra said. "Remind him I still owe him a beer. I'm going to lose you guys in a couple of minutes. I'll have the bourbon iced up for you Texas, California."

The air to air frequency they were using only had a range of maybe fifty miles, on a good day. Now that they were flying in the mountains, it might be less.

Ten minutes later, Clary received clearance from Denver to split off and head to Idaho. Delta and Joss continued north and Joss called Canada Customs to have them met at Lethbridge. Even though they were over an hour away, things were busy in the cockpit. Joss was working on one of the two displays, setting frequencies for Lethbridge Approach. Delta was entering the Lethbridge co-ordinates on hers, plus the approach and runway map. Joss calculated their air speed and distance to the border and radioed the time they would cross the border to Denver Control.

Denver acknowledged the transmission, then turned them over to Edmonton Control as they were now close to entering Canadian air space.

Joss's next task as co-pilot, was to dial in the ATIS frequency in Lethbridge and obtain the latest weather and runway information.

She radioed Edmonton Control once they had crossed the border and was then told to contact Lethbridge Tower for instructions. Having done that, they were given clearance to land and once on the ground, she switched to the ground frequency and was told where to taxi the airplane to and to wait for customs.

Now, Delta gathered all the airplane documents, her passport and pilot's licence. Joss, her passport and licence. They had been directed to taxi next to the fuel tanks set up just beyond the small terminal at the Lethbridge Regional Airport. They were guided by a ground crewman once there and shut the aircraft down. The customs agent walked over to the aircraft once the propeller had shut down and walked around to the rear of the wing on the pilots side.

Both Delta and Joss exited the airplane. The agent, first went through all of Delta's paper work, then Joss's, stamped both passports and was off. That's when the ground crew man asked and was told to fuel up the airplane.

While he was doing that. Both Joss and Delta walked into the terminal and used the washroom. Delta paid for the fuel with the card Piper had given her, then both women walked back to the Piper, checked the level of the fuel in the tanks and took off headed to Richard's ranch.

The sun was headed behind the snow capped mountains when they turned on final approach to land at the ranch. It still being March, there was still snow on the ground bordering the runway, which was clear and dry.

That it was cold out, was evident by seeing Sandra wearing her Hubba Bubba racing jacket zipped up to her chin. Sandra had already put her PC-12 NGX to bed beside the other PC-12 and PC-24 in the hanger. Her duffle bag of clothing with purse on top was on the ground beside her and the hanger door was slowly shutting. Moving over to the next hanger, she entered the man door and its main hanger door began to open, revealing the empty interior. Joss had been at the controls from Lethbridge and now deftly swung the Piper around in a blast of high speed engine, moved forward slightly to straighten out the nose gear and shut the engine down.

By this time, the hanger door was fully open and Sandra advanced on the nose of the Piper with an electric tugger, which she attached to the nose gear.

"Oh my God!" Joss exclaimed as she exited the Piper. She quickly went back inside and came back wearing an insulated jean jacket which she was buttoning up as she came back out. Picking a wing each, Joss and Delta helped push the Piper into the hanger and Joss quickly ran over to the side of the doorway and hit the close button mounted there.

Wrapping her arms around herself, she frowned at the other two women. Delta was wearing an insulated ski jacket and pair of insulated gloves, she was smiling. Sandra was out right laughing. She reached into the pocket of her also insulated jacket and pulling a wool watch cap out of it, pulled it on her head and over her ears.

"It's only -12," Sandy said. "What are you going to do when it really gets cold?"

"Go back to Texas," Joss said. "You guys are nuts living here."

Grabbing their luggage and purses, the three women made their way to the house. Joss was hurrying, by the time they reached the house, Joss had a hand on an ear trying to get it warm. Sandra punched in the security code to unlock the door and Joss rushed in side, dropped her bags on the floor and began to blow on her fingers and rub them together. As Sandra moved down the hallway to disarm the alarm system beeping away, Joss heard the forced air furnace kick in. Sandra had already removed her jacket and now tossed it on a living room chair. She went to the air tight fireplace, opened the door and soon had a fire roaring away in it with the door partially open.

Joss rushed to it and stood in front of the blazing fire bouncing up and down, trying to get warm.

She turned her back to the fire and saw Sandra filling up a kettle with water and place it on the stove to boil.

Delta had also removed her jacket and was now standing beside Joss in front of the roaring fire. She, however, was not bouncing up and down and rubbing her hands and ears like Joss was.

"I guess you didn't check the weather before we left," Delta said. She undid a couple of buttons and showed Joss the heavy T-shirt she had underneath her heavy cotton shirt.

Her front now warming up, Joss removed her jacket and turned her back to the fire. She saw Sandra spoon two spoonfuls of something from a jar into three large coffee mugs, pour a healthy portion of white rum in them, followed by filling them with hot water from the kettle and rigorously stirring them. She walked into the living room and handed Joss and Delta a cup.

"Mud in your eye," Sandra said, and took a deep pull. She put her cup down on the fireplace mantel and making sure the dampers were wide open on it, closed the door.

Joss took a tentative sip of the liquid, then a much deeper one.

"This is good," Joss said.

"Hot rum toddy," Sandra said. "Just the thing for a cool day. Your old man says he's three hours out."

Joss took another sip and nodded her head. It had taken them just over seven hours to arrive. Richard must be really pushing the Cherokee to make it in just under eleven hours. The phone rang at that point, Sandra walked to the portable handset on the coffee table, looked at the phone number and answered it.

"Hey Clary," Sandra said. "I guess you made it ok? Ya we just got in. Ok I'll tell her. See ya."

Sandra hit end and placed the set back in its charger base.

"Clary made it home ok," Sandra said. "Now, before your old man gets here and mine arrives to take me home, I want to show both of you and especially Delta, something."

Sandra picked up the TV remote, turned the set on and hit a few buttons, then a password and scrolled through a number of files and finally selected one. An image came on the screen and Sandra paused it. It was a long range video shot of someplace that looked familiar to both Joss and Delta. It was a large clearing surrounded by tall cedar trees and there was snow on the ground. That it was a movie location shoot was obvious from the number of cameras, lighting systems, trailers and huge generator units located all around the clearing.

"That's the Moroccan location shoot for your 'Platinum Mines' movie Joss," Delta said. "Remember?"

"Ya," Joss said. "It was a couple of years ago. Until just now, the coldest place I had ever been. That's a drone shot. I don't remember any drones being used at that time."

"Very good," Sandra said. "You both get another hot rum toddy for that. Yes, it's a drone, no, it's not part of the movie shoot. Give me your mugs. I'll refill them for you while you watch the rest."

The video restarted then. At first it just showed the goings on at the movie shoot, then turned and zoomed out and refocussed on a group of six men just inside the tree line four or five hundred yards away. Two men went to a large machine gun set up on a tripod and loaded it. Another two men placed pointed objects into tubes and placed them on their shoulders. The other two men stood with large binoculars to their eyes.

Then, almost at the same time, the men with the tubes and the men at the machine gun were blown violently off their feet. Large mists of red came out of their chests. Seconds later the two men with binoculars to their eyes suffered the same fate.

Two figures dressed head to toe in white and light grey clothing approached the fallen men with assault rifles at their shoulders. One was tall, the other shorter and a wisp of blonde hair was visible coming out the back of its balaclava. This figure watched, rifle at its shoulder while the taller one rolled each of the bodies over and took pictures. They both melted back into the trees. The drone then refocused on the movie shoot, saw nothing untoward was happening there and the picture shut down.

Sandra handed the two shocked women another mug of steaming liquid.

"That was not in the script," Joss said.

"No," Sandra replied. "That was real. Real people died. Very quickly, very deadly, very silently. Nobody but the dead and the killers ever knew about it."

"Who??? Why??" Joss asked.

She was very pale now. Her left foot was rapidly tapping the floor. Delta had her right hand covering her mouth.

"The Moroccan Government received credible intelligence that an Iranian backed Libyan terrorist group was going to hit the movie," Sandra said. "They contracted an NGO contractor to handle the situation.

"Remember that group of four skiers when you were taking your ski lessons? The one with the one smart ass skiing backwards? That was the team which had been sent to handle the situation."

"Oh ya," Delta said. "I remember them. They were having a ball. I saw them leave a couple of days later in a PC-24....Wait a second."

Sandra raised her glass and did a little bow.

"You always were sharp Delta," Sandra said. "Moroccans paid us a pretty penny for that job, as did the movie's insurance company."

"So you knew who we were even back then," Joss said.

"Duh ya," Sandra said. "We also had a lot of money invested in the movie.

"Look girls, the whole point of me showing you this was to make a point. Our organization does a lot of work like that. All around the world. Sometimes, like your kidnapping, they are made public. Most times, they are like the Moroccan job and nobody hears anything about them. A lot of the time, nothing at all happens. We spend a week or more on site, nothing happens and we get paid and go home."

Sandra took another sip of her drink and looked each woman in the eyes.

"Out of one thousand combat soldiers, maybe, one will become a special operations operator. Out of a hundred special operations operators, maybe one will be chosen to do what we do. Out of one hundred of us, maybe five will be alive after five years. Another three will melt down. One will have enough and pack it in."

Joss now began to understand just how special Richard and Sandra were.

"The teams of our organization are made up of those one percent," Sandra continued. "Black team is the best of those teams and Richard is the best of all of us. It takes a very special person to be able to do what we do girls. When we are on the job, we are cold hearted unfeeling killers. We have to be. Off the job, we feel it, we feel it just like you girls do. Unlike you girls, we know how to process it all.

"It's like George and all the F1 drivers. On the track they are deadly to each other. Off the track, most of them are friends. Yes, George knows what I do, my kids do not. Richards sons know what he does, their wives do not. Now you know."

"What happens next?" Delta asked.

Sandra shrugged her shoulders.

"Our team is basically retiring," she said. "We are to busy with the racing stuff right now and don't need to jeopardize that, or our organization. That is another big difference between our organization and most others like ours. We keep what we do as secretive as possible and only take jobs that we can prove will save lives, not to further some governments agenda."

"What does Olga do outside the organization?" Joss asked.

"She's one of Richard's minions," Sandra replied. "Well, actually, she's the boss minion. She's almost as good as Richard is doing that stuff. She has an understanding wife and two kids at home. The wife thinks she is an investment banker that, at times, has to go on extended business trips."

Sandra's cell phone beeped.

"Well, my ride is here," she said. "See ya in Bahrain."

Chapter Eighteen

It had been a busy six months since the action at Fun and Sun. Joss had done a number of interviews, all of them on Skype from the living room at Richard's house, with CNN, Entertainment Tonight, Fox News and several social media bloggers. That was before the Formula 1 season had begun. She had no commitments this year and could spend her time at the Hubba Bubba garage for the whole race. Everyone knew she was friends with Anna and Sandra and didn't make a fuss over it. The media was more interested in Anna and the expectations of the race team this year. As Joss had predicted, now that she was out of the lime light, she was forgotten.

Being her first year at the team, Anna had struggled a little for the first few races. Placing in the top five at first, now, she was most always second to Georges first. Hubba Bubba, while winning all the races, had their work cut out for them this year. Red Bull was close, as was Aston Marton. Ferrarri kept finding ways to shoot themselves in the foot and were in third place, barely, as Macleran was right behind them in the standings.

Clary was relatively busy. She was still handling Joss's day to day requirements and now, was doing research for the security company for Brigette. When she was to busy, Delta was always around to help her out.

Delta now had a stable of ten PAs she managed. Five were from new Formula 1 drivers or the better Formula 2 drivers. Others were employed by recording artists or actors. Other than occasionally having to put out the odd fire, Delta was generally not all that busy. She was having a blast with Joss and Sandra at the Formula 1 weekends.

Olga and her wife attended all the European races. While not as much of a smart ass as Sandra was, she had a great sense of humour, as did her wife. They fit right in with their now close knit group.

Joss was five months pregnant and just beginning to show. Richard was ecstatic about it and, if anything, more attentive and loving than ever. A new PC-24 with extended fuel tanks had been purchased for the clandestine operations and Richard had registered the old one to himself. While he and Joss, still flew in the Archer and Cherokee when ever they had the chance, the long commutes now were made with the PC-24. While Joss had stopped any alcohol consumption the minute she had found out she was pregnant, she still partied with the others and had just as much fun. Richards two sons and their wives commuted to the races with them and Joss enjoyed their company. Father and sons were getting along fine now and other race teams finding out that the boys company were making prototypes for Hubba Bubba, had contracted them to do the same.

Richard's other concerns were doing well. Like he had told Joss when they had first met, his money worked for him, not he for the money. Joss had spoken to Richard about maybe selling her Texas ranch. She wasn't there much anymore. After a session of Richards questions, Joss had decided to ask her mother if she would like to move in. Her mother had readily agreed and with Joss's encouragement, had rented her house in Brownsville out. But she had insisted on building her own house next to the main house to live in.

Other than they had more fancy expensive toys, like driving an Audi, airplanes and clothing than most people did, Joss and Richard acted like the normal type people they really were. At home, they went for long drives, rode horses in the woods around Richard's place, or flew to some new destination to experience something.

For the first time in many, many years, Joss was under no pressure to do anything. Anything but enjoy the life they had worked so hard to make happen.

Well, almost. Richard always had that special box in the baggage compartment and still wore the special watch that would blink red when it had to. So far, it had not.

So far.

Don't miss out!

Visit the website below and you can sign up to receive emails whenever R.P. Wollbaum publishes a new book. There's no charge and no obligation.

https://books2read.com/r/B-A-DWJC-RVXIC

BOOKS 2 READ

Connecting independent readers to independent writers.

Also by R.P. Wollbaum

Baren und Adler

Baren und Adler

Bears and Eagles

Bears and Eagles

Eagles Claw

Eagle's Talon

As Eagles Swarm

Bears Maul

Desert Eagle

Eagle's Nest

Wind Riders

Oaken

Wind Riders Zebra

White Ghost

Standalone

Cal's Quest Part 1
Joss Lynn

Watch for more at www.bearsandeagles.com.

About the Author

R.P. Wollbaum and his faithful companions Lady and Baron, live in the foothills of the Rocky Mountains in Southern Alberta Canada.

When not busy composing a new novel, he can be found exploring North America in 'Da Buss'.

Read more at www.bearsandeagles.com.

www.ingramcontent.com/pod-product-compliance
Lightning Source LLC
Chambersburg PA
CBHW051331020726
47501CB00007B/2033